Osmosis

A novel by Donald Skiff

Published by Donald Skiff
Copyright © 2011 by Donald Skiff
All rights reserved
ISBN 978-0-9832003-1-4

There is no "they." Indeed, there is no "we," for I cannot find the boundary line between you and me. We permeate each other.

— Gary Blanchard

To those in my life through whom I see.

Government Agents Can Read Your Thoughts

Special to The Post by Greg Thompson

An official of the U.S. government admitted today that "certain agents" of the government have the ability to read thoughts of nearby people. Speaking on condition of anonymity, the official said that these agents are equipped with electronic devices implanted under their scalps that detect the electromagnetic waves that are given off by everyone over a short distance.

"They can't actually read your mind," he said. "It's only what a person is consciously thinking in words or sometimes clear images that can be detected." As a demonstration, he asked the reporter to look at his watch. With his eyes closed, he reported the time seen by the reporter. It was evident that the official was equipped with one of the devices.

The main use of these devices is in investigations in which traditional interrogation techniques are not possible, for example in verifying the truthfulness of informants. When asked about the number of these devices deployed within the government, or what agencies were involved, he declined to comment.

The technology for such detection of brain waves is being studied by both government and private organizations. One Australian company has claimed that it has a low-cost device that is worn like a helmet, which can detect and transmit brain waves to a nearby computer, allowing a person to exert mental control over mechanical devices. The company is looking for investors to help bring the device to the market

Contents

Scene 1

Meredith usually avoided having to take the elevator at rush hour. The crush of people and their smells, the feeling of being trapped, and hating to say, "Excuse me, please" six times as she pushed her way to the door always made her feel like an animal on its way to the slaughter house. But she had dawdled outside at lunch today, the first warm day of April.

She was near the back of the car. The man behind her, she could tell, was pressed against the wall. She hadn't noticed him when she got on, but now she felt how tall he was. Next to her a young woman was watching a video on her phone, and Meredith could barely hear music from the woman's ear piece. Another woman was in front of her, pressed against her breasts, squeezing the breath out of her.

The faint sound of an electric guitar drew her attention to the video. It was Eric Clapton, she recognized immediately, his eyes closed, drawing the music from the 2003 televised "Concert for George" out of that glorious guitar—and Meredith was transported back to the night she had first watched that concert from her bed, sobbing uncontrollably over the loss—all the loss represented by the death of George Harrison, one of her idols in her youth. Paul had lain on top of her, kissing her tears, trying to bring her back to him, but the weight of his body was the weight of her loss, and Clapton's guitar solo in the middle of "Something" was her wail.

Tears welled up, but the press of bodies in the elevator kept her arms pinned and she couldn't reach inside her purse for a tissue. Her eyes were fastened on that little video screen. Her memory furnished the full resonance of the music. Her body was suddenly hot, and she tasted the saltiness of tears streaming down her face.

Then suddenly there was release; the pressure of bodies eased and cool air wafted over her face from the open door. Several people left the car. Meredith managed to dig into her purse, but a woman's hand appeared beside her offering her a tissue. She murmured, "Thank you," and dabbed at her makeup.

A few minutes later she made her way to the doors and, dazed, exited the elevator. She never looked up to see who had given her the tissue, and she remembered nothing about the woman with the video except a mass of dark hair with a white wire trailing from under it. The song "Something" kept running through her head. At her desk all afternoon, she felt Paul's weight on her, holding her in the world that seemed to be flying away.

Memories of listening to the Beatles' music, lying stoned in a tangle of young bodies, smelling the sweet smoke mingling with incense and perfume, lips kissing her, all came flooding back. She had an impulse to go online and try to find that video, but she kept the data entry form on her screen and pretended to work.

Finally it was after four o'clock, and she shut off her computer and looked over the wall of the cube, where Dolly sat looking up at her. "I need a drink," she said fervently.

Dolly instantly closed her computer and grabbed her purse. "Yes, you do."

Scene 2

The next day, she made sure to take the elevator before the rush. There was only one other passenger. As soon as she entered the car, however, she knew. *He's one of **them**,* she thought. *Oh my God!*

"Yes, ma'am," he said quietly. "I am. I wish I could turn it off when I'm off duty, but I can't. I'm sorry."

She didn't say anything—actually, she was trying to think of something to reply that wouldn't sound totally stupid. It made her furious to know that he knew what she was thinking, maybe even before she knew. She'd read about these people and how they had the ability to read thoughts in other people's heads. Some kind of secret government program to help search out terrorists.

"Most people," he said, "don't think so much in words, anyway, unless they're rehearsing what they intend to say aloud."

She blushed slightly, and smiled uncomfortably. "I feel so vulnerable!" she said aloud.

"Sure. We do, too. It's hard to say something to civilians, because everything we think is already colored by knowing what they are thinking. I try to hold my tongue until somebody actually speaks, and then respond to their words. But it's hard."

"I can imagine. I guess I just have to relax, don't I?"

He looked up at the floor display, watching the numbers go up—*6, 7, 8, ...* "Yes, ma'am. Me, too."

She looked at him, and noticed that she had been avoiding that. "I'm curious, of course." She wondered how she had recognized him so quickly. His clothes were ordinary, he needed a haircut, but he was clean-shaven.

"They try to train us to be invisible," he replied to her thoughts, "but it's hard. I try to smile at people, but a lot of them guess right away, and the fear shows in their face as fast as it does in their thoughts."

"How far—how far away can you read people's minds?" Her curiosity was getting the better of her.

"Just a few feet, really. If there's a lot of people around, it's hard to know who is thinking which thoughts." He laughed. "If you want to stay anonymous, keep close to others. We get people mixed up."

An idea hit her, and she spoke it as it came, "I can imagine it would be hard in a crowd—you wouldn't know who was thinking those thoughts about **you**." Her smile was attractive.

He laughed. "Exactly."

She became bold. "You wouldn't know who wanted you to hit on them."

"Ouch. But yes. I'm naturally kinda shy, but sometimes . . ."

"So, tell me—what's it sound like, other people's thoughts?"

"I can't hear your voice, just your thoughts, and they are all scrambled up usually, like my own. Sometimes I'm not sure whether they are yours or mine. They are just thoughts, like images, fragments mostly."

"Sounds confusing."

"It's a curse, actually."

"Hmmm."

"Feels good to run into somebody who isn't scared of you."

"Guess I don't have anything to hide. I like to be up front with people."

"No mixed messages from you."

Her laugh was music. "How did you get into this business?"

"Looking for a job after Afghanistan. In D.C. there's all kinds of unusual jobs."

"You have a kind of implant, don't you?"

He tapped his head with the flat of his hand. "A tiny chip. But you have to go through training, and they program the chip gradually—otherwise you'd go nuts!"

"And if you decide to leave, you turn in your chip?"

"It's a felony not to. They hunt you down."

"Are you in the CIA?"

He looked at her without replying.

"I guess you can't say. But are there any like you who **aren't** in the CIA?"

He laughed. "Good thing you can't read **my** mind!"

9

She was quiet for a minute, then asked, "I bet the divorce rate among you people is pretty high?"

"I heard that one coming. In a word, yes." He looked up at the floor display again—*23, 24, ...*

"I hope this isn't too personal, but . . ."

"I was married before Afghanistan. She couldn't wait."

"Sorry to hear that. But what I was wondering—do two of you, ahh, 'mind readers' ever get together?"

He nodded. "I know what you mean. They try to discourage it. It gets weird."

"Ever think about getting out?"

"Every day."

She looked at him. "My floor."

"Yes. Good to meet you."

"Maybe again."

"Hope so."

As the door opened, she moved toward it, thinking *Me, too.*

She left the elevator without looking back.

"Me, too," he said aloud as the door closed.

Scene 3

She sat alone at her favorite spot: a little table in the corner of the restaurant, where she could see the whole room at once. She'd rather have had company, but she needed to do some shopping before returning to work, and talk tended to use up the time.

In the booth next to hers, a man and a woman were leaning toward each other, talking. A waitress interrupted them briefly to bring their orders. In the next booth sat a man with his back to her. She could see that he was watching the images on an iPad and listening with earbuds. Farther on, three women were engaged in an animated but apparently confidential conversation. *Gossip, for sure,* she thought. In the other direction, two men at the same table were each reading a newspaper and taking occasional sips from coffee cups. Two booths were temporarily empty except for dishes left by recent patrons. A busboy pushed his cart next to one and began clearing the table.

Music, all but inaudible through the noise, played through speakers in the ceiling. She watched the counter people busily taking orders and retrieving food through the stainless steel pass-through to the kitchen. A young waitress appeared beside her, quickly took her order and disappeared in the back.

She was thinking about the mind-reader she met yesterday in the elevator. A shiver of something—excitement?—made the hair on her arms stand up. *"Those people" could be all around us,* she thought. She wondered how she had detected him the moment she stepped into the elevator. Some sixth sense had told her that he was "different." *How mysterious the mind is!*

She had just taken a paperback out of her purse to read when the waitress returned with her sandwich, so she put it back. She and the waitress smiled at each other without speaking. In ten minutes she had finished eating. Dropping a bill on the table, she picked up her check and headed for the register.

As she passed the man with the iPad, he spoke to her without looking up. "Good morning."

Startled, she turned and saw that it was **he.**

"It's afternoon already," she managed to say as he looked up at her, smiling.

She was torn. "I'd love to sit and chat for a moment, but I have to run some errands before I have to be back at my desk."

"Yes, I know."

It unnerved her. She smiled, and rushed on. By the time she was on the street her face was wet with perspiration. The cool air felt good. Her heart pounded.

From his booth, he watched her go. His smile was as much from appreciation of this attractive woman as it was from the humor of the situation. Humor, mixed with irony. Could he ever have a normal relationship, or was he, like a Catholic priest, forever wedded to his work? He glanced quickly at the couple he had been monitoring. They were oblivious to him, seeing, if anything, just a man with a little computer spending his lunch hour reading the *Washington Post*. He decided that they were no longer interesting, so he picked up his check and left.

It never stops, he thought as he headed down the sidewalk among the lunch-hour crowd, *six meters—they told us it would be constant, as long as people are within six meters.* Only the people walking in his direction were really readable; those coming toward him appeared in his mind as quick flashes of thought, gone before he could figure out who it was that he was picking up. They had also told him that he'd get used to it, as one gets used to tinnitus, that ringing and buzzing that some people hear all the time. But if you tune it out too much, then you're sure to miss something important when you're monitoring.

She was interesting, he mused. *She was nervous, but most people get freaked out. There's no talking to them if they know.*

And if they know, they can be dangerous. People talk. A few operatives have been killed because of fear. But that's not unusual in the Company.

He decided to make a report on the couple he was monitoring in the restaurant. Turning down an alley, he pulled out his cell phone and pressed a key.

Scene 4

"This woman in the elevator—what do you know about her?" His boss leaned back in his chair. Behind him through the glass wall, the city looked gray and sad.

At least yesterday the sun was out, Doug thought.

His boss swiveled around and looked out the window. "What can I say? It's April." He turned back and paused, waiting for a reply. "This woman in the elevator?"

"She's nobody of interest."

"You're sure?"

"She was clearly flustered when we met. I don't know how she picked it up, but she did. And then it was like I had only one arm or something."

"She knew about the operatives."

"Who doesn't? At least anybody who reads the papers knows about us."

"C'mon, Doug. There's something else going on, isn't there?"

Doug took a deep breath and grinned. "She's very attractive."

"And, just by accident," his eyebrows arching as he paused, "you've run into her two days in a row."

Doug, his frustration showing, asked, "You want somebody else to monitor her?"

The boss waved his hand. "Just use common sense, Doug. If she appears frequently, we'll put somebody on her. Meanwhile, don't initiate anything."

"I can handle it."

"You're vulnerable, dammit! You don't know who this is!"

"Okay, okay." He turned to leave.

"Don't get yourself killed," his boss said to his back, "just to get some ass."

The remark felt like an insult, but Doug blew it away. It takes practice to not think near your boss. He reads minds, too.

Scene 5

Doug saw her in the crowded elevator on the way down. Remembering what his boss had said, he caught up with her anyway on the way to the street, feeling guilty and daring and charged up. "Hi," he said, alongside her.

She started, and turned to see who had spoken. Her face softened. "Hi, yourself."

"I'm not supposed to do this—and maybe you'd rather I didn't."

She smiled. "Will I regret it?"

"Maybe. But just for lunch?"

"You already know what I'm going to say, right?"

He ignored the question. "The same place we bumped into each other?"

She didn't bother to reply. *This is kinda fun,* she thought.

"Yes it is," he said aloud.

They found a table at the far end of the restaurant. "This is Dutch," she said, looking straight at him.

"You're very positive about things."

"Life's too short . . ."

". . .to play games."

"But," she added, "we are, anyway, aren't we?"

"A kind of infinite game."

Her eyebrows went up just a little. "You read James Carse."

He smiled.

"Or did you pick it up from me?" Her head tilted slightly, a Mona Lisa smile on her face.

"Isn't that what Carse said, flirting is an infinite game?" He liked that look.

"No winners or losers. One hopes, anyway." She picked up the menu and scanned it.

"Last time you had the grilled tuna."

Her expression turned quizzical, and she stared at him. "I don't know if I can handle this."

"Sorry. You're feeling vulnerable again."

"Again?" Now she was frowning.

"When we met in the elevator, that's what you said."

"You know a lot about me, but I don't know much about you."

"Okay." He put both hands flat on the table and spread his fingers. Looking down at his hands, and then up at her, he said, "First, know this: monitoring other people takes effort. In a place as noisy as this, it's about all I can do to hear your spoken words. I was being flip—playing the game."

"Is it always going to be this hard?" Lines formed between her eyebrows.

A waitress appeared beside them, placing glasses of water before them. "Hello," she said brightly.

They both looked up at her. Meredith spoke first. "Grilled tuna."

"Make it two," Doug said. "And I'll have coffee with cream."

The waitress pointed to the creamer on the table. "One coffee?"

"Two," said Meredith. Then as the woman left, she looked at him. "I don't even know your name."

"Doug."

"I'm Meredith. But you knew that, didn't you?" Her voice was guarded.

"No I didn't. And I'm not very good at this."

"All right, hello, Doug. I'm glad to meet you—I think." She smiled.

Doug put his elbows on the table and rested his chin in his hands. He looked into her eyes. "I'm very glad to meet you, Meredith, even if you have me off balance."

"How could I have **you** off balance? You read my thoughts!"

"You have no idea how much power you have in this!"

She shook her head. "Bull shit."

He grinned. "No, it's not. I feel like a little kid, trying to keep up. And you don't think much before you speak."

The furrowed brows again. "What's **that** supposed to mean?"

"It means that I can't read your thoughts before you've already said them aloud."

She smiled. "Really?"

"Really."

"Good!"

Their coffee appeared, and Doug stirred cream into his. Meredith shook an envelope of sweetener, tore it open and emptied it into her cup. He watched her, and when she put her spoon down, he lifted his cup between them. "To infinite games."

She touched his cup with hers. "Thank you, Professor Carse."

"Have you read his latest book?"

"After *Games?*"

"Yes. It's *The Religious Case Against Belief.*"

"No. Doesn't sound like my kind of book."

"I got interested in Eastern religions while I was overseas. Took up meditating—which really came in handy in learning my job."

"Really? How . . ."

The waitress came with their sandwiches. "Here, you go."

In a softer voice, he said, "You have to learn how to quiet your own mind before . . ."

"Oh."

"And," he began, then took a bite from his sandwich, "right now it's not very quiet."

She laughed. "You mean you're not always in control?"

"I'm not always in control."

"I have to admit, I like to be in control—most of the time, anyway."

"May I say, 'I know'?" Then, before she could speak, "Not from reading your mind, either!"

Her easy laugh put them both at ease, and they ate silently.

After a few minutes, she said, "I got trapped in the elevator the other day. No, no—not that way! It was just packed with people, and I couldn't move. I was definitely not in control."

"What happened?" He wiped his mouth with his napkin.

"I started to cry."

"Because you were pinned?"

"Partly, maybe. But there was a woman next to me playing a song on her iPhone, and it reminded me of another time when I was held down."

"Hmmm?"

"No, it wasn't like I was being raped or anything. It was just a very intense experience."

Doug shook his head slowly. "I get the impression that you live your life very intensely. Very deliberately."

"But it seems to happen to me."

"I guess it goes without saying that my line of work has some intensity to it."

That head tilt again. "Do you like your work?"

"Sometimes. I can't talk about it, though."

"Oh. I understand. What **can** we . . ."

"I do have a life, actually. Or, I did."

"Tell me."

"Uh, mmm, oh, boy. Well, I got married right out of high school. Seemed like the thing to do."

"Meaning," she smiled, "she was pregnant?"

"Oh, no. It just felt like that's what you did. Neither of us went to college. But then, I realized I wasn't doing anything with my life. So, I joined the army and ended up in Afghanistan."

"Which she wasn't happy about."

"Right."

"I just realized . . ." She picked up her coffee cup just as the waitress arrived with the refill pot. "Thank you," she said to the woman. "I just realized that you're a lot younger than I am."

He smiled. "Not that much."

"That much."

"Make a difference?"

"It's just that I hadn't noticed before. No, it doesn't make a difference—right now."

He finished his coffee. "Okay, now that we have that out of the way—where were we?"

"You enlisted."

"Actually, I went to Europe and India and kicked around for a while before I enlisted."

"A while."

"Three years."

She made an elaborate gesture of pulling her phone from her purse, and pretended to speak into it. "Hello, Mother? He's not as young as I thought."

17

Doug laughed. "Told you."

"She couldn't wait, huh?" She pursed her lips.

"It was a long time to wait."

"Okay. I won't pry."

"Now you know my secrets—do you have any?"

She sighed. "For a first date, this is getting pretty deep."

"Okay. They can wait. Actually, I have to be someplace."

She looked at her watch. "Oh, lordie."

"Looks like we both have to be someplace." He picked up the check.

"Dutch!" as she reached in her purse for her wallet.

They hurriedly negotiated the bill and the tip, then went toward the register.

"I'll pay it," he said, "You go on."

She put a hand on his arm and looked at him. "Enjoyed it. Thanks." Then she was out the door.

He sighed, then smiled as he handed the check and money to the cashier.

"Yes, ma'am," he said to the woman just before she asked, "Was everything all right?"

There was a strange look on the cashier's face as he turned and left the restaurant.

Scene 6

"Was that **him**?" laughed Dolly when Meredith sneaked into her cube.

"Shhh!" She blushed.

Dolly came around the partition and sat down next to Meredith. When Meredith didn't say anything, Dolly held out her hands and shrugged, a big grin on her face.

"We just happened to meet on the way to lunch, and he asked me."

"Wel-l-l-l?"

Meredith grew serious. "I really can't talk about him," she said.

"Aww," her friend whined, and then said, "I saw you at The Egg Place."

"Just a friendly lunch." Meredith opened her computer.

"Is he married?"

"No."

"Sure?"

Meredith looked at her and smiled. "I don't think so."

"He looks young."

"Please—it's too soon to talk about it."

Dolly leaned close to her and spoke softly, "Was he in the elevator with George Harrison?"

Meredith grinned. "No."

"Just asking."

"Dolly, I have work to do!"

"Bye."

Meredith took a deep breath and let it out slowly as she began typing.

Scene 7

She stood off to one side and watched people get off the elevators. *Maybe he left before I did,* she thought as car after car emptied into the cavernous lobby. But her patience paid off. She turned and walked toward the front doors, knowing that he would see her. That way, he had a choice, whether to catch up with her again or not. She didn't know if he might be with his fellow workers—**operatives**, she corrected herself.

She was out on the plaza before he touched her elbow. "Turn left," he said quietly, then dropped back.

He's being discreet.

Halfway down the block he caught up with her. "Some people from my office," he said without looking at her. "Let's go to that little deli in the next block, okay?"

She took his cue and kept looking straight ahead. Then she couldn't contain it any longer, and burst into laughter. "I feel like I'm in high school again!"

He looked at her then, and caught her eye. "I feel a little like that, too. But my boss is a cautious guy."

"No consorting with civilians?" She was still smiling.

He slowed down until they had dropped a little way behind the people in front of them on the sidewalk. "Some of it is that—it's 'the Company,' after all . . . oh, shit!"

A slow, thoughtful smile. "You slipped."

He nodded. "I wish this was a two-way channel."

"Like walkie-talkies, or those little wrist things **certain people** wear?"

"Hard to be spontaneous when everything is a charade." He touched her arm. "Here's the deli."

They lined up at the counter and ordered separately. Nothing was said between them while they waited at the counter. When she got her order, she found a small table toward the back and sat down, waiting for him. Out the window, crowds moved by on the sidewalk in both directions. Occasionally someone stepped off the curb and dodged between vehicles to cross to the opposite side.

Then she was aware of how long it had been since she had sat down. She scanned the other customers who were standing up by the counter—he was not one of them. *What happened to him?*

She slowly unwrapped her sandwich, frowning at it. When her cell phone rang, she nervously dug it out of her purse. The phone said, "Unknown Number."

"Hello."

"Sorry, ma'am. Have to call you later."

She started to reply when she noticed the connection had been broken. Closing the phone and dropping it into her purse, she picked up the sandwich, then put it back into the paper and wrapped it up again. Her stomach ached. *What had happened? Did one of his buddies see him, and he didn't want to be seen with me? Is he off on an assignment? Is he running from someone? Is this the way it's going to be?*

She tried to be angry, but the lump in her throat said otherwise. Completely dejected, she went back to her cubicle, laid the wrapped sandwich on her desk, and tried to work.

"Hey, you look like somebody ate your cupcake," Dolly said, hanging over the partition. Gesturing toward the sandwich, she added "And it's not in that deli wrap."

"I got stood up—no, **abandoned** in the Ninth Street Deli."

"By your mystery man?" Dolly came around the partition and sat down in the cube. "What happened?"

"I guess he got called away just as we were about to have lunch. I was at a table waiting for him to get his order, and he just disappeared! A few minutes later he called and apologized, but couldn't talk."

Dolly smiled slyly. "He already has your cell number?"

"I didn't give it to him. I don't know where he got it."

"Obviously, he was motivated." She put her hand on Meredith's arm. "He'll be back."

Meredith absentmindedly fingered the wrapper on the sandwich. "I've been thinking about all the reasons this isn't going to work."

"You're hungry. Eat. And in between bites, tell me why this guy isn't a catch."

"He's not a catch!" Meredith exclaimed. "I'm not invested in this."

"Obviously, you are." Dolly sat back in the chair and crossed her bare legs.

Meredith smiled. Dolly was a woman on the prowl. The way she dressed, the way she talked, the way she walked, all were a Victoria's Secret waiting to be told. Next to her, Meredith felt like a Kansas schoolmarm.

She didn't used to feel that way. In her twenties, she made her way among men with confidence and that bit of lid-lowered seductiveness that attractive women enjoy—what they used to call in Hollywood "the 'come hither' look." A couple of disastrous relationships—and twenty years or so of natural deterioration—subdued the seductiveness. Instead, she grew stronger, more confident of herself in a different way. She didn't want to need. Mostly, she didn't want to be needy. She took a nothing job in the big city to be in on the excitement. It wasn't New York, but there was plenty of night life—jazz clubs and parties to be invited to, with or without a man. She didn't try to compete with the young women. She said she didn't need to. It didn't bother her to see the beautiful bimbos on the arms of freshman congressmen. Most of them couldn't carry on a conversation about James Carse.

She wilted. *Infinite games,* she thought. *Is this one of those? If it is, maybe it's not what I want, either.*

"I'm waiting." Dolly, smiling, looked steadily at her.

"He's younger. But that doesn't seem to matter to either of us—at least at this stage of the game. But he disappears once—is that an omen?"

"You've had, like, one lunch with this stranger, and already you're keeping score. What happened to my mature, confident woman friend who can blast an asshole off his bar stool with three words?"

Meredith smiled. "You're right. Thank you." She took a bite of her sandwich.

Dolly reached down and picked up Meredith's gym bag from the floor and held it up. "You work out twice a week. You can press sixty pounds. You run ten miles a week. You make me feel like a flower, maybe pretty, maybe smells good, but in ten years I'll be old, and you'll still be stunning and strong and smart—too smart for **this** place. And maybe too smart for **him.**"

"Okay, love. I hear you. Now, let me work it off!"

Scene 8

It was three days. He called once, rather late at night, but thirty seconds into the call—right after he had apologized again—the connection dropped, and he didn't call right back. She got the impression that he wasn't close by. His call said, "Unknown Number," just like the last one. She had no way to call him.

One night she downloaded "Concert for George" and wallowed in Eric Clapton playing the bridge for "Something." She looked for some pot she had stuffed in a jar somewhere, but couldn't find it. She thought of calling Paul, but her better judgment kicked in just in time.

Her phone said, "Unknown Number" again. She hesitated before opening it. "Hey."

"Hey." He waited a moment, then said, "I'm back."

"Really back?"

"Really back. I had a work emergency. That's all I can tell you."

"You know—" she began, "You know how I felt vulnerable because you had a power that I don't have?"

"Hmmm. Yes."

"I have another vulnerability if there's no way I can reach you."

"I'm sorry—I couldn't even wait for my sandwich!"

"Goddamn it, that hurts!" she almost screamed.

"You're right. I'm sorry. You know, I can't do my thing over the telephone. I'm pretty dumb sometimes. That didn't come out right."

"You don't know how close I came—how close **I am** to hanging up!"

"I hear you that you feel vulnerable because you can't reach me. I'm desperately trying to figure out a way to do that right now, but I'm upset that I've upset you and I feel like shit and I can't think straight. Can we meet someplace?"

Meredith reached over and pulled a tissue from its box. Wiping her eyes and taking a big breath, she said, "I hate being a needy woman!"

"There's a little bistro right around the corner from you. Will you meet me?"

"How do you know where I live?" She didn't know whether to be thankful or wary. He must have access to directories—easy to find her.

"I feel like I should apologize again. I should have asked you. It's just one of those things I do a lot, look people up. Meet me?"

"All right. Give me fifteen minutes."

"Make it thirty. I'm farther away than you are. Thank you, Meredith."

She knew the bistro well because she often ate dinner there. And it was comforting that they knew her there. She took another deep breath. *Do I not feel safe?*

She refreshed her face and walked to the bistro. He was waiting at a corner table. The night waiter smiled at her and started toward her, but when he saw that she was going toward Doug, he bowed slightly and withdrew. She actually smiled at his discretion.

"Hey." Doug smiled. She half expected him to rise, but he didn't.

"Hey." She sat down across from him.

"I've missed you, too," he said, and she remembered, *he is reading my mind.*

They sat silently for a few moments, just looking at each other. She noticed for the first time that he had a wisp of gray in his temples.

"I'm older than you thought," he said, reminding her of their conversation at lunch.

"I wish I were."

"Older?"

"Older and maybe wiser."

The waiter appeared. They looked up at him, both distracted. "How about a glass of wine," he suggested. "You like Pinot Grigio, don't you?" looking at Meredith.

She burst out laughing. "You're reading my mind!"

Doug thought it was hilarious, but the waiter looked mystified.

"Two of them," laughed Doug.

After the wine had been set before them, Doug took a slip of paper from his pocket and offered it to her. On it was an address of a Web site. "It will ask you for a password. Your ID is 'infinite,' and your password is 'games.' I think you'll remember that, but you have to memorize the address."

She started to take the slip from him, but he held on to it. She looked up at him.

He shook his head. "Sorry. You have to memorize it."

"Right now?"

"Yes."

The address looked at first like a random group of letters. "How ... Oh, I got it! It's James—"

He touched her lips and shook his head.

"My god, you **are** careful, aren't you?

"Nobody else can know this. Just us." He wiped the lipstick from his fingertip with a napkin.

"What's on the web site?"

He smiled. "So you can reach me."

They touched their glasses of green-gold wine and relaxed--finally.

The next morning before breakfast, she ran her usual fourteen blocks and beat her best time by six minutes.

Scene 9

Doug sat on a small cushion in the middle of a large, loft-like room in Arlington, his legs folded, his hands on his knees. Lined up along the walls were pieces of furniture arranged as though waiting for the moving van—or a high school dance. In one corner was a low bed—seemingly just a box spring and mattress on the floor. A small wooden table sat in another corner, next to a refrigerator and range and a nondescript cupboard. "A home like that of a struggling grad student in temporary quarters," he had described it.

He sat motionless, his eyes closed, for forty-five minutes, when a timer clanged in the "kitchen." Standing up slowly, working his legs and stretching his back, he walked toward the bathroom, leaving his cushion in the middle of the floor. He showered, dressed, turned out the lights and left for work.

Downtown, he ate breakfast in his usual restaurant and took the elevator to thirty-five. Touching the identification screen with his open hand, he passed through several doors to his office.

A woman entered immediately after him, and stood in the doorway without speaking.

"Yes, I can make that," he said to her.

She smiled, but didn't move.

"Coffee, yes, thank you," he replied.

He smiled to himself after she left, and looked at his watch. Opening his laptop, he typed in an address, then his identification and password. There was already a message from her, sent late last night, "I'm just testing the system. You do this yourself?"

He responded, "I'm not as old as you thought." No greetings, no names, just bare bones communication. He logged out, erased the history item and closed the laptop.

Fifteen minutes later, he was in his boss's office, along with two other operatives. The woman entered with coffee, said nothing, and left, closing the door quietly behind her.

His boss, Tony, leaned back in his chair and asked, "Well where are we? George?"

George opened his notebook computer and read his report from it.

"Well, said the boss, "that's disappointing."

"Yes," said George.

"Okay, stay with them. Doug, your assignment worked well, didn't it?"

"We nailed him," said Doug. "Even after it was over, he had no idea what had happened. I suppose he thought his group had a mole."

"Good. Stay loose. There'll be something coming up this afternoon, and I don't think it will take you to Dakar." He sat up in his chair and looked soberly at Doug. "I'm concerned about this babe, Doug."

Doug didn't say anything. "I know, I know," replied his boss. "So you ran a background on her. With a mind like I guess she has, what's she doing, entering data for an insurance company?"

"I depend on my gut all the time, Tony!"

"I'm afraid you're depending on your dick. Dicks lie all the time."

Doug frowned, but didn't reply.

"Andy, you take her on. Monitor her, but don't make contact. And don't let her see you and Doug together. Get her stats from Doug."

Andy nodded but didn't say anything.

Tony waved the three of them away, and turned around in his chair to look at the skyline.

Andy followed Doug to his office. Both men opened their laptops. Doug selected a folder in his machine and transferred it to Andy's computer. Andy studied the files in the folder for a moment, then looked at Doug and said, "She's been around."

"That doesn't make her an agent."

"Doug, I'll be above board on this. If she's okay, I won't mess it up for you."

"Thanks."

After Andy left, Doug resisted an impulse to log into the private web site and give Meredith a heads up. He hesitated, then closed his computer. *Got to be straight with her, and got to be straight with the Company,* he thought.

It was another three days before he had time for her again. He wasn't particularly worried about how she might be taking his absence because they had parted on good terms, and there weren't any messages from her on their web site.

Scene 10

Meredith looked for him every day at lunchtime, and every evening when she ate at the bistro around the corner. But she was determined not to be greedy. Or needy.

Peering over the cubicle partition, Dolly admitted to being bored with Meredith's love life. "But I admire your strength, lady," she said.

"I need to do some things for myself." Meredith continued to type into her computer.

"More things? Jesus. Bravo. But what things?"

"There's a meditation retreat at the Spirit Sands Conference Center this weekend."

"You going? Awesome."

"Want to come?" Meredith smiled up at Dolly, knowing what her answer was going to be.

"Not me. My idea of a great weekend does not include sitting for hours on a cushion, chanting in Nepalese."

"No, it wouldn't. But they don't chant. You just have to sit very still, and listen for 'that still, small voice' to give you wisdom." Both women laughed.

"Tell you what. You're going out there on Friday, right? Well, how about Thursday you and me go to Barney's and have dinner and maybe meet some interesting men? You're not engaged yet to this Doug, are you?"

"No, but I don't think—well, on second thought, okay."

Dolly extended her fist for Meredith to bang it. "Yeah, maybe if you get lucky you'll have something to confess to the priest or monk or whatever it is."

"They don't have confessions!"

"After all, being a monk is a very boring kind of life. He could get a little bit of pleasure out of hearing the confessions of a sexy broad once in a while."

"They don't have confessions!"

"Bummer."

"Bummer? What kind of word is that—sounds like something out of the sixties."

"You would know!"

Meredith's face changed. "You know," she said quietly, "the other night I downloaded the Concert for George Harrison."

"I bet you cried all the way through it," Dolly said, gently.

"I did."

"You know, I've never seen that video. Could we play it sometime?"

"Only if you promise not to laugh at me!"

"How long can you keep it?"

"Oh. That's right. It will only work until, let's see, Thursday."

"Then the horses all turn into mice and run away."

"And the beautiful gown turns into rags."

"I'll give up the concert for a chance to meet some princes in Barney's. You need some more princes in your life, Meredith. Especially before you go sit on your wild butt for a weekend."

Scene 11

"You'll like this assignment," said Tony. Behind him through the window, the sun was shining on the city.

Doug looked through the sheaf of papers. "Where's the Cayman Islands?"

"South of Cuba, northwest of Jamaica."

"What's there?"

"One of the world's biggest centers of financial shenanigans."

"So I get to sit in hotel bars and drink mineral water and keep my ears open."

"There's a few people we're interested in. They live pretty high, so it should be fun for you."

Doug continued to read, and Tony swiveled around to look out the window.

"Yes," said Tony to Doug's thought, "there's the business about the babe."

Doug smiled as Tony turned back around to face him. "Don't suppose I could take her along."

"You out of your gourd? Your associate will be somebody from our office."

"Who—Kathy?"

"She's real solid, and she can shoot the tip off a cigar. You just may need a good backup."

"She doesn't like me. I wouldn't want to be caught in friendly fire."

"All right. We'll find someone else. But I don't want you to have **too** much fun."

"How much time—how long do you estimate we'll be gone?"

"Depends on how well you do your job. Get the data in a week and you're on the plane home."

"And we leave tonight."

"Ten-thirty plane. Stops once in Charlotte."

Doug stuffed the papers into the envelope. "We're tourists, right? 'Manager and his secretary' off for a little 'business' trip."

"You don't want to be a married couple, because you might get tripped up in different stories."

Doug looked at him. "You mean, she's not a reader?"

"Kathy's not. I don't know who they can get." Tony was obviously ready for the conversation to be finished.

"Tell 'em I need a reader! Otherwise, it's all on my shoulders."

"Okay, I'll try." Tony waved Doug out of the office, and picked up the phone.

In his own office, Doug looked at his watch and pulled the papers out of the envelope again. He opened his laptop and sent Meredith a message: "Maybe a week. Later."

Caribbean in April? Light clothes. Swim trunks. Doug sighed. *Be fun to take her.*

But the young woman in the cab that picked him up that evening was not Meredith. Nice looking—nobody would question his wanting her along as his "secretary."

Doug looked up at the cab driver, who gave him a signal that he was one of them.

And, obviously, so was she. "Hi," she said brightly, "I'm Janet. Here's our story: We've worked together for about five years, and I'm indispensable to your work as a systems analyst. I know more about you than you do about me," smiling sweetly, "but that **is** the way it always works, isn't it?"

And then to his unvoiced question, she answered, "Yes I do read. I'm not very good at it, but I won't embarrass you."

And he picked up what followed in her mind: *I've been on sixteen assignments so far.*

"Sixteen."

"Yes." Janet looked at him and smiled. "We could almost pose as husband and wife, finishing each other's sentences."

"I haven't worked with other readers much," said Doug.

"You're used to being in control."

He grinned.

They went over the assignment, repeating every name they were supposed to connect with or monitor.

Sounds like a fun vacation, came from the cab driver as he pulled up at the airport unloading zone. Outside the cab with their luggage on the curb, Doug handed him his tip.

"Thank you, sir! Have a good flight!"

They were waved through security. As one of the TSA people looked at him, Doug picked up *That's them.* He wondered how the Company managed to get all the clearances organized, given the sheer numbers of operatives passing through.

On the plane, he and Janet practiced their silent communications. The mental noise in the aircraft was incredible; the two of them had to learn what each other's thoughts "sounded like" so they could sort them out of the hubbub that swirled around them. Once in a while, one of them had to say something out loud to clarify the dialog. *This conversation must sound pretty strange to anybody listening in,* she thought.

Doug liked her sense of humor. She approached the assignment like a professional actor, pausing at times to try a different way of "saying" something. When they intentionally thought in sentences, as people tend to do when they're rehearsing what they're going to say aloud, their communications went easier. *We might try that as a regular thing,* she thought.

"Good idea," he said.

The first leg of the flight took only an hour and a half, but they had to hurry to catch the connecting flight to George Town. Once again in the air, they ordered drinks.

I like gin and tonic, usually, she thought. *Maybe a glass of white wine with a meal.*

I go for Sapphire martinis, if I can relax. If things get tense, I'll drink Poland Spring and explain that I have stomach problems.

He ordered and paid for both of them. After they had consumed the drinks, they relaxed. The three hour flight to Grand Cayman was long enough for them both to doze. It was four A.M. by the time they got their luggage. They caught a cab to their hotel and went right up to their room. Without discussing it, they were circumspect in their preparations for sleeping, and occupied separate beds.

Doug did wonder, as he turned the light out, what she would have done if he had suggested sleeping together.

I'm comfortable with you, she thought very intentionally, *please don't spoil it.*

Gotcha.

Both of them smiled in the darkness.

Scene 12

In the morning, Janet awoke to find Doug in a bathrobe meditating on the balcony. She showered and dressed in a white pants suit, sunglasses perched on the top of her head.

"There's orange juice in the fridge," Doug said through the open door without turning his head.

She browsed the refreshments in the refrigerator. *Even fresh limes!*
You like lime in your gin and tonic?
Hmmm. Yes. There's also bitter lemon in here.
Give me ten more minutes, please.
Right.

Janet hung up clothes from her luggage and straightened her bed. Doug rose from his cushion and came inside. "Nice day," he said as he disappeared into the bathroom. She went out on the balcony to look at the incredible blue of the ocean. There didn't seem to be a beach close by, only a kind of rocky shoreline.

"Okay, I'm ready," he said, putting on his watch and taking his sunglasses from the night stand. He, too, was wearing white slacks, and a pale blue sport shirt.

In the hotel restaurant, they kept their conversation out loud, like normal tourists. Doug checked his phone for coverage, then while they waited for their breakfast he went on line to look for a message from Meredith.

"Thanks for telling me," was all she had written.

"Your wife?" Janet was teasing; she had read the dossier about him the day before, and she knew he wasn't married.

He just smiled.

" 'Thanks for telling me?' That's a wife who is pissed off." Doug had forgotten himself as he read the message, and of course Janet had picked it up.

"I move my lips when I read," he joked, but he was embarrassed. "No, we just don't know each other very well."

Their breakfast arrived, and they ate silently.

Outside, they walked down toward the water. The rocky shore was a disappointment—obviously not for flip-flops.

"You bring a suit?" she asked.

He hesitated, and she added, "A swim suit."

"Yes, but it doesn't look promising," he answered.

"There's the hotel pool."

"That's probably better, anyway, to make connections."

The rocky shoreline near the hotel was covered with what they called "ironshore," an accumulation of limestone embedded with fossils of marine animals. A brochure in the hotel said that there were beaches nearby, but apparently the Company had saved money by putting them up in a second-rate hotel. It was still picturesque.

They ambled over to the pool and sat under an umbrella at a table. Children were playing in the water.

Doug looked at Janet. *Who are we supposed to meet first?*

She smiled sweetly. "Isn't this delicious?" *His name is Roger Bean. Tall, gray hair, will be wearing a Panama hat with a blue feather in the band.*

"Sure beats the city." *People still wear Panama hats?*

She looked around through the glass doors to the hotel. "You know, it's lunch time already. We slept late!"

A rich baritone voice said, "Honeymooners are supposed to sleep late." They looked up to see a tall white man in a Panama hat.

Janet laughed. "No, we're not . . ."

"Well, you look sweet together." Roger Bean sat down at their table. His thoughts carefully said, *Good to see you both. I've read about you. Impressive résumés. Meet me at the rocks down there at four P.M. It's pretty deserted.*

Are you a reader? Doug asked, but got no response, so assumed the answer was "no." "We're enjoying the warm breeze," he said aloud. "Oh, sorry, this is my secretary, Lucy. I'm Daniel Thomas."

Roger Bean took his hand. "Good to meet you, Daniel and Lucy. No doubt we'll run into each other."

"Lucy" put her hand out. "I like your hat," she said.

"Thank you. Now, if you'll excuse me I have to meet someone for lunch."

The three of them stood and went into the hotel, Bean separating himself from the couple to greet another man.

"I'm not hungry after that breakfast," said Janet.

"No. Do you want to go back up to the room?"

"Yes."

Scene 13

Janet opened the little refrigerator. "I don't usually drink this early in the day, but we have until four o'clock, don't we?"

"We're 'on vacation,' right? Make one for me, too."

She turned and looked at him, unsmiling.

"Please?" he added.

"I'm just teasing. It's part of the role playing we're supposed to be doing."

"I know, I could tell." He picked up a large envelope from his open suitcase. "We could be looking through our documents."

"Lime?"

"Yes, thanks."

He sat in an easy chair near the open balcony doors and began leafing through the papers. "Bean has an associate—Lewis Alsten."

"I suppose we'll meet him, too." Janet brought the gin and tonics over and handed him one. "Bean is going to introduce us to our targets. Maybe we should make ourselves more visible around here beforehand. Maybe a dip in the pool before four."

I'm sure they will notice you in a bikini.

She smiled. *That's the idea, isn't it? Why else would they pick me to come down with you?*

You're not just a decoy. They originally chose somebody else— definitely not the decoy type.

Why the change?

She hated my guts, for some unknown reason. A big chip on her shoulder. I didn't want to take a chance if we got into a tight place.

She took a big sip from her glass. *I'm glad. This is a nice place to work.*

She pulled a chair up next to his and they spent a couple of hours going over their documents and communicating mostly in carefully expressed thoughts. The gin gave the work a comfortable easiness.

Doug stood up and stretched. "Okay, I've had enough. I think I'll change."

After he had put on his swim trunks, he sat down on the balcony to wait for Janet. She appeared in a few minutes clad in a next-to-nothing pink bikini, with a towel over her shoulders.

"Nice," said Doug. *Am I allowed to appreciate a fellow operative? Part of the role, isn't it?* "Thank you."

Out of the corner of his eye, Doug caught a glimpse of a dark man with a camera on the lawn across the street, then casually walking along the sidewalk. The camera had a very long lens attached to it. Doug turned and looked more carefully, and the man lifted the camera and seemed to be photographing some palm trees down the street.

Oh, oh. We may—it might be that we're being watched.

Janet looked in the direction he was looking. The photographer, dressed very touristy in shorts and a brightly colored shirt, turned and walked between some buildings and disappeared. *So soon?*

Let's play it as it is. Lock your suitcase and we'll go down to the pool.

Both of their bags had combination locks as well as built-in theft alarms. They went out, making sure the balcony doors were locked and the door to the hall was secure.

Janet, in her bikini, attracted many eyes at poolside. She stepped down into the water and pushed off. Doug, sitting on the edge of the pool, shook his head and smiled. *It's just skin,* he thought, *we all have skin. Did evolution do this to us just so we'd propagate?*

She swam back to where he sat, smiling at him. "Your mouth is open," she said.

"You're enjoying it, too."

"Of course!"

He dared not push himself off the edge and into the water. *What's so strange is knowing that in an instant she could pull a pistol out of that bikini and drop a bad guy. How did she ever get into this business?*

She caught only part of all of that, and looked quizzically at him. Then she splashed water on him and swam back across the pool. Stopping at the far end, she looked back at him. She was thinking something, but he couldn't catch it. She held up her left wrist and pointed to it. *The time! Of course.* He looked at his watch. Three thirty. He nodded to her and stood up.

Janet lifted herself easily out of the water—she was quite strong—
and walked around the pool dripping water off that gorgeous body,
grabbed her towel from the chair and joined him as he started for the
door. "The water was wonderful! You should have come in."

Inside the room, it was all he could do to keep his hands to himself.
While she went into the bathroom to change, he slipped out of his trunks
and into street clothes.

At five minutes to four, they were again in the sunshine, walking
toward the blue ocean.

Scene 14

The three of them stood at the edge of the ironshore, facing the Caribbean. The rough rocks prohibited walking farther in ordinary shoes. Roger Bean shook both their hands and said, "When we go back to the hotel I'm going to make a show of inviting you to join me for dinner at seven today."

He's really stiff, thought Janet.

Doug picked up a stone and threw it into the surf. *This is a big deal he's trying to pull off.*

"How many people will be there?" she asked Roger.

"Six, altogether. Two of them are your targets, so we'll make sure you each get close to one of them. Lewis Alsten is the other one, and I'll see that he sits next to me. So both of you will be opposite us—keep an eye on us. If I use my napkin, listen to me." *If I use my napkin, listen to me!*

Gotcha. Doug nodded, forgetting that Roger was not a reader.

"That was clear," Janet said, "but in the restaurant, there'll be a lot of noise pollution." She glanced up at Roger.

"I don't think this is going to be dangerous to you. But be alert."

"I think somebody was taking pictures of us on our balcony a few minutes ago," said Doug.

Roger looked down at the two of them. "Was she wearing that bikini?" He was smiling.

"That could very well have been it," laughed Doug.

"When we go back to the lobby, start to go up to your room. I'll call you back." He turned and casually made his way from the ironshore toward the hotel. *Don't hurry after me.*

Janet and Doug ambled back, stopping to watch a big sea bird fly overhead. "Bet there's a camera strapped to him," Doug said.

She looked at him. *Relax, Doug.*

Yeah, I know. He stopped and turned to her, taking her hands in his. *This is part of the role, okay?*

She nodded and smiled.

But I have to admit I'm nervous. I feel responsible for your safety.

She leaned into him and raised her face to him. "Kiss me. We're supposed to be lovers, remember?"

It was a kiss that would have fooled a movie director. When it was over, they stepped apart and just looked at each other for a moment. Then they turned and walked toward the hotel.

Don't overdo the role-playing, she thought, looking down at his trousers.

His face grew hot. *I'm not very good at this game.*

Yes you are. You are very good. She laughed. *Just stop worrying. I can take care of myself.*

As they rounded the pool, they returned the smiles of several people who had been watching them come up from the shore. *We performed well!* thought Janet.

Inside the lobby, they headed for the stairs.

"Oh, Daniel and Lucy!" called Roger. They turned to see him standing with several other people near the desk. He walked toward them, saying, "I'd love to have your company at dinner tonight. Can you make it, or do you have other plans?" His smile was wide.

Doug and Janet looked at each other, then at him. "We'd be delighted," Janet said.

"Excellent! Let's meet at the hostess station." Roger shook Doug's hand, then took Janet's hand just a little tenderly. Doug thought he was going to kiss it, but he didn't.

Up in their room, Janet smiled at Doug and said, "That was sweet, Daniel."

When he started to reply, she put her finger to his lips. *Something's different here.*

Doug frowned. *What?*

I'm not sure. She began snooping around the room.

Doug watched her. *A real pro.* Then he said, "Lucy, you know I love you?"

She swept across the room and into his arms. "Oh, Sweetie!" *There's a camera in the drapes. Don't look. It's at the very top left.*

He kissed her again, passionately, thinking all the while, *This is getting out of hand!*

*Oh, boy, **is** it!* She pulled away. "I'll be right back." At the bathroom door she turned. "Okay?"

"Okay." He pulled down the bedspread and took off his clothes. By the time she undressed and returned, he was under the sheet, holding it open for her. She slipped into his arms. *Keep the sheet over us. We don't want to end up on YouTube.*

For a moment, Doug felt weird, knowing that the little camera in the drapes was recording their every movement. But he promptly forgot everything but the soft, smooth body in his arms.

Scene 15

"Ah, there you are!" Roger Bean reached out and took Janet's hand. The hostess led them to a table in the corner of the big restaurant, with Roger leading Janet by the hand. "I asked for the quietest table in the place," he said. "Our friends will be here momentarily. Please sit." He pulled out a chair for Janet, pointed to Doug's place next to her, and took a seat opposite them, with his back to the corner.

When Roger saw the others arrive, he waved grandly at them. "I hope you don't mind having our lovely couple between you," he said to the two strangers. "Daniel is a systems analyst with EDS, and Lucy is his right arm! Where he is called, she goes, too. A wonderful arrangement, don't you think?" Gesturing to one of the men, he said, "I want you to meet Wolfgang Zeit, who is a brilliant investment counselor, and Heinrich Handel, the best money salesman in the Caribbean. They have a very large office here in Grand Cayman, as well as branches all over Europe."

Daniel stood and shook hands with the two men, and Lucy allowed them to hold her hand for a brief moment.

"My dear," Roger said to Lucy, "you look flushed. I hope you didn't get too much sun on your first day here!"

She smiled. "I guess I'll have to switch to a stronger sun-block." She and Daniel exchanged glances.

Just then, Lewis Alsten arrived, and was introduced all around. As soon as he sat down, a waiter approached to take their drink orders.

Roger shook out his napkin and touched his lips with it. Thinking carefully, *I'll see to it that you stay clear-headed, okay?*

Daniel and Lucy both ordered gin and tonic. When the others had ordered their drinks and the waiter was about to turn away from the table, Roger caught his sleeve and whispered something to him, pointing out some item in the wine list. The man nodded and left.

"I took the liberty of ordering a very fine Pinot Noir to go with our dinner," he said to the group. Is that suitable for everyone? It's one of the best California wines ever produced—MacPhail Sangiacomo Vineyard Pinot Noir 2007, from Sonoma County."

"Thank you, Mister Bean," Lucy gushed. "It's so nice to have somebody around who knows good wine!"

And the dinner progressed. Daniel picked up a lot of negative thoughts from Wolfgang Zeit, most of it directed at Roger Bean. *What a windbag!* he was thinking. *It's a good thing he has lots of money. I wouldn't want to spend any more time with him than I have to.*

Lucy, on the other hand, was noticing almost glee from Heinrich Handel, the salesman beside her. He thought, *I know people like him. He'll drink more than the rest of us put together, and then I can simply hand him a pen to sign his name. A sitting duck.*

Lewis, Daniel noticed, said and thought very little. At least, he could pick up very little from the quiet man. He did seem to be watching everything that was going on. Roger dominated the conversation the whole evening, talking about everything—the weather, the economy, the "honeymooners," as he called them, and the free market, especially as it existed on the Caymans.

Somehow, the subject came up of money laundering. Roger took a strong permissive stance about smart investors protecting their assets by passing them through various organizations to hide their source. "Government wants all of our money!" he ranted.

It became apparent that this was just a preliminary meeting. Both sides were watching each other, trying to assess the weakness of the other, looking for clues that the other was as it professed to be: an investment firm about to offer a package to a rich American. The two Germans drank heavily, finishing two or three cocktails before dinner, and then polishing off the expensive wine. Daniel and Lucy each had a small glass of Pinot Noir. Their gin and tonics were nothing but seltzer water with a twist of lime. *It's awful to waste that good wine on these drunks,* he thought. Lucy nodded and laughed brightly. If he didn't know better (unless somebody behind the bar made a mistake), he would have thought that she was really tight. Her red face in the beginning, however, had faded. *That was cute, about the sun block.*

Was I really that red?

You were indeed.

Roger wiped his mouth on his napkin. *Okay, we've gone as far as we can. Let's break this up.* "Folks, you'll have to pardon me, but I've reached my pumpkin hour. You young folks can stay as long as you want—order more wine if you like. They'll put it on my tab."

Daniel stood up. "I think I'm ready to call it a day, too. Lucy, we have some work to do in the morning."

At that point, everyone at the table stood, shook hands all around, and thanked the host, Roger (the "rich investor") for the wonderful meal. The Germans seemed as anxious to leave as the Americans.

Up in their room, Doug and Janet sat limply in the easy chairs and let their breath out. Doug gestured with his eyes toward the camera. "I am really bushed. I did eat and drink too much!" he said.

"My lobster was fabulous!" Janet said.

I guess we need to talk about our arrangements.

You mean where do we sleep?

With that camera up there, it will look strange if we suddenly go back to sleeping in separate beds. But I'm also feeling weird about it. I don't want to complicate our assignment.

You're right. Suppose I get modest and insist on separate beds. A girl has the right to set the pace of things, doesn't she? "Daniel, sweetie, this afternoon was truly wonderful, but I don't want us to get too used to all that togetherness. Do you know what I mean?"

"Not exactly." He looked at her and thought of how she had felt next to him earlier.

Ooh, I know. she thought *We kinda let the cat out of the bag, didn't we?* "Let's sleep in our own beds. I'd really be more comfortable. Do you mind?"

"No problem. It's your call. But I don't have to like it, do I?"

"I know, I have a Puritan streak in me, from my family."

"All right."

"When we get back home, I want you to meet my family." She smiled softly at him and went into the bathroom.

He turned down both beds and turned out the light. After they were both in bed, they said goodnight. Much later, the camera picked up only the sound of rustling bed clothes. After a while, it stopped.

Scene 16

The next morning, they showered, dressed, and went down to breakfast carrying their laptops. Afterward, they found a spot in one of the common rooms where they were not in range of any of the hotel's surveillance cameras, and set to work on reports for Roger.

"Turn off your wireless connection," Doug said. "No point in taking chances."

"Right."

So far, neither of them had noticed anything about the targets that indicated more than greed. Roger's money laundering remarks had not stimulated any similar thoughts in the Germans. But the Company had reasons to believe that they were getting money from groups in the United States and funneling it to terrorist groups overseas.

Roger was not pleased with their reports—or, at least, with their findings. And the fact that someone had bugged their room and someone was possibly taking photographs of them, all pointed to something more dramatic than greed in the situation.

"I need to light a bigger fire under them," he said later as they walked along the neighboring beach. "Daniel, I'm going to hire your services as a systems analyst so that you can be included in the negotiations that will set the fire going."

"Do you want me only as an observer, or do I participate actively?" Daniel was nervous. He wasn't a systems analyst in fact, and he felt vulnerable in that role.

"Leave that to me. I'm in contact with others who will feed me garbage and I'll pass it on to our friends. If you can merely absorb some of the main points so that you can appear to participate, I think we're good. Lucy, I'm not sure how we're going to use you in this, so put on your bikini and lie around at the pool—only don't get too much sun!"

I don't like this, she thought to Daniel.

Daniel nodded, half in response to Roger and half to her. *I don't either, but we can work something out.*

Roger and Daniel agreed to meet at four o'clock, where they could be seen as developing ideas for the potential investment plan. Daniel and Lucy returned to their room, aware of the camera in the drape.

Daniel received a call on his cell phone. Someone had sent him a photograph of him, Lucy and Roger conversing on the beach. There was no message. He frowned. *What's this about?*

Lucy looked at the photograph. *Somebody is guessing that we're working with Roger?* Aloud, she said, "Well, that's a nice picture. Wonder who took it."

A few minutes later, Roger phoned their room phone. Lucy picked up the phone, and before she said anything aloud, her face registered shock, and then she hung up. "Roger is leaving," she said simply. *He said to forget the whole thing!*

Something is happening—we'd better contact home. "Oh, that's too bad. He was an interesting guy."

Just in case it isn't what we think it is, be cool. She took her cell phone from her suitcase and pressed a key to get her voice mail. When it connected, she entered a three-number code and waited. A moment later, she hung up. "Oh, damn!" she said. "My brother is ill!" She looked at Doug. "He's been in chemo therapy."

"You need to be there. I guess our vacation is going to be a short one." Daniel looked at his watch. "I'll call the airline and see if we can get a plane out."

Lucy took his arm and turned him toward her. Putting her arms around his neck, she said softly, "I'm sorry. I was looking forward to this week."

Daniel kissed her gently. "You need to be with your family."

And so they left Grand Cayman to return home and their "real" lives. In the air, Janet held Doug's hand for a long time. *At least, I'm glad we had the time we did. Whatever went wrong with the assignment, I don't think it was our fault.*

Doug laughed. "I threw a towel over the camera as we left."

Janet smiled. *Should have thought of that last night!*

Scene 17

They were picked up at Reagan International and driven immediately to an office downtown. Doug and Janet were debriefed separately, and they didn't see each other again. Doug found out that apparently their targets had been tipped off, and had left the island in the middle of the night, after which Roger had been contacted to immediately cut off the whole operation and return to D.C.

Doug arrived at his loft late that evening, and immediately checked the Web site for a message from Meredith. There was none. He sent her one, "Returned early. Dinner tomorrow?"

There was no reply when he checked just before going to bed, but in the morning she had written, "Same little place?"

"Six-thirty?"

"Good."

He reported in to Tony, who had already received word from the Company. "Don't sweat it," Tony said, "can't win them all."

Doug asked, "My associate—she have a phone number?"

Tony looked at him and laughed. "Forget it, lover boy. That's verboten; you know that!"

"I just thought we had some unfinished business when the plane landed."

"I have no doubt. Consider the case closed."

"Any chance we might work together again?"

Tony shook his head. "Forget her. Period."

But Janet was hard to forget. Even if he were interested in Meredith, he would like to stay in touch, at least.

Who are you kidding? came the reply. He had forgotten Tony was still within mind-shot.

"Incidentally," Tony added, "you'll be pleased to know that your 'other' babe has been cleared. Andy gave her a clean bill. You know she works out at that gym around the corner? She's knocked around, but above board all the way."

"Thanks." Doug closed the door and returned to his own office. He wondered how Meredith would take the news that she had been checked out by the Company. Or that anyone had had reason to want to. Would she blame him?

It was a moot point, he decided, and didn't need to be brought up at this stage in their relationship.

Scene 18

Her waiter recognized him when he arrived at the bistro, and led him to a table in the back. "Pinot Grigio?" he asked.

Doug looked at him. "I've been here once, and you remember what I drank?"

The man smiled. "I remembered that you were with Meredith."

"She must be a regular."

"Very regular. We take care of her."

"Wow. That's great."

"I'll bring your wine." He disappeared into the back room.

Doug thought about Meredith—how different she was from Janet. Janet was smart, sexy and playful, and a very competent operative. But he felt a wall around her, as though she only let him see of her what she chose to reveal. Meredith seemed softer, more vulnerable (as she reminded him several times). She was quite attractive, and at one time must have been a real knockout. If he had to choose between them— something he apparently would never get the opportunity to do—he thought Meredith would be his choice.

But at this point, he wasn't even sure the choice would be his. He felt as though she had offered him something tentatively, and that he needed to be careful not to blow it.

The waiter returned with two glasses of wine just as Meredith appeared at the table. She smiled at both men, and sat down. "He saw me coming," she said to Doug.

"Good to see you." Doug was a little surprised at her beauty, as though he had forgotten, in the intense Caribbean sunlight.

"I hope you had an interesting adventure," she said, and thought clearly, *I'd give anything to know what it was!*

"Sometimes, even my assignments don't go as well as expected." He immediately regretted saying that. It could be dangerous for her to know too much about his work.

"Oh, I'm sorry to hear that," she said. "I, on the other hand, had an interesting weekend."

"Tell me about it." He watched the beginning of a smile at the corner of her mouth.

"You can probably read all about it from my head!" She laughed.

"No, I want you to say it." Doug made a show of settling himself in his chair to listen.

"I went on a meditation retreat."

"Really! What kind of meditation?"

"Mindfulness—they have another word, Vipanna, or something like that."

"Vipassana."

"That's it. We sat for hours and hours. My back was killing me. I finally had to sit in a chair."

He leaned toward her on his elbows. "Now that it's over, what do you think?"

"Oh I guess I'll go again, but not for a while. I need to do something about my back."

"I can give you some help there," he said. I sit every day for a half or three-quarters of an hour. It gets easier, if you sit right."

"And I have an admission—I went out on the town one night, too." As he looked surprised, she added, "With a girlfriend. We got snockered." That was what she really wanted to tell him.

"But it was fun, I gather."

She hung her head, then looked up at him, a guilty-little-girl look. "For a while it was. I got sick in the cab home."

"Ouch."

"I promised myself, 'never again.'"

"I can imagine. I've said that myself."

"Why do we do those things? I'm an adult woman. I know what four martinis do to me."

He laughed. "Do you want a therapist's advice?"

"No!" Meredith smiled wryly. "It was a rhetorical question."

"Okay, have you recovered enough to eat some dinner now?" Doug picked up a menu.

"Oh, yes—that was before the retreat."

They ordered food, and exchanged small talk for an hour. He was aware that he wasn't picking up much from her thoughts. It was as though she were completely up front all of the time, responding and initiating without thinking.

Then, over decaf coffee, she suddenly said, "You slept with her, didn't you?"

The shock showed on his face. He hadn't picked that up from her thoughts, at all.

She hung her head. "I'm sorry. That was mean."

Doug didn't say anything, wondering how he could explain and knowing he did not dare. The heat of his guilt swirled in his brain. Desperation showed on his face.

"Doug, forgive me! That started out as a joke, a bad joke. You don't have to tell me anything. I don't want to know!" Her eyes were filling up.

He didn't know what to say next. *No, I didn't? How did you know? It was a mistake? I'm sorry?* Everything he thought of turned into an admission. The little she knew of his work meant that she would know too much if he admitted he was on an assignment with a female.

"I met someone I used to know," he lied.

Meredith took out a tissue and dabbed at her eyes. "Damn it!" she said, "I didn't want to know! It was just my paranoia, guessing at what could go wrong."

Something told him, however—and he couldn't be sure what it was—that it was more than a guess. This woman had a gift. He remembered how quickly she identified his "skill" the first time they met in the elevator. He wanted to talk about it, but this was obviously not the time.

She turned around to look for their waiter.

"Hey, let's not stop here," he pleaded. "At least, let's finish the evening on a better note. Please?"

She had caught the waiter's eye, and as he approached, she said, "Doug, you didn't deserve that. I can live with the knowledge that you had sex with somebody else, but I'd rather not. I hate this need of mine!"

Doug handed a credit card to the waiter, who disappeared again. "I don't want to leave it like this," he said. I don't know what to do."

"I don't know why this is so goddamn important to me," she said huskily. "I was doing perfectly well before I met you." She looked up at him. "What have you done to me?" She managed a sad laugh.

"Something clicked in that elevator," he said softly. "I don't know what it was, either. Our minds are pretty mysterious."

"Well, yours is. You know all about mine!"

"Not true. I get glimpses of thoughts from you, but there's so much more about you that I don't know. And I want to—I want to hear it from your lips, not from your thoughts."

Meredith sighed, and was silent for a moment. "I know that I've been followed," she said slowly, "not so much physically, but people have been checking up on me. Is that your doing?"

He shook his head. "Someone in my organization noticed us together, and they are very careful. They told me yesterday that you're safe." He laughed.

Her eyes widened. "The CIA was investigating me? That's hilarious!"

Doug put his finger to his lips, then he smiled. "They are a thousand times more paranoid than you are." He immediately regretted saying the word.

But she was feeling more at ease. "So they also know you slept with her." A wry smile.

"I'm sure." Then he added, "I wish I could talk about it."

"I don't want to know!"

"Okay, what do you want to know about me—that I can tell you?"

She laughed. "You know, it used to make me uneasy that you could read my mind. Now, that's the least of my concerns!"

"Okay, to start—what?"

"First, can I trust you with my heart?" She held up both hands. "Stop. No. That's not what I want you to tell me. I have to hear it from my heart. MY heart."

"Then what?"

"I want to know your history, I guess. I'm curious how you got into this line of work, aside from what you said in the elevator, that you just picked up this job because it looked interesting. Or can you not tell me that?"

"They picked me more than I picked them. I took a battery of tests for civil service, and I guess my scores pointed in this direction. I've always been interested in the mind and how it works. I'd read all the books on psychology and consciousness and neurology—what I could understand, anyway. They put me in a couple of classes, and then asked if I'd take the chip in my head."

"You stood out from the crowd." She tilted her head in that curious way.

He waited. "Okay, what else?"

"Where'd you grow up?"

"Cincinnati."

"I've been there. Pretty city, with the river and the hills."

"How about you?"

"I grew up in California, went to Berkeley, poked flowers in the guns of kid soldiers. Smoked pot and experimented with a lot of stuff. Including sex. Tried it all. Finally decided I'd had enough."

"So then you got married and settled down in Omaha."

She looked quizzically at him. "Is that what they said in their dossier? No, I did get married—a couple of times—but never lived in Omaha."

"I was kidding. What did you study in Berkeley?"

"Biology. Psychology. Took some graduate courses in neurology."

"How'd you come to read James Carse?"

"I took a course from him at NYU in religion." She smiled. "I liked his class, but religion always irritated me."

"You'd probably like his later book."

"Maybe."

"You get into encounter groups or anything like that?"

"Oh, yes," she said, "Spent most of two summers at Esalen. Big Sur is so beautiful!"

"Ever hear of Jack Gibb?"

"Heard of him. TORI, or something like that."

"He was before my time, really," said Doug, "but I was in some intentional communities and his theories came up a lot. Trust, Openness, Realization, Interdependence …"

"We do have some things in common, don't we?" She reached over and touched his hand. "I'm sorry about that tantrum."

"It wasn't a tantrum."

"With all I've done in my life, I can't judge other people."

Doug smiled. "It didn't sound like you were judging. You were just reacting to something you didn't want to hear."

She looked into his face. "I want to keep talking. Would you come up to my place?"

"Sure."

When the waiter returned, Doug signed the check and they walked out together. The spring evening smelled fresh and clean. The short walk to her apartment was mostly in silence, except for the noise of the city around them. Inside, both were calm.

She put her key in the lock. "I'm feeling giddy," she admitted. Opening the door and entering, she held it for him, her eyes on his.

A shriek came from another room, startling Doug.

Meredith laughed. "My cockatiel," she said. "He's called Chick. He always greets me when I come in." She left to attend to the bird.

The apartment was tidy—sparsely furnished, with a few framed black and white photographs on the walls. He looked closely at a couple of them. "Your photographs?"

She returned with a yellow bird on her shoulder nibbling at her earring. "A hobby of mine. I had a job once, a kind of PR person at an intentional community in Canada. That's where I learned to develop my own."

"Nice work."

"Thank you." She went into the open kitchen. "You want more coffee?"

"No, thank you."

"Something else to drink?"

He smiled. "You don't have to be a hostess. We came up here to talk."

"Role playing, I guess." She returned the bird to its room and came back. Then she took Doug by the hand and led him to the sofa. "Come sit with me."

They sat silently for a long time, still holding hands. She sighed.

"What's the sigh for?"

"Just letting go. All the way up here I was anticipating. Silly school girl."

He looked at her face. She was smiling at the far wall. "Anticipating what?" And then he thought, *Making love?*

She laughed. "Oh, not **that**. Just **this**." Looking at him, she said softly, "Odd, isn't it, how **that** comes up so quickly—sex?"

He laughed. "I was about to pontificate about evolution and all that, but that's not what I want to say." It was clear to him, however, that sex was not very far away from this moment. "I'm feeling really mellow. This is where I want to be right now, sitting on a sofa with you."

Meredith kissed him, lightly, on the lips, then they both smiled and she did it again.

Settling back, Doug thought, *I'm really turned on, but I don't want this peace to be over.* Aloud, "You said at the restaurant that you wanted to keep talking."

"Yes." She thought for a moment, settling back on the sofa beside him. "When I'm alone, I analyze, all the time. I analyze my motives, other people's motives, other people's meanings in what they've said— it's a bad habit. Being with you, I just want to **be here.**" She took his hand again and turned her face to him.

Doug picked up nothing at all of her thoughts. *Amazing,* he thought.

"Yes it is, isn't it?"

He sat up quickly. "What?" Turning to face her, leaning his arm on the back of the sofa, he asked, "What did you just say?" His heart was pounding.

"I just responded to your word 'amazing.' It **is amazing**, isn't it?" Her eyes were half closed.

"Meredith, I didn't say it!"

She opened her eyes and thought a moment. "How did I get that word? You said it!"

"No, I didn't. I **thought** it."

Furrows appeared between her eyebrows. "You did?"

"Yes. You read my mind!"

"No, no. That's **your** shtick. I clearly heard you say it."

Doug leaned back again, dumbfounded. "Okay," was all he could manage to say. His mind was going crazy trying to take it in. *Tell me again!* he thought, very intentionally.

She was silent, watching him. Then, "Are you okay?"

He was trying to quiet his mind, to pick up what she might be thinking, but it was hopeless. Nothing clear was coming, and it was all scrambled up with his own wild thoughts.

"I guess I'm imagining things. You know how sometimes we think we experience what we want to?"

"You want me to read your mind?" She tilted her head in that way he liked. Her hair, reddish blond, slightly curly, hung alongside her cheek, caressing it. One strand curled toward the corner of her mouth. He wanted to touch it, but he didn't want to break this spell that he felt. "Maybe," he said. "I don't want something artificial to separate us."

"I can't read your mind," she said simply. "Sometimes I wish I could, but I can't."

"You do believe me when I say that most of the time I can't read yours, either?"

She frowned. "I don't know how it works. I can't imagine, even, how what's in one person's mind could be communicated somehow to another mind."

"Sometime I'll describe it to you the way it was described to me. But not now, okay?"

"Okay." She turned and lay back down on the sofa, pulling him with her.

Scene 19

Doug went home after a while so he could sleep and get cleaned up for morning. A part of him was analyzing his situation, their relationship, and whatever it was that she possessed—the "gift" that he was convinced she had.

Another part of him was basking in her aura. He had never given much credence to the concept of an aura, even though he had heard about it during his time in India. But now, it felt real. There was something very special about this woman. He could smile at her jealousy and her lack of confidence, but from first meeting her he felt she had some kind of power beyond that of just a strong woman. He had known strong women. In fact, it seemed that most of the women he found himself with were assertive and confident. Perhaps, he had decided, that's the kind he was attracted to, or else the kind that found him attractive. One of his lovers told him years before that she usually connected with "accommodating" men. He guessed that was him.

Janet was strong, but it was her body that gave him an almost electric thrill to look at and to touch. She was physically perfect, and of course she knew it and used it to get what she wanted. Well, no, he guessed, there was more to her than that. She was very competent. Still, . . .

It occurred to him that he was finding fault with Janet in order to ease some of the guilt he felt about having had sex with the younger woman. Making love to Meredith was a completely different experience. It was as though their souls had merged. *Wow,* he thought, *wouldn't Janet have fun with that idea!*

The notion that our minds extend outside our bodies seemed ridiculous. He once loved a woman who was convinced that thoughts exist as vibrations. Higher thoughts were on a different vibrational level than ordinary thoughts. Of course, this chip in his head certainly was picking up **something** from people around him. He didn't know how it worked, and he wasn't convinced that the engineers who designed it knew how it worked. He'd heard that they stumbled on it, somehow picking up those "vibrations" in a machine that was developed for something else. The probes they used to try to locate the source turned out to work in reverse—they transmitted certain signals from the machine into the brain, and a person could identify patterns that were transmitted.

Years before, biologists had found that they could cause animals and people to sense things such as odors or colors when electric probes stimulated certain areas of the brain. People could experience panic attacks or wonderful bliss from nothing more than electric tickling among the folds of the brain. Monkeys and other animals were implanted with electrical circuits that stimulated the erotic centers in their brains, linked to levers in their cages. "Whenever they pushed the lever, they had an orgasm," one researcher told him. "If we hadn't cut the power, they would have kept pushing that lever until they dropped over dead. They weren't interested in food or sleep."

"Ever try it on yourself?" he had asked the fellow, but he never got a straight answer.

Perhaps, Doug thought while riding the subway to his office, *the wiring to my chip is also transmitting, and Meredith is simply sensing that signal. The original machine worked in that direction, after all.*

Trying to disregard the cacophony of thoughts of other people near him in the car, he closed his eyes and focused on his breathing. Slowly the thoughts—even his own—became softer and all but disappeared beneath the regular mechanical rumbling of the wheels of the subway train. Sometime later, he was stirred by the force of subway brakes approaching his stop.

Doug joined the other automatons trudging up the stairs to the street, and along the crowded sidewalk to Connecticut Avenue and his building. The jammed elevator to thirty-five seemed worlds away from the sofa in Meredith's apartment, where soft silence lay over them like down.

Scene 20

"Shall we try the deli again?" he asked as they reached the street.

"Do you have to be careful?"

"Nope," he laughed. "You've been cleared."

"I'm relieved." Meredith was as relaxed as he. Her face brightened often in a smile as they walked and talked.

At the counter in the deli, waiting their turns, she quipped, "You won't abandon me again if you get a call, will you?"

"I promise."

At the table, they watched the passing crowds outside. "Right now, I can't imagine why they hurry," he said.

"Maybe what they want isn't sitting across the table from them in this noisy little room."

Doug took a bite from his sandwich and put it down. After a moment, he said, "I have an admission to make."

"Oh." Meredith stopped and looked at him. He picked up her thought, *Here it comes.*

"No, not that," he said, smiling. "It's only that I keep thinking—bad habit—this is almost too good to be true."

"Which means, I guess, that we're no longer in an infinite game?"

"I could lose."

She held his eyes with hers and said softly, "Or I could."

"I keep telling myself that it's too early for this."

"'**This**' meaning . . ."

"Meaning I'm feeling very vulnerable. I don't want to lose you. And I think it's too soon to feel that."

"Too soon for promises?"

"My head says 'Be careful.'"

"Doug," she said seriously, "we're not kids. We've been here before—at least, I have. This is a very scary part of the trip."

He took a deep breath and let it out slowly. Meredith ate from her sandwich without taking her eyes off his.

"Okay," he said finally, picking up his sandwich, "it's lunch time, and we have our food, and the logical thing to do with it is to eat it while it's here. We'd only regret it if we chose not to eat while we could."

She nodded slowly. "Life is short."

They both smiled at the layers of meaning in what they said, and continued their meal.

Scene 21

Doug and Meredith had dinner nearly every evening, sometimes at his loft, sometimes at her apartment, and often at the bistro around the corner. He introduced her to his "meditation studio," as he called his loft.

"This big space separates me from outside interference. Transcending the noise in my own mind is difficult enough when I'm not involved in separating my thoughts from those of others."

"It's a wonderful space." She laughed. "You're like a monk here in your monastery."

"You said you had pain trying to sit in meditation." He pulled out several cushions from a closet. "Try sitting this way." He demonstrated a half-lotus position. "The main thing is to get your pelvis tilted, so that your spine can curve upward in balance."

Meredith sat on one of the cushions and folded her legs. "My slacks bind—they're too tight for this."

Doug took a shawl from his bed. "Take off your slacks, and put this over your legs to keep them warm. You should always wear loose clothing."

After trying a higher cushion and making adjustments to the position of her legs, she said she felt balanced.

"Imagine a string attached to the top of your head," he explained. "It's pulling you straight up, and you don't want the string to break, so you go with it—straight up. There, that's it. Now let your arms relax. You can fold your hands in your lap, or put your hands on your knees. At first, it will seem you're straining to maintain that upright position of your spine, but those muscles will hold you up. With practice, you'll be able to sit like that indefinitely."

"I feel tense, trying to stay like this," she said.

"It'll get easier. Do that every morning, even if it's only for ten minutes at first."

She looked up at him. "Are you going to join me?"

He grinned, and settled onto another cushion beside her, facing her. "I'll keep an eye on you now and then, and remind you if you're slumping."

The two of them sat quietly for a while.

"I'm supposed to be counting my breaths?"

"That's one technique. Use it if it helps you stay focused. When thoughts come to you, just notice them and let them go, and go back to your breathing."

Doug found that Meredith's thoughts drifted into his awareness. He was surprised that her thoughts seemed to have a different "flavor" or "sound" from his own. Perhaps, he considered, it was just that he was used to how his own thoughts and fragments seemed to him. After a while, he could tell that she was getting uncomfortable, so he said, "Okay, that's enough for now."

She groaned softly as she straightened her legs. "I don't know if I can do this," she complained.

"You can if you want to," he assured her. "Just make sure your back is upright. You'll be able to tell after a while. If your legs hurt too much, we can get you a little bench that allows you to fold your legs under you. Some people prefer that. Be gentle with yourself."

She stood up, wrapping the shawl around her legs. "This is pretty. I could wear this to a party!"

"It's yours," he said. "It does look good on you."

"I was just kidding!" she laughed.

"I'd be pleased if you took it."

"No, I'll leave it here so I can wear it the next time we meditate together." When he smiled, she said, "That is, if my presence doesn't distract you too much in your own meditation. All my wild thoughts floating around the room!"

"I'll let you know if it does. Actually, your presence is very distracting most of the time I'm near you, and it doesn't have anything to do with your 'wild thoughts.' When I'm sitting, all of that stuff gradually fades, anyway."

"What's left?"

"A deep peace. It doesn't always work, but when it does, it's wonderful."

"I doubt whether I could ever get to that place. How long have you been meditating?"

He hesitated. "About ten years."

"Please teach me. I desperately need peace," she said softly.

He shook his head. "I can help you with your posture. You'll need a real teacher to guide you once you've gotten the fundamentals."

"Do you have a teacher?"

"I haven't had in several years. I need one, too."

"What does a teacher do?" She sat back down on the cushion.

"You talk together. Nobody else knows exactly what's going on in your own mind, so you have to tell your teacher. He or she can interpret what you say you're experiencing and tell where you are in your practice. Otherwise, you can go around in circles and never learn to let go of what you need to." He laughed. "Even my little chip can't tell me exactly what you're experiencing."

"Isn't that interesting that nobody can know what's in somebody else's mind. With all our science!"

Doug sat down next to her. "You will have to tell me."

"And you will have to tell me—at least, everything the CIA allows."

They looked for a long time into each other's eyes.

Scene 22

Stephanie, the department secretary, came into his office. She stood silently until he looked up.

"Good morning, Stephanie," he said to her. "I have an appointment for maintenance? What time?"

Stephanie continued her silent communication.

"Okay, I'll be there. Thanks, Babe."

"I'm not your babe," she said aloud, her face sober.

He blushed. "You are absolutely right. As helpful and efficient and as beautiful as you are, you are not my babe. I apologize."

"That's okay," she said, smiling. "I've called you worse." She turned and left the office.

Doug looked at his watch and went back to work.

That afternoon, he caught a cab to the Pentagon annex. It was time for the regular checkup of his chip. Randy, the technician, greeted him with a smile and a silent question: *How's the little gadget working?*

It seems to be losing its sensitivity. Crowds are not so unbearable as they were.

Randy's eyes lit up. *Part of that is to be expected,* he thought, *you're accommodating to the noise level.*

"But I think I'm missing some signal. There's this woman ..."

"Ah, cherchez la femme. You have a hard time hearing her—with or without sound, right?"

"No," Doug replied. "Just without sound. She has a very clear voice. But sometimes she surprises me when she speaks, because I haven't heard her getting ready to say it."

Randy grinned. "That's because she doesn't want you to know what she's thinking. Some women are quite good at that."

"As a matter of fact, I wanted to talk with you about her. I think she can read. Not well, and not all the time. Maybe it's just me she can read."

They both laughed.

"Well," Randy said, "let's see how this little gem is working. Then afterward we can try to understand women." He fitted a kind of helmet on Doug's head, and plugged a cable into it. Turning to the computer behind him, he brought up a screen filled with small graphs, each one changing from moment to moment. He studied the screen for a moment, and said, "Looks normal to me." He removed the device from Doug's head.

Randy was also a reader. In fact, he was the first member of the organization to have the chip implanted in his head. He was continually experimenting with the equipment that supported the program. His latest invention was a device for transmitting status data from the chips carried in the heads of operatives through their cell phones. An application downloaded into the phones picked up the data and phoned it to his lab from anywhere in the world.

Even so, Company regulations required all operatives to show up periodically in person for "maintenance," which in reality was simply a security check to make sure the chips had not been transferred to somebody else's head. Each one was traceable by GPS, but that alone could not guarantee that it was legally implanted.

"The next generation," he had told Doug gleefully, "will have remote relay ability. What you read can be relayed to someplace else—maybe an ap for your phone to anywhere."

He sat in his chair and touched his fingertips together thoughtfully, making Doug smile. *You're such a geek.*

"Yes, I am that," Randy said, grinning. "But tell me about this female who has you going."

"I've wondered if the chip was maybe somehow transmitting, as well as receiving. Could that happen?"

"You mean, she can read your thoughts but not other people's?"

"She won't even admit that she might be reading. And I can't very well ask other people, unless they have clearance."

"You want to bring her in for a test?"

"I don't think she would do that. What I'm wondering is whether this happens naturally to some people."

"It has happened. Have you tried to test her at different times?"

"Yes. It seems to happen only if she's aroused somehow."

Randy's eyebrows went up. "Aroused?" He grinned broadly.

"No, not sexually. Emotionally."

"Interesting!" He went to a cupboard and brought back another device, similar to the one Doug had worn. "This thing costs about three hundred bucks. Some Aussie company is trying to build a market for it in the gaming field."

"What's it do?"

"Transmits thought waves!" He put the device on his own head and went to the computer. On the screen was the image of a small cube, seeming to float in space. "Now, I'm going to pull that thing toward me!"

In a moment, the cube seemed to grow, and then to shrink again. "I can even make it disappear." The cube faded out, and then returned. He took the device off his head and turned to Doug. "My thoughts are doing that! And it works through the wireless router to this computer. I could do it from anywhere in the range of the wireless net."

Doug was impressed. "How long does it take to learn how?"

"You could probably do it in five minutes. Everybody's different."

"So that proves that my thoughts can be transmitted—at least to the headgear."

"Your lady could be receiving. I have to exert some will to make this thing respond, but maybe she does it without realizing it."

"Then why do we need these chips?" Doug asked, tapping the side of his head.

"Reliability. The Company wants consistency."

"Wow."

"The thing is, if I can transmit my thoughts—or my intentions, because we don't know exactly how it works neurologically—it's only a matter of time before we can control external devices at some distance, like a robot, just with our minds."

Doug laughed. "Come to me, my pretty one!"

Randy slapped his thigh. "Don't you wish! Controlling other people is probably a whole different thing."

"And you get to play with this stuff all day?"

Randy grinned. "Actually, I have another maintenance coming in in about a half hour. You're supposed to be gone."

"Okay, I'll leave. I appreciate your ideas, though."

"Be patient but be persistent."

69

Randy put the device back into the cupboard and pretended to go back to his computer. Doug slipped out the door and went back to the office.

Scene 23

They lay naked on Doug's low bed, pretending that the slow-turning ceiling fan was a breeze on a tropical island. The loft was warm, and it was only May. "Wonder what it's going to be like in August!" said Doug.

"I guess we'll sweat together." Meredith turned to face him. "Isn't that just one of the things that you meditate on, 'just noticing,' and then return to your breathing?"

He grinned. "For a **real** challenge, we could meditate together like this. I don't know how to slow down my heart right now."

She smiled. "Have you read anything about Tantra sex?"

He smiled back at her. "I have, a little. Some years back there was a lot of stuff about it. What I heard in India was that it's a lot more complicated and ritualized than just feel-good sex."

"Ever tried it?"

"No. I didn't have time to really look into it while I was over there, and I got turned off by the popularization of it here. If it's a path to enlightenment, I'm not ready for that much depth yet. Why—have you looked into it?"

"I had a lover once who was convinced that he had, at least once, seen God while he was having an orgasm, and he kept trying to get it back."

"Sounds like the people who have tried peyote and want to find that path again."

"The most intense orgasm I ever experienced was when I was high on pot." She was propped up on her elbow, looking at him.

He looked at her out of the corner of his eye. "Sounds like you have done it all."

She rolled over against him and threw her leg over his. "Not all. Until just recently, I had never made love to you. That is a very big thing."

He pulled her on top of him. You are the most exciting woman I've ever known!"

She turned her head, and her hair brushed against his face. He closed his eyes, and she continued to sweep her hair against him. She could feel his heart beating under her breast.

And his mind grew quiet as his body began to respond.

Scene 24

Lunch together at The Egg Place became routine. Since they didn't have to worry about others seeing them together, they enjoyed walking hand in hand. Meredith seemed to glow with a new-found security, and her laugh was hearty and frequent. She reminded Doug often that he was staring at her.

"I can't help myself," he said.

"We're like teen-agers."

"My grandmother would say, 'Taint fittin', at your age."

"Where's your grandmother?" Meredith wanted to know all about his past, since she couldn't know much about his present when away from her.

"She's dead now, but she lived all her life in Kentucky, not far from Cincinnati. She and my granddad had a little tobacco farm down in the hills, with a mule and a bunch of chickens. We used to go down to visit during the summer."

Meredith laughed. "Wonderful! My grandmother was an uptight bitch. She wanted to control everyone. The family revolved around her. I left for Berkeley as soon as I could. I suppose she's who I was rebelling against."

Back on the crowded street, the two continued to chat, building that subtle weave of relationship that comes only with time. Nothing seemed to break the spell.

They stood close together in the packed elevator. The crowd didn't bother Meredith, but she kept her fingers entwined with Doug's. Most of the other occupants looked upward at the floor number display. The two exchanged a glance and a smile.

Well, hello, Daniel! Doug, startled, looked around. The greeting came clearly through the almost impenetrable thought-noise in the crowded car. In the far corner, Janet smiled brightly at him.

Lucy! He smiled back. *What are you doing here?*

I've been transferred. You in this office too?

Wow! Yes. Thirty-fifth floor.

73

Just then, Meredith's fingers tightened on his. He looked down to see her staring up at him, her eyes wide. He leaned down to whisper to her, "An old friend."

Her expression didn't change, and he felt a knot build in his stomach. By the time they reached her floor, the romantic spell from lunch was gone. Meredith let go of his hand and worked her way out of the car without saying anything or even looking at him. He did see that she glanced at Janet—a quick, almost frantic scan of faces, that fastened immediately on the other woman, just as the doors closed.

Oh, oh. Janet had caught Meredith's look. *You are in big trouble, my friend.*

Doug didn't know what to say or think. He managed a weak grin in Janet's direction. By the time they reached their floor, the car was almost empty, and she had moved closer to him. *Is that the 'pissed off wife?'* she asked.

He nodded. Leaving the car, he tripped on the threshold, but caught himself.

"Careful!" Janet said, grabbing his arm.

He turned to look at her. "I **am** glad to see you," he said.

"But you would have preferred different circumstances." She was laughing that bright little expression of fun that he had loved on Grand Cayman. "So tell me where Mister Angelo's office is. I'm to report to him."

"Tony," Doug said. "The last office down there," pointing toward the end of the aisle.

"Where's yours?"

"This one." Doug opened his door.

"Well, I guess I'll be seeing more of you," she said. That thick reddish-blond hair was pulled back into a ponytail. Her clothing was businesslike, but did not hide her curves.

"Yes—stop by when you can. I'll be in all afternoon." Doug watched her glide down the aisle. Inside him was a chaos of mixed feelings. He sat down at his desk and opened his computer.

Meredith had already left him a message: "I assume that is SHE."

He replied, "We need to talk. I'm changing my plans for this evening—can we meet?"

Her response appeared immediately. *She must have been waiting,* he thought. "You betcha. My place, 7PM."

It wasn't a suggestion. She wanted to be on her home turf, and she wasn't in a mood to cook for him.

An hour later, he saw Janet being escorted to an office on the far side of the cube farm. He waited, trying to figure out what to say, how to handle this situation. He had all but forgotten Janet, thinking that they would not be likely to cross paths in the huge organization of the Company.

But here she was. She knocked once, and opened the door. "Hi," she said. "Good time?"

He waved her in silently.

Janet started to say something, then stopped. "Wow, your mind is turning somersaults!"

I thought I'd never see you again!

I caught that. Surprise, isn't it? She pointed to a chair opposite him, and he nodded. *I didn't even know you were at this office.*

I am glad to see you. Doug managed a smile.

You said that before. But I am getting that you have mixed feelings."

He merely nodded again.

Look, I don't want to cause problems. We can just keep some distance. You have your lady—and she's very pretty! We should have been more professional down there, anyway.

"You must have replaced Andy," he said aloud. "I didn't even know he was leaving." His voice was flat.

Just then his desk phone rang. It was Tony. As Doug hung up, he said, "He wants to see both of us."

"Oh, shit."

They went down the aisle to Tony's office. Tony had his back to the door, facing the skyline. "Close the door," he said.

They waited.

Swiveling his chair back to face them, he said, "I didn't realize that you two were together on Grand Cayman. I didn't recognize your name when the order came through. Now, here's my problem—" He sat upright in his chair. "I cannot have any hanky-panky between my operatives. This is a serious business we're in!"

"Of course," replied Janet. "I will ..."

"You will treat each other as fellow officers. You will limit your contact with each other to official business!"

"Right," said Doug. He was feeling easier about the situation. Regulations can sometimes work in a person's favor.

Janet looked at him quickly, then back to Tony. In the voice of a cute little girl, "We'll be good!"

Tony's face broke into a wide grin. "Yes you will!" With a wave, he swiveled back to the skyline.

Doug walked Janet over to her office. "You have guts!" he said, smiling.

She looked up at him. "I could read him like a book. His shell is not very thick. He just wanted to scare us with his 'ferocious bear' look."

"He got my attention."

"And you got off the hook, maybe?" She smiled, touched his hand, and went into her office.

Doug went back to his office feeling more than a little relief. *Saved from myself!*

I heard that way over here! He looked around, but saw no one looking at him. Reddening, he closed the door.

Scene 25

Meredith was shaking as she returned to her cubicle. She looked over the partition—Dolly hadn't returned from lunch yet. She opened her computer and sent a message to Doug. Just as she clicked "Send," a waft of perfume announced that Dolly was back.

"Wow, do you look awful!" Dolly sat down and pulled the chair closer to Meredith, and asked quietly, "What's going on, babe?"

"An **old friend**," Meredith replied, turning away from her computer.

"Oh, oh. Not, I gather, **your** old friend."

"We were in the elevator, coming up just now, and it felt like a bomb went off!"

"What?" Dolly frowned. "What do you mean?"

"Doug reacted to this woman in the elevator like—like fireworks went off in his head." Meredith looked at her friend. "I'm back to square one!"

"Okay, okay. He met up with someone he knew—maybe someone special. You just need to talk with him before you go off the deep end."

Meredith's computer beeped at her. She turned around. The screen read: "We need to talk. I'm changing my plans for this evening—can we meet?"

Dolly, looking over her shoulder, "You betcha!"

Meredith typed those words, and added, "My place, 7PM." Then she logged off and turned around to Dolly.

"You got it, girl!" Dolly laughed. "Stand up straight! Now, what do you know for sure?"

"I caught the name, 'Lucy.'"

"He spoke to her? What'd he say?"

"Uh, I don't know. Y'know," she said slowly, "I don't know if either of them said **anything**!"

"You said Lucy."

Meredith looked at her, furrows forming between her eyebrows. "That's weird. I don't think either of them said anything. I just **felt** the fireworks.

"Who's Lucy?" Dolly insisted.

"I don't know." Her face changed, her eyes widening. "Doug told me one time that I read his mind."

Dolly took Meredith's hand. "I thought **he** was the mind reader."

"Maybe that's a two-way street? Lordie, I don't know."

"Well, you got something goin' on with this guy. Stay cool." Then hurriedly, "Hey, I got to go to work." She stood up and went into her own cubicle. Over the partition, she said, "Tonight—**call me,** okay?"

Meredith smiled at her. "Thanks."

"That's what friends are for," Dolly sang, as she disappeared behind the partition.

Scene 26

On the subway, Doug's mind was still full of apprehension. There was no question about whom he would choose, if it came to that. His relationship with Meredith, new as it was, was becoming more important to him than he could express. But there was no denying his attraction to Janet. She was beautiful, charming and smart. Six months ago he would have pursued her enthusiastically. *Maybe that's how evolution works,* he thought, *young and energetic make for better mates because they are more apt to produce offspring with a better chance of surviving to produce their own offspring.*

He smiled at his own overblown analysis. The simple fact was that Meredith did something to him that Janet didn't. He didn't know quite what it was—she seemed to have more depth to her, and that appealed to him. He remembered being with Janet on the island, responding to her beauty and charm, and how quickly and positively he had been ready for sex. He could picture her in the bikini, swimming toward him, and hoping that his erection didn't show. When she said, "Your mouth is open," he wondered if she knew. In all likelihood, she did.

With Meredith, his response was more than just genital; he wanted to envelope her and be enveloped by her, to merge their bodies, somehow. The softness of her breast in his hand took his breath away. *That's odd,* he thought, *I can't remember what Janet's breasts felt like.*

The screeching of the subway wheels as they rounded the bend just before his stop brought his mind to the present. He needed to get Meredith to know—as she said, "in her heart"—that he wanted only her.

It seemed she took a long time to answer his ring. But she buzzed him in without saying anything in the intercom. As she opened the door, her face was stony. Her eyes looked as though she had been crying. She stepped back to let him in.

He sat on a chair near the table. "Tell me," he began, "what I did?"

She sat down across from him without speaking. Then, "I hate this neediness in me."

"But ..."

"You didn't do anything. Well, yes you did. You practically ejaculated when you saw her in the elevator!"

Doug's eyebrows rose. "No!" He tried to remember just what had happened.

"You called to her—'Lucy!' and your heart was pounding!"

The expression on his face changed to astonishment. "You heard that?"

"Clearly."

"I didn't speak. I hadn't even seen her in the elevator until she called me—in her thoughts. And I answered the same way—I **thought**, 'Lucy! What are you doing here?' Neither of us said anything out loud."

Meredith looked at him. Tears welled up in her eyes. In a tiny voice, "She reads minds, too?"

Doug rubbed his face with both hands, then looked directly at her. "You are not supposed to know this. You are **really** not supposed to know this, okay?"

She wiped her cheek with her fingertips. She didn't know how to respond.

"She and I were on an assignment together, **somewhere**. We were playing roles, and her name was supposed to be Lucy. In the elevator, she called me by my role name, Daniel. It was a shock, not only because she used that name, but also because we were never supposed to see each other again, for security reasons."

"So how did she turn up here?"

"Somebody screwed up. She was transferred to our office."

"And she's the one you slept with." It was not a question but a statement.

Doug dropped his eyes and toyed with a pencil on the table. "Yes. It was part of the roles we were playing."

"I won't ask." Meredith got up and pulled a tissue from a box, then sat back down.

He sighed.

"So, fucking other women is part of your job description?" She could barely get the words out.

"No," he said, and paused. "Maybe."

She covered her face with her hands. He couldn't tell if she were still crying or not.

"I'm sorry."

"Stop!" she almost screamed. "I don't want that!"

She blew her nose on the tissue, then got another. "I can live with it! I'll bet I've fucked more men than you have women."

Doug sighed again. There was nothing he could say.

"I can live with that," she said again. She laid both arms on the table and looked across at him. "I threw a fit the other day when you first told me, and I got over it. It's okay that you slept with her. What I'm trying to deal with right now is that she is here, now. Do you understand that?"

"Of course."

"I can't—I won't **try** to compete with her."

He put his hand on hers. "You don't need to, Meredith."

They sat without speaking for a long while. They were both thinking the same thing: that a wayward lover is hard to believe, even when their intentions are pure—at the time. It's like dieting to lose weight, or trying to stop drinking. Temptations abound.

"Let's sit on the sofa, please?" She got up and offered him her hand.

"You said something today at lunch," Doug began after they had sat down again, "something about our being like teenagers. Maybe this is part of that."

"Yes. That was the good part. This is the other side of it." She looked at him, her head resting against the back of the sofa. "I hate the feeling that I'm losing something. I may not be **that** much older than you," (now smiling,) "but I keep feeling," (now serious,) "that life is passing by too fast, and I never took the time to **just be.**"

He reached over and pulled a bit of hair back from her cheek. "Well, if we're both teenagers again, we have a lot of years ahead of us to **just be.**"

She shook her head slowly and smiled again. "You are such a smooth talker."

"My body has been tight all afternoon. Do you have anything to drink in this place?"

She gestured toward the kitchen. "You know where it is. Make me one, too."

When he returned with the drinks, she said, "You're right—I don't have to compete with Lucy, or whatever her real name is."

"Janet."

"With Janet. If she is working with you, I will have to deal with her again. I only caught a glimpse of her in the elevator—she's young and she's gorgeous—but it might help if I got to know her. Is that possible?"

He pursed his lips. "Our boss insisted that we have nothing to do with each other unless it's on company business."

"So, no happy hour chats."

"Definitely not. But ..."

"But **I** could have a happy hour chat with her."

"Do you know how to get to her?"

She looked at him from the corner of her eye. "Remember how we had lunch—**almost** had lunch together at the deli, before you skipped out?"

He thought a moment. "I happened to see you coming out of the elevator."

"I had been waiting there twenty minutes before you came out of that elevator."

Doug looked at her, and they both burst out laughing."

"You'll find her," he said, still laughing.

"I know her to see her. That's all I need."

"I have no doubt."

He leaned over and took her into his arms.

Scene 27

The next day, Meredith left work early, telling those near her that she was "going to work out at the gym."

Dolly looked at her quizzically. "I thought you went on Wednesdays."

Meredith winked at her. Dolly's eyebrows went up.

"I'm hunting," Meredith whispered, and slipped out.

In the big lobby, she took a position against the wall next to the elevators, set her gym bag on the floor and waited. She wasn't sure when Janet would appear, if at all. But she was patient.

When her prey finally appeared, Meredith was a little shocked by the beauty of this creature she was stalking. She had remembered the face and the hair, but not the body. For an instant, she forgot what she was going to do. Then, very clearly, she thought, *Lucy!* As she thought it, she smiled at the irony. "Lucy" had started all this by calling to Doug as "Daniel."

Janet was just as startled as Doug had been. For a second, she thought it was Doug calling to her, but immediately recognized that it was not. She looked around. There were many people exiting the elevators and spreading across the lobby. Then behind her stood "the angry wife!" She almost dropped her gym bag, but caught it and herself, and smiled sweetly at Meredith.

Meredith walked up to her and put out her hand. Janet, confused, took it.

"I know, your name is Janet, and we have something in common," Meredith said.

"I'm sorry, but ..."

"Daniel."

Janet's eyes widened, and then she smiled again. "You know a lot about me."

"And you may know a little about me. I'd like to change that. Do you have time for a drink?"

Janet stammered, "I would, but I'm on my way ..." She held out her gym bag—which was identical to Meredith's.

Meredith picked up her bag, held it up for Janet to see, then, "Why don't we go together?"

Walking toward the front doors, Janet looked quickly at her bird of prey. She wasn't sure what this woman wanted from her—perhaps she would shove her into the path of a bus or something!

I know you can read my mind, Meredith thought to her, *and I don't want to embarrass you or cause you any problems. I just want to know you better.*

Janet looked at her. "Why?"

In the simplest words, I'm in love with Doug and I want to protect that relationship.

"Oh." Janet pretended she just figured out who Meredith was. "You're ..."

The angry wife! But you knew that, didn't you?

They turned off Connecticut Avenue toward the gym. Janet looked at Meredith and frowned. "He must have told you an awful lot!"

Nothing classified—I hope. Then, aloud, "Sending thoughts is hard! Suppose we just talk quietly." She smiled.

Janet relaxed a little. "That 'angry wife' thing was a joke," she said, "or supposed to be. I don't want your man, uh ..."

"My name is Meredith. Sounds better than 'angry wife.' I'm not his wife, not even close. I just like some clarity in my relationships, and that's all I want from you."

Janet's expression changed. "I'm sorry we ..."

"No, you're not. I don't want you to be sorry. Those things happen. I just want to know from you what the situation is now."

Inside the gym, they went to the locker room. Nobody else was there. Janet sat on the bench and put her gym bag on the floor. "I just said I don't want your man. Doug's a very nice man, sweet and smart and good looking. But we have a professional relationship that would be seriously affected if we became involved. And I'm committed to that. Okay?"

"That sure sounds clear," said Meredith. "I realize that I'm at a disadvantage with Doug because of his chip. He can read me but I can't read him, except through the regular channels. I've trusted him—I still trust him. I have had a full life, and I'm not under any illusions about how easy or hard it is to be faithful. I just needed to connect with you so that you were not going to continue to be a mythological figure." She smiled.

"Mythological? I'm flattered."

"The myth was in my head. I just wanted you to become real."

Janet put out her hand and said gently, "I'm real. Feel me."

Meredith took her hand and the two of them smiled at each other. Then they changed into their gym clothes and went up to the treadmills to warm up.

On the machines, Meredith forgot for a moment that Janet could read her. *My god! Look at that body! I can't blame Doug for wanting to mate with her!*

At which, Janet burst out laughing.

"Oops!" Meredith turned up the speed of the treadmill to work off her embarrassment.

But she went home that evening feeling a lot more secure.

Scene 28

Doug was cooking dinner for them in his loft. Meredith stood nearby most of the time, sipping on a glass of wine and watching him. "You are full of surprises," she said.

He grinned without looking up. "I hope this isn't a surprise for me."

"What is it—or do you want me to be surprised?"

He took a big sip from his wine glass. "If I tell you, and mess it up, I can't tell you that's the way it's supposed to look."

"Okay. It smells good. How much time do I have?"

"Ten minutes."

"I want to look at your books." She wandered off to the brick-and-board bookshelves next to the bed. A moment later, she exclaimed, "My God! Look at all the Ken Wilber!"

"I spent almost ten years trying to absorb him."

"I think I've read two of these books."

"You're welcome to take any of them to read."

She walked back to the kitchen area holding a book. " 'The Simple Feeling of Being,' she read from the cover. "I don't think I ever saw this book before!"

"From what you said the other day about wanting to just be, maybe this is what you need right now." He continued to stir something in a pot, looking over his shoulder at her.

Meredith opened the cover. "It says it's compiled and edited by several other people. Is it Wilber's writing?"

"Yes. They pulled out passages from his other books and put them together."

She read further from the book, "It says it's 'a collection of the specifically spiritual aspects of his work.' "

"I liked it," he said. "I hadn't realized how passionately he writes when he talking about spirit.

"I had a hard time following him—he's obviously so brilliant, I can't keep up."

"Well," Doug said, serving some kind of dark sauce over yellow mounds in two large bowls, "I think we're ready to sit down." He brought the bowls to the table.

"Now, can you tell me what it is—or is supposed to be?" Meredith laughed.

"Portabella mushrooms on polenta. This calls for red wine."

She sipped from her Pinot Grigio. "You mean I can't stay with this?"

"You can drink anything you like. But I'll pour you just a bit of this Pinot Noir I discovered recently. Actually, it's the same variety of grape as what you have."

"Only fermented with the skins. I grew up in California, you remember."

They sat down at the table, and he raised his glass. "To—uh—**to be!**"

"Just—to be!"

"The simple feeling of being," He said. "Wilber had it right, didn't he?"

Meredith tasted the polenta. "Mmmm. Wonderful!"

"Thank you."

She picked up the other glass he had poured and tasted it. "Wow. That is smooth. It still has the fruity tang to it that I like in the white."

They ate in silence for a few minutes, then he asked, "Did you connect with Janet?"

"I did." She had a half-smile on her face.

"And are you going to tell me about it?"

"You're worried."

He laughed. "Not really. If it had gone badly, I know I would have heard before this."

She pretended to pout. "You have me all figured out, don't you?"

"No. And I don't really think I would have heard. I just made that up."

She got up and went to the refrigerator. "If you don't mind, I'll stay with the white," she said, pouring another glass of wine. "First, I think you have good taste in women." She looked at him and laughed. "That is some female."

He smiled and nodded. "And second?"

"She assured me that she is not after you. I believe her." Sitting down again, she continued, "I'm also fully aware of the power of erotic attraction."

He frowned. "And so …"

"And so I just hope you and I can stay up front with each other."

He put his hand down flat in the middle of the table and looked straight at her. "I'm in."

She put her hand over his for a long moment, then picked up her fork. "Meanwhile, our polenta is getting cold."

They ate in silence for a while. Then he looked up to see her dabbing her eyes with a tissue. "Meredith—something you haven't said?"

She suddenly began sobbing. "I'm sorry. It's not about you or Janet."

He waited for her to continue, then got up and brought a box of tissues to the table.

After her sobs had subsided, she wiped her eyes again. "I was at the other point of one of those triangles. They ended up separating. I've never been able to forgive myself."

Doug watched her, saying nothing.

"There were children. It was a disaster for everybody!"

"You didn't cause it all by yourself. He should have known what he had to lose."

"I loved him. But afterward, I couldn't stand the sight of him. I don't know quite why."

"How long ago was this?"

"Maybe two years, a little more." She looked up at him, her eyes glistening. "When I went to confront Janet, I felt rage. It's so stupid!"

"At her? At me?"

She laughed. "No. At me, for that other thing. Somehow, I was her— and of course she was wonderful about it! She was totally honest with me, and she was totally aware of what I was going through—my fear of losing you. She promised me that she would not pursue you, partly because she was aware of how badly it would go for her career."

"Our boss laid it on the line to both of us."

"If he hadn't …No, I won't go there!"

"If he hadn't, I would have had to lay it on the line to her."

She reached over and squeezed his hand. "Would it have been hard to do?"

"You know, I used to go down to the marina and just hang out, watching the yachts come and go. I wanted that kind of life. But I knew that I didn't want to live the kind of life it would take to get there. I lusted after those sleek cruisers on the Potomac, and I've lusted after the BMWs I see all over this city. I know what it's like to want something I can't have."

"But a BMW doesn't drive up to you and invite you to climb in."

He laughed. "Not exactly."

"I used to be very free with my body," she said. "It felt good to be lusted after. But after a while, it didn't any more." She smiled at him. "I'm very lucky I never contracted anything worse than crab lice!"

"I'm glad you didn't give up on sex altogether."

She pursed her lips and kissed the air between them.

Doug smiled. "It would be a shame to waste all that passion and sensuality—and that body."

"You think," she began, drawing her head back and looking at him, "that the principle function of a human body is to fuck?"

"That's a good question," he laughed. "In evolutionary terms, it probably is. But being the imaginative creatures that we are, we've found a few other things that are enjoyable, as well."

"Such as?"

"Sitting and talking to another human being—one who is smart and bright and quick and passionate."

"Or driving a BMW?"

"That, too."

"How about eating a delicious meal?" She stood up and collected the plates from the table.

"And leaving the dishes for a later time when the smart and quick and passionate woman is not around." He stood up and took the dishes from her and put them into the sink. "Let's go where we can talk and touch each other at the same time."

"I'd like that."

Later, he turned to her and ran his fingers through her hair. "There's one function we forgot."

"What's that?"

"To love somebody."

"Hmmm. Yes. Do you know—that's the first time that word has come up between us?"

"Was it overdue?"

"I think it showed up at just the right time."

Scene 29

Meredith continued to meditate, sometimes with Doug in his loft but most of the time in her own apartment just before going out for her daily run. It meant that she had to get up an hour earlier, but she was determined. They experimented with several kinds of cushions and benches, and she finally settled for a high cushion that she could straddle so that she was supported on her spine and her knees.

She bought several books on meditating, some of which were by Buddhist teachers and others not. "Mindfulness in Plain English" was one she read several times because it concentrated on the act of meditating, without so much of the tradition—especially the Hindu terminology.

"It's going to take me a long time," she told Doug when they had finished sitting one day. "I'm a slow learner."

He laughed. "You're being funny. But don't think in terms of getting somewhere. It will only slow you down."

"If I realize that I'm having an enlightened moment," she quoted from one of the books, "then I am no longer having an enlightened moment."

He sighed. "Slow learner, indeed."

They got to their feet and stretched. "I want to talk with you about something," he said.

They moved to the sofa, and she looked at him expectantly. She suddenly realized that this situation no longer made her feel panicky.

"A number of times, you have picked up my thoughts."

She smiled. "You've told me that before, but I haven't believed you. I did wonder if that chip in your head transmitted both ways."

"My tech guy says probably not. He thinks you may have a natural ability."

"You're discussing me with your tech support? This is like when I found out you were looking into my past." Her face was serious, but not angry.

"He wants to run some tests ..."

She shook her head. "No. No. No."

"Okay. I told him I didn't think you'd do that. But are you okay with our trying some things out just between us?"

"So you don't think it's your little chip gone haywire?"

"No, I don't think so."

"So what do we do—you think of a color and I'll try to guess it?"

Doug grinned. "No parlor games. Here's what I've figured out so far—the times when **I think** you have picked up my thoughts have been when you've been, shall we say, emotional?"

He saw the look on her face and laughed out loud. "Maybe like right now?"

She scowled even more deeply. "All I'm picking up at this moment is that you're making fun of me!"

"I'm not! Honest."

"Well, I guess the first time," she said, "was when I heard you say 'Lucy'."

"Hmmm, yes, I remember that."

"Well, was that when **I** was 'emotional'—or **you** were?" She had a twinkle in her eye.

"That's a thought. We won't discard it yet. But you were, uh—frightened?"

"To put it mildly, yes. You want to frighten me again to find out?"

He held her chin up and kissed her on the lips. "No, Love, I don't want to do that, ever again."

"You are so slippery!" She laughed.

"Then there was the time you picked up 'amazing' from me. I don't remember exactly when that was, do you?"

"Yes. It was the first time you were in my apartment. You said, 'amazing' clear as day."

"Oh, I remember. No, I didn't say it. I was thinking how amazing it was that I could not pick up anything at all from your thoughts. Then you said, 'yes it is.'"

"I was talking about how good we were together and how good I felt after our talk. So that one doesn't count. I wasn't even emotional then. I just felt good."

"That's right. Okay, that doesn't count as emotional—although feeling good is an emotion, isn't it?"

"Wait," she said, suddenly thoughtful. "Lucy wasn't the first time."

He looked at her. "When was the first?"

She looked stunned. "The moment I first laid eyes on you, in the elevator."

"But you didn't echo anything I said, did you?" Doug was trying hard to remember that moment. He remembered being struck by her, somehow. She had seemed to **understand** something about him. Her thoughts were something like, "He's one of them. Oh, my God!"

"Oh ... my ... God," He said. **That** was the first time! He remembered wondering how she had identified him. He couldn't now remember what, if anything, he had been thinking when she entered the car, but it would have had something to do with her, as he saw her. He would have wondered, as he often did, how a stranger was going to react to him if they found out he could read their mind. He knew right away that she guessed, because he had responded vocally to her reaction. "Yes, ma'am, I am **one of them**," he had said. She didn't freak out, as most people did. She **knew** and she was curious!

"You saw me," Doug said. "You really saw me, didn't you?"

"I don't know what it was, but it felt like I just recognized you." She tilted her head in thought without taking her eyes off of him. "It's not like I'd ever met anyone else with a chip in their head—or even without the chip, who could read my thoughts. How could that be?"

"And how was it," he said, "that just about every time we have been together, you have finished my sentences for me, or understood immediately (at least most of the time) what I was trying to say. It was as though you and I were on the same wavelength."

Meredith frowned. "That may be going a bit far."

"Then, when I got back from my assignment and we met in the restaurant, you said, 'You slept with her, didn't you?' Right out of the blue—maybe you didn't know for sure, but that was not a tentative question, and at the time you didn't even know I was with a partner on the assignment, much less that she was female. Maybe you would say it was only 'women's intuition' or something, but would you have said it that way if you didn't know **something**?"

She didn't say anything. Her mind was full of replays.

"Still going a bit far? And how did you know that the Company was checking you out?"

"I don't know. I had a hunch. Is that mind reading?"

He didn't answer right away, letting her think about it. Then, "That first time in your apartment, you said something about being a silly schoolgirl, 'anticipating,' and I asked you 'anticipating what?' but what I was thinking was about making love. Then you laughed and said, 'Oh, no, not that.' Now, I'll admit, maybe we were both thinking the same thing because of the situation, but it's one more thing to wonder about. That was just before you echoed my thought about 'amazing.'"

"So what does it all add up to?" she asked. "What are we going to do with this information, even if it is, as you suggest, indicative of something?"

"Wow," he laughed. "You sound like my science teacher!"

"I guess I'm still skeptical."

"Skeptical is good. Let's at least think about all this for a while, okay?"

"Okay."

Scene 30

Weeks had gone by since that discussion. Once in a while, Doug would look up at her suddenly, noticing something, but not saying anything about it. They were comfortable with each other, and his ability to anticipate what she was about to say became ordinary. It was just how they were together.

Then one day they were meditating together in the center of his loft, sitting in their island away from the noise of other people's thoughts. He heard her move, and opened his eyes. Meredith was still on her cushion, but she had bowed her head until it touched the floor, with her hands covering her face. He thought of the Muslim men he had seen during their prayers, in almost that same position. She was sobbing silently.

He waited, sensing that she was dealing with something personal, perhaps very deep. Meditation sometimes brings up memories or realizations that overwhelm a person. Once in Afghanistan he had gone through something similar, suddenly being aware of the war around him, not as combat but as human struggle. The issues of the war were far away both physically and spiritually. He felt as though he were simply a pawn in a gigantic game, programmed to act out his part. He could die or he could kill—or both—and it wouldn't make anything better or worse. He was overcome with sadness, and it was several days before he recovered from it.

Meredith's shoulders continued to shake. Doug moved off his cushion and sat beside her, his hand placed gently on her back. He wanted to lie down and embrace her, kiss away her tears, chase away her agony, but he knew she had to finish.

Long minutes later—he marveled at how time is so different in different circumstances—she stopped sobbing. She slid forward on the polished floor until she was prone; her head turned toward him, her hands now simply a pillow under her face. She opened her eyes and smiled at him. Her face was streaked by dried tears. He lay down next to her, keeping his hand resting on her back.

"Wow," she whispered, and then thought to him, *I didn't know all that was in me. It was like a milkweed pod exploding in the sunlight.*

95

"Do you want to talk about it?"

"No," she said, "I don't need to." She reached out a hand and touched his face, then closed her eyes.

After a while, he thought she had fallen asleep, so he quietly got up and took her shawl from the bed and spread it over her. Going to the kitchen, he began heating water for tea. He sat at the table, waiting for the water to boil and waiting for her experience to run its course. It was clearly a profound thing she had gone through, a private catharsis, perhaps.

When the water boiled, he poured himself a cup of tea.

A little while later, she gathered herself and stood up. She folded the shawl and returned it to the bed, then joined him in the kitchen. Smiling wanly, she put her hand near the tea kettle to see if was hot, then turned it on again. "So much suffering in the world," she said, standing next to the stove, waiting. She wasn't looking at him, but seemed lost in thought. He did not try to read her thoughts.

Finally, she poured her cup of tea and sat down.

"Are you okay?" he asked gently.

"Yes."

He watched her face, looking for clues. Her eyes were cast down toward the floor. Her silence stirred apprehension in him. Finally, he couldn't stand it any longer. "Are **we** okay?"

She looked at him and smiled sweetly. "Of course, silly."

"I didn't want to intrude, but I was getting nervous."

"I'm sorry. It's like I've been away, isn't it?"

"Yes."

"My face must be a mess," she said, getting up and going into the bathroom. In a moment she returned, the streaks gone from her cheeks. "Better?"

He smiled. "Do you know how much I've come to love you?"

Meredith reached over and took his hand. "This is all your fault, I think. I never felt anything so deeply before I met you."

"I hope that's good."

"I feel as though I've turned some kind of corner. I don't know what it is, but I will never be the same."

He looked at her, waiting, hoping that she would tell him more.

"I can't tell you more, not yet anyway."

The surprise showed on his face, and she grinned. "Yes, I did, didn't I?"

"You read my thoughts."

"Just a glimpse." She stood up and moved her chair around the table next to his and sat down. "Doug," she said, her face next to his, "something is happening to me, and I need to find out what—and why."

"What are you going to do?" A small lump was forming in the pit of his stomach.

"I don't know yet. I've been reading that book by Ken Wilber—'The Simple Feeling of Being'—and it's speaking to me."

He managed a wry smile. "You really were ready for him, weren't you?"

"He is still way over my head. It's all I can do to keep my head above water as I read, but it feels like I'm on the verge of something. I **have** to find out!"

Doug gestured toward the book shelves. "There's almost everything he ever wrote over there, at least up to a few years ago."

"Thank you. But I may have to go somewhere else for a while."

"Where, to India, or Tibet, or ..."

"I hope not that far."

"I hope, too."

Scene 31

Dolly looked worried. "Hon, you don't look good," she said, looking over the partition. "What's going on?"

Meredith smiled, the dark crescents under her eyes belying the smile. "Goin' through some stuff."

"You want to talk? Let's have lunch." Dolly lived other people's lives. She recorded Oprah Winfrey's interview program on cable so she could watch it at night. Even though she enjoyed being sought after sexually, she knew that it was just surface activity, a game that occasionally allowed people to touch each other in a deeper way. Men, after they had done their male animal thing, sometimes would open up to her with their hopes and fears and frustrations. Orgasm was a key in a lock that revealed the hurting child who was kept hidden inside. She loved that helpless child. She could nurture and comfort and absorb the pain of others.

"You used to talk about the games people play," Dolly had told Meredith once. "Games are exciting and fun! Winning or losing—it doesn't make much difference, after all. It's like sex—you set them up so they think they're in control, but then they come pleading for your boobs. It's a power game. I don't understand that 'infinite game' thing you've talked about. Sounds like maybe something an old married couple might play. I'm not ready for that yet."

Meredith had some doubt that Dolly would understand what she was going through, but she knew that Dolly understood the need for a shoulder to lean on and a sympathetic ear to just listen. "Yeah," she told her friend, "I'd like some company for lunch."

At the far corner of The Egg Place, Meredith managed for a time to keep up the mindless chatting that goes so well in a big-city lunch. Dolly waited until their sandwiches arrived and the conversation slowed before asking, 'Now, will you tell me?"

"Well, you know I've been meditating for a while."

"Yes, sometime after you started with Doug."

"Lately, I've gotten into it really deep, and a lot of things come up for me."

Dolly took a bite of sandwich and put it down. "What kind of things?"

"Old feelings, that I had thought I was through with, like guilt over leaving a friend in a tight spot twenty years ago. Heavy sorrow about my relationship with my dad that never got resolved. Sadness, I guess, is most of it. I haven't been the kind of person I wanted to be—that I thought I was."

"It comes up in meditation?"

"Yes. The other evening I totally lost it. Doug and I were sitting at his place, and I just fell apart."

"Sounds like the way I get sometimes when I've had too much to drink."

"How do you handle it—after you sober up?" She smiled.

"It goes away."

"This hasn't gone away. I'm really depressed."

"You need a shrink, it looks like."

"Maybe. I did that a couple of years ago, when I broke up with Paul. Then, I just felt all this shame over tearing his family apart. This is different. I don't really think I'm a bad person now, but there's all this suffering, and I've contributed to it." Meredith hung her head and poked at her lunch with a fork.

Dolly reached across the table and lifted her chin. "Meredith, look at me. You are not a bad person! Everybody falls short of their own image of themselves sometimes."

"I know."

"So, what's happening in your life right now, besides meditation?"

"Doug, of course. Mainly Doug."

"You haven't said much about Doug lately. What's happening with him? Did his 'associate' come back into his life?"

"No, I don't think so." She looked at Dolly. "I'm not good enough for him."

"What? That's bullshit!" She said it loud enough that people nearby looked at her.

"No, it isn't. He has so much integrity! And he sees right through me."

"Of course he does! He reads your mind! So," lowering her voice, "what's he said lately?"

"That's just it! He doesn't say anything. He says he loves me."

One eyebrow went up. "Oh, I see. Yeah, **that's** depressing to hear."

"No sarcasm, Dolly, please. I'm serious! I know he loves me. And I know I'm not good enough for that love."

"Wow. I'm not going to talk you out of this, am I?"

Tears welled up in Meredith's eyes as the two women looked at each other. Their sandwiches sat almost untouched on their plates.

"Look, Meredith," Dolly said, "I love you too, and don't tell me you're not good enough for that!"

Meredith smiled weakly. "You're sweet."

"So what can we do to get you through this? It will end, you know. The feeling will end."

"I don't know."

"Okay, after work, I'm coming over to your place, and we're going to think of something that will kill the time while we wait for it to end."

Meredith didn't say anything.

"You supposed to get together with Doug?"

She shook her head. "He's off on an assignment someplace."

"So you need company. I'll cook dinner for you—no, we'll cook together. And we'll get snockered and you won't have to go home drunk because you'll be home already." She collected her purse and stood up. "Right now we're almost late, and you know how guilty that makes you feel. Wrap your sandwich in a napkin and let's go back to work."

Meredith, almost in a trance, stood up and walked with her friend to the cash register.

100

Scene 32

Riding home on the subway, Meredith still seemed to be in a trance, walking woodenly, silent, not seeing anything. Dolly took her by the arm and guided her to her apartment. She glanced occasionally at Meredith, worriedly.

Inside, Dolly answered the welcoming shriek of Meredith's cockatiel. "Hold on, you crazy bird!" She led Meredith to the sofa. "Sit, woman."

Then she went into the bedroom and came back with the yellow bird on her shoulder.

Meredith waved a hand at her. "Put a diaper on your shoulder! He'll shit on you!"

"That's my girl! You are present after all!" But she retreated to the bedroom and came back properly protected from the bird's droppings. "Now, I know that they say a depressed person shouldn't drink, but I'm here to change things. You want wine or gin?"

Meredith smiled and shook her head in disbelief. "You are something else, Dolly."

"**Doctor** Dolly to you!" she said as she disappeared into the kitchen. While she was gone, Meredith sighed deeply and leaned back in the sofa.

A few minutes later, Dolly returned with two glasses, clinking ice cubes. "We can discuss what you have in your refrigerator after we relax."

Meredith took a sip of her drink. "That is strong!"

"I couldn't find any limes," she replied as though that explained it. She sat down on the sofa next to Meredith.

"All I have is lime juice. It's still good."

They drank silently. Chick, the cockatiel, was still on Dolly's shoulder, pulling at her earring. Meredith looked at the bird and chuckled. "He is such a character."

"If he gets my ear, he's going back in his cage."

"As I said," Meredith mumbled, "That is a strong drink!"

"Now," began Dolly, "when **I** was seeing a shrink, she told me that if I was depressed, it meant that I was mad at myself, and that usually meant that I was really mad at someone I couldn't afford to be mad at. Who are you mad at that you can't afford to be mad at? Me?"

Meredith laughed. "How could anybody be mad at you?" She leaned over and kissed Dolly on the cheek.

Dolly turned to face her. "If you're going to kiss me, do it right."

They did it right.

As they separated, Meredith said, "Oh, my god! I'm sorry!"

Even Dolly seemed stunned. "I guess that **was** a strong drink."

"I'm sorry!" Meredith seemed close to tears. "I've been so bound up for days, ..."

Dolly started to say something, then cleared her throat. "You don't have anything to be sorry about. **Never** apologize for kissing somebody you love."

"It wasn't appropriate."

Dolly burst out laughing. "Will what's his name—Chick—care? I sure don't care."

"I do love you, Dolly."

"And I love you, too, Meredith. That doesn't mean ..."

Meredith looked her. "Mean what?"

Dolly blushed. "Jesus Christ, woman!" She put her drink down, took Meredith's glass, which by now contained only ice cubes, and set it next to hers, turned and embraced her. "Do it again!"

The cockatiel flew off Dolly's shoulder and alighted on the top of the drape.

Afterward, they were silent for a long time.

"You want another drink?"

"Oh, god no! That must have been straight gin."

"Should we be feeling bad?" Dolly looked at Meredith and grinned. "You have my lipstick all over your face."

"You know, I don't feel bad. I guess I was embarrassed, but I'm not anymore."

"What do you feel?"

"Better than I have felt all day." She looked at her watch. "And I'm hungry!"

Dolly stood up and held out her hand. "C'mon, let's see what's in the refrigerator."

Later, as they sat at the table and ate leftover chicken and salad, Meredith propped her chin on her hand. "Thank you, Doctor Dolly."

Dolly smiled. "It called for something drastic, but I didn't expect anything quite **that** drastic."

Meredith began laughing. "I had been obsessing over all the reasons I had for feeling guilty about my life, and then I kiss another woman, for which I should feel guilty, and I don't."

"In Russia, men kiss each other all the time."

"That's true. It's a form-ality." Meredith stumbled over the word. "I'm still drunk!" she laughed.

"What we did was no formality." Dolly looked at her steadily.

"No. It was not. It was from the heart."

The next day, both women avoided speaking about the incident, until Dolly finally asked, "Did you ever get your bird down off the drape?"

"Yes," Meredith laughed. "I have him trained. If I stand still near him with the diaper on my shoulder, he can't help himself—he flies right to me. And when I walk into the bedroom, he flies right into his cage."

"Wow. I need to take lessons from you. I have this, uh, **bird** I'm trying to train …"

"Thank you, Dolly. I think you broke my dark spell."

"**We** broke your dark spell. I just held your hand while you jumped out of it."

Scene 33

Doug was gone for almost two weeks. He and Meredith exchanged cryptic messages every couple of days. She did not write about Dolly's 'intervention.'

She kept up her meditation practice and her daily runs—except for that awful day before Dolly took her in hand. She and Dolly went to a jazz club one Friday evening, and both had a good time. Men approached them and struck up conversations, but they declined invitations to more intensive interactions. Her depression lifted some, although she still had occasional 'minor crises' as she was sitting on her cushion. She wished that she had a teacher to help her through those times, but she stayed with the process, and each time seemed to resolve the issue.

She also began to notice, when she was around others, that strange thoughts sometimes seemed to float through her mind. At first, she assumed that they were from her own troubled mind. Soon, however, she was able to separate them from her usual thoughts, and realized that she was actually picking up the thoughts of other nearby people. It wasn't a pleasant realization.

Is that what's really going on? she wondered. *I don't want to read people's minds! I have too much on my mind as it is!*

Curiosity claimed her. At lunch with Dolly, she paid attention to the cacophony of thoughts around her, and occasionally she identified a fragment as Dolly's.

Dolly was looking over Meredith's shoulder at someone, and seemed to be thinking something like, *I wonder if that's a toupee.*

"It probably is, if it looks like it," Meredith said quietly. Dolly started, and looking at Meredith, asked, "What did you say?"

"Gee, I don't remember. I was just muttering to myself, I guess."

Dolly frowned, but didn't reply.

Meredith had found a new game. When she read Doug's thought the night of her meltdown on the cushion, it made her uncomfortable. But at least with Doug, she thought that it might even out the imbalance in their relationship. She was not prepared to allow others to know. Besides, she found it very difficult most of the time to tell which thoughts came from what people. Her ability to read was not selective. A couple of times when she had determined that a thought had come from one person it turned out to be the wrong person.

Once, going down in the elevator, she clearly 'heard' a thought conversation between two people. They were thinking very intentionally. Obviously, they were operatives from the thirty-fifth floor. She smiled. Wouldn't they be surprised if she said something that would tell them that she 'heard' them! But she looked at the two men whom she assumed were conversing and tried to memorize their faces. *Agents look so ordinary!* she thought—and then almost clapped her hand over her mouth. They could also 'hear' her! But there were several other people in the car, and she pretended to be self-absorbed.

Meditating on her cushion at home, she occasionally caught fragments of thought from outside her apartment, but she couldn't identify the people and mostly couldn't understand what the thoughts were about. On the street, she found that her mind became a buzzing confusion. She dug her iPod out of a drawer and wore the ear buds often in public so that her music drowned out all thoughts.

Why haven't I been aware of this before? Is it actually something I've gotten from Doug? I sure didn't notice it before. I don't like it. It feels like I'm eavesdropping on people, and I don't want to do that.

When Doug joined her for lunch the day after he returned, she asked him, "How do I shut it off?" He didn't know what she was talking about at first, but then it dawned on him.

"Are you really reading?" He was delighted.

"You said, that first time we met in the elevator, that it was a curse. Now I know what you meant."

He looked thoughtful, and she could watch his mind working to piece together what he wanted to say. All she got were disconnected words, and a lot of repetition. Finally, he said, "We had to go through several weeks of training to deal with it. And even then, they programmed the chip to start very slowly so we could adjust to the whole experience."

"The first time I was out on the street with the crowds, I thought I was going to throw up," Meredith said. "It was like that wild, frantic feeling you get when you've had way too much to drink, and you wish you could die or something."

Doug looked at her, hesitated, then said, "You have to meet Randy."

She shook her head. "I don't want this! I don't want to do this! And I don't want some geek to get all gee-whiz over something as personal as this. It would be like having a new OB-GYN resident gaping at my vagina!"

"Okay, okay. But I don't know what to do. What do you want me to do for you?" He looked concerned for her.

"I wish I knew," she answered, then thought, *How did it happen that I met you and now I'm doing this?*

Doug shrugged. *"Fate?"* He laughed.

"I try to turn it off sometimes. But it's like trying to turn off my own thoughts when I'm sitting on my cushion. It just adds more shit to the pot!"

He laughed again. "An interesting metaphor."

Her face grew serious. "I had a meltdown while you were gone."

"Another one after the night in my loft?"

"Yes. I got so depressed one morning I couldn't even do my run—that always clears my head, but I couldn't get out the door. I finally went to work, and Dolly took one look at me and just enveloped me with love and caring. After work we went to my apartment and she got us drunk before dinner. She was wonderful!"

"Dolly is a good friend, isn't she?"

"I'm in love with her." She said it simply, the way it was.

He looked at her carefully, trying to see what that meant.

Meredith laughed. "No, not that way! Well, I don't know. Maybe. But it doesn't have anything to do with us."

Doug felt his heart beating. *Why am I scared?* he thought.

She put a hand on his. *Don't be.*

He slumped back in the seat and put his hands in his pockets. Smiling, *The primitive part of my brain is panicking. The reasoning part is saying, 'relax.' It's good that you love somebody.*

"You are number one. I think that you will always be number one. I missed you." Her head tilted, and he watched her earring, almost hidden in her hair, swing next to her neck.

I want to make love with you, he thought, *right now. Let's get a cab and go someplace.*

Her eyelids lowered ever-so-slightly. *You mean it?*

He pulled his cell phone out of his pocket and pressed one button. After a moment, he said into it, "Stephanie, I'm going to be out this afternoon. Call me if there's an emergency. Thanks."

Meredith's eyes were shining and her mouth was open. She reached in her purse and pulled out her own phone.

Scene 34

Later, in her apartment, they lay together, touching each other with every available bit of skin. In the intensity of passion, they had both cried and laughed.

Now their heads shared a pillow, their lips separated by inches, their eyes caressing each other. "When I was feeling so low," she whispered, "I thought I wanted nothing more than to have you hold me. But I would not have been much company for you."

"Dolly held you?"

"Yes."

"I'm glad."

"You make me feel safe—and okay to be who I am."

"The other crisis—the one you had while I was gone—you want to talk about it?

Meredith lifted her head and took off her earrings. "It seemed more of the same—feeling guilty and worthless for all the suffering I've caused others. It's like there was this door in my soul that had not been opened—maybe all my life—where all my shame was stored. On the cushion, I let it open."

Doug touched her cheek tenderly. "And now?"

"I've explained it to myself. I know that's not enough, but it's the best I've been able to do so far. I know that it was like a festering sore, sitting there in my unconscious all those years, and it was good to let air get to it. I cannot have compassion for others without having compassion for myself. I did things in my life for which I have regret, and for which I was and am responsible, but I did the best I could with the knowledge and wisdom I had at the time. I cannot judge my past actions completely on values and insights that I have today; it's like blaming a cat for eating a pet bird."

"Bravo," he whispered.

"You understand." She smiled.

They lay there quietly for a long time. Then she began to pick up something from him, something that felt horrible, that she wanted to push away. It persisted.

"I killed someone," he said hoarsely. "Last week. I couldn't stop to think of alternatives. If I hadn't shot him he would have shot me and my partner. In all the time I spent in Afghanistan, I never killed anyone that I could see die. They were always just figures running around in the distance, and we rained rounds on them. Some of them fell down. They were like the bad guys in the video games—totally impersonal, totally evil. Or like a flock of ducks flushed from a pond—you aim your shotgun in the general direction, and probably hit one or two."

He stopped for a minute. "This was different. When he fell, I wanted to try to save him, the way I would have one of my buddies in my scouting unit. He just looked at me, and I felt as if it were me, looking out of his eyes at me, his murderer. It was all I could do to run away and escape before we were discovered. It's haunted me ever since. In training, they kept at us, trying to make us forget what we had seen so we could go on with our mission. I dream about it."

"It must have been terrible." Tears welled up and ran down her cheeks to the pillow.

"I had to turn in my gun for ballistics. I haven't been able to go back for it."

Her brow creased. "This was in this country?"

Doug didn't answer. Instead, he said, "I've never done that before."

There was a long silence, and the thoughts they shared became mixed together so that neither of them was sure whose thoughts they were. They were just thoughts, arising and fading away and being replaced by others. Meredith was close to tears the whole time. Doug, as usual, swallowed his tears until they solidified in a lump in his gut.

They must have slept, for it had grown dark outside. Doug eased himself out from under Meredith's arm and got out of the bed. In the bathroom mirror he looked at the stranger there. Touching his head where the chip lay hidden under his scalp, he wondered if all he had heard through that chip, all the whispers and cries of suffering people, were changing him. It was hard to remember the other thoughts, the playful, the angry, the stupid, the sublime thoughts that could have revealed to him, had he paid more attention, the humanity around him.

He remembered a long time ago, when he attended a Quaker meeting out of curiosity, the silence of the service. In the middle of the silence, he heard a voice saying simply, "Pay attention." It had startled him, for no one had actually spoken. Later, he thought it was amusing, that he had heard voices, for he didn't believe in spirits or telepathy. Something in him, though, took note of it. *Why do I remember that now?*

"What do you remember?" She came up behind him and pressed her body against his back. She kissed his neck and laid her cheek against his shoulder.

"I remembered something that happened to me a long time ago." He told her of the incident.

"Maybe," she said without taking her cheek away from him, so that he felt her words as well as heard them, "it's time for you to pay attention again?"

He turned around and embraced her so powerfully that she finally gasped for air. "Wow," she said, "you sure have **my** attention."

Scene 35

Doug, after daily nagging from Tony, finally went to retrieve his gun from Ballistics. While he was in the neighborhood, he called Randy. "Got a minute to give me some advice?"

"I got about a half hour," Randy said, "that enough?"

"I'll be there in five minutes."

Randy was seated at his computer, a complicated device on his head making him look like something out of a sci-fi movie. He swiveled around. "Sup?"

"You remember my telling you ..."

"The babe who reads."

"She's doing it more. And she's doing it when she wants to."

"Awesome! Bring her over!"

Doug shook his head. "She won't come. She hates it, really—like I do sometimes."

"Hmmm. She could really help us, if we could run some tests, and some functional MRI on her."

"I promised her I wouldn't ask her again. I tried."

"So what can I do for you?" Randy's interest was waning.

"She keeps asking how to shut it off. It's driving her crazy."

Randy brought his fingertips together, thinking. "Beats me," he said. She doesn't have a chip that we can reprogram." Then he looked up at Doug. "She doesn't, does she?"

"No, of course not."

"You're **sure**?"

"C'mon, Randy, she's not somebody's agent!"

"And she's not some Hindu yogi who's been up in a cave for forty years, either. People don't just suddenly get the ability to read thoughts!"

Doug's shoulders sagged. "So you don't have any advice about how to ease it up for her?"

"Sorry, Man." Randy turned back to his computer, the wires dangling from his headpiece clicking against each other.

Doug went out and closed the door quietly.

Scene 36

When Doug and Meredith walked into The Egg Place, they saw Dolly sitting alone in a booth. Meredith went over to her. "Hi, Doctor Dolly."

Dolly's eyes lit up. "Hey, babe! I thought you'd be out somewhere with …"

"Yes, he's right here." She turned to motion Doug over.

"I'm glad to meet you, finally!" Dolly said to Doug, extending her hand. "Come eat with me."

Meredith glanced at Doug to get his reaction. Doug grinned and put out his hand to Dolly.

"Sit, please!" Dolly was beaming.

They slid into the booth opposite her.

"I'd like to say that I've heard a lot about you," Dolly said, "but your friend seems to be keeping you under wraps. I just gave them my order, but I'll wait for you. This is a treat!"

Meredith noticed that Dolly was wearing her lowest-cut—at least her lowest-cut **work** blouse. She glanced at Doug, and saw that he noticed, too. "He's been wanting to meet you, too," she said, the corner of her mouth curling up just the slightest bit.

Doug said, "Meredith tells me that you took care of her last week when she needed a friend."

"I had a friend," said Meredith.

Doug smiled at Dolly. "Thank you."

Dolly smiled uncertainly, glancing at Meredith. Meredith smiled back, mouthing the word "okay." And to Doug, she thought, *She's nervous.*

"I see that.

Dolly kept smiling at them. She leaned over toward Doug and whispered, "I understand you read minds!"

Doug grinned and threw up his hands. "Found out!"

Meredith touched Dolly's hand and winked at her. "He turns it off around friends," she said.

"Well, that's a relief!"

"So, now we can all relax." Meredith looked up just as the waitress approached. "Glad you're here," she said to the woman. "We're starving!"

The three of them exchanged small talk. Dolly was clearly studying Doug, but she seldom stopped talking.

Meredith said, "Doug and I were thinking of going out tonight for some jazz. You want to come with us?"

"I'd love to. I was just in a little place out on Georgia, called Red Mango. It's a restaurant, but they have a little combo in the bar that I liked a lot. I think they play tonight."

"Great," said Doug. "How's the food?"

"Actually, I don't know." She touched her lips with her fingertips and laughed. "I had Margaritas for dinner."

"Well, I'm game," said Meredith, and looked at Doug, who nodded. He was obviously enjoying Dolly.

"What's the combo?" he asked.

"I don't know their name," Dolly said. "Keyboard, standup bass and a saxophone. He plays a little trumpet, but mostly tenor sax. He's really good."

"Do you want to meet there?" asked Meredith. "That's not far from you, is it?"

"We can drive you home," Doug said.

Dolly asked Doug, "Where do you live?"

"Arlington."

"That's pretty far, isn't it?" Then she said, "But I guess that's close to …" and stopped.

"The Pentagon," Doug finished.

"But you work all the way up here."

"Subway. It isn't so bad."

Meredith chimed in. "Doug has this enormous loft."

"Good for parties!" said Dolly.

Meredith looked at Doug. "Are you a party person, Douglas?" Doug was a little outside his comfort zone with the conversation, and Meredith was enjoying it more than a little.

"Douglas!" exclaimed Dolly, laughing. "It sounds, uh, **judicial**!"

"I don't think he's a party person, Dolly," Meredith said, an impish smile on her face.

They finished their lunch and made arrangements for meeting that evening, then all three took the elevator.

So, what do you think of her? Meredith asked Doug.

He frowned slightly, and shook his head. There must be other readers in the car. Meredith tried to turn off her thoughts, but the more she tried, the worse they got. Dolly look at her strangely, but said nothing until they got out of the car.

"What was all that?"

"What?" Meredith pretended.

"Doug gave you a funny look. Did somebody fart?"

"No," Meredith laughed. "It was an inside joke."

In their cubes, Dolly gushed. "He's very cool."

"Not exactly **cool**," laughed Meredith.

"No, I mean ..." She stopped when she realized Meredith was teasing her. "Oh, forget it!"

Scene 37

When Meredith and Doug arrived at the Red Mango, Dolly was perched, all legs and cleavage, on a bar stool, and hovered over by the bartender. "Ah, here you are!" she gushed. It appeared that the drink in front of her was not her first of the evening (and likely not the last).

The restaurant itself was bright and colorful; the bar was small and dark and intimate, isolated from the restaurant by swinging doors. A small stage in one corner held musical instruments, chairs and microphones. Doug thought that microphones would not be needed in such a small room, but that was before the place had filled up with patrons. At the moment, there was only one other couple in the room, seated in a far corner.

"We can eat in here," Dolly said. "The musicians will be here soon—they've already left their instruments."

After they had seated themselves near the stage, the bartender took their orders. Doug and Meredith both ordered gin martinis. Dolly merely lifted her empty glass and smiled for more at the bartender.

Meredith grinned at Dolly. "You fit this place like it was yours. You could be the main attraction."

"You wouldn't know it to look at me, would you, that I like to hang out in bars."

"Well, I wouldn't go that far."

They had ordered their steaks and nearly finished their drinks when the musicians strolled in, accompanied by two women, dressed similarly to Dolly.

"Doug's getting a treat tonight," Meredith said. Her martini had smoothed her mind, and she barely noticed the thoughts coming and going from the people around. It was easy for her to identify those of Doug and Dolly, but she couldn't quite figure out just how. When the music began, she was pleased that it drowned out the myriad thoughts whirling through her brain.

The sax player, especially, appealed to Meredith, reminding her of Paul Desmond, who had played with Dave Brubeck in the 1960s. Desmond had played mostly alto, but this fellow sang to her with his tenor reed. *What is it about music that makes life worth living?* She thought.

This kind of music, especially, seems to get right into your emotional system—so personal! Then Doug realized that they were leaving Dolly out of their conversation. "Jazz," he said aloud, "gets right to your guts, doesn't it?"

"Maybe your guts," Dolly responded, "my groin." She finished off her drink, closed her eyes and smiled.

Meredith looked at Doug. *We may have to carry her home tonight.*

I've had my ration for the evening. I have to drive.

When they had finished eating, and the musicians had gone on break, they were able to talk a little. Dolly had a permanent smile on her face. "This is good," she said. "I love good music, good booze and good friends." She lifted her glass.

"Dolly," Doug asked, "where do you come from? Are you from around here?"

"Honey," she drawled, "I don't talk right to be from here. I grew up in Detroit."

"Motown," he said.

"When I was a kid my folks would sneak me into bars so I could hear the music. It's in my blood! By the time I was sixteen, I had guys twice my age taking me to the jazz clubs."

Meredith laughed. She was feeling wonderful. "So how did you wind up doing data entry? That place doesn't feel like the kind of place you would want to work."

"Same as you, honey. It's a job. I was in sales for a while—I like to be with people, as you know," touching Meredith's arm, "but I hated the pressure. Here, I can put in my time and think about something else, and at five o'clock the day is mine!"

Doug turned to Meredith. "How about you?" he asked. "Is it 'just a job' for you, too?"

"Of course. I came down here from New York after I, uh, broke up with a guy up there."

"You were doing this kind of work there?"

"She was an **intellectual**," Dolly broke in, carefully enunciating the word. "University professor!"

Meredith laughed. "Hardly," she said. I taught a little as a grad student. One of the slaves."

"Oh, that's right," Doug said, "that's when you took James Carse's course."

"Yes." She leaned against Doug's shoulder. "You know, I'm smashed."

Just then the music began again, and the conversation gave way to listening and swaying, eyes closed, to a mellow rendering of "Frenesi." Meredith could remember an old recording by Artie Shaw, and she had heard Dave Brubeck playing it in San Francisco. *Frenesi means 'frenzy' doesn't it?*

Something like that. Not much frenzy in this, though.

I'm glad. I like it like this. I heard Brubeck do it once.

My mom had a record of Artie Shaw.

Dolly looked at them. "You know, it's like you two are **so tuned in** to each other!"

"Remember, he can read my mind," said Meredith, and looked into Doug's eyes.

"I'm jealous!" Dolly laughed. "Of both of you!"

Meredith leaned across the little table and kissed Dolly lightly on the lips.

Dolly looked at Doug. "Your turn!"

He grinned and complied.

"Now, both of you, wipe the lipstick. People will talk." She got unsteadily to her feet and, taking her purse, headed for the rest room.

Meredith whispered in Doug's ear, "I think we should get her home."

"Right. We all have to work in the morning."

Meredith got up and followed her friend. When they returned, Meredith said that they were ready to leave. Doug paid the check and the three of them walked out of the room full of music and emotion into the quiet of the suburban night.

Doug stayed in the car in front of Dolly's apartment while Meredith took her up and put her to bed.

As they drove to Meredith's apartment, Doug said, "There's something warm and wonderful about her beneath that gaudy exterior."

"Yes there is. She'd make someone a great companion. I just wish she were looking for love in a safer way."

Scene 38

Meredith had the uncomfortable feeling that she was being watched. Several times when she arrived at her apartment, there seemed to be someone standing around, as though he were waiting for somebody. Once, she saw him look at his watch, then put it close to his face, as though he were having trouble seeing it. She thought about telling Doug, but she wasn't sure that her premonitions were real.

One night after work and dinner at the bistro, she opened her apartment door to find a strange man sitting on her sofa. Quickly reacting, she started to back out and close the door again, but someone else blocked her way. "Step inside, please, ma'am," he said quietly.

Her heart raced. *Rapists don't say 'ma'am'* she thought.

"I wouldn't know, ma'am," the man on the sofa replied to her thought.

Oh, oh. The goddamn CIA!

He smiled.

"What do you want from me?"

We need your help she heard him think.

"Is this about Doug?" she asked aloud.

"Well, no, actually." He was fumbling for words, and his thoughts were jumbled. "You are a remarkable woman," he said finally.

She pulled her cell phone out of her purse, but before she could use it the other man gently took it out of her hand. *I want to call Doug!*

Sorry, ma'am. He doesn't have anything to do with this, and this doesn't have anything to do with him.

Meredith became angry. "Are you arresting me?" she demanded.

"No."

"Then leave!"

"We need your help," he repeated. "You have a special ability, and you can help us."

"Okay, I can read thoughts! So can you! Probably half the goddamn CIA can read people's thoughts!"

He sighed. "The difference, ma'am, is that we have to have implanted electrical devices in our heads, like your friend Doug. I understand you know about all that. You don't seem to need one."

"Probably lots of people can do that," she said. "Why pick on me? I don't even know how it all works."

"What we would like to do is examine you to see how it all works. You won't be harmed in the least, and we'll protect your anonymity."

Her fear was lessened, but her anger was not. "So, I'll be like those poor souls who have been abducted by aliens and probed and examined and impregnated and who knows what else?"

He smiled. "We've been blamed for that, too. No, we're only asking you to help us."

"I can refuse?"

"Well, we'd rather you didn't."

"Give me my goddamn phone! I have a right to legal representation!"

The man sighed again. "Look. I'll be completely honest with you."

"I should trust you, right?" Her contempt was plain on her face.

Just then her phone rang. The other man, who was still holding it in his hand, looked at it. "It's him," he said to the man on the sofa.

"Don't answer it." He pursed his lips. "Find out where he is."

The other man took out his own cell phone and touched some keys. In a moment, he spoke some numbers, and waited. Then, "okay."

He scrolled his phone and selected an application. A moment later, Meredith could see a map displayed on his phone. When she tried to move closer to see more, he turned his back to her. "Looks like he's on the subway, maybe ten minutes away."

The man on the sofa stood up. "Ma'am, we're not here to make trouble. We do need your help. Your country needs your help. If you think you can do that, please call this number." He handed her a blank business card with only a telephone number hand-written on it.

The two men walked out and were gone.

Five minutes later, her doorbell rang. She went to the intercom. "Hello?"

"Meredith, I called you!"

She buzzed him up without saying anything. Her heart was racing again, and she was breathing hard when he tapped on her door. She fell into his arms, sobbing.

Scene 39

Doug was furious. "Damn Randy!"

"What do they want from me?" Meredith was frightened again.

"I think they just want to run some tests, maybe functional MRI, to see if they can figure out the mechanism your mind is using to read thoughts. They know enough, from all the operatives they've implanted, to suspect how you do it."

"I told them that I felt like I was being abducted by aliens for experimentation."

He looked at her, amused. "Probably not far from the truth."

"And they knew where you were! They just punched up some numbers on a phone and they were tracking you on the subway. They left just before you got here."

She showed him the card the man had given her. He looked at it and said, "I could check the number, but I doubt that I'd find out anything. It's probably one of those one-off numbers, to be used only by you and then abandoned."

They were both still standing next to the door. The cockatiel was screeching from the bedroom. "I'll be right back," she said.

Doug threw the deadbolt on the door and sat down at the table in the kitchen. When she returned, Chick was perched on her shoulder, eyeing Doug sideways. "Would you fix me a drink?" she asked.

"Vodka and lime?" He took a bottle out of the freezer and laughed. "I never heard of keeping vodka in the freezer."

"Sometimes I just want a taste, and it goes down easier if it's ice cold."

"You chug it right from the bottle?"

"Yep. Just like my grandpa."

Doug thought that was funny. "Your old grandpa taught you to drink straight liquor?"

"It was his way to keep from killing my grandmother. Besides, what's in those martinis we had the other night? Almost straight gin."

"Anyway," he said, changing the subject, "I don't think those people will harm you—whether you cooperate with them or not. They can't afford to risk the publicity. They may annoy you for a while." He mixed their drinks and handed one to Meredith.

"Don't they make people just disappear?"

"Maybe, rarely. But can you picture the brouhaha if some reporter from The Washington Post were to pick up on all this. You're too visible."

"I don't know what I'd do if I didn't have you to back me up—just getting your perspective makes it seem bearable."

"I can't do much, officially. But I can make it known around the office that you're being harassed. It's not like you're an international spy." He paused. "Are you?"

Meredith picked up a kitchen towel from the table and threw it at him.

Doug finished his drink and clinked the ice cubes in the glass. "I saw the report on you when Andy checked you out. You were, quote, **uninteresting**."

They both laughed at that. "If they only knew," he said, "how very interesting you really are."

Meredith smiled at him. "If I weren't still shaking from that home invasion, I might throw my body at you."

"Tell you what—I'll go in and run a hot, sudsy bath for you to soak in for an hour. Would that stop your shaking?"

"Let's try it." She drained her glass.

While Doug was running the bath water, Meredith did a strip-tease for him, finally picking up her clothes from the floor and throwing them into the bedroom. Looking at herself in the full-length mirror on the door, she said, "I'm sorry I don't have a twenty-year-old body any more for you."

"I can afford to be generous toward that kid who did get your twenty-year-old body," he said, holding out his hand to help her into the steaming tub. "What I get is so much more."

"Sit with me and talk while I get rid of the shakes."

"I'm sure you know what this is doing to me."

She craned her neck to see, her eyebrow lifting.

He sat down and watched her for a long time.

She slid down in the water until only her face was above the surface. She smiled. "So what I need to do is write a letter that tells all about this, seal it and give it to somebody to open it in case I disappear or something happens to me."

"Give it to somebody—like The Washington Post?"

She eased herself out of the water enough to look at him. "I don't know. Could I trust them?"

He grinned. "**Them** is a very big company."

"Doug!" She sat up suddenly.

"What?"

"I was under water—almost all of my head was under water—and I heard what you said! I **think** I heard it. You said, 'give it to somebody like The Washington Post.' I've never heard somebody talking when my ears were under water!"

"I never thought of that. It's true—the pressure of the water restricts motion of the ear drums."

"They do play music at swimming pools, where the speakers are under water and designed for the pressure. But the ordinary voice doesn't penetrate the surface. I must have heard your **thought** as you said it."

"And that signal **can** penetrate, apparently. Wouldn't Randy love to hear **that**!"

"Don't you **dare**!" she cried, splashing water on him.

Doug grinned, and pulled a towel from the rack and dried his face. "I think you may have stopped shaking," he said. He stood up and pulled all of the towels off the racks, as well as those on the shelf overhead.

Meredith stood up in the tub. "I don't need that many!" she laughed. And then as he slipped out the door with them, she realized what he had done. "Doug! You sonofabitch! Bring me a towel!"

She stood for a moment in the tub, beginning to shiver. "Doug! I'm freezing!"

When it was apparent that he wasn't coming back with a towel, she stepped out of the tub and pursued him in the bedroom. He hadn't expected her to get water all over the apartment, so she took him by surprise. Wrapping her wet arms around him, she pushed him onto the bed and fell on top of him. By that time, both of them were laughing hysterically. She rolled around on him until his clothes were soaked.

He reached down and pulled the bed spread over them, and rolled the two of them up in it like a mummy.

It didn't take long for them both to become warm again.

Scene 40

Meredith was becoming settled in her meditation practice. Her knees no longer hurt, and she found that her back was becoming stronger. At work, she sat up straighter and was less tired at the end of the day. With that and her regular physical workouts, she felt stronger and had more energy than she'd had since her high school soccer days.

She felt calmer, too. She was not as apprehensive when Doug got called out on assignments and was incommunicado for periods of time. She seldom tried to read other people's thoughts, choosing to respect their privacy. She didn't need to look for an advantage over others through her gift. If anything, it gave her more compassion when dealing with difficult people or circumstances.

Dolly noticed the change. "You were never as scattered as I am, but you seem quieter lately, not withdrawn, but like **serene.**" She was sitting in Meredith's cubicle, drinking a coke.

"I guess I'm learning to accept things more. I don't get so scared or depressed as I used to." She smiled at her. "I haven't had any big crises since you helped me through that last one."

"Well, just remember, I'm here if you need me."

"That goes both ways, love."

Dolly pulled her hair back into a pony tail and tied it with a rubber band. "How's Doug?"

"He's gone again." She made a face. "He's **always** gone!"

"With all the trouble in the world, I guess there's a big demand for mind readers."

Meredith put her finger to her lips. "We're not supposed to know some things."

"You get messages from him, though, right?" Dolly pointed to Meredith's computer screen.

"Sometimes. Nothing yet this time."

"You get time on your hands, let's you and I do something."

Meredith thought for a moment, then said, "You want to come over my way and have dinner at the bistro?"

"Tonight?"

"Yes."

"Okay."

After quitting time, going down in the crowded elevator, Meredith was picking up the usual mixture of thoughts. She glanced around at the other passengers, trying to be discreet about it. One man caught her eye.

Evening, ma'am, he thought. Obviously, he knew her, but she didn't recognize him.

Good evening, officer.

He suppressed the quickest of smiles.

Meredith's face felt suddenly hot. She turned away quickly, and spoke to Dolly, "I need to make one stop around the corner when we get on the street."

Dolly gave her an odd look, but nodded without saying anything.

When the elevator reached the big lobby, Meredith pulled Dolly aside, pretending to look at her shoe. She watched until the operative had exited through the main doors, and then said, "That guy knows me, but I don't know him. Give him time to get away before we go out."

Dolly looked at her. "What's going on, girl? You are red in the face!"

Meredith laughed. "I think he works with Doug."

"That mean he reads minds too?"

"Maybe. I thought he might say something to me."

Dolly took her by both shoulders and looked in her face. "Are you in trouble, or are you getting paranoid?"

Meredith laughed again.

"That's not an answer, Meredith. C'mon."

Her shoulders sagged. "Okay," she said finally, "I need to tell you something in private. Let's go to my place instead of the restaurant. I'll fix us something and we can talk."

On the street, Meredith hailed a cab instead of heading for the subway. In the cab, she explained, "He's probably not following me, but this is better than the subway."

Dolly continued to watch her with a worried look. "And here I thought you were so calm!"

Meredith laughed. "I really am. But I'm also being careful."

At her apartment door, Meredith put her key in the lock and paused. She sighed, turned the key and opened the door. *I **am** getting paranoid!* she thought.

Only the shriek of her cockatiel greeted them.

"Okay," said Dolly, "fix us a drink and then talk. I can't stand this suspense!"

Meredith went into the bedroom to retrieve her bird, then went into the kitchen. "You want a drink like those you made for us the last time you were here?"

Dolly laughed and followed her into the kitchen. "I don't rightly remember what I put in those."

"Then what you get is a single shot of vodka with Rose's lime juice."

They carried their drinks to the sofa. Meredith took a sip of the tangy drink and set the glass down. "Dolly," she said seriously, "I'd trust you with my life. But I need you to know that this has to be just between us, okay?"

"You're really a spy from Tajikistan. I knew it all along."

"No, I'm an ex-hippie from Berkeley. But you knew that. This is different. A couple of months ago, I began to hear things—people's thoughts."

Dolly's eyes widened. "You have a chip like Doug?"

"No. I don't know how it started, or where it came from, but just like Doug, I can hear things that people are thinking—sometimes. And not very well."

"And you didn't tell me?" Dolly looked troubled.

"I'm sorry. It's complicated, but at the time I couldn't deal with it. I didn't want it to be happening, and I didn't want anybody to know.

Dolly raised a finger. "Wait—that guy in the elevator a few minutes ago—he knew?"

"Yes. And I don't know why he spoke to me—in thoughts. That's why I was **paranoid**, as you put it."

"So they don't like other people reading minds like they do."

"Well," Meredith said, taking another sip from her drink. "not exactly. They sent some guys to my apartment. They were here when I walked in. They asked me if I'd help them. They want to know how I read thoughts."

"Holy smoke!"

"Yeah. It scared the life out of me. You know, you walk into your own home and there's a couple of hoodlums sitting there waiting for you."

"And you without your pepper spray!"

"At first I thought I was going to be raped or murdered—or raped **and** murdered. But they didn't do anything to me, except keep me from calling Doug. They just talked to me, very calmly. My heart was going a mile a minute."

"What'd they want you to do?" Dolly finished her drink.

"They asked me to come down to **someplace**—I don't know where—so they could run some tests on me, to see how I do it."

Dolly, her face stony, picked up both glasses and went into the kitchen. "And you've been reading my mind all this time without me even guessing it?"

Meredith got up and followed her. "Dolly, it's not like that! For one thing, it's hard to do. And I would never—what, **eavesdrop**? on your thoughts!"

Without responding, Dolly handed Meredith her drink and returned to the sofa.

They sat without speaking for a few minutes. Finally, Meredith said, "Dolly, you are my best friend! I meant it when I said, 'it goes both ways.'"

Dolly set her glass down and reached for a tissue. Her eyes were filling with tears.

"I was afraid," Meredith said, her voice hoarse. "I still am. I didn't want you to get mixed up in it, because I didn't know what was going to happen. I even thought of writing it all down and sealing it in an envelope and giving it to you to open in case I disappeared or something."

Dolly dabbed at her eyes.

Meredith took her hand. "I wasn't going to say anything at all, but today when you said 'I'm here if you need me,' I felt awful, keeping all this from you. You deserve my honesty, Dolly."

"I'll be all right. Give me some time to process this." She looked at Meredith. "I keep thinking ..." And then she stopped. "But you read my thoughts anyway. I don't have to tell you anything!"

"Dolly, please! I don't read your thoughts—only once in a while I pick up something, but I wait for you to tell me what you want to say."

"You don't know how humiliating this is!"

"I do! I do! Remember I've been with Doug all this time, and I have felt just as vulnerable as you do right now! I learned how to trust him, and I hope you can come to trust me, too."

"It's like you're suddenly somebody else, somebody I don't know!"

"I'm not!" Meredith was now also close to tears. "If I could turn it off, I would. But I can't. I try to ignore it—most of the time, I try to ignore it, because it's—it's a curse! That's how Doug described it, the first time we talked."

They sat in silence for a long time. The cockatiel hopped from Meredith's shoulder to Dolly's and began tugging at her earring. Dolly impatiently brushed the bird away.

"Here," Meredith said, taking Chick from Dolly's shoulder and removing it to the bedroom. When she returned, the bird was objecting vociferously from its cage.

Dolly was staring at the far wall. "I keep thinking of all the times we've shared stuff with each other, and ..."

"I should have told you right away ..."

"No, let me finish. I'm always straight with you, you know that."

Meredith nodded.

"But sometimes I could be thinking something that I wouldn't want you to hear."

"Of course! I understand that! Dolly, if something like that would happen, I'd tell you right away, so we could get clear with each other. I wouldn't think any less of you, no matter what you said—or thought. I promise!"

Dolly's eyes were red-rimmed, but she smiled at Meredith. "Okay," she said hoarsely, "now, you said you'd feed me. I trust you!"

The two of them went to the kitchen and rummaged around for dinner. As Meredith set a pan on the range to make an omelet, Dolly went up behind her and hugged her, laying her head on her friend's shoulder. "I always knew you were special," she said softly.

Scene 41

On Saturday morning, Meredith felt relaxed and comfortable. She showered and sat on her cushion for nearly an hour, when something began to gnaw at the edges of her attention. Focusing on the sensations in her body, she tried to see it from a little distance, to let go of it. It had to do with Dolly, but she couldn't identify it. Her abdomen was tense, so she tensed it even more and released, several times. The tightness remained.

When they had parted, both had seemed to be over the tension caused by her not telling Dolly right away about her discovery that she was reading thoughts. Now, she wondered if there was still something lurking between them. One of the things she loved about Dolly was the way she spoke her mind and then seemed to let go of whatever was bothering her.

But that wasn't it. She wasn't picking up something from Dolly. It was in herself, and it was about kissing Dolly. Then a half-memory emerged from a long time ago, a dark fog settling over her.

In her early twenties, she had once participated in a drug-clouded, awkward-schoolgirl kind of orgy that hadn't gone well. Six or seven people fumbled in the psychedelic darkness, fondling each other, kissing and touching, playing with every kind of sexual feeling they could imagine. At first it was a lark—abandoning all inhibitions, enjoying the freedom from all the rules. She felt orgasm after orgasm. Then, mysteriously, it transformed into something hideous to her. She had been lying on top of her best friend, kissing her almost feverishly, wanting somehow to swallow her or be swallowed by her. Her friend suddenly pulled her face away, gasping for breath. "What are you doing?!" she cried.

Meredith became aware that a boy was attempting to put his hand between her legs, and his fingernails had scratched her thigh. She rolled over and roughly pushed him away. Her friend moved away from her without a word. The hash they had been enjoying was now anything but enjoyable. Confused, she crawled into a corner and began to cry. The music was too loud, too demanding, too distorted—impersonal and violent. After what seemed a long time, someone turned the music off and people began quietly to leave. The odors of sweat and sex in the room made her nauseated, and she fled to the bathroom.

All the feelings from that scene from so long ago flooded back once more as she sat on the cushion. Her shame struck like a fist in her belly, and she doubled over, sobbing.

After a long time, she lay exhausted, still straddling the cushion, her face on the floor, her eyes closed. Rolling over onto her side, she became aware of the room again, of the texture of the carpeting against her cheek, the feeling of dried tears on her skin, their echo still resounding in the pit of her stomach, faintly sore from her sobbing.

That friend whom she had so unthinkingly violated in her drug-muddled passion that night had emerged once more—in Dolly. *Of course it was sexual,* she thought, *I let that part of myself off its leash. For just that moment it was loose again. Whatever it is, it does not define me, and I don't have to fear it.*

Dear Dolly, she just took it in, and she kissed me back, and then she let it all go. Of course I love her sexually. How could I not? Don't we all have those feelings about the ones we're close to? Admit it—acknowledge it, and move on! It's too late to resolve that relationship with Heather—she probably doesn't remember it either, after all these years.

Meredith gathered herself once more, and resumed her perch on the cushion. Wiping her cheek with the back of her hand, she took a deep breath and closed her eyes. *May Heather be well. May she be free of enmity and danger. May she be free of suffering. May she be happy. May all creatures be well. May they be free of enmity and danger. May they be free of suffering. May they be happy.*

She sat there, resting. *May Meredith be well,* she thought, opening her eyes and slowly getting to her feet. *May she be free of enmity and danger. May she be free of suffering.* Dropping her cushion in the bottom of the closet, *May she be happy.*

She took a deep breath and let it all go.

"Why don't you tell me about these things," asked Doug when she told him about her experience some time later.

"It's my own mind," she said, "I can't tell you everything that goes on in here." She tapped her head. "I have to deal with my own demons, or they can never get tamed."

Doug pulled her to him and kissed her, but he still didn't understand. "I want to ride in on my white charger and rescue you from your demons."

With her arms around his neck to keep him from moving away, she leaned her head back and looked into his eyes. "Yeah, there's a part of me that wants that, too. But I have to slay my own dragons."

Doug nodded. "I know you do," he said.

Scene 42

Meredith sent Doug a message on their special web site, but he never replied to it. So when he called her and said he was home again, she was relieved. "I wouldn't make a very good army wife," she told him. "The suspense is awful!"

In the bistro that evening, they caught up with each other's lives—at least, he caught up with hers, since he couldn't tell her anything about his assignment. "How's the meditation going?" he asked.

"Pretty good. My mind jumps around so much I am constantly having to stop it and go back to my breathing. I read something in Ken Wilber's book ..."

"The one you borrowed from me—'The Simple Feeling of Being' or something like that?"

"Yes. He said that while meditating you have to be sure you're directly experiencing something, like your body, instead of just thinking about it. That made sense to me, because that's what I've been doing—thinking **about** things."

"I only managed to sit a couple of times on this trip. I miss it."

"I've noticed that each time, it takes me, like, a half hour to get to that place, you know, where everything suddenly quiets down."

He chuckled. "I've described it as like when you're driving a car and you don't realize that it's in third gear, maybe going up a little grade or something, and then suddenly it goes to fourth gear, and it's noticeably quieter."

"It's like 'ahhhhh,' this feels like home!"

She cut a piece of chicken on her plate and picked it up with her fork. Pausing with it in mid-air, she put it down again.

"Something wrong with it?"

Meredith looked at him. "I can't eat it." She stared at the meat. "It's my friend, Chick."

Doug started to laugh, and then stopped. "You're serious."

She took a drink of water. "It just hit me, just as I was about to put it in my mouth. What's the difference between that bird and the one in my apartment who loves me?"

He almost reminded her that the cockatiel would make only about one mouthful, but decided that she would not find it funny. "I guess there isn't much."

She pushed her plate away. "I'm sorry. I can't eat it. I just can't."

"Okay, we'll get something else." He signaled to the waiter. "There's nothing wrong with the food," he told the man, "but we don't want it. And we'd like to see the menu again."

"Doug," Meredith protested, "I didn't mean that you couldn't eat yours!"

The waiter looked puzzled. "It's not good?"

"No, it's fine. We just want to change our dinner. We'll pay for this, too." Doug motioned for the waiter to take both plates.

In a moment the manager came out of the kitchen, carrying two more menus. "I'm sorry the food wasn't to your liking," he said, in broken English.

Meredith put her hand on his arm. "Marcel, it is good. I just don't want to eat any meat right now, and Doug is joining me. Do you understand?"

"You want vegetarian?"

"Yes," she said, smiling. "You understand."

Marcel took back the menus. "I will fix you a magnificent vegetable plate!"

"Thank you!"

She turned to Doug. "I'm sorry!"

"Don't be sorry," he said, "Lots of people don't eat meat. I've thought of it myself."

"It's come up during my sittings a few times—thinking about compassion. There's a little blessing one of the writers told about, something like, 'May I be happy, may I be healthy, may I be free of suffering,' and then you say it—or think it—for others, those close to you, other people, and then other creatures. At first, it struck me as contrived, or something from Sunday school. But then when I actually did it—while you were gone, I was worried about you, and so I said it, 'May Doug be happy,' and the whole thing, and it made me feel better. Or at least I didn't have as much trouble letting go of my thoughts of you."

Doug smiled and touched her hand. "That comes from the metta chant, an old Buddhist chant. Metta means 'loving kindness,' and the whole chant covers all creatures in the universe."

"And how could I say, 'May all beings be free from suffering,' then go out and eat one of them? At first, I tried to rationalize it and say, well they die instantly, they don't really suffer. But that sounds so hypocritical! Killing is not loving kindness!"

His expression sobered. "Don't I know!" he said softly.

"Oh, I'm sorry! I forgot!"

"It's okay."

"I can't judge others," she said. "I just have to deal with this for myself. And just then, when I started to put that piece of chicken in my mouth, it hit me!"

The bistro manager arrived with two plates, mounded with an assortment of roasted vegetables, two small bowls of sauce, and a small dish of various cheeses. "Pour sauce over or dip it," he said, demonstrating. "You didn't say vegan, so I brought you cheese, too—for protein!"

Meredith touched his arm again. "Thank you!"

"Enjoy. S'on the house!"

To more profuse thanks from Meredith and Doug, he withdrew to his kitchen.

Doug smiled at Meredith. "You have an admirer."

"I'm overwhelmed." She took his hand and closed her eyes for a minute. Then, picking up her fork she dipped a piece of roasted red pepper in the sauce and tasted it. She pronounced it "wonderful!"

Later, in her apartment, they discussed her decision for a few minutes. "I have to think about this some more," she said. "It's hit me that it's a very big thing. It's not just about whether I eat chicken, is it?"

"Everybody has to draw the line for themselves."

"It feels important."

"You've been changing while I was gone," he said.

"I guess I have."

After a moment, she said, "Oh, on that subject, I told Dolly about my reading thoughts."

He pursed his lips. "How did that go?"

"Awful, at first. She felt I had blind-sided her, that all this time I was reading her mind and she didn't know it."

"Yeah, I could understand that."

"But we finally sorted it all out. I think she'll be okay. But what started it was coming down in the elevator after work, somebody sent me a thought. He just said, 'Evening ma'am' and I knew he was talking to me and nobody ever says, 'ma'am' except you Company guys. I didn't recognize him, but I assumed it was somebody from your group. I answered him before I thought about how that acknowledged to him that I heard his thought. I got rattled, and Dolly and I dodged him—even took a cab home—'cause I didn't know what he was up to."

Doug frowned. "Wonder who that was. My boss knows, of course, and maybe one other—oh, and Janet—but it's not general knowledge. Maybe the word spread from Randy's group."

"So Dolly naturally caught that something was up, and I had to tell her the whole thing. I swore her to secrecy, but she was only upset about my not having told her before."

"You are so bloody honest!" he said, the frown gone.

"I don't want to deceive anyone. But wait a minute! You said Janet knows about me?"

"Hmmm. I did say that, didn't I? I don't think so, actually. I don't know why I said it. I haven't spoken to her since you told me."

Meredith looked at him steadily.

Doug laughed. "You have that look. You're not sure you believe me—right?"

"I believe you if you tell me. I really do." She smiled. "But there's always that little girl inside of me that is terrified."

"Terrified? That's a strong word."

"It's a strong feeling. It's not me, though—I do trust you to tell me what's important. Just that when I think I've grown up, **she** comes up with her little-girl fear. You know those old drawings of a person with two little demons on his shoulders, one with horns and a tail and the other with a halo?"

"Yeah, I have them, too."

"You do?" She tilted her head in that way he loved. *I guess that's part of the little girl in her too,* he thought.

So I shouldn't kill her yet? she asked.
Doug smiled. *Never. I can live with the occasional fear.
I hope I can.*

Scene 43

After mulling over her decision through the weekend, Meredith decided that she had to tell Dolly about her decision right away. She didn't want Dolly to continue to think she held anything back from her. Leaning over the partition between their cubicles, she waited until Dolly finished entering a screen of data. "You have plans for lunch?"

Dolly looked up at her. "Sounds like I do now."

"I have something I want to bounce off you."

"As long as it's not harder than a marshmallow!"

They laughed together. The tension that began when Meredith told her about being able to read thoughts was pretty much gone, although she knew that Dolly hadn't forgotten it. Only on rare occasions did it come up, and always with humor.

Going down to lunch on the elevator, Dolly watched Meredith carefully for signs that she was connecting with another of those men from the thirty-fifth floor. But walking together across the big lobby, their conversation was light and easy.

After they had found a booth in The Egg Place, Dolly spoke first. "Is this something top secret?"

"Oh, no, nothing like that. It's something I've been thinking about for the past few days, and I'd like to hear your thoughts on it."

They looked at the menu for a few minutes, and when the waitress came with their water, Dolly ordered a cheeseburger. Meredith ordered a garden salad.

"What do you know about vegetarian diets?" she asked Dolly.

"Not much. Why?"

"I had a strange experience Friday at the bistro with Doug. We had ordered their broiled chicken, but when it came I couldn't eat it. I think I don't want to eat meat any more."

Dolly looked at her, slightly amused. "Are you going Buddhist on me?"

"No, not exactly. I just got in touch with something in me that doesn't want to cause any animal to suffer."

Dolly thought about that for a while. When the waitress brought their food, Dolly looked at her cheeseburger. "You should have told me sooner," she said.

"Please, don't think that. This is my thing—I'm not out to change the world. I won't try to convince you or anything. I just need to live with that little voice inside me."

Dolly picked up her sandwich then put it down again.

"Dolly, go ahead and eat!" Meredith poured dressing on her salad and grinned. "I promise I won't stare at you as you eat that poor cow!"

Dolly hesitated, trying to interpret Meredith's joke, then decided that it was really all right to eat her sandwich. They both laughed and ate their lunches.

After they had finished, however, Dolly became serious. "You've been my friend since you first came to our office," she said. "I always knew that you were special—you're smart and you're caring, and I've always been really comfortable around you. You know that, don't you?"

"Yes. You've gone out of your way to make me comfortable, too—and to feel cared for. I love you for that. Does this change anything?"

"I don't know. I feel like maybe you've outgrown me or something. You can read my mind! And now you are going up on another level, or something. It's like I don't know how to be a friend to you anymore. You're up on this higher plane, and I'm still down here, grunting and farting and eating animals like a Neanderthal or something."

"No! It's not like that! I don't want that!" Meredith felt tears welling up in her eyes. She dabbed at her cheeks with a tissue. "Look, we both have to go back to work. Can we continue this after work?"

Dolly sighed. "Okay." She sighed again. "I'll just have to live with this hamburger sitting in my stomach all afternoon, refusing to go down."

Meredith looked at her, and they both laughed.

After work, they decided to eat at a Middle Eastern restaurant near where Dolly lived. "I'm sure I can find something I can eat there," said Meredith.

Over martinis before the food arrived, they picked up their earlier conversation. Dolly still showed disappointment over Meredith's decision to be vegetarian. "I know it makes sense," she said, "but I can't imagine not having meat in my life. I don't know what I'd eat—it sounds so complicated!"

"One thing I can see is that when we go out to eat together, I need to think about what I'm going to eat. That's all. Maybe I'll want to go to different restaurants, where I can get a good vegetarian meal sometimes. It's just a matter of protein, and there are a lot of alternative sources of protein."

"You're not going to get into macrobiotics and that sort of thing, are you?"

"No. I will just substitute something for the meat I usually eat."

"And you won't look down your nose at my Polish sausage or corned beef?"

"Absolutely not."

By the time their meal was served, both women were comfortable again They had a long conversation about the nutritional value of lentils and rice.

Scene 44

In spite of their talk, Meredith felt a new distance between Dolly and herself. They ate lunch together often, but Dolly seemed reticent. She didn't initiate topics as much, and her responses to Meredith's side of their conversations sometimes seemed abrupt.

Meredith spent more and more of her lunch hours alone, sometimes walking the streets, immersing herself in the bustle of the city. She picked up thoughts of passersby and occasionally tried to piece together stories of people from the fragments she heard.

Then one day, she clearly heard, *If you hear this, say hello.*

It startled her, and before she had time to consider it, thought, *Hello,* and looked around the crowd to see where it might have come from. Her first reaction was to expect to see one of the men from the thirty-fifth floor—a group she had come to be able to recognize from their demeanor and dress.

Don't look for me, please. Go over by that mailbox.

This seemed weird, and Meredith had a moment of apprehension, but moved toward the mailbox as requested. Surely, someone recognized her!

Thank you. Forgive me, but I'm trying to stay incognito.

You have me at a disadvantage! she thought, *You know me but I don't know you.*

Sorry. Give me a minute, just a minute—please?

Something about the tone of the request—not, as with a voice speaking, the physical tone, but the emotional tone—touched her. *All right,* she answered.

Do you have an implant?

No.

How do you hear my thoughts?

I don't know. It's new to me.

A hand touched her arm, and she turned. A young man, rather unkempt and pale, stood beside her. She watched his eyes as he thought to her, *I know there are more of us, but I haven't found any—except the CIA people.*

You are roaming the streets calling for others?

I don't know any other way to connect. I'm going out of my mind! He did look desperate.

Meredith wasn't sure how to respond to this stranger. Perhaps he was mentally ill—but he was clearly able to hear her thoughts! "Let's sit somewhere," she said, smiling at him. "That bench over there."

They walked together to the bench and sat down.

"Thank you," he said, "I'm so relieved to find someone else like me!"

"Tell me something about yourself—no, wait." She glanced around and saw a fast-food restaurant nearby. "Are you hungry?"

His face lit up with gratitude. "I haven't eaten in a couple of days."

"Then we can talk better over some food," she said, taking his elbow and steering him toward the restaurant. Inside, in line, she said quietly, "Anything you want."

Her maternal side had been captured by this poor creature. He ordered a hamburger and fries and a soft drink. She ordered a garden salad and coffee. They sat at a table in the far corner of the room, and he immediately began to eat. She waited until he slowed down.

"Where are you from?" she asked.

He took a long draw from his drink and then wiped his face with a napkin. "Baltimore. I walked all the way here."

"Like Diogenes," she said simply. For some reason she thought he just might know about Diogenes.

"He smiled. "But I don't have a lantern." She was right.

"Looking for an honest—what?"

"About six months ago I began to hear voices." He smiled again. "I wonder how many people have truly heard voices like this."

Meredith's heart was pounding. *Other people, too!*

That's what I was thinking!

"Please. Back to voices," she said, "I'm having a hard time distinguishing your thoughts!"

"I thought I was going crazy. I made the mistake of telling my mom, and right away she made an appointment with a shrink. He didn't have a clue. He prescribed some pills, but I knew I didn't need any pills. It took me a while to figure out what was going on in my head. I'd be sitting in class and I could read the thoughts of everybody around me. I'd get so upset I'd go into the john and throw up."

"I know the feeling," she said, propping her head with her elbow. "It's like being in a crowded room and everybody's talking at once."

"I knew that I couldn't be the only one it was happening to. If I was, I'd **really** go nuts! I read something on line about the CIA having special operatives who had chips implanted in their heads, and they could do what I could do—least that's the way I understood it. So I came here. I hitchhiked a little bit, but walked most of the way. How far is that?"

"I don't know, maybe forty miles. Did you think the CIA could help you?"

He looked at her with desperation in his eyes. "I don't know! I even wondered if they had planted one of those things in my head!"

She felt his head in about the place where Doug had said his chip was implanted. Nothing like a scar, only very dirty hair. "I don't feel anything. If you have an implant, then I must, too."

"I kept calling, like I did you. Once, a guy stopped me and started asking questions I didn't understand. He felt my head, too. He scared me!"

Meredith half-smiled. "I can well imagine!"

"How did this happen to us?!"

"I don't know," she said. Her mind was whirling. What should she do—call Doug? No! She could trust him, she decided, but it might put him into a dangerous position.

"Your mind is really scrambled right now!" he said.

"It sure is. I'm trying to figure out what we should do."

"I don't want to make any trouble. This just came on you recently too—also?"

"About a month ago it started. What's your name?"

"Dennis Watson."

"How old are you?"

"Seventeen."

"You're still in school?"

"I just graduated from high school."

"Anybody know where you are?"

"No. I knew if I told my mom she'd freak out."

"She's probably freaked out now. You have to call her."

Dennis looked pained.

"Do you have any ID on you?"

He pulled out a wallet and showed her his driver's license. It didn't look like there was any money in the wallet.

"Okay," she said. "We may be able to help each other, but you have to do what I tell you, okay?"

He shrugged. "I guess."

"You're intelligent enough to know that I could get into big trouble—right?"

"I'm sorry."

She dug her phone out of her purse and called Dolly. "I have an emergency, and I have to go home," she said. "Call me on my cell in about two hours. If I don't answer, send somebody."

"**What**?" Dolly exclaimed. "Meredith, what are you getting into?"

"Please, love, don't ask right now. Just call me later, okay? And tell whatshername I'm off for the afternoon. **I'm okay!**" She hated to cut Dolly off, but she didn't want to have to explain. *But why did I tell her to call me?*

Because you're not sure about me, right? He grinned at her.

Her shoulders sagged, and she managed a weak smile. "What am I getting myself into?"

"I don't know. What are you thinking about?"

"Oh, of course. I'm sorry. I am going to take you home and get you cleaned up. Meanwhile, we need to talk—a lot. It's been a long time since I've been responsible for somebody besides myself, and I'm trying to figure this all out."

"I don't know your name, either." Suddenly he seemed older.

"It's Meredith Handen. I'm going to do something my parents always warned me never to do—take a stranger into my home. Because something tells me we need to get to know more about each other."

He laughed. "I cannot imagine you getting yourself into a situation you couldn't handle."

"Well I have, and not too long ago, either."

She stood up and let him take the tray and trash to the bins by the door.

"Dennis."

He turned and looked at her.

"I am not your mother."

He grinned. "That's for sure."

They caught the subway and got to her apartment within a half-hour. Inside, she pointed to the bathroom. "Throw your clothes out to me and I'll wash them. Shampoo your hair! There's a robe on the door."

"You sure you're not my mother?"

"Go!"

When he closed the door, she had a sudden attack of panic. *What am I doing?*

Even through the closed door, she caught, *You got me!*

She emptied his pockets and stuffed his clothing into the washer. She resisted the impulse to look through his wallet. He also had car keys, a tiny pen knife with a flashlight, and sixteen cents in change. He also had a very expensive handkerchief, still folded and apparently unused.

In a little while he appeared, wearing Doug's robe. *Doug. What am I going to do about Doug? He could return at any time!*

"Who's Doug?"

"My boy friend. **I hate that expression!** My man friend."

"Is he going to walk in and see me like this?" Dennis looked serious.

"No, don't worry about it. The thing is—he's one of those guys with an implant."

"Oh, shit! I'm sorry. Oh, shit! Where's my clothes?"

"They are just now going into the spin cycle. Relax."

"I'm a sitting duck for a jealous CIA lover!"

Meredith couldn't suppress a laugh. "He probably won't show up tonight."

"**Probably**?"

"He's a very reasonable man. But you could put him into a precarious position because of your 'gift.'"

"You call it a gift?"

"Gift, curse. Anyway, he might be bound to turn you in if he knows about you."

Dennis screwed up his face. "Turn me in? What'd I do wrong?"

"Nothing. Except to not let your poor mom know you're not in a ditch someplace with your throat cut." She pulled her phone out of her purse. "I'm taking a chance using my phone for this, but call your mother. Now."

"I don't know her number."

"Yes you do."

Dennis took the phone and dialed. "Hi, Mom, it's me."

Meredith could hear the screeching from the phone, but not the words.

"Yeah, Mom. I'm okay. I'm in D.C., and some lady is helping me." More screeching. "She's real nice. Yeah, she gave me something to eat."

He listened to the screeching for a moment, then held the phone out to Meredith. "She wants to talk to you."

"Hello, Mrs. Watson. Oh, I'm sorry—that's Dennis's name. Yes, he's fine. He was kinda lost in the big city. I made him call you right away because I knew you'd be worried. No, I don't know where he's going from here, but I'll see that he at least has a bus ticket back to Baltimore. Oh, I'm just a good Samaritan helping out a kid in distress. My name is Meredith Handen, and Dennis is in my home. Okay." She handed the phone back to Dennis.

Dennis talked with his mother—mostly listened—for a few minutes, and promised her several times that he would return home. As he hung up and handed the phone back to Meredith, he laughed and said, "She's pretty mad."

"I never had any children, but if I had, I would have been mad, too." She took his clothing out of the washer and put them into the dryer. "We'll have you presentable in just a few minutes."

"Thank you, Ms Handen."

"Now let's talk about this mind reading thing for a minute. That's what brought you to our nation's capitol, isn't it?"

"I can't handle it!"

"Now, think for a minute. What are you hearing in your head right now?"

"Well it's a lot quieter right now. I keep thinking about what I need to do, and I can hear little bits of your thoughts—at least I guess they're your thoughts."

"Okay, I'm hearing about the same thing. We're sharing our thoughts together, and I don't find it too disturbing. Do you?"

"No. But sometimes it gets so crazy I could scream."

"Yeah, I know that feeling. But I've learned I can turn down the volume some. Not all the time, but some times. Did you ever meditate?"

"You mean like sit cross-legged and hold your breath?"

She laughed. "Not as drastic as that. There's a kind of meditation called 'mindfulness meditation' that is very simple, and when you get used to it you can quiet your mind down a lot. Even people who can't hear other people's thoughts have found that it's really helpful. I can show you how to get started, but the main thing is, you'll have to use some discipline and stay with it. Sit for an hour every day. I can give you a book that tells the basic procedure. Can you do that?"

"An hour every day?"

"Sitting very still for an hour. It's hard at first, but it gets easier."

"I don't know."

"Do you want to get the voices under control?"

"Yeah."

"Okay." She collected his clothing from the dryer, shook them out and handed them to him, gesturing with her head toward the bathroom.

He smiled, took the clothes, and disappeared.

The phone rang. It was Dolly.

"Hi, love," said Meredith. "Thanks for calling. I just wasn't sure when I called you, but everything's fine now. And you'll be pleased to hear—you with your ideas about higher planes—I have a young man in my apartment, whom I have fed, bathed and dressed. And I made him call his mother."

"Meredith, are you out of your mind? How old?"

"Seventeen. A couple of years younger, and you could have reported me!"

"Where did you pick him up?"

"On Connecticut Avenue, during lunch."

"So when are you going to tell me **all**?"

"Tomorrow or the next day. I have to teach him to meditate before I send him home."

"You wild, wild woman!" Dolly sounded as though she was doubled over with laughter.

Dennis apparently had waited until Meredith finished her phone call before coming out of the bathroom. He was clean and dressed. His hair was combed. "Is that what you think of me?"

Meredith had started to say something about his metamorphosis, but his question stopped her short. Then she laughed. "If you knew Dolly the way I do, you'd know why I made a big joke of having you here. If she thought I had picked up a man and brought him here for sex, she would have cheered me on. But she was worried about me. That's all."

"I guess I don't understand older women," he said.

"You will, Dennis, you will."

"Okay, now what?"

"Lesson number one." She took a couple of cushions from the sofa and put them in the middle of the floor. After showing him how to sit— his young bones adapted readily to a full lotus position—she pushed on his back. "Your back has to be straight, or you'll be in pain in a short time."

When he was in a suitable posture, she mounted her own cushion. "Let's try it for ten minutes. After we have some dinner, we'll sit again."

When she heard him groan at one point, she said, "Back straight!" After the ten minutes, she got up and went to the kitchen. "Okay, come out here and set the table for us. You're going to have to eat vegetarian tonight—that's all I have in the freezer—but you can have two of these dinners if one doesn't fill you up. I've heard about how young guys eat!"

"What is it?"

"Palak Paneer. It's Indian, with cheese, rice and spinach. And I guess some beans. It's all food your mom fixed for you, but with some different spices. I love it."

"Why vegetarian?"

Meredith grew serious. "This is new for me. I just got to thinking about how I always ate without considering where it came from. I'm not trying to convince anyone else, but personally I just don't want to have an animal killed just to feed me. Not when there's so much other food I can eat."

150

"I had a girl friend once who went vegetarian. We all thought she was weird. I guess she was weird, though, in a lot of ways. She kept talking about animal factories."

"Yes, a lot of people come to that decision at some time or other."

"She finally went back to her cheeseburgers and pepperoni."

"People do that, too. How's your Paneer?"

"It's a little weird. But it's good. You eat this all the time?"

"I keep things like this in the freezer, but I eat out a lot, too."

He stopped eating. "Why should we care about animals? They're not people."

"They feel—just like we do."

"But they don't talk or think."

"Have you ever killed an animal?"

"Well, yes, we shot rabbits."

"How close were you when they died?"

"I don't know. I didn't pay much attention."

"Let's stop," she said. "We can talk about this another time."

"Is there going to be another time?" He looked at her.

Meredith's heart moved in her chest. "I sure hope so," she said huskily.

As they rinsed the dishes and put them into the dishwasher, she gave him more suggestions for meditating. Then she said, "Let's try it for a half hour."

Dennis looked skeptical.

"Really, you'll get a lot out of it if you keep it up. The voices won't be so unbearable. I promise."

They sat silently for a half-hour, then moved to the sofa to talk about all the things that had brought them together—the voices, his leaving Baltimore to search for an answer, his calling to her just as she entered the range of his thoughts. And they talked about what he was going to do—she urged him to return home and develop his meditation practice, and to keep in touch with her. "You and I have something very special in common. We can help each other, and if there are others with the same curse or gift or whatever you want to call it, we might help them and they might help us. Will you do that for me—please?"

She made a bed for him on the sofa. "We'll talk again in the morning, okay?"

"Thank you, Ms Handen."

"Meredith."

"Meredith."

After she had gone into the bedroom and the lights were all out, he thought to her, *Thank you, Meredith.*

"And thank you, Dennis. You gave me a lot today."

Scene 45

When Meredith awoke in the morning, it was a minute before she noticed that her bedroom door was closed, which reminded her of the guest on her sofa. She pulled a robe around her and peeked out. Dennis was asleep. Dressing hurriedly, she gave her hair a quick brush and went out of the room.

The sight of Dennis sleeping made her heart lurch. She wanted to touch him, but instead she went into the kitchen and started water for coffee. She dug out a couple of boxes of cereal from the top cupboard—she couldn't remember how old they were—and set out bowls and spoons.

The coffee grinder was a problem. It would wake him, for sure. So she puttered around the kitchen, occasionally peering around the corner to see if he was still sleeping. *What the hell am I doing?* she thought.

The two meditation cushions were still in the middle of the living room floor. She squatted over hers and settled on it like a hen on eggs, and closed her eyes. In five minutes, her mind went into fourth gear, and then into fifth. Occasionally, she heard him move a bit on the sofa, and opened her eyes to make sure he was still asleep.

There were thoughts—not really thoughts, but more like impressions that she was picking up. She guessed that he was dreaming. A warm, soft, maternal glow flowed over her, a fog of feeling reminding her of the clouds spilling off Twin Peaks in San Francisco. She basked in the glow for a minute, then let it go, along with the thoughts and images of so many years ago.

Good morning, Meredith.

She opened her eyes. He hadn't moved except that his eyes were open, watching her. "Good morning, Dennis."

They stayed like that, looking at each other, this totally new experience that both of them were trying to figure out the meaning of. Eventually, she rose from her cushion.

"Do you drink coffee?"

"No, do you have some orange juice?"

"I do. While you freshen up in the bathroom, I'll fix us something to eat. There's a brand new toothbrush in the top drawer. It's yours."

Dennis stumbled into the bathroom like a four-year-old just awakened, his legs unsteady, his eyes unfocused. Meredith suppressed a sob before it moved from her heart to her mouth. The racket of the coffee grinder helped erase the feeling, and by the time Dennis had appeared, she was all business.

"We'll eat something, and then it's another half-hour on the cushion," she said, not looking at him. "And then we have to talk about your plans."

They ate in silence. She avoided looking at him. Already she was feeling bereft. His thoughts were of home, of fear, of some blackness that she couldn't interpret.

Her phone rang. She didn't recognize the number. "Hello."

"Uh, is Dennis Watson there?" It didn't sound like his mother.

She looked at him and mouthed "It's for you!"

He shook his head.

"Can I tell him who is calling?" Brisk, business-like, impersonal.

"It's Candy. I'm outside your apartment." A very young female, very uncertain.

Meredith pressed the mute button. "It's Candy. She's right outside!"

His eyes widened.

"Well, do I let her in?"

Dennis hesitated, then looked pleadingly at Meridith.

"Ring my bell," she said to the phone, "and I'll buzz you in." She walked over to the intercom and waited for the door bell. Pushing the buzzer button, she turned to look at him. "Your world is catching up with you."

A minute later she opened her door. A young woman was just outside, reaching for the knocker. "Come in, Candy."

Candy saw Dennis standing there, waiting, and rushed into his arms, crying. "I thought you were dead!" was muffled by tears and his shirt. *At least it's a clean shirt,* Meredith thought. There was a lump of a different sort in her stomach.

She closed the door. "Let's sit down, shall we?" Meredith took a chair opposite the sofa, and noticed that the blanket and pillow were still crumpled up there. The two young people ignored them.

"How did you find us?" Meredith asked.

"Dennis's mom had your phone number, and we Googled you." She turned to Dennis. "I had been calling your phone for days, and you didn't answer. Finally your mom answered. You had left your phone on the charger."

Dennis had not said anything. Finally, in a wooden tone, "I thought you never wanted to see me again."

"I'm sorry!" She burst into tears again.

Meredith studied the young woman. Short, bobbed hair, faded blue-gray T-shirt with some rock group pictured on it, tight jeans, platform shoes seemingly made of straw. A fanny pack. Three rings along the edge of her left ear. Nice body. The girl seemed not to notice the tear streaks on her cheeks.

"Do you two want some privacy?" she asked, hoping for a negative response.

Neither responded. Candy faced Dennis. "I was afraid you went off to kill yourself!"

"I didn't think you cared," he replied, barely audible.

"Oh, Dennis! I **do** care!" They embraced again.

Meredith sighed. "We were just about to talk about Dennis's plans," she said. Matter-of-fact, adult speech, belying the turmoil going on inside her.

Dennis looked at her, then at Candy. "Meredith reads minds, too."

A drawn-out, breathless, "**Really**?" She looked at Meredith. "I was afraid Dennis was going bonkers!"

"I was," he said. "Now I'm not. Meredith is trying to get me to meditate. She says it will help quiet the voices."

Candy's eyes were wide. "How did you find her?"

Meredith and Dennis both laughed. "I said he was like Diogenes, searching for an honest man."

Candy frowned. "Oh, like the Greek god?"

"He wasn't a god, just a philosopher. A cynic, actually." Dennis smiled at Candy. "You hate it when I get into stuff like that!"

155

"I don't hate it, I just don't understand you sometimes."

"You know, don't you," said Meredith, "that Dennis has a gift?"

"A gift that's a curse," he added.

"It's scary!" exclaimed Candy. "He can read my mind! I was afraid I couldn't handle it."

"It's hard for everybody," Meredith said. "I went through that with somebody else, and a friend of mine went through it with me. It takes getting used to."

Candy looked at Dennis. "I have my car. Will you go home with me?"

Dennis looked at Meredith, pain showing on his face.

"If you don't," Candy continued, "your mom will come after you."

"Dennis," said Meredith, "you've found me. I'm here, and I will be here, if you need me. I'll give you my email and phone number. You will get through this!"

He slumped. "I felt like there was hope again. Going back feels like going into a black hole."

"Dennis!" Candy exclaimed. "I'll be with you. We can get through this!"

"I can be here for you, Dennis," Meredith said. "You can't live here, but if you need a place to crash again, here it is."

"Thank you!" There were tears in his eyes.

"Okay, go. Keep in touch. We both have a lot to learn from each other." She scribbled her address on a note pad and handed the sheet to him.

Candy stood up and took Dennis's hand to help him up. "Thank you—may I call you Meredith?"

"Of course. Dennis, take your tooth brush. I put some cash in your wallet. And here's the book I told you about."

He went into the bathroom and returned carrying the toothbrush. Walking directly to Meredith, he put his arms around her and kissed her soundly on the cheek.

Meredith held the door open until they had disappeared into the stairway. Then she collapsed on a chair and sobbed.

Scene 46

Dolly watched her from the moment she exited the elevator. When Meredith sat down in her cubicle, Dolly was already seated in the visitor's chair.

"All right, **give**." Dolly crossed her long legs. "My god, your eyes are red again!"

Meredith sighed. "He's gone. His girlfriend found him and took him away."

Dolly shook her head. "Well, you certainly managed to pull yourself down off the pedestal I had you on." She was grinning broadly.

"It's not what you think."

"No? What do I think? You, of all people, know what I'm thinking!"

"I was being funny yesterday when I told you about him on the phone. He was just a lost soul, wandering the streets trying to find a kindred spirit."

"Kindred—how?" Dolly still had the grin on her face.

"He hears people's thoughts."

Shock replaced the grin on Dolly's face.

"Yes. Strange, isn't it?" Meredith booted up her computer and turned back around. "He's had this for six months, he said, and he thought he was going crazy. His mom even sent him to a shrink because he was hearing voices."

"Why did he come to D.C.?"

"He knew about the operatives, and he thought he might get some advice or some help. Ran into one operative, which was disastrous, so he was looking for somebody—anybody—who might be able to help him. He thought if he called out silently that he might connect with somebody else like him."

"And he found you."

"Amazing, isn't it?"

"So you took him home with you."

"That's why I called you. I realized that I didn't know anything about this kid. He could have been schizophrenic or something."

"But he was just a lonely boy." Dolly grinned again.

"You have a dirty mind."

"Do I now? So tell me—you said you 'fed him, bathed him and dressed him.' Those are your exact words."

"I was trying to entertain you," Meredith laughed.

"Well you certainly succeeded! You should have seen the images in my head."

"He was hungry. He hadn't eaten in two days. He was filthy—he had **walked** all the way from Baltimore!"

"Nice catch for you!"

"I felt sorry for him."

"Of course! I'd do the same thing, wouldn't ..."

Meredith raised her hand. "No I think you would at least pick a clean boy." It was her turn to tease.

"True. I don't have time to wash 'em up first. Now, you say he's gone back to his girl friend?"

"She found me on Google! His mom gave her my name and phone number."

"Hard to compete with those young chicks."

"Seriously," Meredith said, "I'm worried about him. He's really having trouble with this thought-reading business. He was frantic when he found me."

"I'm wondering how his girl friend is handling it."

"I gathered that she left him at one point. When she came to get him she seemed to regret that. But the problem won't go away. I tried to teach him how to meditate—that's how I deal with it—but he'd have to stick with it, and I don't know if he will."

Dolly put her hand on Meredith's knee. "You certainly have an interesting life!"

"I have interesting friends."

"And lovers."

"True. Now, unless you have some other urgent questions, I have work to do."

Dolly got up and returned to her cube. "Fascinating!" she muttered.

Scene 47

At last there was a message—such as it was—on their web site. "Probably a couple of days. Missing you."

Meredith wondered how she would tell Doug about Dennis. She wanted to protect him and Dennis both from the unpredictable actions of the Company. As it turned out, Doug knew more than she realized.

At dinner at the bistro, he asked her, "What's this about a kid from Baltimore?"

"Who told you about that?"

"My boss. I gather they are still keeping track of you—your phone, anyway."

She had a moment of rage, but waited for it to cool before speaking. "I have to get away from this town! I'm getting more paranoid by the day!"

Doug put his hand on hers. "You have to let it roll off of you."

"Well, you signed up for this shit—I didn't."

"Okay, let's enjoy our first evening together in a long time. I missed you."

Meredith looked at him. "You're not going to ask about the kid from Baltimore?"

"Oh, I did, if you remember. The question is out there, but I'm more interested in how you are and if you missed me, too."

The waiter brought two glasses of Pinot Grigio, but didn't linger. "They are very discreet here, aren't they?" said Doug, watching him return to the kitchen.

"They are wonderful. Wait just a minute." She signaled the staff visible through the pass-through, and the waiter returned. "I want a single shot of Grey Goose," she told him.

Doug's eyebrows went up.

"I need a quick start," she laughed. When the waiter returned with the shot, she dashed it off in one gulp. "Now," she said, "bring on the gol-durned cat!"

Doug guffawed at that. "You, my love, were never a mouse!"

"Okay," she said after chasing the vodka with a sip of her wine, "I have this problem with protocol. If I were to tell you something—something short of treason, but still relevant to your job—would you be honor-bound to tell your people?"

"I can't answer that categorically, but first, let me tell you something I probably shouldn't but I have to anyway."

He lowered his voice. "The kid from Baltimore already made contact with one of our operatives—seems he was trolling for other readers on the streets of D.C. But he chickened out when the operative asked him a couple of questions. They followed him, and saw him connect with you. When you called Baltimore, they collected the number. As far as I know, they did not monitor your phone call. Now, what do you want me to know?"

"Oh, my god!" Meredith put her head down on her arms for a moment. Then, "So you know he hears thoughts like I do. It's been driving him crazy, and he came here thinking that he might find someone to help him with it."

"I can't think of anyone better than you to do that."

"I fed him—he didn't have a dollar on him—and took him home with me to talk. He had walked all the way from Baltimore—that's forty miles! And he was a bit soiled, so I cleaned him up and put him up for the night on my sofa."

Doug smiled at her. "Like a stray dog. I presume you told Dolly about this."

Meredith laughed. "She thought it was great!"

"She was probably jealous."

"Probably. But nothing happened. Doug—nothing happened!" Her brow was furrowed.

"I didn't ask," he replied calmly. "I'm not jealous of a teen-aged boy."

"I'm relieved. I didn't want it to look …"

"So we can forget that part of it, okay?"

"You know I love you!?" She looked at him tenderly, her head tilted, her earring swinging gently.

"I don't think the Company is interested in him at the moment. If he is reading, they might want to keep track of him, just in case."

"Like they are keeping track of me?"

"Yep."

"Okay, so what's for dinner?" She sipped from her wine, smiled, and opened her menu.

Later, in Meredith's bed, Doug admitted to "just a tad" of jealousy. "I know it's stupid. I don't have any doubts about you. You are not a person to hide anything—I learned that the first time I met you! And even if you slept with the kid, I'd get over it pretty quick. We aren't teenagers any more."

"You know," she laughed gently, "There was a moment, after we had gone to bed—he was on the sofa, of course—when he sent me a thought, just 'Good night, Meredith,' and I wanted to take him in my arms. He was so young and vulnerable! It was a feeling like you have with a cuddly little kid, a maternal thing, I guess. At the same time, I was aware that he was not a little kid. Do you understand that?"

"Sure. None of those feelings of affection and lust and all—Eros— are completely separate. It's a life force. It's part of our genetic makeup."

"When I was young and sticking flowers into rifle barrels, we told each other the same thing. We were all for doing away with the cultural taboos."

"Well I didn't grow up in California like you did. Midwestern culture was still pretty conservative. But I had my share of fantasies."

Meredith rolled over against him. "All my fantasies of the past couple of weeks have been about you. Almost all."

"Tell me about them."

Scene 48

Her first email from Baltimore was not from Dennis; it was from Candy. "i hope u dont mind if i write u. im worried about den – hes still brooding. i try to get him to medtate but he wont. he mite listn to u. he luvs u."

Meredith wrote back as soon as she saw it. 'I don't have Dennis's phone number. Does he do email?"

Apparently, Candy was emailing from her phone. She sent Dennis's phone number and email address within an hour.

"Dear Dennis," Meredith wrote, "Candy wrote me that you are having problems. That girl cares about you, and so do I. You can get through this, I promise! Call me or email me. Let me know what you are going through. You and I can help each other! Love, Meredith."

She didn't hear from him for three days. Then one evening he called her while she was watching a very bad drama on television. "You saved me from myself," she told him. "Now what can I do for you?"

"I don't know. I can't seem to keep myself together."

"Do you have a job there?"

"No. When I go in for an interview, I mess myself up. I can tell when they are not interested and just waiting for me to leave."

"Okay, do you want me to come up there? Can we meet somewhere and talk?"

"Oh you don't need to do that," he said, but he sounded as though he would like her to come.

"How about tomorrow evening. I'll catch the train and be at Penn Station around seven. Can you pick me up? Do you have a car?"

"No, but I can meet you there, and we can find someplace to talk."

"Okay. Let's do this together, Dennis. We can do it!"

"Bye."

Meredith put down the phone and doubled up her fists. "Aghhrr!" she roared. She tried to go back to the television program, but gave up almost immediately. Open the freezer, take out the vodka, down a healthy swig, and wait for the release. In ten minutes, she felt normal enough to call Doug.

"You want me to go with you?" he asked after she told him. When she didn't reply, he said, "I didn't think so."

"Were we that dense at seventeen?"

"Our folks would probably say yes."

"If I call you when I leave Baltimore, would you meet me at the station and take me someplace and fuck my brains out?"

The phone seemed to go dead for a moment. Then she realized that he was laughing so hard he couldn't speak. In a few minutes, he said, "Anything you want, my love."

On the train north, she was grateful that she'd had the foresight to take her iPod with her. She settled back with some soft jazz in her ears and tried to relax. She had no idea what she could do with or for Dennis. She knew only that she had to try.

Wouldn't it be wonderful, she thought, *if Dennis and I could have a chip removed from our heads and all this would be over!*

That made her wonder about Doug. Would he always have his chip? Right now, he and she were fairly balanced, because they shared their thoughts without even having to speak. It was often confusing to them both, but there was no situation in which either could hide themselves from the other. On the rare occasion when she picked up something from him that was obviously to do with his assignments, she managed to drop it or push it out of her consciousness by thinking about something else. She chose not to wonder about those thoughts.

Maybe she could tell Dennis about that. The curse they shared didn't have to take over their lives.

Maybe if we find other people in our situation, we could create a support group. Like the AA groups, someone would stand up and say, 'Hi, I'm Meredith, and I'm a mind reader.' And then everybody would answer, 'Hi, Meredith! We already knew that!'

She smiled at the image, but she knew that it wasn't funny. *You'd think that this gift or curse would give us some kind power over other people, but it doesn't seem to work that way.*

Wes Montgomery playing Misty brought her thoughts back to the present, with the train softly swaying to the music and the romance that was "always already," an expression she had read in Ken Wilber but

163

which seemed to relate to her own fantasies more than to some kind of ultimate reality. *Reality isn't what it's cracked up to be.*

But reality was slowing the train down to stop at Penn Station in Baltimore, where she had to try to connect all over again with a young, desperate man-boy and get him to live his life instead of fighting it.

He was standing on the platform when she alighted. *So far, so good.*

She gave him a hug, and when he clung to her she didn't push him away. "There's a café not far from here, I'm told," she said finally. "Sofi's Crepes—do you know it?"

"I've seen it," he said. "I've never been there."

"It might be too noisy for us to talk. How far is Lafayette Street and Charles Street?

"A couple of blocks."

"Do you know of another place you'd like better?"

"No, that's okay."

The evening was warm, so they were perspiring by the time they reached the café. It wasn't very quiet, but it smelled heavenly. Meredith hadn't eaten before catching the train at Union Station. "Did you eat?" she asked him.

"I had some chips and a coke."

"Super. We'll have something really good!"

They found a booth toward the back of the café, and soon had soft drinks, with crepes on the way. Meredith liked the atmosphere. When they tried to talk, though, she felt she had to speak loudly to be heard. *If you can hear this, say hello.* She had to laugh at her mimicking his call when they first met.

Hello.

She sighed. *You seem down. Are you depressed?*

Yeah, I guess.

Tell me what's going on?

He hesitated. *I just don't feel like I have any way out of this.*

You know something? I have felt that way myself.

You have?

One day I was on my lunch hour, walking along the street with all the people, and my mind was going bananas with all the noise. I was afraid I had lost my best friend in this big city because she was so intimidated by this curse I have, and my lover was out of town and I was afraid he might not ever come back. I felt so lonely it was all I could do to keep back my tears. Then I heard, If you can hear this, say hello.

Dennis smiled.

You can never know how that felt to me! Even though I was a little scared, and kept telling myself to ignore it, I said hello. And there you were! Meredith reached across the table and took his hand. *And taking you in and spending that time with you gave me a sense of purpose.*

What purpose, taking in strays?

No! She covered her face with her hands, then grabbed her napkin to soak up her tears. *Goddamn it! No! You are not just a stray!*

Dennis was shocked at her emotional response. "I'm sorry!" he said aloud.

Just then their food arrived. The waiter gave Meredith a strange look, glanced at Dennis, and withdrew.

"Let's eat while it's warm," she said, wiping her face with her napkin.

Dennis was upset at having caused her tears, but he didn't know what to say to her. They ate silently—she picked at her food, but was still smarting from his remark.

Finally, she said, "You are not the only one who has suffered."

He hung his head.

After a while—eating was taking a long time—he apologized again. "I think of myself as a victim of this thing, and it seems nobody understands how hard it is."

"Do you think I don't understand?"

"Well, yes, I guess so. But you're an adult, and you're able to figure out stuff."

"When you were roaming the streets of D.C. looking for a needle in a haystack, did you think there were others like you out there?"

"Yeah, I thought there must be—that's why I was there!"

"Did it occur to you that they—if they were there—might be suffering as much as you were? Feeling just as misunderstood as you?" Meredith took a bite of her crepes.

"I guess I didn't think of that."

She put her fork down and took both of his hands in hers. "You and I both did some healing that day and that evening. I am so grateful to have found you, because it tells me that I am not alone. Somebody knows how I feel!"

"Yeah," he said, "that's how I feel, too."

"So why are you still feeling sorry for yourself?"

"I don't know. If I was living in D.C., we could get together and talk and stuff. Then I might feel better."

"Dennis, meeting you gives me hope that we are not alone with this! There must be other people who are going through exactly what we have gone through and are still going through."

He looked up at her. "How do we find them?"

"How did you find me?"

"You mean we have to go out on the street and call for people to say hello?"

She smiled. "It worked once. Have you tried that in Baltimore? Have you tried it at school?"

"I'm finished with school. I graduated."

"Were you planning to go to college?"

"I didn't like school much. I never felt like I fit in."

"Well, how about the places where other kids hang out? What if, while it's still warm, you order a coke and sit at an outdoor table where people are, and put out the call? If they say hello, invite them to sit and talk for a minute. I bet they would be grateful."

"I'd feel conspicuous, sitting there all day by myself."

"Then take your computer! You see people all the time sitting with their computers in coffee shops and even in the parks. You don't even have to have it turned on!"

He laughed. "Yeah, I've even seen some homeless guys, sitting with computers that don't even work—it's like the ones who walk down the street with old dead cell phones, pretending to talk to people—pretending to be normal."

Meredith smiled. "And you wouldn't want people to think you were one of those."

"Will you do it with me?"

"Sure! But I have to work every day. We'd have to do it when I can, okay?"

His face brightened. "Okay!"

She looked tenderly at him. "Oh, Dennis! You can do this! Just don't give up—please?"

I love you, Meredith!

And I love you, too! But not just you. And you don't love only me. We both have people who love us and deserve our love. And there's a lot of people who might be strangers to us but deserve our help and our compassion. We can't save the world, but we can make a difference to a few. Maybe even a few who are like us.

You sound like ...

She blushed. "Like Sunday school?"

He nodded.

"Sorry! I don't want to do that. It's just that I have hope—since you found me—that there might be others like me, who could be helped if we knew each other."

Meredith took a credit card from her purse and laid it on the check. "I need to feel like this gift I have—and it's not really a curse—is for the good. It's not just mine."

When the waiter returned with her card and the receipt, she signed it and collected her things. "Now, I have to get back home. Will you stay in touch with me, and not make me call you every time?"

He nodded, and they moved out of the booth and onto the street. On the walk back to the train station, they agreed to exchange emails daily, even if they didn't have anything important to say. And they would figure out a way to go into places together–with their computers—and "put out the call."

On the ride back to D.C., Meredith felt at peace. She was doing something, at least, not only for Dennis but for herself—and maybe for others, too.

She took out her phone and called Doug.

Scene 49

The next evening, she told Doug about the plan to "put out the call." He thought it was a good idea, if it worked. "But I don't want to be involved in it," he said. "I don't even want to know who or how many fish you pull in."

"I don't want you to know. Your associates will probably catch on to it anyway before long. We'll try it in Baltimore, rather than here. If we caught a CIA fish we'd just have to throw him back anyway," she laughed.

"So you'll be spending a lot of time out of town?"

"Well," she said, "you do."

Doug was thoughtful. Pursing his lips, he finally said, "Uh, remember—**I never told you this**, okay? You might try a place like Silver Spring."

She looked at him, frowning.

"I've heard some talk that there might be some bass up there in the streams."

"Oh, Doug!"

"I'm not a fisherman, myself. Never cared for it. I just hear talk now and then." He didn't break a smile.

"Thank you."

"I'd be glad to loan you my car, but I don't think it's a good idea."

"I'll look into the transportation. Must be a lot of commuters."

Meredith sent an email to Dennis, suggesting that they try to put out the call in Silver Spring on the following Saturday. She told him that she just had a hunch that they might find someone there, and run less risk of encountering operatives. Public transportation was readily available from both Baltimore and D.C. And she asked, "Do you have enough money for the bus?"

His email reply said that he had the money, and he'd bring his computer and cell phone.

On Saturday morning, she set out for Silver Spring. They had agreed to meet at the Greyhound terminal on Fenton Street and Silgo, then scout for outdoor locations where people would pass. While neither of them knew the city, they were both confident that they could find it and each other. Both had their cell phones and computers with them. Meredith felt giddy when she got off the bus from D.C. This was a real adventure!

The meeting place turned out to be less crowded than she had hoped. There were people walking everywhere, but it wasn't as busy as the streets of D.C. on a weekday. Still, they needed to develop a mode of operation, and this should work well at least for that. They walked down Fenton into a busier block and sat at a table outside a restaurant.

"This feels strange, doesn't it?" Meredith said after they had ordered soft drinks.

"Yeah, it's nothing like the crowds in the city.

"I have an idea," Meredith said, "why don't we separate, sit at separate tables. A stranger getting our call might be more likely to approach one person than a couple. Do you think?"

"Unless we're pretty far apart, they might hear both of us at the same time and not know which one called."

"So, let's play this out. A man—like that one there—walks by and one of us calls, and he says, 'Hello.' He will probably stop and look around for the source of the call. One of us waves to him and invites him to sit down."

"If we're sitting apart, it may get complicated."

"You're right," she replied, "we'd be better sitting together. They might feel safer responding to a couple, and it simplifies the situation."

"Yeah, and I guess it doesn't matter which of us calls to them—they couldn't tell just from the thought."

The main thing is that we need to look safe and welcoming. This is going to take them by surprise, remember."

A woman and a small boy walked by. Meredith nudged Dennis.

If you hear this, say hello, thought Dennis, as clearly as he could.

The woman glanced at them as she passed, but showed no sign of hearing the call.

They sat there for an hour, exchanging occasional remarks, and repeating their call whenever someone walked past or entered the restaurant. They caught no fish.

Finally, Dennis said, "I don't think Diogenes would have sat in this place waiting. It's not like sitting in a boat in the middle of a lake waiting for a nibble. This isn't fun."

"It's not, is it?" Meredith answered. "We could sit here a year without meeting anyone. What should we do?"

"How about a mall? Aren't they pretty busy on Saturdays?"

"Good thought. But I didn't look for malls when I was checking out this town."

Dennis opened his computer and turned it on. After waiting a few minutes, he announced, "There's WiFi hot spot here." He logged in and searched for malls in Silver Spring. "Got one!"

Meredith moved around to see his screen as he searched for a route. "The city buses come right down Fenton and go to the mall. About five miles."

"What's the schedule?"

"Uh, looks like one should be coming by in about twenty minutes. They don't run as often on weekends."

A half-hour later they were stationed inside a large mall food court. There were people all over. "It's really noisy, isn't it?" Dennis said.

"But a much better fishing spot."

If you hear this, say hello, thought Meredith, very clearly.

Almost an hour of repeated calling passed before they both heard an answering *Hello!*

They looked at each other. *Bingo!* thought Meredith.

We're sitting with computers in the food court, thought Dennis, and they both looked around. A middle-aged man, partly bald, clean shaven, was walking toward them.

Won't you sit with us for a moment, please? thought Meredith, smiling at the man.

This is remarkable! he answered, taking a seat at the table.

"Hello," she said, extending her hand. "We've been searching for other people like us."

Dennis, shaken, shook hands with him. "I'm Dennis Watson."

"George Randolph."

"Meredith Handen."

"You have a very original approach," said Randolph. "Are you from Silver Spring?"

"No, I'm from D.C. and Dennis is from Baltimore. He found me just last week using this approach, and we hoped it would put us in touch with others."

"What made you come here?"

"Well, we wanted to be away from D.C., first of all, and someone hinted to me that there might be others like us here."

Dennis looked at her quickly.

She turned to Dennis. "I'm sorry. I was afraid to tell you. Doug—very obliquely—suggested this town. He had heard at the office, I gathered."

She turned back to Randolph and thought, *I have a friend who has an implant.*

The CIA? he replied.

I think so. He hasn't told me.

Can you trust him?

Yes. But I want to be honest with you. The Company knows about me, so they may be keeping track of me.

Randolph clasped his hands on the table and looked at Meredith. *I try to be discreet. I can tell you that I know others and know of still others. But we don't know what the CIA will do if we become public.* He looked around the big room, which was filled mostly with young mothers and their children. The noise level was like that in a sports stadium before a game.

You mean, thought Dennis, *there are really others like us?*

He nodded. *We have a kind of support group that meets and shares stories and problems. I'm sure you know there are problems.*

I even thought about suicide, Dennis thought.

Yes.

Meredith thought, *We'd be so grateful if we could meet others.*

If the CIA knows about you, it's difficult for us to communicate. As I said, we try to be discreet. I need to talk with my group. Can you meet me again next Saturday, same time?

Here?

Yes. I won't look like this, but I will again answer your call. "Makes a good password, doesn't it?" He smiled and stood up. "It's been nice meeting you both. Good luck—and be careful!" He turned and walked away. Meredith thought she saw another man get up from a table across the court and follow him as he disappeared in the crowd.

"Oh, lordie," she said to Dennis, "I hope that was a friend of his and not an operative!"

"What should we do now?"

"Well, we can stay here and continue our calling. Personally, I am really charged up. I'd love a drink, but you can't go with me."

"There's a bar in the mall," he said. "I'll sit here and have a coke and keep calling, if you want to go have a drink."

"Oh, you sweet boy!"

He grinned. Meredith turned and went down the mall corridor. The bar was dark and cool. She sat at a table far from the door and ordered a clean gin martini. As soon as the drink arrived, a strange man approached from across the room. "Afternoon, ma'am," he said.

Lose yourself, officer!

He did not appear to have heard her thought, so she guessed he was not an operative. She smiled at the man. "I'd prefer to be alone," she said.

"Oh, that's okay," he said, sliding into the chair opposite her. "I'll just be here a minute. I'm meeting somebody also."

Her smile remained as she said quietly, "You will get up from that chair and go back into your cave, or I will have a policeman here in thirty seconds." With one hand she pulled a small spray vial from her purse and opened her cell phone with the other. She kept her hands on both of them.

The intruder left without a word, and she took a large swallow from her glass. *Dolly should have seen that!*

Meredith emptied her glass and walked to the bar to pay. She could see the man sitting again at his table. He did not look up. Just outside the bar, she caught, *If you hear this, say hello,*

Joining Dennis in the food court, she said, "I could read you all way to the bar!" She laughed. "I just scared off a guy trying to pick me up."

He grinned. "You probably know karate, too."

"Sometimes I manage to keep my cool."

Dennis stood up and stretched. "My backside is getting sore," he said.

"You want to call it a day?"

"It **is** getting boring," he said. Maybe that guy will lead us where we want to go."

"It's past lunch time. You hungry?"

He smiled. "Smells really good here."

"Okay, let's get something. You go ahead and get what you want, and I'll stay here and watch the computers."

Buoyed by the alcohol, the promise of success and her growing comfort with this young man, Meredith leaned back in her chair and watched him. He was more in his element here, and seemed confident and relaxed. *I forget sometimes how much I like men!* Then, *Be careful, Meredith—you are on dangerous ground!*

I didn't catch all of that, Dennis responded from the service line, *but I can tell you've had something to drink!* He turned around to face her, and grinned broadly.

She covered her red face with her hands.

Scene 50

Saturday night and all day Sunday she spent with Doug—as much as possible enveloped by his strong arms. It was hard for her not to tell him about Silver Spring. She wondered how connecting with other readers would affect her relationship with him. The two of them were gradually accommodating to the fact that their every thought, almost, was instantly shared between them. It made some of their conversation irrelevant, or at least redundant, but it also necessitated explanation of some of those very personal thoughts and feelings that are not ordinarily shared, even between intimates. They were emotionally naked when they were together. And just as with physical nakedness, it's hard to protect one's defects from display.

Meredith lost her self-consciousness about her aging body. She teased him with, "What you see is what you get!"

"Promise?" he stroked her back—at least the part he could reach, considering that much of her body was pressed tightly against his.

They ate vegetarian when they were together, in spite of her protests that he could eat what he liked. They meditated together in the middle of his "Great Room," as they had begun to call it.

Only very occasionally did anything seem to separate them. Once, when Meredith picked up his clothes from the bed before they lay down on it, she felt the heavy, hard sheath of his firearm nestled in them. "I thought you didn't carry that any more," she said to him.

He was silent for a moment. "I don't usually."

"That's all you can say about it?" She looked at him, a hint of fear showing on her face.

"There's a situation," he said cryptically. She knew enough not to ask for more, but her apprehension increased.

Why would someone, she wondered sometimes, as solid and yet sensitive as Doug was, choose to be in a profession where life and death decisions are instantaneous and frequently arbitrary? Where obedience to authority came before personal judgment? She considered herself worldly, as opposed to provincial: authority made her suspicious, and categorical pronouncements aroused her skepticism. However, she felt deeply her vulnerability to the judgments of others simply because she was crippled by her own doubts about her character.

This new gift of hers—and she thought of it more and more as a gift, rather than a curse—was changing her way of seeing the world. Thoughts about people in general that formerly would have struck her as naïve now seemed almost profound. The earth may not be the organic Gaia that James Lovelock and Lynn Margulis proposed in the 1970s, but it contains the whole of life as we know it, and all of that life is tightly interconnected. What she was experiencing might be a blip on the screen, or it might portend another step in the evolving complexity of humanity.

She tried to get this across to Doug, but the barrier of officialdom interfered. He said he didn't doubt her insight—certainly the fact of her gift suggested something more—but if he could sense other people's thoughts by means of his implanted electronics, it seemed to him more mundane philosophically, if not technically. He didn't want to think about the implications of everyone on earth having the capability that his implant afforded him and a few other—trusted—people. "Wouldn't it simply raise the stakes?" he asked. "Wouldn't it create a different kind of arms race?"

It was inevitable, he argued, that the government (hopefully ours) would somehow discover how Meredith's gift worked and proceed to control it in some way. That's why he wasn't so concerned about protecting the privacy of the self-described "readers." Still, he respected her desire and would do all in his power to help protect her. Especially her.

Doug thought it fortunate that he could be close to her as she discovered her gift and tried to come to grips with its implications. His position with the Company gave him access to information that would be denied to ordinary citizens. Even though he could not pass on much of what he knew or heard, he could be a kind of buffer between her and the impersonal juggernaut of government.

That she was special—far beyond remarkable—he had not doubted since he first met her. He was as surprised as she when her gift of sensing the thoughts of others manifested itself, simply because it had been to him a technological achievement. Now, it was becoming apparent that the gift was not unique to her. The "kid from Baltimore" was probably

175

just the tip of an iceberg that would soon be a widespread phenomenon. The Company knew it, too. Doug was still furious with Randy for tipping off his superiors and bringing the goons to harass Meredith. It was undoubtedly just the beginning.

Still, he had other, even more pressing issues to resolve. "Tomorrow," he told Meredith, "I'll be out of touch for a while again."

She looked at him for a sign of reassurance, but saw none. "Take care of yourself, Doug. There's more I want to say to you and hear from you."

Neither of them slept soundly that night.

Scene 51

Dolly, her chin resting on her hands on top of the cubicle partition between them, watched Meredith stow her purse in a drawer and open her computer. "I always try to get here before you do, just so I can watch you come in," she said. "It's obvious that you live a very interesting life!"

Meredith smiled at her friend. "How can you tell—aside from all the moaning and complaining I do?"

"It's Monday morning. You've had two whole days to get into trouble. Now—how many men have you kissed or cried over since I saw you last?"

Meredith hesitated, then in a small voice, "Two."

"See?"

Meredith drew herself up, one hand on a hip and a defiant look in her eyes. "All right, Ms Know-it-all, how many men have you kissed since Friday afternoon—we won't speak yet of crying over, because the other list could take a while."

Dolly's face fell. "It was all crying, no kissing."

"Poor dear!" Her sarcastic grin turned serious. "Really? You want to talk?"

"Oh, shit, woman! What do I have to tell you? You've been there, done everything! I have this tiny little life, trying to outwit the lowlife men who inhabit the bars in this godforsaken town, freshman representatives from boondock parishes in Louisiana intent only on fucking the local females so when they don't get re-elected in two years they can go back home to their double-wides and pickup trucks and possum hounds and feel important!"

"Wow!" Meredith stood up and stood with her face three inches from Dolly's. "You must have had a terrible weekend!" She leaned into Dolly's face and kissed her lightly and tenderly. From that distance, she watched Dolly's eyes fill up with all the liquid frustration of a wasted weekend. "Tell me," she whispered.

Dolly backed away six inches, and said softly, "You have a supervisor waiting at your door. You better take care of her first." She sat down and blew her nose into a tissue.

Meredith turned around. Gladys was obvious shocked at the emotional scene she had witnessed. She stammered, "Meredith, uh, will you have the Pennsylvania Metro report done today? Mike is asking for it."

"Two P.M. latest. Promise."

Gladys disappeared.

Meredith turned and peered over the partition. "You okay until lunch?"

Dolly laughed and shook her head. "My god! You are something else! Go to work!"

At lunch time they went down to the deli because Dolly didn't want to run into Gladys in The Egg Place. Dolly tried to get her mouth around a monstrous corned beef sandwich, while Meredith nibbled daintily at an egg salad on Jewish rye.

"I gather that your weekend was not what you had wanted it to be."

Dolly snorted, and put the sandwich down. "You could say that."

Biting the end of a Kosher dill, Meredith said, "Something about freshman congressmen from Louisiana."

"Oh, you can spot those bastards a mile away. The professionals in this town are at least sophisticated enough to pretend they want to talk."

"But the assholes are the only available men in the place?"

"I should know better. Liquor dissipates my judgment."

Meredith smiled. "Oh, how I know that scene!"

Dolly wiped her fingers on a napkin and put it down. "Meredith, sometimes I forget that you're different!"

Meredith frowned. "How am I different?"

"Oh, for Christ sakes, you are a saint!"

"I'd think that was funny, but I don't think you're joking. Wouldn't you think a saint would know what she was doing?"

Dolly silently took a bite of her sandwich.

"How many times have you carried this poor dumb soul back home? How often have you known exactly what I needed?"

Dolly made a kissing gesture with her lips.

"You and I," Meredith said, "know what it's like to be a single woman in a big city. Both of us have fallen apart and had the other pick up the pieces. I'm not different than you. Just because I sometimes pick up what other people are thinking doesn't mean that I know any more than they do. You pick up things that I'm thinking, too! You know that?"

Dolly looked down at her hands holding the corned beef sandwich, then looked up at Meredith. "I'm jealous of you."

Meredith looked shocked.

"Sure," Dolly said, "we both get into stuff. But it seems to make you bigger. I just get smaller!"

Meredith pulled her head back as though to take in more of what Dolly said. "There's nothing small about you, Dolly! You don't 'put on airs' as they say down here. That's what I love about you. You say it like it is, and you're almost always right!"

"What d'you mean, 'almost'?" Dolly had that chin-thrust-forward defiance on her face.

Meredith burst out laughing. She picked up a fork. "You going to eat all that coleslaw?"

They finished their sandwiches. Dolly wiped her fingers on the seventh paper napkin she had picked up with her food at the counter. "Funny, isn't it?" she said. "How you think your life has gone to the dogs, but then a friend puts it into perspective. Nothing is changed, except how you feel about it."

"We have this brain that we borrowed from some other animal, and we just added layers on top of what was there. A dog feels like we feel, but it can't think as well. We just need to be touched once in a while, and we can cuddle like a basket of puppies. Sometimes we need to stop thinking."

"See?" Dolly said, "That's what I meant."

Meredith frowned, and Dolly grinned. "You're my favorite puppy."

Scene 52

Meredith and Dennis arranged to meet at the food court in the mall where they had made contact with George Randolph. She was still uneasy about the other man she had seen get up and follow Randolph after they had met. But all she could do was trust, for now at least.

Dennis greeted her with a big grin. "Maybe this is a big day!"

She had brought her computer; he had not. "Should I have brought mine?" he asked.

"No, I don't think so. I probably won't need this. I just thought it would make us more recognizable to them."

They sat down at a table and began looking around at the people in the big room. The thoughts they were picking up were all about eating and children. The thoughts were easy to dismiss—even Dennis remarked about how he was getting used to shutting out the noise of crowds. "When I meditate I notice that my own thoughts usually begin with some trigger, like, a word or something I hear. Words just pop up—I don't know where they come from. But I can separate my own thoughts from what I'm picking up, a lot better now."

"Sounds like you're getting more comfortable."

"I used to fight it all the time. After practicing my meditation, I'm getting better at just letting go."

"Wonderful. Keep it up, Dennis."

Fascinating! The thought appeared to both of them, and they looked around. Randolph was not to be seen in the room.

Hello? Meredith answered.

Clear across the room I could not hear you with my ears, but I followed your conversation in my head! A grey-haired man with a beard was walking toward them. When he got close enough, he said, "You don't recognize me, do you? George Randolph."

Surprise showed on their faces. "You're really different!" said Dennis.

"I try to be discreet," he replied, shaking hands with both of them.

Meredith spoke, "Last week when you left, a man got up and followed you—or that's how it looked."

Randolph smiled. "He was my backup. When we heard your call, we weren't sure you were safe. So he stayed back, just in case."

"So we can meet some of your group?" Dennis asked.

Yes. Because of your connection with the Company, we need to be discreet. I will leave now, going out that door to your right. In ten minutes, go out the same door. There will be a blue minivan at the curb. Get into the back without saying anything, and the driver will take you to our group meeting. Okay?

Wow, Dennis thought, *this is exciting!*

I try to be discreet.

Thank you, George, thought Meredith, *we appreciate this.*

Randolph left, and Dennis looked at his watch. He looked at Meredith and grinned.

"You are enjoying this, aren't you?" she smiled.

They sat down again and Meredith pretended to work with her computer. When Dennis said, "Time," she closed the computer and the two of them walked casually to the door. The blue minivan was waiting for them. Meredith was nervous just opening the door and climbing in, but she didn't hesitate.

As soon as Dennis closed the door after them, the minivan moved away from the curb and into traffic. The driver, who had not spoken, looked into his rear view mirror and said, "George is a real character, isn't he?" He laughed. "He may be right—they might be after us—but I don't think so."

Dennis was delighted. "You mean you're not going to blindfold us so we can't tell them where you took us?"

"If you want, Meredith can blindfold you, if one of you has a handkerchief." He caught her eye and smiled.

"You know my name," she said.

"George told us about you. We Googled you both—not much out there on Dennis, but we found you easily. How long have you been reading?"

"Seems like a long time, but I think it's only a couple of months. Dennis began about six months ago."

"We'll get better acquainted when we get to the meeting."

A few minutes later they pulled up in a comfortable residential neighborhood in front of an older but well-kept house. As they got out of the van and walked toward the house, Dennis was busily working with his phone. He showed Meredith the screen, on which a map was displayed. "I have GPS," he said. "I know exactly where we are."

"We'll get you both back to your bus stations after the meeting," George assured them.

"Thank you," Meredith said.

A youngish woman answered the door and graciously invited them in. The living room was fairly crowded with people, and the noise from their thoughts seemed daunting to the newcomers. George Randolph, shorn of his recent disguise, came over to greet them. "It's noisy, isn't it" he said cheerfully. "They will quiet down in a minute. As you can no doubt tell, they are very curious about you. Come over here with me, and I'll introduce you." He showed them to a couple of empty chairs.

"Okay," he said loudly to the group. "Please take your seats and meet a couple of new readers."

The chairs were arranged roughly into a circle, with several rows where there was space for them. Meredith thought that there must be almost twenty people. She looked at Dennis, who seemed a little bewildered. "Looks just like every other group I've ever been in," she whispered to him. "You can relax."

After introducing Meredith and Dennis to the group, George asked them to say a little bit about themselves and their experiences with reading. "Reading" and "readers" appeared to be the standard terms for what had brought them all together.

Meredith told about how she slowly discovered her gift and her difficulty in accepting it. "You should all know, if you don't already, that I have a very good friend who has an implant. I have never had any reason to mistrust him, but our association is known by the Company, and I have been visited by operatives asking me to submit to some tests—which I refused to do. Through me, they also undoubtedly know of Dennis here. Dennis and I would like to connect with other readers just so we can adjust to this new experience." She turned to Dennis. "Tell them a little about yourself. I don't think you have to hold back anything you want to say."

Dennis haltingly described his experience with the "voices" and his desperation to find others so that he wouldn't feel so alone. "I found Meredith on the streets of D.C. and she saved my life," he said.

George addressed Meredith and Dennis. "This group has been meeting for almost a year and a half, having started with just two of us—Mary Donovan and myself—who were just as desperate as you have described. Mary is one of my grad students at UM. When she came to me asking my advice about how to deal with the voices she was hearing, I realized that I was not alone! I had never had the nerve to speak of the voices I heard because I was sure it would get around that I was going crazy. We met together regularly to share our experiences and give each other support, and gradually got up the courage to put out hints to people we thought we could trust. Eventually, others began to come to us with their own stories. It's been a kind of Readers Anonymous group, and there are even more members besides those present here."

Mary Donovan, who had been the one greeting them at the door, was standing beside George. "Like George said, we are—most of us, anyway—are trying to remain anonymous to the outside world as much as we can. A lot of us have had unpleasant experiences with others who saw our ability as a threat. We know that the CIA has been snooping around, although none of us has been directly threatened by them. It's as though they just want to keep us under surveillance. So we ask that you respect our desires."

Meredith was impressed with how quiet the room became as the different people spoke. The mental noise that had greeted them when they arrived was but a murmur now. "May I ask something?"

"Of course."

"I've become accustomed to the mental noise of crowds of people, and I can handle it much better than I could at first. But I noticed that as George spoke to this group, the noise diminished noticeably. How do you do that?"

Mary laughed. "We discovered it almost by accident. It seems that just as we readers can learn to discriminate between the thoughts of different people near us, we can also learn to quiet our minds so that we don't send out so much mental activity. It's similar to Vipassana meditation, if you've heard of that."

Another woman spoke up. "Some people seem to be able to ignore the noise the same way we learn to ignore the noise we can hear with our ears. It's a matter of focusing. After a while, you don't have to think about it—it's automatic."

Meredith smiled. "Something my friend and I discovered was how much we sort of 'talk' without speaking. It's funny, sometimes, how we have to go back and correct ourselves, like, 'that's not what I meant' kind of thing. When we actually speak, we've already edited what we wanted to say, but with our thoughts it's more spontaneous—and sometimes wrong."

A man raised his hand, but didn't wait to begin, "I have a question—is it different between you and your friend with the implant than it is with 'natural' readers?"

"I don't know yet," Meredith answered. 'Dennis is the only 'natural" reader I'd met before running into George. All my experience had been with my friend. He told me that his experience with people with implants was about the same as with me, except that they went through some training, so they all had the same language to describe it—and to understand it."

Mary, who had left the circle, returned, with her hand in the air. When there was a pause in the conversation, she said, "There's coffee, tea and soft drinks on the table. Please help yourself, and mix it up. I'm sure Meredith and Dennis would like to be out of the spotlight for a while."

The noise levels—both audible and mental—in the group went back up as people broke into separate conversations. Dennis followed Meredith to the refreshment table. Then another young man approached him and began to ask him questions. Later, Meredith noticed that Dennis seemed more at ease, chatting with others in the group. She got into several different conversations herself, feeling comfortable with this group of people who shared her gift/curse. Several people asked her to exchange phone numbers and email addresses with them. By the end of the meeting—several hours later—both of them were grateful for the new connections they had made and for the knowledge that they were not alone in their new situations.

In subsequent weekends, they met with the group, the numbers and the makeup of which changed from week to week. Just knowing that there were all these other people like them allowed both Meredith and Dennis to relax more and more in their gift. And gift it was, as they became more skilled at using it.

Candy, on the other hand, seemed intimidated by Dennis's growing skill—and more by his widening circle of acquaintances, both among their peers and among his fellow readers. He told her a little about these without revealing their identities, and she sensed her own shortcomings in his eyes. She felt he was gradually outgrowing her.

Scene 53

Back home, Meredith also began to sense a reticence from Doug. He didn't smile as much, and he didn't ask her personal questions. She felt conflicted about it, because she was afraid she might slip and reveal something about her new friends, but she wanted to keep the exciting intimacy she had with him. All that came up, of course, when they were together, even though neither of them spoke of it directly. Finally, she couldn't stand it any longer. "Doug, I'm afraid for us."

He looked at her. "Yeah, me too. I know that you're meeting other people, but I don't dare ask about them. I guess it's the same problem I have with my work—I can't talk about it with you."

"I almost never pick up anything around you that seems to relate to your work. How do you do that?"

"Hard work," he said. "You know, everybody pushes stuff down out of their consciousness, but the process itself is mostly unconscious. Like things we do that we're ashamed of. I have to do it intentionally. It's part of our training, you know, because we're not supposed to reveal a lot of things we know, even to other operatives. What they don't need to know, we don't talk about or even think about when we're around them, because it could be dangerous." He laughed. "You know, when you and I first got acquainted, my boss was suspicious of you, and I had to keep my thoughts about you out of his reach."

"He was suspicious of **me**?"

"Yeah, he didn't believe that you could pick up on my ability so fast unless you were maybe an agent or something."

Meredith snorted. "It was **I** who was feeling vulnerable!"

"That's what I told him. But all he had to go on was what I told him, and I guess my bias showed." Doug reached for her hand. "It still does. But I have to be careful of what I notice around you. I try to forget some of those things, because I might put two and two together later."

Her expression became serious. "I must be really transparent to you!"

He grinned. "It's what I love about you. Not that I can figure you out—you surprise me all the time—but you're so upfront with your responses to people. Like you're not afraid to be yourself. I'm always catching myself wondering, 'What will they think of me?'"

"C'mon, you're not a pleaser!"

"You'd be surprised." He laughed. "See? I am so used to protecting myself that I think you'd be surprised at who I am inside!"

She put her arms around his neck. "I have an inkling."

Doug kissed her. "And I'm aware," he said quietly, "That it's because of my job that both of us have to be careful. It's like this big weight hanging over us, ready to come crashing down at any minute."

"I hate not being able to share everything in my life with you!"

"Yeah, me too."

Meredith smiled. "I remember, that was the last thing you said to me as I walked off that elevator after meeting you for the first time. 'Me, too.'"

"And I was just echoing what you had just thought."

"There is something to say for this mind reading business, isn't there?"

"I've wondered if I could ever learn how to do it without this gadget in my head."

She studied his face for a moment. "I think it might be wonderful, but I keep telling myself that you are just the way I want you, just as you are. I don't like the idea that you are tethered to the Company, that's all."

So we make the most of what we have.

Yes.

She released his neck. "Now, why don't you go out and make us your special Margaritas?"

"You know what those things do to you," he said over his shoulder as he went into the kitchen.

"Exactly."

She went into the bedroom and covered Chick's cage. Chick murmured plaintively then was still. Dropping her clothes on the bedroom floor, Meredith went out to meet him.

187

Scene 54

Meredith and Dolly were having lunch at The Egg Place. "You are glowing!" Dolly said.

Meredith smiled slyly. "I'm learning how to live," she said, "from you."

"Poor dear!" Dolly laughed.

"Next thing you know, I'll be wearing heels to work."

"Oh, no! Not that!"

"You know? That's one thing that I think is so silly! And uncomfortable!"

Dolly grinned. "Remember—I've seen your legs. They shouldn't be kept hidden!"

"Cleavage, too?"

"Cleavage especially. I love to see men's faces with their tongues hanging out."

"Speaking of which, how was your weekend?"

Dolly hung her head. "I'm so ashamed!" she whispered.

Meredith became serious. "Really?"

Dolly grinned broadly. 'No, but probably I should be."

Meredith shook her head. The two of them stood up to leave, and Meredith followed Dolly to the door, watching how the woman moved. *Wonderful!* she thought. *She is so in touch with who she is.*

Meredith had been troubled recently by feelings that came on during her meditation sessions. Only when she was with Doug did she manage to relax about misgivings regarding her past. He was so accepting of her that she almost believed in herself, but without his support her doubts always returned. She wished she could be as unselfconscious as Dolly.

Naturally, Dolly didn't see her the same way. They were having dinner a couple of weeks later, when she said, "Meredith, you are the sexiest earth mother I ever knew!"

"Earth mother?" Meredith laughed.

"I was always the wild one," Dolly said, "Nobody ever took me seriously. Sex was the only thing I had going for me. You, though, were born wise."

"Oh, brother!" Meredith said. "You didn't know me then!"

"No? So, tell me!"

"I was one of those California Hippie flower children, trying everything, refusing to take any responsibility for what I did. I don't think I grew up until I was in my forties, and then not very much. Looking back on my life, I cringe at the stuff I did."

"But you went to college and studied and graduated," Dolly said. "You told me you studied psychology and biology and all that. I flunked out of every school I went to."

"Yeah, and in grad school I fell for my professor and totally destroyed his marriage."

"You did that, all by yourself? He couldn't help himself?"

Meredith stopped and thought. "Well sure, he could. I was so conceited I thought I could get any man I wanted. And I never gave a thought to what might happen to his wife and kids."

"Kids do get the short end of the stick, don't they?"

"The older one was a boy—he'd be just about Dennis's age."

Dolly looked at her friend. "So that's why Dennis?"

"Maybe. It's occurred to me."

"Dennis is your chance to make it better?—your life?"

Meredith dropped her eyes.

"I'm sorry, Meredith. That wasn't nice." Dolly reached over the table and put her hand on Meredith's arm.

"It's probably true," Meredith said softly. "But nothing will make up for what I did."

"Who broke it off?"

"I did. I was with him when he drove away from his wife and kids, and they were standing in the yard, crying. I couldn't handle it. I tried to act as though it wasn't my problem, but it was. Not long after that, he and I were in his apartment watching television, and there was this farewell concert for George Harrison after he died—'Concert for George'—and we thought it would be cool to hear all those old songs again. Eric Clapton was playing 'Something in the way she moves,' you know, and Paul was turned on by it. He was singing along—to me—and I just fell apart. I kept thinking about those days when we all thought 'anything goes,' and people had to take care of themselves, and the ones

189

who suffered were just not grown up enough or something—but then I knew that if we don't take care of each other we're just animals. Everything Paul did to get me out of it just made it worse, because he wasn't thinking about anything but right then, how could he get me to stop crying—and crying was what I needed to do. And what I needed to do after that was to leave him."

Dolly didn't say anything for a long while. "Don't take this the wrong way," she said, "but have you cried over Paul since then?"

"Yes. Many times."

"You carry a big fucking load on your sweet shoulders!"

Meredith sighed, then took a deep breath. "We all carry the whole world, don't we?"

"I don't know if I can handle that!" Dolly was frowning.

"Maybe none of us can. All we can do is try. Somebody has to."

"So I should care about those guys who just want my body?"

"Dolly, don't ask me! I care about you—those guys you sleep with are just part of the whole rest of the world. They may be cheating on their wives, but they are ..."

"Don't say it! If I go out with a guy and I start to care about him, I'm going to end up crying in my beer for the next week."

"Sorry, babe. I can't lay stuff on you. I want you to be happy. I want you to be healthy. I want you to be at peace with the world—with yourself. I wish I knew how to make that happen, but I don't."

Dolly looked at her through misty eyes. "I love you, too."

"Maybe that's the best we can do."

Scene 55

Doug was sitting in his office sorting papers when Janet knocked at the open door. "Got a minute?"

He gestured toward a chair. "Sure."

"May I?" She had a hand on the door knob. He nodded.

"I know you and I are not supposed to fraternize," she said quietly, "but I don't know who else to talk to."

"What's up?"

"I need to get out."

"Hmmm," he said, "you know it's possible. And it comes at a cost."

"Yeah, I know. They told us in training."

"If you changed your mind later, they might not take you back."

"That's not a problem for me. I need to get out from under this—this—cloud of paranoia. Everything I do here is fake. No matter what the high principles are that we supposedly work for, at the end of the day I know I'm trying to screw somebody."

"Who is also trying to screw somebody else."

"Can I say that? Can I tell my grandchildren, if I ever have any, that I did what I did because somebody else was trying to screw somebody else?"

Doug propped his chin on his hands. "Sounds like you need a pep talk."

"Fuck the pep talks! It's all for a good cause! We'll all sleep better with the bad guys collared!"

"You no longer believe that, I gather."

"Do you?" Her eyes flashed fire.

He pretended to cower behind his arms. "Holy smoke!"

She leaned on his desk. "Doug, do you sleep well?"

He smiled. "I gave that up when I got my GS-12."

"You're in this for the money?"

"Maybe at first I was. I just needed a job, and this sounded exciting."

"Yeah, it did to me too. I pictured myself like the Secret Service guys, posing with their sunglasses and wrist radios."

"The bureaucracy swallows all."

"See? Cynicism pervades this place!"

He sat up in his chair. "What would you do instead of this?"

"I don't know. I have a degree in education."

"No kidding? That's an interesting transition."

"I majored in psychology. I thought I could learn a lot here."

"I've learned a lot," Doug said.

"Have you? Really?"

"Really. Not a lot of it would go into the training manual, though."

"I've heard that there are natural readers," she said quietly.

"And?"

"Maybe I could help them."

"They won't let you keep your chip."

"I know, but ..."

"And you signed a non-disclosure contract."

Janet looked at him silently.

"You could go to prison for a long time if you violated that contract."

"But there must be things I could do to help!"

"I have one more caveat."

She looked at him, waiting.

"Removing your chip involves surgery. They have to open up your scalp and pry the chip off its mounting, and then they have to pull the probes out of your brain."

"But **they** put them all in!"

"They had a lot invested in your coming out of **that** surgery intact."

Her brow furrowed.

"You don't check the oil in a used car just before you sell it."

"You think ..."

"I don't think anything," Doug said. "I have no reason to doubt the integrity of government surgeons."

Janet stood up. "That's not exactly what I wanted to hear, but thank you just the same."

"You're welcome."

As she opened the door, he added, "Janet—good luck!"

She smiled wanly and closed the door behind her.

Scene 56

George Randolph and Mary Donovan were sitting at a table outside a Starbucks in Silver Spring when Meredith arrived. She found herself smiling at the fact that George was not wearing a disguise other than sunglasses, but the two of them smiled back.

"This early fall weather is awesome, isn't it?" said Mary.

"Awesome is sure the word." Meredith took the chair that George gestured toward, then looked around.

"No operatives in sight that I've seen," George said.

"Thank you for meeting with me."

Mary touched Meredith's hand. "We've been wanting to get better acquainted," she said. "There's a lot about this that nobody seems to know, and the only way we have to learn how to deal with it is through each other."

"I don't think I can contribute very much."

"I don't think that's true," said George. "So far, there's no single source of information. It must be an attribute of human consciousness that has only recently appeared, and I haven't been able to find any scholarly writing about it at all."

Meredith looked at him. "I'm sorry, but would you mind taking off your sunglasses? I like to see your eyes when you're talking to me." She looked down. "I guess that shows my lack of confidence, doesn't it?"

"Of course. Not 'of course' it shows your lack of confidence, but of course I'll take them off!" He complied, and exchanged glances with Mary. "Our friend here has asked me the same thing, many times."

"The eyes are the windows of the soul," Mary quoted. "George has a very deep soul." She smiled at him.

"I've wondered," Meredith said, "if there are degrees of this ability. I know people who seem to be able to see right through me," she laughed, "but I don't think they could read my thoughts."

"Well, if it's an evolutionary development, I'd think that it has been a long time coming. It could be that some recent event has triggered its manifestation."

Mary touched his arm. "George is our theory person."

"What is your field?" Meredith asked. "I gather both of you are in the same field?"

"History—although Mary majored in biology in her undergrad studies. What are your interests?"

"I studied psych and biology at Berkeley, and dabbled in neurology as a grad student at NYU."

"And now you're in business in D.C.?"

Meredith looked at him quickly, frowning. "Did I tell you that in one of the meetings?" And then she laughed. "I guess we can't have many secrets from each other, can we? I'm in a no-thinking job for an insurance company right now. I've considered it an interim thing for a couple of years."

Mary tilted her head. "A time of recovery?—or is that too personal?"

Meredith smiled. "You are very perceptive. Yes, you could say that. And it's not too personal."

"As you said," George replied, "secrets don't last long in this group. It's good, though. I think people hide too much."

"Spoken by one who loves disguises!" Mary laughed at George, who turned pink.

"Touché." He looked from Mary to Meredith. "It's a game I play. I still have a nine-year-old boy in me."

"So the 'being discreet' thing is a game?"

"Yes!" Mary laughed again. "Some of us do have some apprehensions about the CIA and their implants, but we'd be no match for them if they had serious intentions about us."

"There have been a couple of people who have come to our meetings for a while, and then just disappeared. We think they might have been plants."

"Plants with implants." Mary's sense of humor pleased Meredith.

"Could you tell for sure?"

"No, not really. Some members said they detected something different about them, but that was after they had gone."

"I've often thought I'd love to go through their training," said Meredith. "Doug won't—oops—please forget I said that!"

George smiled. "Your **friend**, who remains unnamed, won't tell you about the training?"

"Thank you. No." Meredith's face became hot.

Mary leaned toward them. "If George's theory is true—if this is an evolutionary uptick—then we all need to know how to do it well! Having an us-versus-them conflict going on with the CIA or any other group will just make it harder for everybody!"

"If—and I admit, it's a big if—if that's true, it's probably the biggest thing to happen to the human race since we dropped out of the trees and moved onto the savanna."

"And there hasn't been anything written in the neurology journals?"

"I think," George said, "it's too new. The journals won't touch a new idea until they think it can be defended by published leaders in the field."

"Either that," Mary put in, "or the CIA is squelching all publication—or, worse, is capturing all the researchers!"

All three laughed. "Sorry," Mary said, "my paranoia is showing again."

"Actually," George continued, "There is a lot out there from the fringes of science, like Dan Siegel, a psychiatrist who has written a lot about the brain and meditation. 'The Mindful Brain' for example, and 'Mindsight,' a term he coined about the mind's natural ability to discern very subtle clues to other people's states of mind. But the crucial difference for us—and the CIA—is the seeming existence of some kind of energy field outside the brain that other minds can detect."

"**Some** other minds," added Mary.

"One thing he did contribute, at least to our group, was about the importance of meditation practice. We found that we could learn to have a lot of control over this thing just by using Vipassana meditation."

"I stumbled on that myself," said Meredith. "I had begun meditating before I noticed what was happening to my mind around others."

The three of them continued their conversation for a time, until Mary interrupted. "I hate to break into this, but I have to be back in College Park in an hour. Can we pick it up another time?"

On the train back to D.C., Meredith felt elated. *It's becoming more and more a gift, and less and less a curse,* she thought.

Scene 57

Meredith was at her usual table in the far corner of The Egg Place, eating and reading a book. She wasn't particularly interested in what was going on around her. The crowd of thoughts were at a reasonably quiet level—she was getting better at ignoring them.

"Hi."

She looked up to see Janet standing next to her, smiling. A moment of uncertainty gave way to something more comfortable. "Hi."

"You're engrossed in your book, or I'd ask if I could join you."

Meredith smiled. "Sure, sit down. I have only about twenty minutes left in my lunch hour, but I'd enjoy putting my book away to chat with you."

"Actually, I have a request. Would you be willing to meet with me sometime in a more private time and place? I need some advice."

Meredith's forehead furrowed. "Is this about Doug?"

"No. Definitely not."

"I'm not sure what I could offer to you." Meredith smiled. "Sorry— that didn't come out right. Tell me what I can do for you."

Janet switched to thoughts, *First, I know that you are a reader.*

Meredith was startled. *How do you know that—through Doug?*

No. I picked it up from others in the organization. They don't know I know.

My God, I'm a marked woman!

That brought a smile between them.

This has to be quick—this place is crawling with people.

Okay, meet where? When?

Seven this evening?

Meredith wondered if Janet knew that Doug was to be in a conference that evening.

Yes, I do.

Meredith sighed. *All right. Where?*

I'll be in a cab to pick you up on the southeast corner of Connecticut and Eye. Blue Cab.

Sounds serious!

"It is," Janet said aloud, "but I've been enjoying the fall weather, haven't you?"

For the remaining time, the two chatted about nothing at all, and when Meredith had to leave, she collected her things, stood and said, "So I'll see you later!"

Meredith didn't look back as she paid her check and returned to work.

All afternoon, she thought about what Janet might want from her. A niggling little worry that it might have something to do with Doug in spite of what the woman had said, came and went several times. She stood and looked over the partition at Dolly. "I need a friend. Are you my friend?"

Dolly looked up. "You betcha."

"Have a quick bite with me after work? I have to be someplace at seven."

"Sure. Maybe a martini?"

"No, I have to be clear."

"Well, all right, then, party pooper!"

At quitting time, they took the elevator down together and found a little sandwich shop that was not crowded.

"What's up?" asked Dolly, after they had ordered.

"I am to meet **the other woman** at seven, and I don't know why."

"And you're about to explode."

"Maybe it isn't all that serious." Meredith gave her a weak smile. "She says it doesn't have anything to do with him."

"And you'd like to believe her, but in light of past experience …"

"Exactly."

"Okay, love. Here's the way it is. Right now you are your own worst enemy. If it was me, I'd get fortifications to help me relax."

"I don't want to be relaxed. I want to be really clear-headed, even if it's bad news."

Dolly shook her head. "You are something else, Meredith."

"When she told me she didn't want him, I believed her. I guess I still do. But she may be about to tell me something I don't want to hear."

"What'd she say?"

197

"She wants advice."

"Which could mean anything at all."

"Anything."

"You want me to come with you?"

Meredith smiled. "No. But thank you anyway."

"I didn't think so. But I'd come and bring the boys, if you needed me."

"You're sweet. You and your boys."

"Go with God, as they say. You can do it. And call me **immediately afterward!**"

At seven, Meredith was standing on the corner when a blue cab pulled up. She opened the door and got in.

"Thank you, Meredith. I know I don't deserve your attention ..."

"Stop it! That's over with!" Nevertheless, she looked at Janet with the question in her mind.

Yes, it is.

Meredith sighed and slumped back in the seat. *Why do I always wonder?*

It's in our genes.

But that's not what you wanted to talk about. Meredith looked at the young, beautiful agent as the woman slowly disintegrated. *Okay, I'll help if I can.*

I have to get out. Out of the Company.

Meredith frowned. *But why do you come to me?*

I know—I've heard—that you are in touch with people. She studied Meredith's face.

These people you say I'm in touch with—what could they do to help you?

Janet's eyes seemed to hollow out, even as they filled with tears. *Support, I guess. I don't know.*

Meredith frowned. *I don't know anyone outside the Company who could help you get out.*

No, that's not it! I know the procedure. It's moral and emotional support I need. I don't know anyone around here—my friends and family are all out West.

The cab pulled into a little park and stopped. Meredith looked around, suddenly apprehensive.

"It's okay," Janet said. "I told him to come here. I just wanted a private place for us to talk. I know the driver. He'll wait as long as we want."

But we still need to talk like this, right?

Right. Now, here's the story—my story. I've become really cynical about my job. I feel like my function is to deceive people, and I'm not comfortable with that anymore. I want to resign from the Company and let them take their chip out of my head. But then I will know too much. I've signed a non-disclosure contract, so I have to be really careful about what I say after I get out. Since this group I've heard about probably knows a lot about the program already, I won't be taking as big a risk connecting with them. And I'd like to help them in whatever way I can do it safely. Does that make sense?"

How do you know they would want to be contacted by you? Meredith was becoming increasingly uncomfortable.

I don't. I'm just hoping.

Meredith turned to face her. *This feels very weird to me. I'm not accusing you of anything, but how would the group know to trust you? You could be a plant.*

Tears were steaming down Janet's face. *I wish I knew how to convince you!*

It's not me you'd have to convince.

But I'm a stranger to them. At least you know me!

Meredith laughed. "What I know about you isn't the best recommendation I could think of."

Janet covered her face and sobbed.

"I'm sorry, Janet. I didn't need to say that. We crossed that bridge a long time ago." Meredith pulled a tissue out of her handbag and touched Janet's hand with it.

"Thank you." She took the tissue and wiped her eyes. "I need to tell you something, just to keep things straight between us." *I told Doug that I wanted to get out. I didn't tell him anything else—I swear!*

The weirdness grows!

I'm sorry!

And so, here we are, skulking around to talk with each other because your employer wouldn't like to hear that we even know each other. I have a dossier in their files, too, you know. And you want me to introduce you to some people I may or may not know, who would be even more suspicious of you than I am. And my connection with you lies in our having slept with the same man, who also cannot know of our contact or your intentions.

"Bizarre, isn't it?" Janet's voice was husky and strained, but she smiled. "There's something about this ability that feels wonderful to me—that offers a hope for humanity that is in direct opposition to the paranoia and adversarial stance epitomized by my employer. Does that make sense?"

"Of course it does. I can't help but sympathize with your request. I also can't help but want to protect certain people—if I knew them. What I need is to know you better. Everything else hinges on my trust level, doesn't it?

"How do we do that?"

Let's think about it for a couple of days. In your job, you must have learned some ways to get privacy. This cab idea was very smart. Maybe we can rent a car and go someplace for a weekend.

All right. Janet smiled again. *Thank you!* To the driver, she gave directions to a subway station.

"I'll get in touch with you," Meredith said, "indirectly. You'll know it's from me."

Were you ever a spy? A hint of mischief showed in her face.

They both laughed as the cab pulled into traffic.

Scene 58

Meredith and Doug had been promising themselves some alone time for a while; Doug had been away on assignments frequently, and the two of them always seemed to have other commitments interfering with their promises. One weekend appeared to be open for both of them, and so they turned off their cell phones and hid away in his loft. The one avenue with potential for interruption was his pager; that could not be defeated.

They had had dinner on Friday evening at the bistro near her apartment, and found a 24-hour grocery where they could stock up on food for the weekend. "It feels like we're an old married couple," Meredith remarked as she pushed the cart among the produce tables.

"I was thinking more along the line of honeymooners," he said. "Watching you pick over the onions and potatoes reminded me how much I enjoy watching the way you move."

That particular line from George Harrison's "Something" stood out for her as he said it, and she stopped, her stomach tightening ever so gently. She turned and faced him. "When we get home," she said softly, "would you please sing that song for me?"

His face registered uncertainty; he had a vivid memory of her talking about the song and how it had affected her in the elevator just a day before they met.

"I love the song," she said. "I want to change the associations I have with it."

He grinned. "Obviously, you haven't heard me sing."

"That doesn't matter. It matters that it's you." She leaned against him and kissed him lightly.

Several times in their shopping, they found themselves in different aisles in the store, and communicated by thoughts about which brands of food to buy.

Meredith: *I like Newman's Own Italian salad dressing.*

Doug: *Do you want to make waffles from scratch, or should I get a mix?*

Meredith: *As long as we put a good yogurt on it, it doesn't matter to me.*

Doug: *I'm almost out of Grey Goose—I'll get some more.*
Meredith: *Do you have Cointreau for Margaritas?*
Doug: *I have triple sec.*
Meredith: *No, no, no. Too sweet.*
Doug: *Ah, a discriminating palette! Cointreau it will be.*

Lugging their grocery bags up to his loft, they laughed a lot. Forgotten for the moment were the heavy issues that usually occupied their minds. As Doug stored away their supplies, Meredith made their first Margaritas of the weekend.

"Oh, I love this little lime squeezer!" she said. "Mine is hard to use. I usually don't have fresh limes, so I use Rose's, but it makes the Margarita too sweet for me."

She carried their drinks to the sofa while Doug selected several jazz CDs.

"Life is good," she said, holding her glass up for him to touch it with his.

They drank to a good life, and shared erotic thoughts.

Then a single word, *Janet*, slipped into that stream of domestic bliss in their minds.

Both of them registered shock. Doug put his glass down and looked at Meredith.

"I don't know where that came from," she said, flustered. She knew very well where it had come from, but was afraid to think more.

"Has she …?" he began.

Meredith's shoulders slumped. "Yes. I wasn't going to tell you."

"Hmmm. I don't know what to say."

"I know. She told me that she had said something to you, but we avoided that subject."

Doug looked concerned. He picked up his glass and finished the drink. "I don't want to ask you what I really want to know."

"I'm sorry. I think I could have kept from saying anything, but keeping my mind from it is a lot harder."

"Can we stop it here? Can we agree that it didn't come up? At least, for the weekend? I don't want it to be here, with us, not now!"

"All right." A hint of a smile tugged at the corner of her mouth. "Sing to me."

Doug sat with his hands clasped together touching his lips, reminding Meredith of someone praying. Then he got up and turned off the stereo.

They arranged themselves on the sofa, facing each other. Her expression was of delight; his seemed a little sheepish.

"Something in the way she moves," he began singing softly, "attracts me like no other lover, Something in the way she woos me, Don't want to leave her now, You know I believe her now," and he hummed the six-note measure—and the implications—that finished the verse without words.

As he began, Meredith leaned back and closed her eyes, the smile lingering at her mouth even while tears formed at the corners of her eyes and drifted slowly down her cheeks.

Then, when he began the alternate verse, she joined him in singing, her eyes open and shining, "You're asking me will my love grow, I don't know, **I - don't – know**!" the song going from soft and tentative to clear and loud, a joyous parody, "You stick around and it may show, I don't know, **I - don't – know**!"

Then they clung to each other, the rest of the song forgotten.

The next morning they lay in bed holding hands, their faces on one pillow, almost touching. Suddenly Meredith laughed.

"What's funny?"

"We were. I will never again hear that song without thinking of the two of us, slightly tipsy, singing our hearts out, '**I – don't – know**!"

Doug smiled as he asked, "So what about Eric Clapton?"

Her face lost its grin. "It may take you learning to play the guitar to erase that part."

He dug his fingers in her ribs and she squealed like a teen-ager. Soon they were thrashing around on the bed, the covers flung to the floor.

Eventually they quieted down and lay there panting, their perspiration turning cold under the ceiling fan.

"How about those waffles you promised me?" teased Meredith.

"With walnuts and strawberries and yogurt—and just a touch of maple syrup."

"Okay, you mix them up and start the waffle iron while I shower, and I'll watch them while you wash off that sweaty body I love so much!"

After a breakfast sweet with syrup and moon-eyes, they put on their clothes and ran Meredith's daily route. "I don't think the shower was supposed to come before the run," Doug said breathlessly.

"So we'll just have to do it again!"

"Together?"

She grinned at him and spurted ahead. By the time they had finished the fourteen blocks, both were breathing hard and laughing. Their second showers took much longer than the first.

Doug set their cushions out in the middle of the floor as Meredith dried her hair. "We sure have the sequence of things screwed up," she said. I meditate **then** run, **then** eat breakfast!"

"This is called **unwinding**—isn't that what we wanted to do today?" He watched her as she wrapped her robe around her and kneeled over her cushion.

"Breathe," she said without looking around.

An hour later, as they stood and stretched their cramped legs, their mood was less of playful puppies and more of quiet appreciation for what they shared.

For two days they avoided the one subject that neither of them could completely erase from their thoughts: *Janet.*

On Sunday afternoon they sat quietly reading, Doug with a copy of "New York Review of Books" and Meredith in the middle of a book: "Mindsight: The New Science of Personal Transformation." The quiet pool of their shared thoughts was in fact a river, flowing smooth-surfaced but deep, with bubbles of association rising from the depths, as they read: "The vulgarization of Darwinism that sees the 'struggle for existence' as nothing but the competition for some environmental resource in short supply ignores the large body of evidence ..." "The term 'mindful brain' is used ... to embrace the notion that our awareness, our mindful 'paying attention or taking care,' is intimately related to the dance between our mind and our brain." Then *"George Randolph"* and *"Janet asked ..."*

"I have to go," Meredith said suddenly, rising from the soft folds of the sofa.

Doug looked up, startled. "What's wrong?"

"I have to think," she replied, then turned to face him. "Being with you really does unwind me." She smiled sadly. "But reality is bigger, and there is a fence between us right now."

Doug frowned. "Did I miss something?"

"I hope so." She collected her purse and her book, leaned over him to kiss him tenderly, and was gone.

Doug still sat, unable to move, unable to comprehend, the newspaper suspended in his hand.

In the warm September Sunday, Meredith held back tears as she walked to the subway.

Scene 59

Dolly watched her friend come out of the elevator and walk silently to her cubicle. Peering over the partition, she said, "You said you'd call me."

Meredith looked up. "Sorry, love. Actually it was not as bad as I was afraid it would be."

"Well, that's a relief!"

"And it was worse."

"Oh, shit." Dolly disappeared from the partition and immediately appeared again at the door. She sat down. "It's about Doug."

"Well, yes, in a way." Meredith took Dolly's hand. "But I can't tell you. I'm sorry!"

Dolly's face showed her disappointment. Her voice broke as she asked, "Okay. What can I do to help you?"

"I don't know." She smiled. "But Doug and I had a wonderful weekend!"

"I'm glad. I'd be doing handsprings if I didn't know there's something else."

"There's something I have to do. It feels like the right thing to do, but I'm afraid it might be absolutely the wrong thing."

"Please don't say you're leaving!"

"No." She looked at Dolly, her eyes misting. "I can't leave. I have to face this."

"Then I'll face it with you—if you'll let me."

Meredith turned to her computer. "Let me think, please?"

"Okay." Dolly retreated to her own cube.

Near quitting time, Meredith looked over the partition. "My place?"

"Absolutely."

The subway ride was somber. Meredith kept thinking about Janet, wanting to help her do something Meredith felt was admirable, and yet not absolutely sure that Janet was really who she said she was. The whole thing could be a CIA setup. She had had only that brief connection with Janet months ago. The paranoia that the Silver Spring group exhibited could very well be justified. Meredith did not want to become a tool of the CIA. Whether or not Janet's request was genuine, Meredith didn't want to involve Dolly in her muddlings with the Company and the Silver Spring group, because she wanted to protect her from any fallout or miscalculations. But Dolly was the only person Meredith knew well enough to talk to about it, and she needed another opinion besides her own.

Dolly sensed the gravity of Meredith's problem, and didn't try to cheer her up—at least until she found out what was wrong.

In Meredith's apartment, Dolly went first to the kitchen and fixed drinks for them both.

"I hope this isn't as strong as the last time we did this!" Meredith said, smiling.

The two women sat on the sofa and clinked glasses. "To easing our burdens," said Dolly. "Now—I know you are in some kind of bind. And I know that you don't want me to know certain things about this bind. I'm here to be a friend, in whatever way I can. So tell me what you can tell me."

"Dolly, I would not hold back anything from you just to keep a secret. Even if someone asked me to keep a secret, I would at least tell you that much. The reason I've been so vague with you is that I'm afraid of getting you embroiled in something I have no control over and I'm not sure would be safe for you."

"Okay. But just know, Meredith, I would put myself on the line for you—at any depth it takes. I'm aware that Doug is an agent, and that the people he works with cannot be trusted. I suspect that all this has to do with your 'gift' or whatever you call it. You can read my mind, but I cannot read yours, or anybody else's. So where do we start?"

"Remember I had an appointment with 'the other woman?'"

"Who, it turns out, is also an agent and a mind reader like Doug—and she's slept with Doug on some assignment."

"Oh, Lordie, did I tell you all that?"

"You must have. Or at least I surmised as much from what you told me." Dolly took a large swallow from her drink.

"Now, two things I wish I didn't have to tell you, but none of this will make sense unless I do. Janet told me that she wants to get out of the Company. It's not easy, and carries serious risk. And she asked me to help her to connect with some folks I've met who have the same 'gift' that I do."

"Wow. You've been in touch with other people like you?"

"Yes. And they are all very nervous that I am closely connected to Doug, who because of his position is for them a possible enemy."

"The safest thing for you to do right now is turn her down. Right?"

"The safest thing for me. Yes."

"But you have a kind heart and you want to help her."

"She hates what they have her doing. She regrets getting the chip implanted in her head."

"Can't blame her for that—even though it would come in handy on Saturday night."

Meredith grinned. "I can imagine the fun you would have."

Dolly peered into her glass. "I'm sure there are some very strong strings attached to having that little piece of hardware."

"Very strong."

Dolly finished her drink and turned to face Meredith. "What if you turned the dilemma over to the other people? After all, what you're agonizing over is about protecting them, isn't it? If Janet is a worm or a plant or whatever you call it, shouldn't they be the ones to gauge the risk? Or do you feel responsible for them?"

"I don't know. You're right—they should be the ones to decide, as long as I give them all the information I have."

"Janet, if she is on the up and up, should be able to understand that. You ready for another?" She picked up both glasses and headed for the kitchen.

"You help me get my mind clear, and you make me feel better, Dolly," Meredith called after her. "I just hope I'm not endangering you."

"You worry too much."

"You're important to me."

"So give me at least half the worry, okay?" Dolly returned with fresh drinks. "We should eat something or these things are going to flatten us."

"If we can't make it to the bistro on our own steam, we'll both have to eat vegetarian here."

"Geez—people keep special drinks on hand for their friends all the time. Not even a pork chop?"

"I have something they say tastes 'just like chicken.' It's mostly soy."

"Okay, let's eat in. It's probably good for my soul, right?"

"I wouldn't guess about that."

Scene 60

It was a small group that met Meredith in Silver Spring, for which she was grateful. She was unsure of her relationship with these people, but she needed their support. And she was there to plead for Janet, who also needed their support. This "gift" that she had been granted from who knew where set her apart from the rest of the world except, it seemed, from this small group of people blessed—or cursed—with the same gift. Janet was in a different situation because her gift was technological and would certainly be withdrawn. At the same time, she had experienced the same difference from ordinary people and could never again feel "normal."

The gift was more than a simple ability; it changed one's sense of self, one's separateness from others—it seemed to demonstrate an interconnecting web of humanity, through which we all are linked into what some have called "the oneness of everything." Meredith resisted that concept, which she attributed to wishful thinking, a New Age mantra, and yet she was drawn more and more into an awareness that the popular idea that individuals are "separate" and isolated was inadequate to explain her experiences.

She felt nostalgia for her youthful, naïve image of the Counterculture as being an awakening, even though through it she had selfishly grasped what she wanted at the expense of other, equally deserving human beings. "Imagine all the people," went the old John Lennon song, "Living life in peace." It tugged at her soul and yet, as she had found out, was so hard to accomplish. This gift seemed to promise to her that the dream was still possible. And yet, here it was, separating her from others even more.

Janet, she felt, had some of the same awareness and some of the same promise. But Meredith wasn't sure. Pushing the young woman into this group could benefit all—or could even destroy the dream.

So she opened herself to the group. George Randolph was there, and his protégé Mary Donovan, and Dennis, and several others. She told them what had happened.

"Just hearing your story," said Mary, "I want to believe this woman. But we've seen so much deception and subterfuge from people in the government, that we're all afraid."

George asked, "There isn't any way that the woman can leave the CIA without losing her implant?"

"As far as I know, no. And obviously, if she goes through with it she will probably no longer be able to do as we are learning to do. But what impresses me about her is her idealism. She has experienced what we experience, and it's convinced her that there is a better way to live. She wants to be a part of whatever we are."

"What does your CIA friend think of it?" asked George.

Meredith sighed. "He's a good person. He said one time that he thinks 'every day' about getting out. But he stays. I'm in love with him but there's this barrier between us that I wish I could break down."

"Does he know about your woman friend?"

Meredith thought at first that he was referring to Dolly. "Oh, you mean the operative. She's not a friend, really. We've had some personal connections, that's all. Doug" she paused, "knows her, and knows that she wants out of the Company. But he and I have not discussed her any further than that. I haven't told him that she wants to make contact with this group, although I'm not sure she didn't tell him. He knows about you all—maybe not individually—and he was the one who suggested, indirectly, that I look you up. We are very careful not to talk about some things."

George said, "I'd like to meet her—maybe in some other venue, where she couldn't trace me to this group. I don't know how to do that, at the moment. I like to be discreet."

Meredith smiled. "Discretion is your watch word."

"Yes. I feel responsible."

"I told her I would contact her—discreetly—to tell her if a meeting is possible. If you tell me where and when you can meet her, I'll pass that on. Is that workable?"

"Yes. Let's say, I'll meet the bus at the U of M stop. She can use your own call, 'If you hear this, say hello.' When I feel it's safe, I'll say hello."

"Wonderful," said Meredith. "I'll get that to her, and then wait until you contact me again. Thank you!"

Back in D.C. the next day, Meredith handed Dolly an envelope over the partition. A note in it read: "Would you please give this note to 'the other woman' who will stop at the building directory on her way to lunch at noon tomorrow? Tell her it's from the angry wife." Inside the envelope was another envelope containing the directions for Janet to meet George.

Dolly looked at Meredith with a half-grin on her face. "If I say it's from the angry wife and she looks shocked, I'll not give it to her, right? It could be somebody else, who will then be scared to death that somebody knows **her** secret."

"You got it."

Dolly tucked the envelope into her purse and said, "This is exciting!"

"I'll be waiting for you in The Egg Place."

That evening Meredith made a point of asking Doug, "Can you make sure the other woman goes down for lunch right at noon tomorrow?"

Doug looked at her intently for a moment, then said, "I think so."

"She should go from the elevator to the building directory, where someone will give her something. If it's not going to work, just tell me before noon."

Doug grinned. "You are getting to be a regular spy!"

"Please don't say that out loud. I'm getting an ulcer over this."

She was sitting and reading over her after-lunch coffee the next day when Dolly arrived, flushed. "She actually smiled when I said 'angry wife.' Then she just put the envelope in her purse and went out the door."

"Thank you, Dolly. Now, let's not say any more about it, okay?" Meredith looked around to see if anyone seemed interested in them.

Is it all right to do it this way? Dolly thought.

Meredith looked at her and smiled. "Fantastic!"

I was there at noon, but when she didn't show up right away I moved across the lobby near the front door where I could watch. She was late, but it was obvious to me that she was expecting something. So I just walked over and pretended to look at the Directory also.

"You are terrific!"

"I'm hungry. Where's the waitperson?"

Scene 61

That evening at the bistro, Meredith and Doug, over eggplant parmesan (hers) and chicken cacciatore (his) "talked" in silence. They had gotten quite adept at conversation within their pool of mind, each recognizing the other's words, able to piece together the inevitable fragments of thought that preceded sentences, ignoring the intruding fragments from other people around them. The waiters gave them sidelong glances occasionally, wondering at their silence even as they often seemed to respond to each other. Once, their waiter approached their table with two glasses and a bottle. "Perhaps a little Pinot Grigio to smooth out the evening?"

They laughed and agreed. "Thank you, Rico," Meredith said. "You do take good care of us."

Rico poured the wine, bowed and left silently. *He's worried about us,* she thought to Doug.

Yes. He thinks we are having problems.

When the waiter returned later to suggest coffee, they made a point of speaking to him and to each other. "We're like an old married couple," Doug told him. "We know all of each other's jokes." Rico, apparently relieved, went to fetch fresh coffee.

Back at Meredith's apartment later, she said, "I don't know how we do it."

"What?"

"We both know there's a fence between us, but we manage to avoid it without even acknowledging it."

"Hmmm. Maybe it's not so different from what most couples do— avoid speaking about the thing between them that both know and neither wants to address."

"The elephant in the room."

Doug smiled. "Yeah."

"I saw a movie some time ago, a French movie, in which the husband was having an affair, and the wife knew about it but she didn't want to disrupt the life she had. So she simply went on as though she didn't know, until she met another man. They were so open and honest with each other that she saw how hollow her marriage was. It didn't end well, as I remember."

Doug looked at her. "Does this feel hollow to you?"

"No," she answered. Then, thoughtfully, "Sometimes."

He sat down on the sofa and pulled her onto his lap. "I hope you know that I'm not unfaithful. I have to keep some things from you that would not be safe for you to know. Do you know that?"

"Yes," she said. "Yes, I know that because I do the same thing. But it's like we're soldiers in enemy armies. Personally, we're lovers. Politically we're on opposite sides of the fence."

"It's not political," he said. "It's really about something much more serious—dangerous."

Meredith buried her face in his neck, and he felt her tears running down inside his shirt.

She lifted her head to face him. "Do you believe in what you do?"

There it was: she was questioning his integrity—no, not integrity—his morality. He had often thought that he knew what he was doing, that his work in the Company was for high purposes, even if he had to perform unpleasant or even ugly tasks in the course of his work. He was paid to betray people, and he wasn't sure that it was not slowly draining his soul. He had felt good—righteous, even—about how he had suffered after killing that man. His suffering was a sign that inside he was still a good person. He needed Meredith to believe in his goodness. But he didn't know how to answer her question.

She waited for him to respond, watching his eyes. Slowly, she wilted in his silence, and closed her eyes. She had hoped that he would reassure her that, even if he felt he must continue in his work, inside he was where she was. In the past few weeks she was awakening to something profound. She had discovered a purpose—or at least a direction—that could give her life meaning. And she wanted him to be there at her side.

She slid quietly off his lap and reached for a tissue. They sat, silent and subdued, for a long time. He reached for her hand without speaking.

"It's this **place**!" she said vehemently, staring across the room. "I watch the tourists, busloads of children, come and stream through the buildings and the museums, full of awe at what they think is the center of the universe. They trace the names on the Vietnam Memorial, touch the souls of young men who went over there and never came back. They look up at Lincoln like he was some kind of god. It's just another Disney World!"

"No," he said quietly, "it's not Disney World. It's a city, with five or six million people, each one trying to live the life they've been handed. Some of us are better at it than others. Most of us feel that we're doing the right thing, at least as close as we know how."

She felt the chill in his words. "I'm sorry," she said. "I don't really believe that about Disney World. The irony, though, gets to me sometimes, the difference between what people say they want and what actually comes out. And I don't believe that about you. I fell in love with you even knowing what you do for a living. I just hate the distance we are forced to maintain between our lives."

"So do I. Lately I've sensed some changes in you, how you see the world, and I think it has to do with your new gift. Maybe also your meditation. You've become more sensitive to values."

"When we're together, I keep wanting to share things with you—things that are really important to me—but I have to be careful, because I'm not the only one who could be hurt." She blew her nose into a tissue she held in her free hand. "See? I can't even talk about that!"

He lifted her hand that he had been holding, and kissed it. "But I noticed that you blew your nose with one hand so you wouldn't have to let go of mine."

Meredith smiled and looked down. "Probably got snot all over my blouse!"

He pulled another tissue from the box and closely examined her blouse, dabbing here and there, his expression serious.

She grabbed his head in her arms and squeezed it to her breast. "If you're going to touch me, don't put a tissue between us!"

He waited a long time before he tried to move, his voice muffled. "I can't breathe!"

"Well," she said lightly, "we all have to make choices."

The spell was broken, but the issue remained.

Scene 62

The email message was terse: "THK U SSSat-day." Meredith didn't recognize the sender's address, but she assumed that Janet had met with George and the group was to meet on Saturday at their usual time and place. That meant, she inferred, that Janet was accepted, at least so far. She phoned Dennis, not wanting to have two email messages that might be linked if someone were monitoring her messages.

It turned out that Dennis knew about the meeting. She didn't mention Janet to him. They agreed to find their own ways to the meeting.

On Saturday, she made an excuse to Doug—which he unhesitatingly accepted—and caught a bus to Silver Spring. From there she caught a cab to the house.

On the way, she thought about how careful they all were to try to protect themselves and each other. It was as though they were revolutionaries, struggling to stay underground. As far as she knew, no one in the group had ever been questioned directly by the CIA; a few strangers had attended meetings in the past and some members had thought they were snoops. Meredith guessed that some of them would be watching Janet closely.

Mary greeted her warmly at the door, and said that George was picking Janet up. Inside, Meredith felt as though she were in the comfort of "almost family." Everyone was talking, and the mental noise was just as chaotic. A few greeted her by name and went back to their conversations.

Here were people whom she could trust and who professed many of the values she was beginning to believe in again. The cynicism she felt about D.C. was absent here, even though Silver Spring is largely a bedroom community for the Capitol City. If the group had first formed out of mutual recognition of a few readers, it seemed to her that it would have formed nearer to the university, where counterculture typically centers. But when she asked several people, she found that the geographical distribution of members of the group didn't seem to have a central place of origin. They came from all over. That told her that the phenomenon that they all shared was widespread. Somehow, that thought was exciting. She no longer felt alone.

Dennis greeted her with a hug, and introduced her to "another reader from Baltimore" whom he had found and persuaded to come with him. "I still call out," he said, laughing, "every time I'm out in public. Ginnie just came up to me and said 'hello' without batting an eye!"

"I'm glad it's working."

"Who is this woman you brought?" he asked Meredith, looking around.

"I didn't bring her, and she's not here yet. I only introduced her to George."

"How did you meet her?"

Meredith grinned. "It's a long story. I'll tell you sometime." She turned to Ginnie and offered her hand. "Good to meet you."

"Dennis has talked a lot about you," Ginnie said.

Meredith looked at Dennis. "I hope it's all good."

"He's in love with you."

"Oh." Meredith's face became warm.

Dennis smiled, but said nothing.

Just then they heard loud voices at the front door. George and Janet had just entered. As they came into the room, Janet saw Meredith and smiled shyly. She was being towed to the center of the room by George, who was trying to get the attention of the noisy crowd.

Meredith marveled at how the mental noise in the room also quieted as the group gave George their attention.

"Some of you know about Janet," he said. "To the rest, she has a special qualification to be here." He paused. "She has an implant."

There was a murmur in the group that Meredith couldn't interpret.

"She says that it's going to be removed. She's getting out of the Company. I assured her that she can still be one of us, because she knows the value of what we do."

A woman spoke up, "I hope you won't mind if I'm direct," she said, "but many of us distrust the CIA. How do we know we can trust you?"

"I don't blame you," Janet said. "All I can do is be straight with you, and let you decide." She looked directly at the woman. "And I appreciate that you are honest with me."

"Are you carrying a wire?" asked a young man. "You know, ..."

Janet smiled at him, spread her feet wide on the floor, and slowly lifted her arms over her head, her hands clasped—revealing that perfect body that had so intimidated Meredith. "Check it out," she said to him quietly.

"Holy shit!" whispered Dennis, standing next to Meredith.

"Okay," the other young man said, his voice trailing off, "I'll take your word for it."

George said to Janet, "I guess you're going to attract some suspicion for a while." Then to the group, he said, "Janet told me that she does not like it that she is hired to deceive people. That tells me a lot about her."

Janet, who had resumed normal posture, said, "I took the job in the Company because I thought I could do something for the country, and I didn't want to go into the military. But after five or six years of it, I'm burned out. This implant is as much a curse as it is a benefit to me personally—I guess you all know what I mean—and I'm ready to give it up.

"One thing I've learned, though, is that most people—me included—hide much of ourselves, out of fear, I guess. Being able to sense other people's thoughts changes the dynamic of interpersonal relationships. We become more honest. It's much harder to hide our thoughts and feelings, so we become used to being kind of transparent. I think it's a good thing. I think it's a wonderful change, and I'd like to help it along. It seems that more and more people are discovering that they have this gift, so maybe it's an evolutionary thing, a step up in our development. I don't know. I'd like to be part of finding out."

A woman asked, "I understand that if you resign from the CIA, you'll have to have your implant removed."

"Yes," said Janet.

"Then you'll no longer have the ability?"

"I guess so."

"Then you won't any longer be one of us, will you?"

Janet's shoulders slumped. "That's the bad part. I do want to be part of whatever this is that you are doing. I have had the experience, and I believe that it's a good thing."

"We have not excluded people who are not readers," George said. "Some come out of curiosity, but most of those eventually leave because they can't feel a part of what we're doing. They don't know what it's like."

"I don't know if I'll eventually feel too different to stay," Janet said. "I've had the ability long enough now that it feels 'normal' to me. And I really want to be involved!"

"But aren't you sworn to secrecy?" asked someone in the group.

"I'm sworn to protecting very specific secrets. I'd be sent to prison if I revealed those things. I can do that—I can honor my commitment and still have a life outside." She looked down at the floor then looked up at the group, and continued, "What you people are doing, at least from what George has told me, is much more important to us as citizens and as human beings than what I was assigned to do for the government. I don't regret what I've done with this thing," she said, tapping the side of her head, "but I'm not proud of most of it. I need to change my life."

There were murmurs of approval.

Meredith stepped up beside Janet, facing the group. "When Janet asked me to help her contact you, I had misgivings. I did not—I still do not—trust the Company, and I admit I was suspicious. There's something precious about what's going on here, and I didn't want to put that into jeopardy. Janet and I have a bit of personal history, which I knew should not affect what happened, so I needed to have my sense of her checked out by someone else. So I put her in touch with George, because I respected his judgment. I'm glad he had the same reaction to her that I did." She faced Janet. "I'm glad you're here."

Janet turned to her and hugged her. "Thank you!"

Meredith turned back to the group. "I'm really new here, and I'd like to hear some of your personal experiences—like how long have you been reading, and how you learned to cope with it. I had a really hard time with it at first, but I'm beginning to get the hang of it. It's like a skill, isn't it?

Several people spoke up with their interpretations of the experience, and soon the conversations broke into small groups. George, the nominal leader, didn't attempt to bring the entire group to focus on one thing. At first, Meredith felt frustrated with the lack of focus, but soon she was exchanging ideas with different people, going with the flow of various conversations. She kept an eye on Janet, however, and on Dennis and Ginnie, to make sure they seemed comfortably included in the activity.

One older man, who appeared to her to be an academic, probably a professor, spoke at length to a small cluster about the theoretic aspects of reading other people's thoughts. "Neurologists have for a long time been able to pin-point locations in the brain of different kinds of mental activity, and in some cases actually stimulate some kinds of response with electrical probes."

Meredith listened at the edge of this cluster as he continued. "The implants used by the CIA are actually little radio receivers. What that means, of course, is that the electrical activity of our brains does not stop at our skulls, but radiates out for some distance. That is a remarkable finding. It also means that some of us can tune into those external fields, without the use of the implant receivers. At first glance it seems almost miraculous, but if you stop to think about how we hear, for example, sensing minute periodic changes in air pressure and decoding those changes into what we describe as sound, then brain waves do not seem so strange. We not only sense the sine waves of varying sound pressure, we can hear multiple tones at the same time, translating the resulting complex wave form into music in our heads. It's only been in the last couple of centuries that we've had the mathematical tool—Fournier analysis—to appreciate what our brains have been able to do for many centuries."

This, Meredith found, was far beyond what she could understand or what she was interested in. Someone else could perhaps explain technically how she could read other people's thoughts, but she was interested in the psychological effects. Dennis had told her that when he first began reading, he was so disoriented that he was afraid he would vomit. After a while, it became for him a nuisance—enough of one to make him consider suicide to escape it. Having discovered others with the same ability—"gift"—he could accept it more, and even begin to appreciate how it expanded his sensing of the social environment.

For her, it seemed a matter of learning to control the perceptual aspects, to be more selective in picking up the thoughts and fragments of other people, to be able to identify individuals in a way that was equivalent to identifying different voices. What the professor had said about the analogy to hearing made sense to her, for she knew that musicians, for example, spent years learning to hear more accurately and more selectively in order to make music. She had attended concerts with friends who could hear discrepancies and anomalies that were completely beyond her perceptual abilities.

She returned home that evening with her head swimming from the overload of information she had tried to absorb. She also felt even more secure, personally, as she became familiar with the individuals in the group.

Scene 63

The next morning, after her meditation and run, Meredith opened her computer to check for a message from Doug. Although he hadn't said he was going away on assignment, they hadn't spoken for a couple of days. The problem that they had discussed—her feeling of distance from him because of his job—hadn't seemed to be troublesome when they parted, but her old fears lurked in the background, especially during meditation.

There was nothing on their private web site, but she had several emails waiting for her. One was suggesting that she check out the blog "Readers Anon." The double-entendre caught her attention—"anon" as "anonymous" and also as "in a little while." The idea that her gift was a expanding phenomenon appealed to her.

The blog seemed to be the work of a young person, who signed with a pseudonym. The latest entry was about the meeting in Silver Spring the previous day!

Without specifying the location, it read: "The CIA was upstaged in a recent meeting of readers in the East. One reader admitted to having a device implanted in her skull, which suggested a connection with the infamous spy network, but she said she was planning to have it removed. The prospect of losing her ability to read did not deter her from the decision, she said, but she wanted to remain a part of the movement that promises a more open and peaceful future for the human race."

Meredith caught her breath. *My God, they're outing her! The Company is sure to find out. Poor Janet!*

She called Doug. "Have you heard anything about the other woman?"

He didn't answer immediately, but finally said, "Yes."

"Can you talk about it?"

"Not now."

"Can I come over?"

"Sure. I'd like that."

"Okay, bye."

On the subway to Arlington, Meredith worried about the development. Could Doug tell her anything? Was Janet in trouble? In danger? In less than a week, the young woman had gone from being "the other woman" to someone she cared about. Meredith could only admire the way Janet handled the questions from the group, especially her unself-conscious display of her body at the suggestion by the young man that she might be carrying a recording device. It reminded her of her own youth, when her body was her ticket to just about anything she chose to do. Later, she had decided that it was a weapon she didn't need. She remembered a line in a book about Gandhi that said something about our assumptions being "weapons we never bought," and how one has to learn how to "throw them away and go, defenseless and undefending, toward whatever the truth may be." She hadn't thrown away her beauty—although she knew women who had—but she could stop using it as a weapon. It pleased her that she could stand before Doug and say, "What you see is what you get," without worrying about whether he thought her beautiful.

Seeing Janet in her gym outfit did make her pause, knowing that Doug had held that body in his arms. Even so, for some reason she didn't think of Janet's body as a "weapon." Dolly, who was closer in age to herself, clearly used her body to get what she wanted—which was male attention and hope for love. Meredith couldn't judge Dolly, however, for she was a true friend. One didn't judge one's friends.

Doug was wearing his sweats when he opened the door. "I was hoping I would see you today," he said.

"You could have called me, you know." She didn't intend it to be a critical reply, but she herself reacted to it. *I'm sorry. That didn't come out right.*

Sounds like both of us are a little tentative today. Don't be sorry. Love means never having to say ...

I am sorry. I hate feeling separate from you!

"Okay," he said." Let's start over. Good day, madam. May I kiss you?"

She giggled, skewing his kiss. She backed off, her face sobering. "Close the door."

When he complied, she put her arms around his neck and kissed him again, passionately and lingeringly.

Then they walked hand in hand to his sofa. "You're worried about Janet," he said.

"Yes. You said you've heard something."

"Nothing official—which is why I can tell you. Someone posted a blog that mentioned her. Not by name, but it was easy to guess."

"You people even watch the blogs?"

He smiled. "Of course. That one's been up for several months. I don't think it's dangerous for her, but I'm sure it will be noted in her file."

"Doug, I'm scared for her!"

He smiled again. "Quite a change from the 'angry wife.'"

"She's a good person. I like her a lot. I was suspicious at first, but she's very open. I can't imagine how she could carry out one of your 'assignments.'"

"From what I've heard, she's very good."

"At spying, you mean." Meredith's eyebrow raised ever-so-slightly.

Doug laughed. "That, too."

Meredith punched his shoulder, and they both laughed.

"Seriously," she said, "could they disappear her or whatever they do?"

"We're speculating, you understand. I don't know anything. As long as she doesn't give away any secrets, she's probably okay. Although, as in any business, a dissatisfied employee usually doesn't get recommended for advancement."

"I wish," Meredith said thoughtfully, "we could talk about all this."

"Me, too," he said. "Something seems to be happening."

"In the Company?"

"All over."

"Tell me!"

He shook his head. "I can't. Besides, from what I know of you, you probably know more than I do."

"Are they following me?"

"Sorry. I can't say."

"They are. Like that line in one of Simon and Garfunkle's songs, 'Somebody's tapped my phone!'"

"You're sure?"

"No. I get really paranoid, though."

"I can't imagine anyone considering you a threat to national security."

"So why would they care if there are people like me who can do what it takes them a million dollars worth of electronics?"

"I can give you the answer that a guy in "Wired" magazine came up with—unsupported by evidence, by the way. First, the Company had a monopoly on this technology, and now, apparently, they don't. They are understandably nervous. The people they send out to listen in on other people may not be as secure as they once were. They may have to up the ante in the mind-reading arms race. Second, what you can do, and what an increasing number of people seem to be able to do, is mind-boggling, if you'll pardon the pun. Potentially, it can change the relationships that people have with each other—and not just in diplomatic circles."

"When we first began seeing each other," Meredith said, "I felt really vulnerable. I said it was okay ..."

"You said you didn't have anything to hide."

"Yes. But it made me nervous, because I didn't know how much you knew about me. And Dolly said the same thing—she was really intimidated for a while."

"But now that you and I are on fairly even terms?"

"Actually, it's a blast! I love that we can communicate privately even in public places. It's better than being able to speak a different language, because other people aren't even aware of it."

"But now," he continued, "it's increasingly possible that we'll not have that privacy, as more and more people—assuming that happens—can read. That's why it's likely to cause major changes in the way people relate to each other."

"It seems to me that it will make people more honest—won't it?"

"On the surface, anyway. But people are bound to figure out how to hide their thoughts, or disguise them, or something. People may gradually get more honest, generally, but there will always be those who will try to beat the system."

Meredith pouted. "I guess I'm still a product of the Counterculture." She sighed a long sigh. "I'm still pretty naïve, even after all these years."

"I'm grateful for that!"

She looked at Doug thoughtfully. "Does that mean that you'll soon be out of a job?"

He shrugged. "Remember—everything I've said today is what you can read on the Internet. There is not much actual research on this phenomenon yet, at least that's available in the academic journals. I'm sure a lot of people are up to their armpits in grant writing these days."

"So I'm wasting my energy?"

"Hell, no. Stay with your work. Watch your mind work. You're a remarkable woman. You have a lot to offer, no matter how all this pans out. Think about how far you've come in learning to do what you do. Some people just get freaked out. Some go nuts. Somebody has to help those people who don't have the gift—they are the real danger."

"What do you mean?" She tilted her head, and Doug was distracted by that little earring, swinging in the hollow of her neck.

"It could become a social issue, or a political issue—probably both. It's like the haves and the haves not. I'm not too sure it won't become a very hot political issue, and I have no idea how it might go. You said Dolly was intimidated—think how a rural Midwest town might react to a rumor that someone in their midst could read their thoughts!"

"The Salem Witch Trials."

"Exactly."

Meredith slumped down in the sofa. "I didn't come over here to hear about a civil rights war all over again."

He held her hands in his.

"So Janet's fate could be one of the less important things I need to think about," she said.

"No. You'll worry about your friends anyway. And the world is going to change in some way—in any number of ways—and you and I and everybody else will adapt to those changes."

"Do you keep vodka in your freezer?" she said, getting up from the sofa and heading for the kitchen.

"Pour one for me, too, please."

She returned a few minutes later and stood over him, glasses in both hands. "You know I love you?"

He reached for one of the glasses. "I am getting that impression."

She sat on the floor across the coffee table from him. "You're so left-brained and logical. You can calmly assess a situation that makes my head spin." She propped her head with one elbow on the table. "But you still care for people."

"I wish I could be as open and spontaneous as you," he said, smiling. "There's a saying, 'reduced to tears' that to me isn't 'reduced' at all—on the contrary. I admire that ability, I suppose, because it's beyond me."

"You have never cried?"

"Not that I can remember."

"Did they ask you that when you applied for your job?"

He laughed. "I don't think so, but they had other ways to test my stoicism."

"I can imagine. But what about the time your wife told you she couldn't wait for you any longer? What did you feel then?"

"I was sad, and angry, and I felt helpless being so far away. I couldn't blame her, though."

Meredith looked at him for a long time.

"If you left," he said, looking into her eyes, "I'd die."

She got up from the floor and came around the table. "Stand up, please." She put her arms around his neck and said softly, "I will never leave you."

They stood there, embracing, their lips pressed together, until their mind pool registered only one thought, and then they turned and went to the bed.

Scene 64

It was after lunch when Meredith's cell phone buzzed. She looked at it to see who was calling. "Unknown number," was all it said, and when she opened the phone there was a text message; "CHK MSG."

It must be Doug, she thought, telling her that he'd left a message on their private web site. But she didn't dare go into the Internet from work. She was sure all computer activity was monitored by her employer. Doug wouldn't have sent her that text message if it weren't important, so she made an excuse to her supervisor, waved at Dolly and left for home.

All he had written was, "TOW is gone! ???"

TOW—"The Other Woman!" Meredith's heart was pounding. Her worst fear, that Janet would face some kind of reprisal, was now a real possibility. Doug's reassurances had become irrelevant.

She typed a response, "Goddamn them!" and signed off.

Meredith paced her apartment. The cockatiel screeched at her, but she couldn't pay any attention to the bird. There **had** to be something she could do to find out what had happened!

In the kitchen, she paused long enough to take the vodka bottle from the freezer and quaff from it. Back at her computer she sent George a message: "YNG WMN MISSING." She was pretty sure he would know what that meant.

She couldn't contact Doug—he'd made it clear that it was an official secret that he had disclosed, and it would not be safe to say more. She would have called Dolly just to let off steam, but decided that it wouldn't be fair to her friend. Not yet, anyway. Every ten minutes she checked her email and Doug's private web site.

Her phone rang. It was George, calling from a pay phone. She told him what she knew, and that she was worried. He knew about the blog from the day before. "I'm sure he didn't think about what might happen from his blog entry," he said. "He's young. I will call him, however, to make sure he doesn't compound the problem. And I'll let you know if I hear anything."

"Thank, you, George. Right now I can't think straight. I'm frantic."

"Understandable. Wish I could help."

After a second swig from the vodka bottle, she went from frantic to devastated. Throwing herself on her bed, she cried for a long time.

Telling herself that Janet must have known the risks before she asked to be introduced to the group, she tried to gather herself and think reasonably. Janet had said that she had family out West someplace. Maybe she had flown away before the Company got to her. But her implant had a GPS circuit in it, so they could trace her wherever she went. There was no way she could disappear so that they couldn't find her.

If the CIA had spirited her off someplace, why would they want to? Maybe she had knowledge that made her a lot more important to them than Meredith had thought. Would they kill her to keep her quiet—or to keep her out of the hands of some other government?

For a minute, Meredith's anger and anxiety transferred to Doug. "He says he cares, but he's just like the rest of those bastards! He's more afraid of them than he cares about people!"

Then she stopped. The alcohol was taking over her reason. In the midst of her emotional state she could still see that she needed to let it go for a while, maybe even meditate to clear her mind. But after five minutes on her cushion, she gave up. Thinking was out of the question. All she could do was feel. So she lay on her bed and looked at the ceiling, letting all her fear and anger take charge of her mind. "Do not **do** anything in this state, she told herself. "It will only make it worse!" A part of her mind stayed present. *This is madness. This is what they mean by madness. I am not mad. I only have to wait.*

Images roared through Meredith's mind, of Janet with her perfect body strapped to a table, diabolical surgeons ripping the implant out of her bloody head. *It's my fault! I should have said I couldn't help her! Now I've killed her!*

She sat up on the side of the bed. Her head was spinning from the alcohol, but she managed to get to her computer and check her email one more time. Nothing. She sprawled across the bed again and fell asleep.

It was dark outside when she awoke, nauseated. Running to the bathroom, she threw up and retched repeatedly. She hadn't eaten anything, so there was nothing to throw up except a bit of liquid.

At least her rage had lessened. Her stomach hurt. She sat on the bathroom floor clinging to the toilet until she was satisfied that the spell of nausea was past. She could hear her phone in the bedroom. Groaning, she made her way on her hands and knees to the phone. The call was gone, leaving only the record, "Unknown Number." She waited for another ring that would indicate that Doug had left a message. He had, several of them.

"I've been calling you. Where are you? I'm coming over."

She pressed his speed dial.

"Meredith," he answered, "are you okay?"

"Not exactly," she said.

"I'm almost at your building. Hang on, Love."

She got enough energy to sit down at her desk. When he tapped on the door, she struggled to let him in.

"My God, you look awful!" he said.

"I lost it." She began to cry again. "I totally lost it!"

Doug held her for a few minutes until he felt her go limp. "Whoa!" he said, "C'mon, let's get you to bed."

He helped her stagger to the bed, still sobbing. After a while, she lay quietly, just looking at him. He sat on the edge of the bed, his face showing worry. "Tell me," he said quietly.

She put her hand over her mouth. "I threw up," she admitted.

"Yes, I can tell. I'll bring you some water. Have you eaten anything?"

She shook her head.

"We'll fix that. Now tell me what's going on."

"I got your message, and I just lost it. I feel like it's my fault!"

"Meredith, it isn't your fault! I just wanted to give you a heads up, because somebody might be contacting you." He went into the kitchen and returned with a glass of water and a wet dish cloth. Gently wiping her face, he said, "Nobody knows where she is."

She took the glass of water and rinsed out her mouth, then spit it back into the glass. "Do you think they took her?"

"No. At least, everybody in the office seemed worried about her. If somebody at headquarters did something, they would at least have told Tony not to worry."

231

"Then where …?"

"First, let's get some food in you. You must have really hit the vodka. Think you can hold it down?"

She nodded and tried to sit up.

"Stay there. I'll make you some toast."

When he returned, she was sitting up on the edge of the bed, a wan smile on her face. "So much for your 'remarkable woman'" she said hoarsely.

"Doesn't change anything." He handed her a slice of toast.

"Where do you think she is?" Meredith nibbled on the toast.

"I don't have the foggiest idea," he said. "But we can relax the security precautions a little bit."

"Why?"

"I've been assigned to see if I can track her down. Tony knows that I will be working with you and anybody else you might suggest."

"You mean they know that I introduced her to the group?"

"Yes. They were watching her, but nobody thought she would just disappear."

"Her GPS would give her away, wouldn't it?"

"Yes. She was a pretty straight operative, and very smart. She knew what she could do or not do."

Meredith wolfed down the other slice of toast. "More," she said.

He laughed. "How much did you drink?"

She shrugged. "No idea."

"I could put a frozen dinner in the microwave."

She nodded. "Did you eat?"

"I'll make it two."

He went back to the kitchen, and Meredith followed him, sitting down immediately at the table. She leaned her head on her arm and looked at him sideways. "So, Mister CIA—what's the plan?"

Doug laughed and pressed the start button. "Our first guess is that she panicked when she found out about the blog."

"She told me she had family out West someplace."

"Montana. But we don't think she would go there. It's more likely she's holed up someplace close by. She might try to contact you."

"Can you track her GPS?"

He looked at her. "Interesting thing—she's gone from the system. Her GPS doesn't reply."

Meredith sat up suddenly. "Does that mean she could be dead?"

"Not unless her implant was also smashed somehow …"

"Oh, Doug!"

The microwave dinged, and Doug took the two boxes out. In a moment, he had served them both steaming on plates, and handed Meredith a fork. He sat down opposite her. "Let's begin with the most likely things, okay?"

"Her murder is not likely?"

"No."

"I wish I could believe that."

"That's why you have been suffering."

She looked up at him. "Yes, that's true." She picked at her dinner.

"Meredith, this is not your fault. It is not your fault. It is not your fault. It is …"

"Okay, I get it. My head gets it. My gut does not."

"She met some people on Saturday, right?"

Meredith looked at him intently.

"Meredith, we're both on the same side here."

"Yes, she met some people. I don't know who, except for one or two. I've already contacted one of them."

"Can we talk to that person?"

"I can find out. They are very suspicious." She stood up.

"Finish your dinner. And then we'll take a drive."

"This makes me very nervous." She picked up her plate and went to the desk. There were no emails waiting, so she sent one to George. "We have help. Can you meet with us?"

In the time it took her to eat a bite of food, a reply came back. "U of M train stop 9: 05."

"He must have been at his computer," she said. "The other message I sent him, he phoned me back from a pay phone."

"We'll drive. We can get there much quicker."

"How quick?"

He looked at his watch. "Eight thirty."

She sent George another message. "Driving. Same place 8:30?"

"Yes."

She turned to Doug. "He's a good person. A professor. He might show up disguised."

Doug's eyebrows went up. Meredith smiled. "You'll see."

When they arrived at the train station, there were only two people on the platform. Doug started to get out of the car, but Meredith put her hand on his arm. She opened the window of the car. *If you can hear this, say hello.*

Doug looked at her strangely. But in a few seconds, the reply came: *Hello.*

"My God!" Doug said.

Meredith smiled at him. "George needs to be discreet."

One of the men on the platform walked over to their car. Meredith waved at him through the window. He bent over so he could see Doug. He was wearing his beard and toupee.

"We are safe," Meredith told him. "Do you want to talk in the car?"

George looked at the other man still on the platform. Meredith recognized him and waved. He waved back, but did not approach.

When George got into the car, Meredith introduced the two men. She was twisted around in her seat, her hand on the top of the seatback. George kept looking at Doug.

Doug said, "Things are pretty much out in the open. We want to get Janet back, but she's not in any trouble. We're just concerned for her safety."

George looked at Meredith without speaking.

"George, he wants to help us. Honest."

I really want to help, Doug thought.

You're a reader, too?

Yes. I have an implant.

George put his hand on the door handle.

"George—do you trust me?" Meredith asked.

He didn't respond.

"Please, George! Can you tell us if she's safe? Just that much?"

He nodded slowly.

Meredith burst into tears. It affected both men. George put his hand on hers.

"Goddamn it, she needs help!" She pulled a tissue from her purse and blew her nose.

"Look," said Doug, "I know that the Company does not always operate on the up-and-up. But right now we're concerned about Janet. We know she's been through a lot. There hasn't been any official action taken—they gave me permission to try to find her, and they know that Meredith helped her to contact you all. Nobody's in any trouble here!"

George tried to operate the window next to him, but Doug had shut off the engine. Opening the door, George waved to the other man to come to them.

"They want to see Janet," George told him when he neared the car. "I think they are okay."

The other man said, "Let me contact her." He stepped away from the car and made a phone call. In a minute, he came back to the car and offered the phone to Meredith.

"Hello," Meredith said, then burst into tears again. Struggling to regain composure, she said finally, "I've been worried sick! Are you okay?" She listened for a moment, then said, "Doug is with me, and you're not in trouble, but we want to see you and talk with you. Will you do that?" After another moment, she said, "Janet, please trust us! We will not abandon you!" A moment later, she closed the phone and handed it back. "She'll see us."

George made room for the other man, and gave Doug the directions. Twenty minutes later, they pulled up in front of a modest home. As they got out of Doug's car, George touched Meredith's arm. "I'm way out of my depth here. I'm trusting you."

She turned and hugged him. "Thank you!"

They were greeted at the door by a woman Meredith had never seen before. She indicated that they should go into a room at the side. There sat Janet and two other people from the Silver Spring group. All had serious looks on their faces. Janet was wearing some kind of helmet.

Meredith spoke first. "This is bizarre," she said. "Janet, Doug has been given the assignment to help find you. You are not in trouble—there are no charges against you."

Doug said, "Tony has been worried about you, too. He gave me free rein to find you and make sure you are okay. That's all. He knows that

Meredith is with me. Nobody else is tracking us—or you, so you can take that silly thing off your head."

That brought chuckles from Meredith and Janet, who removed the helmet. Meredith turned to Doug. "That's how she disappeared from the GPS?"

"Yes."

Janet started to hand the helmet to Doug, but he backed away. "I don't want to see it," he said.

"You still have to be careful?" asked Meredith.

"Could come up later," he answered.

Meredith turned to Janet. "Tell me what happened!"

"Someone sent me an email about a blog, and I panicked. I thought for sure that the Company would come down on me. I had been so naïve, thinking that I could attend that meeting without being found out!"

"Janet," said Doug, "we were worried about you. They knew about the blog, but they had known about the meeting anyway. It was just that you didn't show up at work. I didn't tell anyone about our conversation except Meredith after you met with her. So they didn't know you wanted to get out until the blog was posted."

"I thought what you said in your office meant that they might try to kill me!"

"Oh, shit! No, that's not what I meant!" Doug looked defeated. "I was trying to say 'be careful' because you might be getting into something you were not prepared for. I'm sorry!"

"Mister Spock!" Meredith broke in, "sometimes you are so much in your head that you can't feel what others need!"

That made Janet laugh, but Meredith and Doug were not laughing. The others just looked quizzically at them.

Doug's eyes were misty as he turned to Meredith. "I'm sorry," he said softly. She threw her arms around him. *Me, too!*

Me, too, came from Janet. Then she said, "Okay, now what?"

Meredith looked at the beautiful agent and shook her head, smiling. "And I was telling Doug that I couldn't figure out how someone like you could be a CIA agent."

Janet's face fell.

"Now I see. My hat's off to you."

"I don't understand," said Janet.

"You've got balls."

The two women grinned at each other.

George spoke up, "Okay, now what?"

Doug pursed his lips. "If Janet will go back to work tomorrow morning, my understanding is that nothing will be said to her, and no mention of all this will be in the record. Janet, if you submit your resignation, they will require you to have your implant removed immediately, and your resignation will be processed like anybody else's. In spite of what I said to you a couple of weeks ago, the surgery should go without any problems, and you will simply be left without your ability to read the thoughts of others, but otherwise have no aftereffects. The surgery takes ten minutes, and they will let you go as soon as the anesthesia wears off. I will personally drive you home."

"No, you won't," said Meredith. "I will. Janet and I have a lot to talk about." She turned to Janet. "With your permission?"

"Thank you," Janet replied. "I guess you'll be more comfortable ..."

"Goddamn it, Woman! Forget that! It's history! Okay?"

Janet ducked her head. "Okay," she said softly, and smiled. Then she handed the helmet to someone, went over to Meredith and hugged her.

"We'll see you all soon," Meredith said to the group members as they started to leave.

"You two need a ride to the station?" asked Doug.

"No, thanks, said George. "We'll get there."

On the way back to D.C., Meredith and Janet sat in the back of the car and talked softly, woman to woman.

Scene 65

Janet's separation from the Company was quick and without incident. The reason given in her resignation letter was "for family reasons." She was sent to Walter Reed Hospital that afternoon, and her implant removed. Her blond hair hid the incision, and by dinner time Meredith had picked her up and taken her home in a cab. She never returned to the office on the thirty-fifth floor. Her personal effects there were delivered to her home by courier.

Meredith ordered Chinese takeout for their dinner, and she stayed the night on Janet's sofa. In the morning, after fixing her breakfast, Meredith left for work, making her promise to call if she needed anything at all, and to keep her phone close because Meredith would be checking in on her. Janet assured her that she would be all right. Her head hurt a little, and she was having trouble concentrating.

When Meredith got to her desk, Dolly immediately came around and sat down. "Okay, what's up?"

"A small crisis," Meredith answered. "The 'other woman' resigned."

"Oh, my God!"

"She simply didn't want to do what they had her doing anymore."

"So it didn't have anything to do with Doug."

"No. She got scared, though, and disappeared briefly. Doug and I found her, and she came back to resign properly."

Dolly crossed her legs and leaned back. "Funny, I have the feeling that there's more to it than that."

Meredith smiled. "You may not be able to read my thoughts, but you sure do a good job of reading me, period."

"You were in a state when you left here on Monday. You just waved at me, didn't say a word."

"I had just found out that she was missing. I thought I was responsible."

"So what'd you do?"

"Went home and tried to think of how to find her." Meredith made a face. "I was afraid she might be dead. It was a terrible afternoon. Finally, Doug came over and we worked together and located her."

"Nothing I could do to help, I guess." Dolly leaned back farther in the chair and looked down her nose at Meredith.

"Dolly, at the time I wasn't thinking straight. I drank a bunch of vodka and passed out and got sick. I was afraid the Company was behind it, and I didn't want to get you mixed up in it."

"Exactly the time I should have been there! I could have held your head while you threw up, and wiped your face off."

Meredith laughed. "I forgot to eat, so the booze went right to my head."

"So where is she now?"

"At home. I stayed over with her last night after her surgery."

"She had surgery? Oh, that's right, the implant."

"It left her confused—as you'd expect after brain surgery. But they say she'll be okay in a few days."

"What would that be like, to have a thing planted in your brain and all at once you can listen in on other people's thoughts. And then to have it taken out, and you're normal again."

"When you first got your contacts, didn't they give you trouble for a while?"

"It's like that, huh?"

"With me, it came on slowly. I wasn't even aware of it for a while. It was when I realized what was really happening that I got confused. That young boy, Dennis, who found me on the street? He said that when it came on him he thought he was going crazy. He was hearing voices that were not his. I can identify with that, although because of Doug I knew a little bit. It was still very weird."

"But now, it's normal for you."

"No, not normal. I miss the quiet of my mind. Whenever there are people around, it's like a henhouse in my head."

"You know, when I'm around you I forget that you are continually hearing my thoughts. We just have ordinary conversations."

"I work at that," Meredith said. "I don't want to hear your thoughts, because I trust you to be honest with me. Doug and I have a different way of 'talking'—a lot of it goes on in our minds, without ever being said."

"That must be weird."

"It's not anymore. Especially when we're at home—his apartment is a huge loft over in Arlington, and our minds can be very quiet there—it's like a common pool between us. Every thought is shared automatically. And we know each other well enough that we can tell the difference between his and mine. But they are all **ours**. Does that make sense?"

"In a way, but it feels weird. Do you know the source of the word 'conspiracy?' To conspire is to breathe together. You have a real conspiracy."

"Wow! That's cool! It really fits!" Meredith was delighted. She'd have to tell Doug about it.

"'Course, you won't want the CIA to hear that. It's probably not their idea of the word."

"Thank you, Dolly. Talking with you helps me sort out my life."

"It's mutual."

They went back to work feeling the warmth of friendship.

Scene 66

Meredith and Doug visited Janet frequently in the following days. As the pain from the surgery went away—and her need for pain medication lessened—Janet became more communicative. She got outside nearly every day, walking as far as she was able. She found it very unsettling, however, to be near people and not be picking up their thoughts. "It's like when your ears are stopped up from a cold or something," she said, "there's something missing."

But both Doug and Meredith noticed a lack of affect in Janet's conversations. It was as though she had been traumatized and could not get in touch with her emotions. Her speech, formerly bright and sensitive to the responses of others, seemed flat and factual. When Meredith told her about her meltdown the day she heard that Janet was missing, Janet seemed strangely unaffected. She remembered that she had fled in panic when the blog had reported her attending the meeting in Silver Spring, and remembered the night Meredith and Doug found her, but she described it as though it had happened to someone else.

Meredith felt that the Company should make sure that their operatives are rehabilitated after undergoing the implant removal. There had been an intensive training period when the chips were implanted, but Janet got nothing more than the usual medical attention from her insurance after she was discharged. She did convince Janet to ask for rehabilitation therapy, and they gave her eight weeks of occupational therapy, but the doctors didn't seem to know what to do for her.

"This is going to be a growing problem for employees of the Company," she told Doug. You operatives are giving a lot for your country, and should be taken care of afterward just as those people in the military get."

"One of the things they make you sign when you go in for the implant is an agreement that you will not sue the government if something goes wrong."

"Do you think anyone knows what happens to people when the implants are removed?"

"I doubt it. Maybe they do."

"Are you going to end up like Janet?" Meredith had not previously brought up the possibility of Doug having his implant removed, but she had thought about it.

He smiled. "Janet isn't finished yet. She's still adjusting. I'd give her a few months to learn her own mind again. Isn't it like training for the Olympics or something? When you quit working out every day, you need to come down gradually, let your body adjust to a new routine."

"It's not exactly coming down gradually to have a piece of your mind surgically removed and sent home as soon as you can stand up."

Meredith found that talking to Janet about it didn't help, either. Janet simply seemed indifferent to the problem. "I'm improving just about every day. I'm able to think well enough to read and write. I can remember just about anything I used to. I can even remember the official secrets that they kept telling me that I should never reveal to anyone."

"So you are still committed to keeping those secrets?"

"Why would I not be? I promised I would."

"Maybe I'm just being a mother or something," Meredith said, laughing. "I feel like I need to take care of you!"

"Thank you." Janet's reply was as flat as ever.

Then one day as the two of them sat in Meredith's apartment, Janet asked, "You know that day I disappeared? You said you had a meltdown. What was that like?"

Meredith was stunned. It was the first time Janet had expressed any interest in what others had gone through or were going through. She had accepted the caretaking with polite thanks, but didn't seem to feel gratitude. "When I learned that you were missing," Meredith said, "I was really afraid the Company had done something to you. Actually, it was before I found out—someone sent me a link to a blog. Oh, that's right, you said you saw the blog."

"Yes. I got scared, too. I thought they would be after me, so I ran."

"Well, I didn't know what to do. I was afraid to call Doug, because he's always been so careful to keep the secrets of the Company even from me. I finally contacted George, but he said he didn't know anything. So I felt I was alone with fear and guilt and shame and I don't know what all. I started drinking to calm my panic. That was a mistake."

"But we didn't know each other very well—why were you so upset?"

"Because I thought I was responsible for it!" Meredith sighed and looked down at her hands. "I've been carrying a lot of guilt for a long time over things I've done. I guess it just triggered all that old stuff."

"Have you tried therapy for that old stuff?"

"Oh, yes. And I meditate, but I'm not very far along in the process. That day I tried to meditate, but gave up right away because all I could see in my mind was how I had caused your death or something."

"One of the things they taught us in training was to meditate—mindfulness meditation—where you sit and just observe whatever comes up. Eventually, you get to see that strong feelings are just that—feelings—and you can distance yourself from them so they don't control you."

"I know about that, a little bit, anyway. I thought I was doing pretty well at it, but that day my panic or whatever it was just took over. I've started reading a book called Mindsight, by some psychiatrist, that shows how the mind works with the brain. He mentions mindfulness meditation, too. I should go back and finish the book."

"That would probably be helpful."

Meredith looked at her. "Janet, are you aware that you don't seem to have any feelings?"

Janet looked at her quizzically. "Is that true? I guess I hadn't noticed."

"And your question just now about how it felt when I had my meltdown—that was the first thing I've heard from you since your surgery that even suggested feelings or empathy."

"Why do you think that is?"

"In the military they talk about Post Traumatic Stress Disorder. It's an effect from being in combat, of having to stuff one's feelings in order to survive, and then after the threat is over, they can't get back to feeling things again."

"I know about that. But I haven't been in combat. I've been a little scared sometimes on my assignments, but I got over it pretty quickly."

"I'm wondering if your feelings have been short-circuited by the surgery to remove your implant."

"Interesting!"

"Maybe it's a left-brain, right-brain thing. Do you know about that?"

Janet touched her head where the implant had been. "The right brain is the feeling side, isn't it? That's where the chip was."

"Maybe it's traumatized or something. Doug said I should give it more time before I go jumping to conclusions."

Janet looked at her. "You talk about me?"

"Of course."

"That's sweet!"

Meredith went over to her and gave her an awkward hug. "That's for two things—one, it's for your caring. Two, it's because you seem to be feeling again!"

"You're a strange person, Meredith."

"How is that?" Meredith was still smiling.

"I slept with your lover, and it doesn't seem to bother you. You still care for me—more than I probably deserve."

"We all deserve to be cared for."

"You said, the first time we met, that you didn't want to hear about what happened between Doug and me. I thought it was because you couldn't handle it."

Meredith laughed. "That reminds me of an old joke."

"Tell me the joke?"

"A long time ago, a couple of monks were making their way back to their monastery, and they came to a stream. A woman was standing on the near side of the stream, afraid to wade across. Now, the monks had taken vows that they would never touch a woman. But one of the monks went up to the woman and offered to carry her across. She gratefully accepted, and the three of them crossed the stream. The woman went her separate way, and the monks headed for the monastery. After a while, the other monk said, 'Brother, I can't believe that you touched that woman—after your vows!' The first monk said, 'Brother, are you still carrying that woman? I put her down a long time ago.'"

Janet doubled over in laughter. "Touché!" she managed to get out.

"Doug and I were only beginning to know each other then. If you were sleeping with him now, I'd cut your heart out. Right after his."

244

Tears were streaming down Janet's face from laughing. "I'll certainly keep that in mind!"

Janet's mental condition continued to trouble Meredith, although she tried to heed Doug's advice about patience. She felt that Janet was clearly disabled emotionally, and she thought about how her relationship with Doug might change if he went through the same procedure. Before she met him, she had thought her life was satisfying, if not perfect. She had disconnected emotionally from Paul and didn't particularly want to enter into another romantic relationship.

Now, she was invested in it. And it seemed that she was invested in these other relationships as well, with Janet and Dolly and Dennis—all calling for a different set of responses. She could no longer just be herself.

Scene 67

"Women have trouble with our work," Tony said, leaning back in his chair. Behind him through the window, fall colors changed the feeling of the city, sneaking around corners of buildings, softening the uniform gray of masonry and glitter of glass. "She seemed smart enough, but she was still a woman."

"I wouldn't have guessed," said Doug, "when we were in the Caribbean, that she would quit. She seemed dedicated."

Tony leaned forward, clasping his hands on his desk. "Where are you in all this?" he asked. "You mixed up with her and with this babe you met downstairs, and now with the people in Silver Spring? Should I be worried about you?"

"No. I've got a job to do, and I'll keep doing it."

"Okay, Doug. I'll take your word for it. But my advice to you is to put some distance from these people."

"Yeah."

"Should I put you in for a transfer? Maybe in London you could focus more clearly on your job."

"I'm okay, Tony," Doug said, but there was a nagging doubt in the back of his mind. He hoped Tony wasn't picking it up.

That evening Meredith was in his loft, making a risotto dish with mushrooms and bell peppers. Doug liked to watch her work in the kitchen, sipping a margarita and talking about ordinary things like food and the weather. "I like the produce we get around here," she said, "although there isn't the variety that we used to get in California."

"In another month most of it will be coming from California."

"Or Mexico. Or Chile."

"When I was growing up," he said, "we ate what we could get locally. In the winter we went to the basement for potatoes and apples and rutabagas."

Meredith stopped in mid-stir and turned to face him. "I'm worried about Janet," she said.

"You worry about your friends."

"Of course I do! But she's still not the same person who came to me for help."

Doug shrugged. "Probably not."

"Don't you care?" Meredith stirred the rice again, frowning.

"Meredith, I have to be careful about how involved I get with Janet. Already, my boss is talking about transferring me away from here. Janet—and that group she turned to—are not safe people for me to be around."

"What about me? Am I not safe for you to be around?"

He stood up and embraced her from behind as she stirred the rice furiously. "As a matter of fact, you are not safe for me to be around. And it has nothing to do with Janet or that group—you distract me from my work every day, just thinking about you!"

"I'm serious!"

He nuzzled her neck. "So am I."

Meredith poured a bit of broth into the pot and continued stirring. "I said I would never leave you."

He stepped away from her. His voice caught as he asked, "What does that mean? Are you having other thoughts?"

She moved the pot off the burner and turned to face him. Her eyes were filling with tears. "I don't know!"

He took her hand and led her toward the sofa. "C'mon, we need to talk about this."

"But I need to put the butter in the risotto or it will be a gooey mess!"

"Forget the risotto. You and I are more important right now."

As they sat down she leaned against him and buried her face in his shoulder. "I love you," she said, her voice muffled. "In the beginning, you were inaccessible—not emotionally, but practically. Your work was a big secret that I couldn't share in, but that was okay. Maybe it just made you mysterious and glamorous. You could read my mind, and that was exciting, even if it was scary."

"And now that you can read mine as well, it's not so exciting?"

"It's more! I love it that we have this private little world between us, that we can share our thoughts, even the senseless little stuff that nobody would bother to talk about."

"But now you're caught up in some kind of cause that we can't share."

"I guess that's it," she said, sitting up straighter so she could see his face. "See, we both know it—our mind pool contains it."

"That's a good way to say it," he said, smiling. "And it's making my boss nervous."

"Fuck your boss!" Her furrowed brow suddenly smoothed again. "No, I didn't mean that! I'm sorry!"

He held her face in his hands, gently wiping her tears with his thumbs. "I'm sorry, too. It's true, I'm torn. I want to be fully in your life—I want **us** to be fully in **our** life together. But I don't know what I could do, outside the Company. It's like they hand me my definition, and I don't have to think about who I am."

"I've always heard that—that men are defined by their work."

"And women are defined by their relationships."

She kissed him lightly and said, "I never wanted to be defined by anything outside myself. Is that selfish?"

"Properly selfish, I'd say."

"I guess it isn't possible. We live in a world with other people. They are a part of us, whether we want it or not."

"These questions never stop. Sometimes I go around and around, trying to make sense of it all."

"Maybe we have to let them go once in a while, and let them sort themselves out a little bit, while we go on with living." She stood up. "While we try to make a meal out of gummy risotto."

He followed her to the kitchen. "Well, it smells wonderful!"

She took two bowls of salad out of the refrigerator and put them on the table. Then, trying to stir butter and Parmesan in to the stiff rice, she said, "Wonderful can wait for a day."

Doug took a bottle of wine from the cupboard, uncorked it and poured two glasses. "Wonderful is always here, even with the doubts and the tears."

"You should write that down. Maybe hang it right there on the refrigerator. I forget."

Scene 68

"You're getting awfully hung up on that guy," Dolly said over the partition. "I mean, he's a great guy and all. But I get the feeling you're not living your own life. Why don't we go out on the town tonight? Breathe some fresh air."

"I can't, Dolly," answered Meredith. "He's coming over tonight for the weekend. We're trying to iron out some of our sharp corners."

"Having 'a relationship talk'? Seems like you've been doing that a lot lately."

"Yeah, we have."

"Okay, But if you change your mind ..."

"Thanks."

When Doug didn't show up when he had said he would, Meredith began to stew. Finally, she went online and checked for a message. Sure enough, there it was: "Maybe another week. Love." He was gone on assignment again.

One minute she was worried that he'd get killed, and the next minute that he'd get involved with another woman. *Lighten up, Meredith!* she told herself.

She called Dolly. "He's gone again. Still want to cruise?"

"You betcha. You up for some jazz at the Red Mango?"

"Sure."

"Meet you there in an hour."

It did feel good to walk into that place filled up with the bluesy saxophone. Dolly was where she was expected to be, at the bar, her long legs crossed, her cleavage presented to the young bartender. She greeted Meredith with a wide grin. "Good for you, Girl!"

Meredith perched on the stool next to her. "I'll have what she's having," she told the bartender.

"I'm having fun. Are you prepared to do that?"

"I am. I can't hold it like you can, though."

"Fun?" Dolly's eyebrow lifted.

"Don't tempt me."

"Oh, oh. We're on the muscle tonight!"

Meredith was wearing a short dress with a very low v-neck, something she had not worn in a long time.

Dolly turned to the bartender. "You get two for one tonight," she laughed.

The bartender smiled. "Okay, two for one drinks, then." He was obviously charmed.

The saxophone growled.

Meredith looked around. The bar was half full, but it was early for the jazz crowd. She liked the music—with familiar undercurrents of old, comfortable melodies, yet unpredictable as the individual musicians played with the theme—she could be open and receptive and still feel that security when bits of the original melodies returned.

She avoided the eyes of men—she wasn't here to pick up someone, only to feel she was not alone. She would have enjoyed being in a group of old friends, like the music, full of familiar feelings but stimulated by fresh conversation. The social environment here was just the opposite: the same, tired old lines from unknown people whom she couldn't be comfortable with. Still, when the inevitable happened, she enjoyed the attention—for a while.

Eventually, she asked Dolly if they could sit at a table instead of the bar. The bartender was disappointed, but Dolly was a good sport about it. She could see that Meredith was not really there to get picked up. Several men approached them at the table and offered to buy them drinks, and politely left when they were politely put off. They invited one pair of men to sit for a while, but when it was clear to the men that they would not leave the bar with them, they looked for more promising game.

By midnight, Meredith pleaded fatigue, and they caught a cab home, the music still ringing in their ears. "I'll call you tomorrow—not before noon," Dolly said as Meredith got out of the cab.

The next morning Meredith returned to her routine, meditating for an hour and running her fourteen blocks. The rest of the day she spent reading "Mindsight."

Dolly did call, and admitted that she had told the cabbie to return to the Red Mango, where she spent several more hours. "Didn't find anyone I was interested in, though," she said.

Reading her book, Meredith came across a passage that seemed to epitomize something she was learning from her relationships with Doug and Dolly:

"Wonderful things happen when people feel felt, when they sense that their minds are held within another's mind."

With Doug, it was literal; their minds merged when they were together—the "mind pool" in which they shared every moment, every thought, every feeling. That's why she felt so secure in his presence. That's why the "fence" she perceived in his mind surrounding his work was so distressing to her. It was the one place she could not share with him.

With Dolly, the shared values and experiences of being female in this society meant that they both understood many of the half-recognized signals the world gives to people, the cues to the feelings of others that women seem more attuned to. "Feeling felt" by another meant that one was not completely alone. And they could both understand the other's needs from last night—her own need to escape the garish game of flirtation and her preference for solitude rather than the company of men who didn't share her mind pool, and Dolly's need to keep trying in the face of all the evidence of impersonal game-playing that always left her empty-hearted. Meredith couldn't fill that need for her: the biological imperative.

Meredith hadn't replied to Doug's message the night before. There was a finality to his cryptic "Maybe another week" that left her empty of response. That next evening, however, she needed to connect somehow with him. So she went on line and wrote:

"I know these things need to be short, to not give away too much, just in case. But I need to connect with you with more than a few short words. I hope it's okay.

Dolly and I went to the jazz place last night. I enjoyed the music and the buzz of alcohol, but the superficial contacts seemed totally opposite to the warmth. It even put Dolly and me into a different place—more polite but distant. She's a good friend, but in that place we were in roles that didn't seem us. I played at being provocative, but it didn't feel right, so I asked to leave early. Feeling desired by strange men is not fun anymore. See what you've done to me?"

She walked to the bistro for dinner, and enjoyed the attention from her friends who just happen to run a restaurant. "Pinot Grigio?" asked the manager.

"Of course."

"I can make you a Middle-Eastern dish of lentils and cracked wheat with caramelized onions on top. A garlic sauce to go on it if you want."

"That sounds wonderful! I didn't know you did Middle-Eastern food."

"Just for you. And a little salad."

She smiled and touched his hand. "Thank you."

He refilled her glass without asking, then returned a few minutes later beaming over his offering.

Scene 69

The phone call surprised her. "If you hear this, say hello."

"Dennis!" How good to hear your voice!"

"I've missed you," he said. You haven't been to a meeting in a long time. People are asking about you."

"Oh, she said regretfully, "I haven't forgotten you. How have you been?"

"Wonderful. You remember Ginnie? You met her the last time you came."

"Of course! She answered your call—your own, personal call."

"Well, she and I are an item now. We have such a good time being together and merging our minds."

"I'm so pleased. So you are feeling more comfortable with your gift?"

"Yes. And we're both sending out the call whenever we're out in crowds. It's so different from when I first met you—it's like we're missionaries or something."

Meredith ignored her initial caution about mentioning Janet. "You remember that last time I was there, I was concerned about someone here in D.C. who wanted to have her implant removed?"

"Yes. Janet. She's come back. It's really strange, being with someone who doesn't read but who knows what it's like."

"Oh, I didn't know she had gone up to meetings."

"Yes, she said you and Doug took such good care of her after her surgery. I think she loves you almost as much as I do!"

"That's sweet, Dennis."

"We've been wondering why you haven't come to a meeting lately."

"I will, Dennis. I've just had a lot to deal with lately."

"I hope you do come," he said. "I have a car now. I'll come down and get you if you want."

"Thank you. I will, I promise!"

"I love you," he said before hanging up.

Meredith sat and thought about Dennis and about the group and about Janet. Right then, she felt disconnected from the group somehow.

She was more concerned about her relationship with Doug. It was going to be a long week—or more.

Scene 70

Doug was strangely quiet when he returned, almost moody. Meredith waited, confident that he would open up to her eventually, or as much as he could. She lavished care on him, cooking meals for him and taking the initiative in planning things for them to do. He didn't resist her suggestions. So on the following Friday they arranged to meet Dolly—and a "friend"—at the Red Mango for dinner and jazz.

When she and Dolly were arranging for their dinner together, Dolly asked her to keep her gift and Doug's implant out of any conversation. "I'm afraid this guy might freak out, and I don't want to spoil the evening."

"Of course," Meredith replied with a twinkle in her eye. "I won't even read your mind."

"But I will read yours."

"I won't think, so then you can't."

"Hah!"

She told Doug that Dennis had called, and that Janet had ventured up to Silver Spring. "I think it's a sign she's recovering her right brain."

"I'm glad."

"She has a good grasp of her own mind. She even realizes that she lost her feeling side, although it doesn't seem to bother her."

"I'm sure Janet will recover."

"You didn't reply to my long message," she said. "Did it bother you that I wrote so much?"

"No, not at all. I was just over my head in the situation—I didn't see it until the day before I got home. I couldn't reply."

Meredith studied his face. "Doug, can you talk about it?"

"No." He sighed. "Okay," he said finally. "I feel like shit."

She waited, watching his eyes.

"I need to talk about it, because I don't know how to feel about it. We were overseas—someplace—having dinner with a diplomat and his girlfriend. We—a female operative and I—were there to find out if the diplomat had gotten some information that our people had slipped into our channels. It seemed like a simple assignment—just listen and determine if he had gotten it. It began as a pleasant dinner in a very nice restaurant, very quiet, so it was easy to read them. You know?"

She nodded.

I liked the guy. He'd lost his wife just a few months ago to cancer, and it was obvious he was still grieving. He had no idea what we were there for—we had just met him that morning, and it was a casual, friendly situation. I was posing as a member of the diplomatic corps, a minor level bureaucrat, more or less like him, and my associate was one of our staff members.

While we were waiting for him to say something that would give it away that he knew the information—it was false information, by the way—we discovered that his companion was not his girlfriend at all. She was assigned by his government to find out if he was on the up-and-up, and she was also a reader."

Meredith looked surprised. "You knew that she was reading?"

"She gave it away to us without knowing it. Right away, we closed off so she couldn't read us. I don't think she ever caught on to us. But it was clear that she was on to him and looking for clues to his disloyalty. He was a sitting duck. Our assignment was to feel him out until we could tell if he had received the information, and we did our job. But in the process, we caused him to give himself away to her."

"But wait—do you know if she has an implant, or is a natural reader?"

"Don't know. We're trying to find out."

"If other countries have agents with implants—that could be a big thing for your people!"

"Sure could. Even if they have people who are 'natural readers,' as you put it."

"You think he was in serious trouble with his government?"

"Big trouble. He'd be charged as a traitor."

"And you weren't trying to snag him."

"Not at all. We were there to test our channels, that's all."

Doug sighed again. "You know, a few months ago when I had to shoot that agent, at least he was a dangerous enemy. I hated that I had to do it, but I didn't have much choice—it was him or me. This guy didn't pose any danger to me—or us—at all. But we may have signed his death warrant, even before we turned in our report. I feel like shit!"

Meredith took his hand in both of hers, and pressed it against her cheek. "I'm sorry."

"I don't need to tell you, do I, that all this can't go any further. It could be my neck on the block."

"Of course. Thank you, Doug, for trusting me with it. I've been worried about you. You've looked so forlorn!"

"You know, I was thinking on the trip back—maybe Janet wasn't so …"

"You don't even need to say it."

"I don't know what to do."

"Maybe listening to some jazz tonight will ease your mind a little. You think?"

"I'm afraid I won't be very good company."

She smiled. "You can sit across the table from a gorgeous female who thinks you are so hot. Will that help?"

Before he could answer, she added, "Make that two gorgeous females."

He smiled for the first time since he returned.

257

Scene 71

This time, Dolly wasn't perched on a bar stool, but was seated at a table near the back of the bar, with a man Meredith hadn't seen before. She waved at them as they pushed through the swinging doors. Dolly's outfit was as provocative as ever, but her manner was much more sedate. "You're just in time!" she gushed. "We just ordered drinks."

As Meredith and Doug sat down, Dolly introduced her companion to them. "This is Everett—Everett, Meredith and Doug."

Everett half stood to shake hands with Doug over the table and mumbled the usual greeting. Meredith shook his hand and smiled at him. Everett was older than the men Dolly usually selected, smooth-shaven with gray hair. He had a shy smile. Meredith guessed that he was in government service, rather than a lobbyist. Perhaps an academic brought to Washington on the coattails of an administrative appointee.

The jazz group was not on stage yet, although their instruments were. A waiter brought drinks to Dolly and Everett, and took orders from the newcomers.

"Meredith works with me," Dolly said. "Doug has a very secret job somewhere." Everett, you tell them what you do—I don't understand it."

Everett took a sip of his drink and cleared his throat. "I'm a special assistant to a consultant on domestic affairs," he said, his voice barely audible above the noise level in the room. "I do research, mostly."

"You come from an academic background?" Meredith asked.

"Ohio University."

"Doug grew up in Cincinnati," she said.

"Oh."

Doug didn't offer anything. Dolly and Meredith exchanged glances.

"Meredith and Doug meditate every day," said Dolly. "And they work out regularly. They aren't like ordinary people." She laughed, and the others smiled or chuckled.

"Everett, tell me about your passion," said Meredith.

He thought for a moment, then said, "I build model ships."

The conversation chugged along like that until the musicians returned, when attention was diverted to the stage. Soon, ordinary conversation became impossible anyway. Meredith and Doug exchanged thoughts.

How are you doing? she asked.

I'm okay. How are you?

I'm not struggling with this. Dolly is, though.

I know. He smiled at her. *I'll try to be more present.*

Don't sweat it.

When the music paused for a moment, Doug asked Everett, "You build models—ancient ships or modern?"

"Both," he answered, "I like to do the rigging. It's very detailed."

"I've admired some of those old ship models in museums. Do you construct the rigging right on the model, or on a template and then install it?"

The music returned, cutting off the conversation, but fortunately the waiter returned with fresh drinks and to take their food orders. After he had gone, Everett turned to Meredith. "You're a vegetarian? I noticed."

"Yes, for a few months." They both had to raise their voices to be heard.

"I'm curious. What made you decide?"

"It just came on me one day that I didn't want to eat meat any more." She smiled.

"Ethical?"

"Yes."

"I've thought of it. It seems hard."

"At first, yes. It gets easier. And it seems to get more important."

"Cruelty is such a part of our culture."

Meredith glanced at Doug, whose face didn't change. "There's a part of us that still lives in caves," she said.

Dolly laughed. "That's me—cave woman! I love my meat!"

Laughter all around. "You are my favorite cave woman," Meredith said to her.

Dolly sent her an air kiss. "But I respect anyone who has that much idealism," she said, directing the remark to Everett.

"I was visiting a farm one time," he said, "of some friends, and I had the strangest experience standing near a cow."

The others leaned closer to him, trying to hear.

"It was like I was connected to the animal." He looked around at the others, as though he expected them to laugh at him. "Really. Like there was some kind of communication—but I didn't understand it." He smiled. "Pretty weird, huh?"

"Our minds," Meredith said, "can be very strange sometimes."

Everett nodded. "When I was a teenager, I heard voices. I was afraid I was going out of my mind, so I didn't tell anyone. The voices stopped eventually." He turned and grinned at Dolly. "See what you're getting into?"

Dolly smiled back, but looked sharply at Meredith. She was clearly uncomfortable with the way the conversation was going.

The waiter appeared with their food to the relief of everyone except Meredith, who was watching Everett closely. *If you hear this,* she thought clearly, *say hello.*

Everett frowned slightly, and glanced quickly around but didn't catch Meredith's eye.

Doug—did you catch that? she thought.

Doug nodded, and took a bite of food.

"Hello," said Everett aloud then, looking flustered, he said, "this is really good!" He thrust a piece of dinner roll into his mouth.

Doug looked at Meredith, then glancing at Dolly and back, shook his head slightly.

Meredith looked at him, cocked her head and sighed. They both smiled.

The food, the jazz and the alcohol wrapped them all up in a cozy, innocuous blanket of comfort.

Scene 72

Back in her apartment, Meredith was excited. "He was reading me and he didn't even know it!"

Doug grinned. "You've found another protégé?"

"No. It's just that it feels like the world is changing!"

"Yes it does."

They prepared for bed. Meredith leaned up against Doug's back as he stood brushing his teeth. "How are you doing, my love?"

He paused with his toothbrush still in his mouth and nodded. After rinsing his mouth, he said, "It was good to relax."

"I still love that saxophone."

"He makes that thing talk, doesn't he?"

She put her hand on her belly. "It talks to me—right here. No, maybe lower."

Doug turned around to face her. Smiling, he said, "How about you and I just crawling between the sheets and forgetting the world?"

"I can't think of anything I'd rather do."

"Forgetting the world" worked for a while. Meredith awoke sometime before dawn to find Doug missing from beside her in the bed. She got up and found him sitting in the kitchen. "Doug, are you all right?"

"It keeps coming back," he said without looking up. "Drinking probably doesn't help me sleep, and I woke up thinking about that poor guy. I was so intent on getting the information we needed that I was only faintly aware of the spot it was putting him in with his so-called girl friend. If I'd been more conscious I might have saved him and still gotten what we needed."

"What did your partner say about it?" Even while Meredith was asking about Doug's concerns, a little bit of her was wondering–did he sleep with his partner? She immediately regretted the thought, and hoped that he didn't pick it up.

"She was scared when we discovered that the other woman was monitoring our target's thoughts. Both of us shut off our own thoughts so the woman wouldn't suspect us."

"I don't know how to do that," Meredith said.

"It takes practice. Anyway, my partner let me handle the conversation from then on. We were both anxious to get the job done and get out of there. If we'd gotten caught it would have jeopardized the whole assignment."

"You did what you could." Meredith put a hand on his shoulder.

"It wasn't enough!" He almost shouted it.

She bent over him, her cheek resting on top of his head, her naked body pressing against his shoulder, but after a moment, she had to straighten up from the awkward position. She was also getting chilled. "Come back to bed," she pleaded. "If you want to keep talking, that's okay. I'm freezing!"

Doug allowed her to lead him back to the bed, where she tucked him in like a forlorn child before crawling under the covers beside him. They talked for a long time, until she realized that she must have fallen asleep, for she couldn't remember the last thing either of them had said. He was lying on his back, his eyes open, staring at the ceiling. "Doug, did I fall asleep on you? I'm sorry!"

He turned his head toward her. "It's okay, Love. You're exhausted. Go back to sleep.

"No! I want to be here for you! If you're suffering, then I'm suffering!"

"It's part of my job. They call it 'collateral damage.' Can't be helped."

"But it's your soul that's being damaged. How can you do your job if it makes you so miserable?

He rolled over toward her and pulled her to him. "I haven't worried about my soul in a long time," he said. I'm not sure I even have one."

"I'm not talking about religion," she said, "I'm talking about the deepest part of you, the part that makes you you, the part I've fallen in love with."

"I'm not so sure it's worth your devotion."

Meredith rose up on one elbow. "Well, I'm sure. I wouldn't be here, otherwise. I don't love what you do for a living, but that's not you."

His voice was hoarse as he said, "I should get out, shouldn't I?"

"I should be doing something more with my life than typing numbers into a computer, too. But it isn't killing my soul."

They lay there silently for a long time. Meredith kept trying to keep her eyes open, but eventually she slipped into the dark world where doubts and fears swam through her mind unchecked by consciousness. At some point, horror swirled around her and woke her up, heart pounding, to see sunshine streaming through the window. She looked over to see Doug, still fast asleep beside her, and she felt relieved. She didn't move, afraid she'd awaken him.

Something in her dream still lurked under the surface, something old, something she had known as a child, for now she felt like a child, terrified. She tried to meditate there in her bed, to let her mind rise above the terror in order to identify it. *Come on, whatever you are, show your face!*

It's the same old face you said you love. Doug was awake, even though his eyes were closed. He opened them and smiled at her.

"I wasn't talking to you!" she said. "I wouldn't use that language on you. It was a dream."

"First step in conquering a demon," he said sleepily, "is to challenge it. You want to talk about it?"

"Something out of my early life, I think. It slipped away."

"How about we slip into the shower together, and let all that garbage wash away?"

The spell was broken. She giggled. "My goodness, you are always ready for fun, aren't you?"

"Actually, my thoughts were not so ambitious. I was only thinking how nice it would be to feel your wet body against mine. I doubt if my resources have recovered enough for anything more."

Meredith threw the covers off both of them and got up. "Give me five minutes alone in there, and then you're on."

After their shower, they put on sweats and ran in the cool September morning, stopping for breakfast at a neighborhood café they hadn't visited before.

That afternoon, she sent Doug back to Arlington and took a bus to Silver Spring.

Scene 73

Meredith was shocked to see how much Dennis had changed. He was an adult now; his voice was lower and stronger, and he seemed even taller than she had remembered him. "It hasn't been that long!" she exclaimed.

"He has grown a couple of inches," said Ginnie, his current love, seemingly attached to his arm.

It was a small group present. Meredith was disappointed not to see Janet, but had not called her to say she was coming; she had made a quick decision after spending the difficult night with Doug. "I need to get my battery recharged," she told George Randolph. "I want to feel the energy of this group again."

"Well, you came at the right time," George said. "We're having a visitor this evening, Morgan Brown. Do you know him?"

"The name seems familiar, but I haven't met him."

"He's been reading for over ten years. He's traveled all over the country connecting with other readers. Some people see him as a guru."

"Is there any kind of organization?"

George gave her a quick look. "Well, not officially. We try to keep in touch."

Meredith caught his reaction. "I understand if you're being careful around me," she said.

"Sorry. I try to be discreet." He smiled, and she returned the smile.

"How **is** Doug, by the way?"

"He's okay. He's doing his job."

"And you are also being careful."

She smiled again. "But I met a fellow recently who seems to be a reader but doesn't know it—yet."

George looked interested, and Mary, who was standing nearby, came closer.

"It was a very noisy environment—a bar, with music playing, but he was confessing that when he was young he thought he was hearing voices, and began to worry about his sanity. He was afraid to tell anyone, and he said the voices eventually went away."

"What made you think he was a reader?" asked Mary.

"Just on a hunch, I sent him Dennis's call—'If you hear this, say hello'—and he reacted as though he heard it, even though he didn't say it right away. But then he did say 'hello' and tried to cover it up with some other words. He seemed flustered."

"Is there a chance you could talk with him about it, or was he a stranger?"

"I had just met him through someone else, and I couldn't say anything at the time. I'd like to talk with him sometime, if I can."

George said, "There are a lot of us out there—I'm convinced of it."

"Dennis said that Janet—the woman who had her implant removed—came to the group."

"Yes. Once, I think."

"I haven't talked with her for a long time. Do you think she's still interested in the group?"

"She seemed interested at the time. She ..."

He was interrupted by voices at the door. A man was arriving and being greeted by several members. George excused himself and went to greet him, as well.

Morgan Brown was a tall, brown-skinned man with a ring of silver hair. His rich bass voice carried throughout the house. "Ah, good friends! It's good to see you all again!" He walked into the living room acknowledging people as he came.

"I want you to meet one of our newer members," said George, motioning to Meredith.

"Ah, lovely lady!" Morgan said, extending his hand.

"I'm Meredith," she said simply.

"Have you been reading long?"

"Just a few months. This group has been a wonderful support for me."

"Welcome to a growing club!"

"George tells me that you have contacted readers all over the country."

"Yes—I've met hundreds, and I'm convinced there are thousands of readers in the United States. And I have no idea how many in other countries."

"How do you suppose this has happened?"

"It's time has come," he said.

"What do you mean?" Meredith was feeling just a little uneasy with this man. He seemed so self-assured, and presented a suggestion of something—'charisma' was the word that came to her, although she didn't feel it in her gut, as she had with several people in her life, such as Martin Luther King or Bobby Kennedy. She decided that she hadn't seen and heard enough from Morgan to make a judgment.

"The human race is evolving," he said. "There have probably been readers for years—centuries—but now there is a critical mass of us, and we can finally, very soon, make ourselves known to the world."

"And then what?" she said. "What will happen when these thousands of people come out of the closet?"

He laughed at the connection she had suggested. "I'm certain that there will be a period of adjustment in our culture, just as there has been with gays and lesbians. Only, when we come out of the closet, we won't be the underdogs!"

People had gathered around to hear the conversation. Someone said, "We will have the advantage."

Meredith frowned. "But those who are not readers—won't they be afraid of us?"

"Perhaps, for a time, Morgan said. "There will be a period of adjustment."

"You mean, we'll have the power?"

"That's putting it far too strongly. We readers are a cross-section of the population. Some of us are cut out to be leaders, and others to be followers, just as in the population as a whole."

"What concerns me," persisted Meredith, torn between wanting to just listen and needing to voice feelings that seemed ominous to her," is that if we become an identifiable group—a minority at least at first—will there be people who will fear our gift, and react strongly against us?"

"People fear most those who seem to be what they fear in themselves," offered someone behind Meredith.

"Like the people who fear gay people," added someone else, "are most afraid of their own homosexual tendencies."

"But that's not a good analogy," said Morgan. "A better one is intelligence. Some people are intimidated by people who are more intelligent than they, or more talented, but there isn't much violence that comes from that."

Another man, who had been standing at the back of the group around Morgan, said, "I think there is a real danger of an us-versus-them situation arising, especially if awareness of us grows suddenly—and especially if some of us take an elitist stance."

Morgan turned to see the man. "A good point, he said. "I don't think I know you."

"Gary Blanchard. I'm new here, too. Elaine introduced me to the group, but she's not here today."

Just from his first statements, Meredith was impressed with Gary. "Hi, Gary. I'm Meredith. I liked the way you put it. I have a friend who has known me since before I discovered my gift, and even though we are very close, she is intimidated by all this. We talk a lot about the problem. It's true that she has a not-very-strong image of her own abilities, so I have to be careful of how much I let her know I pick up from her thoughts."

"I have friends like that, too."

Dennis spoke up. "Even Janet, who is still recovering from implant removal surgery, says that she feels inferior now that she can no longer read."

"Maybe," said Gary, "we need an educational program for both readers and non-readers."

George said, "We don't have much of an organization here, but maybe some of us could volunteer to be in a study group or something. According to Morgan, there are other groups around the country who might have ideas—maybe even programs."

Meredith raised her hand. "I'd like to be part of that. I need to feel that I'm doing something about what I'm afraid might become a very troubling situation."

Gary volunteered immediately, as did Dennis and Ginnie and a couple other people.

"At some point this evening," said Meredith, "could we gather in another room and talk about how we want to do it?"

"How about nine o'clock—so we don't interfere with what the whole group is doing now?"

"Nine o'clock. Thank you." Meredith felt relieved. She wandered back to the kitchen and poured herself a glass of wine. *It feels good to be doing something!*

Yes, it does. A young woman whom she hadn't met was at the coffee urn, smiling at her. "I'd like to be in your study group. I'm Sheryl."

"Hi, Sheryl. Thank you."

On the bus ride back home, Meredith noticed how her tension over Doug had dissipated. *Doing something feels so much better!*

Scene 74

On Monday morning, Dolly and Meredith were standing at their "back fence," the partition between their cubicles, coffee cups in hand, laughing quietly together. "The other night, I shouldn't have told you to be quiet about your reading," Dolly said. "He's even weirder than you guys!"

"He's not weird," said Meredith. "He's a reader. He may not know it yet, but he is. I thought you should know."

Dolly looked shocked. "How do you know?"

"Remember that call that Dennis found me with? 'If you hear this, say hello.' I pulled that on him at dinner, and he reacted. He heard my thought."

"My God!"

"I didn't want us all to get into that discussion, so I let it drop."

Dolly pouted and sighed. "And here I thought maybe he'd be a keeper!"

"It changes things for you?"

"I don't know how to be with people like that!"

"People like me?"

Dolly put her hand on Meredith's. "I can handle you," she said. "I know you, and I know that you don't judge me."

"You think that other people who might read your thoughts would judge you?"

"Hell, yes! Even people who don't know what I'm thinking judge me!"

Meredith smiled. "Or envy you."

"Bull shit."

"You think Everett would judge you?"

"I don't know!" she whined.

"I think he's interesting," Meredith said.

"Yeah, you would. What did you think about his communicating-with-a-cow story?"

Meredith laughed. "Actually, I'd like to hear more about that."

"You said he's a reader. Is there any connection, do you think?"

"That's what I'd like to know."

Dolly frowned. "They seem to be everywhere!"

"Well, I've gone from feeling totally alone to feeling like maybe I'm not so alone," Meredith said. "I guess it depends upon your point of view."

"It scares me sometimes. It's like I'm one of the last Neanderthals, or something." She smiled with one corner of her mouth. "A meat-eating Neanderthal that lives in a cave."

Meredith cocked her head to one side. "You **would** look kinda cute in a leopard skin."

Dolly looked past Meredith. "Speaking of Neanderthals, that one has been eyeing us."

"Guess we should do some work, huh?"

"To be continued at lunch?"

"Sounds good."

In their favorite corner of The Egg Place, Meredith asked Dolly, "You're really nervous about Everett?"

"Well, he's a nice guy, and that's unusual in this town. But if he— and I don't mind him being a little bit weird—but if he really can read my mind, I don't know if I can handle that. It puts me at a very big disadvantage, doesn't it?"

"I guess it can, if you are playing games with him."

"What's **that** mean?"

"If you're not saying what you mean, then he might be able to tell that you're being devious, or even lying to him. If you're upfront with him, and honest about how you feel, then he won't get mixed messages from you. If you just make a mistake, or change your mind about something, he ought to forgive that. People screw up all the time. It's no big thing."

"I remember when you first met Doug—you were really intimidated by him. But after you began to read thoughts yourself, it all smoothed out."

"No, that's not how it happened," Meredith said. "I learned pretty early that I could trust him, even if he could read my thoughts. He also made it clear that reading other people's thoughts isn't as easy as it might seem to those who can't. If he's straight with you and you are straight with him, it doesn't matter so much that he can pick up stuff sometimes."

"I've been burned so many times by men ..."

"Dolly, so have I. Eventually, I learned how to tell if they were straight with me."

"Didn't you have that disastrous thing in New York just before you came down here?"

"It was a disaster not because he fooled me. I fooled myself. I knew he was married, and I thought I could take him away from her."

"And you did."

"Yes, unfortunately, I did."

"Well, Everett's not married—I think."

"Then you don't know him well enough to start thinking about getting serious. Right?"

Dolly pouted. "Right."

"But he told you things—he told **us** things the other night that most people would be afraid to admit."

"Yeah, like being in communication with a **cow**. That reminds me of an old Woody Allen movie."

Meredith laughed. "Oh, you mean where Gene Wilder falls in love with a sheep?"

"Yeah, that one."

"Hmmm. Well, did you ever have a puppy or a kitten when you were a kid?"

"Aw, that's different!"

"Is it? Think about it. He told us about that right after we were talking about my becoming a vegetarian. It told me that he recognizes how we are all related. "

"I guess it would. I'm not as evolved as you are."

"Dolly, come off of it! Why do you put yourself down so much?"

Dolly took a bite from her sandwich.

"So, are you afraid he's going to read your mind, or that he's better than you are?"

Dolly ate silently.

"Dolly ..." Meredith stopped. "I'm sorry. I didn't mean to put you on the spot. You don't have to justify your feelings to me."

Dolly looked up at Meredith, her eyes glistening. Meredith reached over and took her hand. "You are one of the most real people I know," she said. "Oh, I am **so arrogant**! Forgive me, please?"

Dolly smiled. "I will if you'll give me one of your tissues."

Scene 75

The study group became Meredith's main preoccupation. The members had exchanged email addresses and agreed to meet in person once a week for the present. Since most of them lived north of D.C., they chose to meet at Gary's home in College Park.

Meredith phoned Janet and invited her to go with her to the meeting. At first, Janet seemed reluctant, but she finally agreed. Gary offered to pick them up at the Metrorail station. On the way, Meredith asked Janet how she was getting along in her "retirement."

"It's harder than I thought it would be," she said. "I found some temp work, but it's kinda boring." She laughed.

"I can imagine. How's your head?"

Janet looked at her. "You mean, how's my right brain?"

"Yeah. Are you feeling more?"

"You're really direct, aren't you?"

Meredith met her gaze. "I don't know what it is, but I'm picking up stuff from you that feels strange."

"It **is** strange. Can we get off the subject?"

"Okay. Sorry. D'you want to talk about the group?"

"I get kinda paranoid with them. I was expecting to, but it's still hard. Some nice people there, but I feel a little bit like a freak with some of them. Like they are examining me, or something. I still want to do something with them—or with somebody, 'cause this thing is going to tear the world apart if it isn't dealt with right. The guys in the Company don't have a clue. There's maybe three people in the whole organization who understands what the chips do."

"I thought as much. I can tell that Doug and I don't process the same way."

Janet looked surprised. "How?"

"I don't know. We can—we have this little shtick that we call a mind pool—and most of the time it's like it's one mind that we're sharing. But then he says something that doesn't follow, exactly, like our mind pool doesn't hold everything that's going on."

"Interesting!" Janet turned in the seat to see Meredith more clearly. "It makes sense, though, doesn't it? Those little probes they stick in our brains are pretty primitive, after all."

"Janet, I don't know if you knew that a couple of Company guys showed up at my apartment—they broke in, actually—and wanted me to agree to come in for some tests."

"No kidding!" Janet grinned. "I'm not surprised. But they let you say no?"

"I tried to call Doug, but they stopped me. It just happened that he was on his way over anyway, and they left in a hurry."

"I could get in trouble if this got back to the Company, but I know that they tried to infiltrate the Silver Spring group. Last thing I heard, they didn't find out much except getting a bunch of names."

"Are you taking a chance, getting involved with the group?"

"I'm sure they are keeping an eye on me. And I'm pretty sure they knew when I turned in my resignation that I had been in touch with you. So they're doing what they do—investigating. Maybe they figure I'll lead them to more fruitful pastures."

"I'm concerned," Meredith said, "that the competition going on between the CIA and the natural readers is just the tip of a very big iceberg."

"What kind of iceberg?"

"A growing **us-versus-them** situation. Readers versus non-readers."

Janet looked thoughtful, but Meredith could not pick up anything from her thoughts that she could identify.

"Janet, something I just noticed."

Janet turned to look at her.

"I'm not able to read you very well at all."

You can't hear this?

"Yes, I could pick that up clearly. But Doug said one time that he could shut off his thoughts so others couldn't pick it up."

"Yes, that's sort of basic training. We had to be able to keep our channels clear."

"You're still able to do it?"

Janet smiled. "I hadn't thought about it, but maybe I can. After all, that is transmitting—our chips were only for receiving. It probably involves completely different circuits. Don't ask me how it's done. I don't know. If I was doing it just then, I wasn't aware of it."

"Could you teach me?"

Janet frowned. "I think I'd be getting into dangerous legal territory."

"Okay, I don't want you to do that. But what if—what if I agreed to go in for those tests they wanted me to do, but only if they would teach me some of those techniques. Do you think they might do it?"

Janet shrugged. "I don't have any idea."

"Or could I trust them? Maybe they'd zap my brain so I couldn't read anymore. Could they do that?"

"They probably could. Would they? I don't know. Some of the stuff the Company does isn't entirely above board. Individuals do things that never get into a report."

"The whole idea—**my** whole idea of this study group is to open up the communications around reading, and trying to short-circuit the us-versus-them tendency. There's a fellow who volunteered to be in the study group—Gary something—who really struck me as thoughtful. He's the one picking us up at the station. We had a visitor at the last meeting, Morgan Brown, who has traveled around the country making contact with groups. He was sort of charismatic but I wasn't impressed with his ideas. He seemed to think that readers would be taking over the world or something. Maybe I misjudged him."

"There's a lot of hysterical stuff on the Internet already. It's creepy."

"I'm glad you agreed to come with me. I've been wanting to get your point of view. I think we need more dialog across the line, and you're in a good position to help."

Janet looked down at her fingernails, carefully trimmed but unlacquered. "It feels odd to me. I know I was determined to get into it before my surgery, but then afterward the gut urgency went away. I'm continuing because my head is still there."

"I'm glad. Two reasons—one, I think the group needs your perspective. Two, I've been wanting to stay in touch with you. We have a lot in common."

Janet looked at her and grinned. "You mean, besides Doug?"

"Besides Doug."

"Y'know, one good thing about this right-brain deficit I have—I don't feel guilty about that any more."

"Guilt is highly overrated."

Gary met them at the station. Meredith, riding in the back seat, noticed that he looked at Janet a lot, and old feelings lurked just under the surface in her mind. She tried not to think about the question that came up—he had said that someone named Elaine had introduced him to the group. But he caught it anyway. *Elaine and I are just casual friends. She heard about me from a mutual friend and called me. No personal connections.*

Sorry. I'm not usually suspicious, but I feel protective toward Janet.

Janet was looking from Gary to Meredith. "I suspect you're talking about me. The conversation suddenly went silent, and Gary was looking at you in the mirror."

Meredith's face became hot. "Janet, you may have lost your implant, but your training didn't disappear. I was feeling protective." She put a hand on Janet's arm.

"Please don't."

"Okay." Sensing a double meaning to the request, she withdrew her hand. A small knot tugged at her midsection.

Gary glanced at the two women, but said nothing.

Six people showed up for the meeting—the three of them, Dennis and Ginnie, and Sheryl. "There are liquid refreshments in the kitchen," Gary said. "I'll make coffee if anyone wants it."

After everyone was settled, Gary told them that George wanted to be part of the study group, but he had other commitments that evening. "And Mary will probably come with him next time, too."

"Good size group," said Dennis.

The rest of the evening they spent getting acquainted and discussing the objectives of the group. Gary offered to scan the Internet looking for other groups or individuals that they could contact. Sheryl said she'd take notes that could be shared with the larger group.

Meredith volunteered to keep everyone in the loop, passing on information among the members. "We can put everybody's name on our emails so whatever happens we will all know it."

"Do we need some kind of private connection as well?" asked Ginnie. "I get the feeling in the larger group that some people don't want us to be too public."

" 'Discreet' is the word." Meredith smiled. "Maybe George will have some ideas on that, but my feeling is that secrecy is exactly what we are trying to get away from."

Janet said, "I'm only one person, but I agree with Meredith. The Company will surely find out about us and maybe even track us. I don't think we can avoid that, honestly. They are very tenacious. The more open and transparent we are, the less interested they will be."

"I hope so," said Ginnie.

Janet waited for a quiet moment, then said, "I have a request. I know I'm the odd one in the group because I can't read you all. But I'd like to feel that I'm not excluded from whatever goes on. If you converse by thoughts, I am left out. Believe me, I know how convenient and tempting it is. Maybe that's why I am so aware of my limitation. It feels sometimes like my ears are stopped up."

"You're right," said Gary, and the others nodded. Meredith's face became hot for the second time that evening. She and Janet would talk about it on the way home.

Scene 76

"Can I come over tonight?" Meredith asked Dolly the next day.

Dolly laughed. "I can tell when you need to talk. You are so transparent. Sure. What time?"

"Whenever it's convenient."

"We can go right from here. Or stop for a martini on the way. Or do you need to keep your mind clear?"

Meredith laughed. "I'd love a drink, but I'd rather talk at your place."

"I've got vodka and lime."

"Super." She paused. "Your place is less likely to be bugged."

Dolly's eyebrows raised, but she didn't comment.

They settled in Dolly's apartment and drank for a few minutes before Dolly asked, "Okay, now what's up between you and the CIA—or is it about you and Doug?"

"Remember my telling you about those hoodlums that invaded my apartment?"

"And tried to get you into their space ship so they could perform erotic experiments on you?"

"Ha, ha. Anyway, I've been doing a lot of thinking lately. I'm in a little study group connected with the Silver Spring group, and we're trying to figure out how to reduce what we think is going to be a lot of public conflict between readers and non-readers. My thinking is that we need to get it out into the open."

"Maybe if all of you people could be made to wear yellow stars on your clothing." Dolly had a mischievous grin on her face, and Meredith said, "Ha, ha," again.

"Well," said Dolly, "as one of the oppressed majority, ..."

"I sure understand your uneasiness. But I'd like to start with getting rid of the suspicion between the Company and the natural readers' groups."

"And so you're thinking about volunteering for that space ship adventure."

"If it were only erotic experiments, I might be more amenable."

Dolly laughed. "You like that idea, huh?"

"I might learn something." Then Meredith's face sobered. "Seriously, I'm wondering if the two sides could become more trustful, we could get somewhere."

"The CIA—trustful? Dream on, girl!"

"But these are people, whatever their jobs are. This thing is going to be a lot bigger than petty espionage. We think there are thousands of readers out there already, and who knows where it's going? The CIA can't stop it, any more than they could stop the civil rights movement."

"If I remember my history, that was not the CIA, it was the FBI under that cross-dresser J. Edgar Hoover."

"Yes, you're right. But it's the mentality that's so dangerous."

Dolly's face was serious. "I got news for you, girl. That dangerous mentality? It's right here!" She pointed to herself.

Meredith sighed. "We are both scared, aren't we? Maybe of two different things."

"I don't know, maybe the same thing—it feels like Germany in 1930. If the fear gets out of hand, all we need is another Hitler to start waving a flag."

"That's what I want to defuse! I don't know how to do it, but we have to start!"

"Okay, you're doing your thing. What can I do? Maybe not dump Everett? Coach him as he learns where his mind is going?" Dolly emptied her glass. "I do have a little experience with this coping-with-the-unknown stuff. Maybe I could do that."

Meredith set her glass down and hugged her friend. "Dolly, I love you!"

Dolly stood up and took their glasses into the kitchen. "I hope I can do it without being drunk," she said. "I do kinda like him in a tentative way. And so far, I'm not jealous of some cow."

Scene 77

Meredith checked her email when she got home. There was a message from Gary.

> Hi, Meredith,
>
> After our discussion the other evening, I've been thinking about you and wondering if you and I have some similarities in our thinking about this phenomenon. I'll try to put it into a few words and if it rings any bells with you maybe we could get together to talk about it?
>
> I heard you speak in meetings about a deep connection not only between people but between all beings, as if this thing we share is evidence of that. I'm not putting it like you did, and I'm fumbling in describing it, but I feel something like that, too. The "us-vs-them" attitude denies this connection. I noticed that you don't eat meat – I don't either. I see our objective in the study group as trying to expanding awareness of that connection.
>
> I hope I'm right, and I hope I'm making this clear. If you'd like to sit and talk about it more, would you let me know? I have a car, so I can come to DC.
>
> Gary

She answered immediately.

> Hi, Gary. I'd love to! Can you make it Wed evening? About 7? I think you have my address. Park in my space – 23 – and ring my bell. Looking forward to it! Let me know if you can't make it then and we'll try another time. Meredith.

Meredith was suddenly hungry, and realized that she hadn't eaten. She took a hard-boiled egg from the refrigerator and poured herself a drink. Still feeling mellow from the vodka at Dolly's, she sat and thought about Gary. She had been impressed with him at the meetings—he seemed thoughtful and balanced, but still sharp in conversations. She laughed at her more visceral response to him—he was very young and attractive—even though she firmly pushed a momentary fantasy out of her mind. She hoped that being with him would not affect her resolve.

As the time for their meeting neared, however, she found herself just slightly giddy. *No alcohol tonight!* she thought.

When he appeared at her door, however, the reality of him displaced any fantasy. "Hi. Have any trouble finding it?" she greeted him.

"None at all."

"Sit over there. Can I get you something?"

"A glass of water," he replied. "I gave up alcohol and caffeine." He laughed.

When she returned from the kitchen with two glasses of water, she sat in a chair across the coffee table from him. "Your email was intriguing," she said. "Tell me more."

He grinned. "I'll try not to tell you the story of my life, but I need to give you some idea of where I'm coming from."

"That's what I want to hear."

"Well, about ten years ago a friend of mine got hold of a couple of joints." He smiled sheepishly. "We were just curious, so we got by ourselves in his apartment and he put on some Pink Floyd album and we lit up. It was the first time either of us had smoked pot."

Meredith smiled.

"I had the strangest—the most wonderful –experience! Listening to that music, it was like all the instruments were out in space, but like I could point to each one, as if the music was coming from a dozen different speakers. It was great! And then when the music was over, I just sort of drifted around."

"I know the feeling," she said.

"But then it was like I was a wave on the ocean. Not on a wave—I **was** the wave—and when I rose up, I could look out and see all the other waves around me. It felt like we were all the same, like we were all the ocean, but just different shapes temporarily!" He sipped from the glass.

"Well, that experience really had an impact on me. I tried smoking pot one other time, but it wasn't the same. There were other people around, and I just felt weird. But I never forgot that first time.

"Then I got involved with a girl, and we got married and that experience just kinda got left behind in our living an ordinary life. You know?"

She nodded.

"Well, then one day I realized that my mind was playing tricks on me. I'd get a weird feeling sometimes, and like I'd hear things—words or expressions, or like somebody laughing—and it was like when you dream—you know?"

"You were picking up things from other people?"

"Well, I didn't know that at the time. I was afraid I was losing it. I tried to talk about it with Carol—that was my wife—but she couldn't understand it. Eventually, she tried to get me to go to a psychiatrist or something, but I wouldn't go. I don't know why. It just seemed like I had to figure it out for myself. I started meditating—I bought a couple of books, and just sat and meditated every day, trying to look at what my mind was doing."

"Sounds very brave to me," Meredith said.

"Carol didn't think so. She thought I was going off the deep end."

"How often did you have this experience?"

"At first it was just sometimes. And then it got more often. Eventually Carol couldn't take it any more. She got scared, I guess, and left. I wanted her to stay, but I just had to find out what was going on in my head!"

He laughed. "I lost a lot of weight. I quit my job and lived on my savings. I sat on my cushion practically all day."

"You seem healthy now."

"Yeah, I got myself together after I figured out that I was tuning in to other people's thoughts. I started experimenting, going out to places and just tuning in. I got so I could identify people even when I couldn't see them, if they were close by. You know, people's minds jump all over the place?"

"I do, indeed," Meredith said. *And now you can hear my thoughts? And now I can hear your thoughts.* He grinned.

"So, tell me more about this connection you had discovered."

"After I found out that there were more people who could read thoughts, it dawned on me—it's just another example of our connections! We permeate each other's minds! Maybe everybody does it, like, unconsciously. You know how you meet somebody and you feel this electricity between you? Or they say something, and you know **exactly** what they're talking about!"

"Even if you're not picking up their thoughts—or you think you aren't."

"Yeah! That's it! It's just a small example of this connection that connects us all!" Gary's face was flushed, his eyes glistening.

"And then you saw that the connection was not only with other people." Meredith's heart was pounding.

He nodded. "You know it too, don't you?"

She suddenly wanted to hug this young man—not out of any erotic impulse but just because she had found another soul like hers. Not like Doug, or even Dolly—she was connected to them in a different way, and they probably would not understand this feeling she had with Gary. Tears filled her eyes.

Gary looked at her, smiling. He didn't even ask—he just looked around and saw the tissue box, and set it in front of her.

For another hour they talked, finishing each other's sentences as thought they had known each other for years. Then she stood up. "Gary, I have to stop. I can't absorb any more. I feel overwhelmed with all this. Can we do this again?"

"I'd love to," he said. "I feel like I'm in love with you!"

"I don't want that," she said gently. "I don't feel like that. It's more like we're related, like we've shared blood or something. Does that make sense?"

"Yeah," he said, his voice breaking. "I know, I just get my feelings all jumbled up together. You've got your Doug, and ..."

"And I'm old enough to be your mother. I don't mean that to be unkind, or deny that I feel something for you. It's just a feeling I've never felt before, and I need to find out about it. I'll spend a lot of time on my cushion!"

Gary laughed, and started for the door. "You and me both," he said.

She caught his sleeve and pulled him close to her. "Thank you for finding me!" she whispered. "We'll talk some more, okay?"

"Okay." He opened the door.

"Gary."

He turned.

"We will change the world!"

He smiled, then walked away.

Scene 78

She found the card with the phone number on it in a drawer, and stuck it on her refrigerator with a magnet. It didn't feel like the time yet. She hadn't even mentioned her idea to Doug until dinner one evening at the bistro around the corner. "I'm trying to let go of my fear," she told him.

Doug looked at her with amusement. "I know that there isn't anything I could say that would influence you."

"Of course there is. I have a lot of respect for your judgment—in spite of an occasional lapse regarding the opposite sex." She gave him that little smile out of one side of her mouth. "And I know, really deep down in my soul, that you want me to be safe. Besides, you have an inside track to information that, even though you might not be able to share with me, it could be pertinent to this issue."

"Have you ever thought of running for office? You have a way with words."

Just then Marcel brought a bottle of wine to their table, with two glasses. "We just received this, and I think it's special. Please, this bottle is on the house, and I'd love to hear your opinion on it."

"Marcel, how could I be critical of anything you brought to me?" She laughed. "But I will try to give you my objective opinion!"

He grinned broadly, poured the wine and set the bottle on the table. "Apprécier le vin!"

After he left the table, Meredith looked at Doug. "So tell me what you think!" She tilted her head in that way that he liked.

"I don't think there's anything for you to fear, not at this stage of things."

"What's that mean?"

"I don't think you are nearly as vulnerable to them as you might have been when they visited you. You've now made friends in Silver Spring, for one thing. People know you. Also—and this is just my sensing of things—the whole subject has become less, uh, **charged**."

"How so?"

"Too many people know about it, and too many civilians are discovering that they can read."

"So they might not even want to talk with me."

"It's a possibility."

"What I want," Meredith said, "is for the subject to become ho-hum. I think that there's a danger in the general public that it might become a political issue."

"I'm sure it will, at some point. When you think about it, it's potentially a cultural dividing issue."

"Exactly what we're thinking! We've formed a little study group to see if we can come up with ways to mitigate that divisive aspect in the public mind."

"Yep," he said, smiling, "you are definitely running for office."

"I don't want to get into politics!" she exclaimed. "I just want to help, somehow."

Doug shook his head. "You are still the barefoot, braless girl stuffing daisies into National Guard rifle barrels, aren't you?"

She grinned at him and sipped her wine. Then she said, "Oh, my God! Taste this wine!"

Doug tasted the wine and picked up the bottle to read the label. "This is expensive vino!"

Meredith caught Marcel's eye through the kitchen pass-through and lifted her glass. He nodded and smiled.

"That settles it," she said to Doug, "I'll call them. Maybe the number doesn't work any more or maybe they'll turn me down. But I'm not afraid of being 'disappeared' or something."

She picked up her menu. "I'm hungry!"

Scene 79

"Please leave a message," said the phone when she finally got the courage to dial the number.

"This is Meredith," she began, then thought that it was probably not necessary. From what Doug had told her, the number was probably reserved for her alone. *Well, anyway,* "I've decided to accept your request, if we can agree upon some conditions. Call me if you are still interested."

With no response by the following evening, she guessed that they would have called already if they were still interested. After the ordeal of struggling to get up the nerve to call, she was disappointed. She picked up her book "Mindsight" and tried to read. A passage from the book caught her attention:

Science has shown that well-being and true happiness come from defining our "selves" as part of an interconnected whole— connecting with others and with ourselves in authentic ways that break down the isolative boundaries of a separate self. Such connections can be created through developing the clear lens of mindsight, which enables us to track energy and information flow within and among us. Cultivating our capacity to sense energy and information flow helps us expand the "self" beyond the boundaries of our body and reveals the fundamental truth that we are indeed a part of an interconnected world. Our "living organism" is the extended community of living beings.

My God! she thought, *He had no idea that what he was writing would become so relevant to what we are going through now! Or did he? Was he a reader already? His field was psychiatry, but he proposed meditation as a means of knowing and integrating the individual mind. And through the ages, meditation has been seen as a path to not only understanding the mind but developing compassion and understanding of others.*

Reading other people's thoughts, even in as primitive way as we're able to now, is a way of extending our sense of self to encompass everything—everybody!

Meredith read to the end of the book, then leaned back and closed her eyes. Now she knew why she had come to this place at this time. Whether there is some higher purpose, some higher power that pulls our strings, she didn't know. But she **felt** something profound about what she was doing.

She remembered Doug's remark in the restaurant about her still being that "barefoot, braless girl stuffing daisies into National Guard rifle barrels," and smiled. Yes, she was. *And there are still a lot of rifle barrels to be stuffed with daisies.*

Just as she reached for her phone to call Doug about her insight, it rang.

"Unknown Number," it said. *Doug? The CIA?*

She pressed a key. "Hello."

Scene 80

Doug sipped his coffee nervously, pretending to read his iPad but watching the door. *She's late. That's not like her. She's always been right on top of things. Maybe she won't show. I can understand that, considering everything. She probably has misgivings about seeing me— that would explain it.*

Then the glass door of the little diner swung open, and **That Body** floated through. Janet spotted him immediately, and smiled as she came to his table. His heart was making itself known. "Hi, Partner," he said.

"Hi, yourself. How have you been?" She slipped into the chair across from him.

The waitress appeared immediately at the table, order tablet in hand.

"Just coffee," Janet told her.

Doug wiped his damp palms on a napkin. "Same old thing. Nothing has changed much," he said. "You recovering okay?"

Janet nodded. "I expected some cognitive effects of losing my chip, but it took longer than I thought to feel 'normal' again."

"So you do feel normal now?"

"Kinda flat, actually. Life isn't as much fun. I guess that's to be expected just from being off the job, though." She unwrapped the napkin from the tableware and rolled up the little paper strip before putting it aside. "You had any exciting assignments?"

"Nothing like the Cayman frolic." He grinned at her.

She smiled as she asked, "How's Meredith?"

He had expected that. She was always direct. "She's doing well," he said.

They were silent as the waitress reappeared with another cup and a steaming pot of coffee. She filled Janet's cup, then topped off Doug's. Pulling a handful of creamers from her apron pocket, she dropped them on the table and left.

"I saw her last week." Janet opened a creamer and poured the contents into her cup.

"I know. She told me."

She looked up at him pleasantly. "So what's up?"

288

It was hard for him to adjust to the knowledge that she could no longer read him—that had always been a part of their relationship, and now he wasn't sure how to be with her. He suddenly recognized the larger problem—he wasn't sure how to be with her, at all. He smiled sheepishly. "It gets in the way, doesn't it?"

Janet's eyebrows raised the smallest amount.

"Sex," he said. "I want to talk to you about something else, and I keep thinking …"

"What else, Doug?"

A knot tightened in his gut. There it was—she was holding him off, pretending that she didn't feel anything for him. He sighed, feeling stupid. "I wanted to ask you about your experience with having your chip removed." Back to business. *Let it go, stupid!*

"Well, the headache wasn't bad, actually. Superficial wound, that's all. But for a while it was like my right brain went into spasm or something. I could think clearly, although I had a hard time remembering some things. That flatness I mentioned—not feeling much of anything—was the biggest part of it."

"But your memory came back?"

"Some parts of it came back right away. The emotional memories—I don't know if I'll ever get those back. It's kind of a shame. I remember feeling things intensely, but now it's like things don't matter to me as much."

Doug took a drink from his cup. "Your voice seems a little flat. You're not depressed, are you?"

"I don't feel depressed. I can get up in the morning and go to work. I eat normally, and I've continued to work out at the gym. That doesn't suggest depression, does it?"

"You told me you wanted to get involved with the natural readers groups."

"I've gone to some of the meetings. I still want to contribute as much as I can. But around them I feel isolated sometimes. I no longer speak their language. It's hard to describe."

"I'm not surprised. I've thought that if I ever did that, it might change my relationship with Meredith."

"Role reversal?"

"Maybe that's part of it. But mostly, it's because we have developed a way of being together that involves mutual reading. We've described it as a mind pool, a shared mental environment. We don't have to talk as much."

"Does it scare you, the thought of losing that?" Janet remained serious—she lacked that playfulness that he remembered from the Caribbean assignment.

"It doesn't scare me so much as it feels like something will be missing."

She looked at him. "Are you considering it?"

He nodded, almost imperceptibly.

Janet smiled. "You and I are different, Doug. Your reactions won't necessarily be like mine. Are you thinking that you'll become like me?"

"Yeah, maybe."

"And you don't like what you see in me now."

"You used to be more ... **playful**."

"I suppose I was. It feels like I was just younger."

"It's only been a few months."

"Feels like years already."

They sat looking at each other for a long time. Then Doug said, "If we had that Cayman Islands assignment right now, it would be very different, wouldn't it?"

"You bet."

"There was an excitement to it then—aside from the job itself."

"It's one of those things that are hard to remember, Doug. I remember what we did, but I don't remember so clearly how I felt."

"I do."

"Doug, it looks to me like we've got two conversations going here. On one hand, I think you are really thinking about getting out, and you're nervous about how it will leave you. On the other hand, I'm getting feelers from you about us. Is that true?"

Doug felt his face grow hot. "I guess that's what I meant when you first sat down, about sex getting in the way."

"So you are thinking of quitting."

"Yes."

"What you will lose—what I lost—is not real, Doug. It's an artificial reality created by a chip. It felt real because we went through that training. We were, in the space of a couple of months, made seven feet tall. I am trying to adjust to being only five feet tall again."

"I guess I can't be seven feet tall forever."

"Was the sexual side of our relationship important because we were seven feet tall?"

Doug thought about that. *Maybe,* he thought, *that had something to do with it. But it felt like I was only myself responding to a fascinating woman—a fantasy figure, sexually seven feet tall.*

Janet touched his hand. "Doug, you'll have to tell me. I can't read your mind anymore."

"Yes," he said, "I guess that was it."

"Some day," she said gently, "maybe I'll get back those feelings again. Maybe I'll remember, too. But right now, I don't even want to. I hope that doesn't feel cruel—I don't mean it to be."

A lump rose in his throat. He felt as though he were going to cry. *Let it go, stupid!*

Doug signaled the waitress.

"Doug," she said, I'm sorry. It was an interlude—a seven-feet-tall interlude. Go back to Meredith."

"Yes. You're right, of course. I've known that all along. It just …"

"And give her my best. She took good care of me when I really needed it."

He watched Janet walk out of the diner. She didn't look back. *I knew when I came here what I had to do. I wonder if Meredith knows what we are going to go through.*

Picking up the check, he paid the cashier without listening to her.

Scene 81

"What's wrong?" Meredith asked, looking at him.

They had just sat down on his sofa with their gin and tonics.

"Thinking about things," he answered, his voice tight. "I saw Janet today." He was looking across the room.

Meredith took a breath. *Here it comes.*

He looked at her. "No, it's not that," he said.

"It's not what?" Her voice was icy.

"I didn't sleep with her. I wanted some information from her."

She looked at him steadily, saying nothing.

"I asked her about her experience with the removal of her chip."

"And?"

She said she had lost a lot of feeling, and memories of feeling."

"Feelings for you?" Meredith was conscious of holding her breath, but she couldn't let it out.

"Well, she said that too, but that's not what I was asking her about."

Meredith burst into tears and set her glass down.

"Meredith—I wanted to know what to expect when I do the same thing!" Doug had the intolerable feeling of lying and telling the truth at the same time. He wanted desperately for Meredith to believe that he was not interested in Janet. But he could remember clearly how he felt in the diner, looking at the gorgeous woman across from him and wanting her so much.

She looked at him through her tears, not sure what she was hearing him say.

"I've had it!" he said. "I want out!"

"Out from us?" she whimpered.

"No!" he shouted. "From my job. From this goddamn chip in my head! I have to end it!"

She leaned her head against his shoulder and sobbed uncontrollably. He wrapped his arms around her and just held her until her crying subsided. "I'm afraid of losing us," he said. "I don't want to stop feeling!"

She clung to him without speaking.

"She's different," he said. "She's flat, like somebody who is depressed. I don't want to be like that!"

Meredith let go of him and leaned against the back of the sofa. He reached for the box of tissues and handed one to her. "Thank you," she whispered.

"You don't have feelings for her?"

"Yes, I have feelings for her. But I chose you. And I still choose you."

She wiped her eyes. "You scared me!"

"I'm sorry."

"You really want to get out?"

"I really want to get out. I don't want my job to be between us."

She smiled. Her eyes were rimmed with red. "I hate being so needy!"

"Janet is the only one I know who has gone through that. I needed to hear from her what I will go through."

"And you no longer have lust for that body?" She was still smiling.

"Let's not go there—please?"

She swung her fist hard against his arm. "**You'd** better not go there!"

He turned and held her face between his hands. Kissing her, he tasted her tears. "I promise."

Scene 82

Meredith fidgeted at her desk. Dolly, glancing over the partition at her, let her alone. She didn't know what was going on, but she knew that Meredith would tell her when she was ready.

Meredith's cell phone rang. She opened it but didn't say anything. Then she shut down her computer, picked up her purse, and left. Dolly caught her eye as she passed, but that glance was the only communication between them.

When the elevator door opened, Doug was inside, alone.

Oh, my God, he's going to do it! she thought.

"Yes ma'am," he said quietly, "I am."

She entered the elevator, pressed the lobby button and turned around to stand next to him, He took her hand and they rode down all the way without speaking. As the door opened, she turned and kissed him on the cheek.

A cab was waiting for them at the door.

"Walter Reed," Doug said to the driver.

Scene 83

Rolling along the smooth floors was kinda fun. He was vaguely curious about why he was there, and where he was going. The woman pushing his wheelchair was talking to someone else he couldn't see. He knew it was a woman pushing only because he could smell her—a good smell. He smiled.

"I'll get the door," somebody said, and then the doors ahead of them magically opened, and there was a motor sound.

Outside the door a car sat at the curb, and the woman—it was another woman accompanying them—went ahead and opened a door on the car. She turned and smiled at him. "Can you stand up?" She reached her hand out and he took it.

His knees were shaky, but he stood, and with her help entered the car.

"Good bye," she said to him, and closed the door. He watched her push the wheelchair back into the building.

For a moment, he was apprehensive. He was sitting alone in the back seat of the car. A driver sat wordlessly in front. Then the door opposite him opened, and the woman he smelled got in next to him. Closing her door, she turned and smiled at him. "You look groggy," she said. "We'll get you home where you can rest." Her face was familiar, but he couldn't remember who she was.

The car started up and for the longest time they moved through the city streets. At one point, he dozed off. When he awoke, she was talking. He couldn't quite figure out what she was saying, so he just smiled at her. It was easy to smile at her. And he loved the way she smelled.

Eventually, the car stopped. She put a hand on his arm. "Do you need help getting out?" she asked. When he didn't answer—he didn't know what he was supposed to say—she got out of the car and came around to open the door next to him. He took the hand she offered him, and got slowly to his feet. His knees were shaking again. "C'mon," she said softly, "let's get you home."

He leaned on her as they made their way into the building. "I don't remember," he said, "how did this happen?"

295

"You had surgery, and you're still feeling the anesthetic," she replied.

"Thank you. You're very kind," he said. His tongue felt thick, making it difficult to speak.

She turned and looked directly into his face. "Doug, do you know who I am?"

He laughed, embarrassed. "I think so."

"I'm Meredith," she said. "Do you know who you are?"

"You're joking," he said, laughing again. "I'm Doug. How do you do, Meredith?"

A worried look crossed her face as she turned away to guide him to the elevator. They stood for a while in front of the door, and then it opened. Meredith led him into the elevator and then turned and pushed a button on the wall. He felt a little unsteady when the elevator began to move, but it felt fun. He grinned at her.

He was startled when the movement stopped with a bang. The door opened, and she gently pushed him ahead of her across a small, bare area to another door. She opened the door and stepped back so he could enter. They were in a very large room that looked like a warehouse, except that the floor was smooth and polished. He looked around.

"You're home," she said.

"This is home?" It did look familiar, as though he remembered it from a dream.

"You don't remember?" Her voice sounded hesitant.

He looked at her and smiled. "I think I'm drunk," he said. I can't remember anything."

She took his arm again and led him to a sofa. "Why don't you relax for a while. Would you like a cup of tea?"

He flopped heavily onto the sofa. "Wow, I've really had a lot to drink!"

She sat down next to him, but on the edge of the cushion. Taking his hand, she said, "You haven't been drinking, Doug. You're still feeling the anesthetic. It will wear off in a few minutes. Do you want some tea?"

"That would be nice," he said. "But can you tell me how did this happen?"

"You had surgery. Don't you remember?"

He frowned, thinking. "We're still in Cincinnati, aren't we?"

That worried look on her face again. "You just sit there and relax, and I'll fix us some tea." She stood up and went toward what looked like a kitchen.

His eyes followed her. She was very pretty, and he liked the way she moved—graceful, like a skater. He remembered seeing skaters in the movies, in New York City. He closed his eyes for just a moment.

"Here's your tea," said the woman standing next to him. She put a cup on the table, then sat down beside him holding another cup. She looked familiar.

He laughed. It was embarrassing, but he couldn't remember who she was or where they were. It didn't look like his home in Mount Adams. "Can you tell me how this happened?"

She carefully put her cup down on the table. He liked her face, but her eyes were filling with tears. "You keep asking the same question, Doug," she said gently. "You just had surgery. They removed your implant."

"Implant?" He was getting a headache from trying to remember. Looking around the room, he said, "This doesn't look like Mount Adams."

"It's not Mount Adams, Doug. It's your home in Arlington." She reached over and embraced him, and he felt her sobbing against his neck. "Oh Doug!" He liked the way she smelled.

"I'm really sleepy," he said, slumping back on the sofa.

Meredith let go of him and stood up. She disappeared for a moment, then returned with a pillow. Dropping the pillow at the end of the sofa, she lifted his legs and turned him so that he was lying down. "Are you warm enough?" She kept a hand on his shoulder.

He closed his eyes, and then a moment later he opened them. He was alone. He lay there for a long time, trying to remember where he was and why his body felt so heavy. Even his arm was heavy, he discovered, trying to lift it off the sofa.

Opening his eyes, he was aware of the darkness. There was some light over there, but he couldn't make out where it was. He turned his head to see more clearly. A shadow obscured the light for a moment, and someone was standing next to him. "You're awake," a voice said.

"It's dark," he said.

"Yes—you've been asleep for hours." Her voice sounded familiar.

He struggled to sit up. The woman took his hand and helped him. He could see her face then. She was very pretty.

"My head hurts," he said. "I'm hungry."

She continued to hold his hand, and smiled. "That's a good sign," she said. "I'll fix you some toast. You didn't drink your tea. Would you like something different?"

He picked up the cup from the table and drank the cool liquid. "Good," he said. "I was thirsty." Then he stared into the darkness, trying to remember.

She left, and returned immediately, setting a dish on the low table. It smelled like warm toast. Suddenly famished, he wolfed down the two slices of toast as she sat and watched him.

"Thanks, Mom." He wasn't sure she was his mom, but he thought she must be. His mind was really confused. "Can you tell me how this happened?"

Scene 84

"Okay, Love, slow down," Dolly said on the phone. "Tell me what's happening."

Meredith was sobbing. She managed to get out, "He's gone!"

"What do you mean—he disappeared?"

"No, I brought him home—to Arlington—but it's like he isn't here."

"He's still under the anesthetic."

"Maybe. But it's been fourteen hours! He can't remember anything! He doesn't even know me!"

"You said that Janet was out of it for some time after she had her chip removed."

"But this is different. She knew me. She just didn't feel things."

"Do you want some company?"

Meredith didn't answer for a few moments. Then, in a small voice, "Yes."

"Where are you, Love? His place or yours?"

"His."

"Okay, give me a half hour."

Still in that small, scared voice, "Thank you."

"Meredith."

"Yes?"

"Have you eaten anything?"

Silence. Then, "I had some toast last night."

"Eat, Woman!"

"Okay."

"Meredith."

"Yes?"

"We've been here before. You can do this. I'm coming over to feed you, but you can get through this. You are one tough broad!"

Meredith managed to laugh. "You know I love you?"

"Of course you do. What's he doing now?"

"Sleeping. I think."

"Has he eaten anything?"

"A little."

"Feed him. And I'll come over and feed you, 'cause I love you."

"Thank you."

"Bye."

Meredith kept the phone against her ear for a long time after Dolly hung up, as though she were desperately holding onto the connection. Then she put the instrument on the kitchen table and went in to check on Doug.

"Hi," he said brightly when he saw her.

She sat on the edge of the sofa and took his hand. "Hi," she said. "You slept a long time. Are you hungry?"

"Yes," he said. He was still wearing the same clothes he'd worn yesterday, and was showing a stubble of beard. His head was bandaged, but she knew that the wrapping was only to keep the plastic cover on the incision.

"You shouldn't take a shower, but you can take a tub bath. Can you manage that by yourself?"

"Of course!" He smiled shyly at her.

She wanted more than anything to help him, undress him, bathe him, touch him—but first she had to feed him—and her. She helped him up off the sofa, and then watched him to make sure he could get into the bathroom. His step was more confident, and he seemed to know where to go. A thought struck her. "Doug, did you get up during the night to go to the bathroom?"

He gave her that shy smile again. "It was pretty dark. I was afraid I'd wake you up. But I found it."

Meredith sighed. "Okay." There was a lot more she wanted to say, that she was glad he was home and that she thought he was getting back to himself, but she was afraid to bring it up again—the big question—did he know her? When he closed the bathroom door, she turned and went into the kitchen. *A half-hour.* Dolly would be walking in any minute. Meredith threw six eggs into a bowl and began mixing them with bits of leftover vegetables and some spices.

Before turning on the stove, she went into Doug's closet and got underwear, socks and some loose pants and a button-up shirt. Laying them in a pile outside the bathroom door, she called to him, "Doug?"

"Hello."

"I put clean clothes outside the door."

After a moment of silence, "Thank you."

She tried to quell the knot growing in her midsection. "You're welcome." She returned to the kitchen.

Dolly rang the bell just as Meredith was beginning to stir the eggs. She dashed to open the door, then back again to stir. "Thank you, Love," she said.

Dolly came up behind her and hugged her. "Where is Doug?"

"Taking a bath."

"Without you?" Dolly peered around her to look into her face.

Meredith had to laugh. "I feel like I'm a stranger to him!"

Dolly began setting the table. "I thought I was coming over to feed **you**," she said.

"Can you make coffee? And set three places, please?"

Dolly gave her a sidewise look. "You want bagels or toast?"

Meredith laughed. "Bagels, please." Then she set the spatula down and buried her face in her hands.

Dolly turned her around and embraced her. Stroking her hair, she whispered, "It's going to be all right!"

They clung to each other, and were interrupted by Doug's appearance. He had shaved and dressed, and greeted them with a wide smile. "Hello!"

Dolly said, "Hello, Doug. I see you have recovered."

"Are you another nurse?" he asked.

"You betcha," she answered. "I'm Dolly."

Doug looked down, as though he were trying to remember something. "Hi, Dolly. I can't remember ..." He looked up at Meredith.

"She's Meredith," Dolly said. "Now, sit down right there and we'll all have some breakfast."

"I'm sorry I forgot ..." he said looking at Meredith, who smiled at him, then glanced at Dolly.

"How are you feeling?" Dolly asked him as Meredith dished out the eggs. The toaster popped up a split bagel, and Dolly reloaded it, watching Doug as she moved around.

"I have a headache," he said. "Did I have an accident?" He touched his head where the incision was under the bandage.

"You don't remember?" Meredith asked.

"I think ..." he began, "I'm not home, am I?"

"Where's home, Doug?" Dolly asked.

The question startled him. "I—I don't know!"

Meredith took a deep breath and let it out slowly. Dolly looked at her and said, "You had some surgery, Doug, and it's affected your memory. You're going to be all right."

Doug frowned, and ate a bite of eggs. Meredith wiped a tear with a napkin.

Dolly bit into a bagel, and with her mouth half-full, asked, "What are some things you can remember, Doug?"

He laughed. "You're fun," he said. "Let's see, I remember our house on Mount Adams. Only I guess it isn't our house any more. I moved away a long time ago."

"Where did you move to?"

He frowned again. "Where's Angie?"

"Who is Angie?"

"My wife, of course!"

"Don't you remember, Doug? Meredith said. "You and Angie split up." She was breathing heavily, fearfully.

He looked at her, wide-eyed. And then his face changed. "She couldn't wait for me."

"She couldn't wait for you." Meredith let out her breath.

Dolly put her hand on Doug's arm. "It will all come back to you, Doug. Give it time." She looked at Meredith. "Give it time."

"Dolly ..." Meredith began, "I can't read him!"

Dolly's eyes widened. "What do you mean?"

Meredith tapped her head. "I can't read him. I can read you, but I can't read him!"

Doug looked at her, frowning. "I don't understand."

"Of course you don't," Dolly said to him. "Meredith wants to help you remember, and she's not sure how to do it."

"He used to be able to quiet his mind—that's part of their training. But it's like he isn't here." Meredith was trembling.

Okay, Meredith, ease up. Don't get him more confused, Dolly carefully thought to her.

"I'm sorry," Meredith said. "Doug, what can you remember?" She was obviously fumbling.

"Oh, lots of stuff," he said. "I remember ..."

"What?"

"My dad's new car. It was a Toyota."

"How old were you then?"

"Nine, I think. Nine."

"Do you remember what year that was?" Dolly still had her hand on his arm.

"Eighty something," he answered. "Maybe eighty five?"

She looked at Meredith. "See? Some things are pretty clear. Could you read any of that?"

Meredith shook her head. "Nothing."

Dolly looked back at Doug. "What color was it?"

"Kinda brown. It had leather seats."

"Good. Do you remember your own first car?"

"Yeah, it was an old Studebaker. It was as old as I was!" He laughed.

Dolly laughed with him, and said, "It will all come back to you."

"I looked in the mirror and I was surprised."

"At what?"

"How old I am!"

She laughed. "I had the same feeling this morning."

Doug seemed relaxed and enjoying the conversation. "You're not old!"

"My God," Meredith said to Dolly, "what would I do without you?"

"Well, you'd probably have made some coffee by now," she replied, getting up from the table. Turning to Doug, she said, "I said I would make coffee. Do you drink coffee?"

"Sure. Just a little cream. Thank you, uh, **Dolly**."

"Tell you what. You two go in the other room and get acquainted while I make coffee and clean up this mess."

Meredith smiled at her gratefully, and got up from the table. "Come on, Doug, We'll let the other nurse clean up the kitchen."

He followed her toward the sofa. "This place really doesn't have any rooms, does it? Except the bathroom. It's all one big room. I like it!"

"You don't remember yet, Doug," Meredith said, "but this is your home. You live here."

"I do? Where do you live?"

"Well, for a while, I'm going to stay here with you. Until you remember more."

"Thank you. I wouldn't know what to do."

"I know. You will." She led him to the sofa. "Dolly will bring us some coffee."

"Is she going to stay here, too?"

"Do you want me to, Doug?" asked Dolly, approaching with coffee cups in one hand and the pot in the other.

Meredith looked at her quickly.

"Kidding!" Dolly laughed.

All three of them laughed.

For the rest of the day, the three of them slowly and carefully led Doug through his available memories trying to find their limits.

Scene 85

The three of them had talked all day, Dolly had gone out for some pastries before lunch, and again before dinner to bring in Chinese. Doug had talked about what he could remember of his life up to about the time he went abroad. He remembered talking with Angie on the phone from Europe when she said she wanted a divorce, but he couldn't remember why he was over there and not at home with her. He remembered nothing about India or Afghanistan or the CIA.

Or Meredith.

After Dolly had gone ("I have to work in the morning."), he and Meredith exchanged small talk, occasionally punctuated with a "stopper" question by her—"Do you remember riding in an elevator?"

"Yeah, when I was a kid. We went downtown and went up to the top of the Carew Tower!"

"Do you remember yesterday, when we rode the elevator up here?"

He frowned and closed his eyes, trying to remember.

"Do you remember my name?"

More frowning. "Meridelle? No, **Meredith!**"

She smiled. "Right. And do you remember the name of the woman who was here all day?"

He grinned. "Dolly. Hello, Dolly!"

She felt, sometimes, as though she were talking with a child. His responses to her questions were often accompanied by expressions of delight, as though this were a game he was enjoying. But when he looked at her sometimes, it was as though **her** Doug were looking out of his eyes, pleading with her to rescue him. Or perhaps, she thought, it was just her own projection. *He is in there!* she thought. *I just have to find the key!*

She got up from the sofa, where they had been sitting most of the day, and paced the big room, trying to think of something that might get his attention—might catch his memory, like a fish, that she could then reel in to her heart.

In a large walk-in closet, she pulled out several pieces of his clothing and brought them to show him. Sometimes he said, "I like that!" but

305

there was no recognition. When she went back to the closet, he followed her. "These are all your clothes, Doug. Do you remember any of them?"

He moved the clothing back and forth on the rod, half-heartedly. Then he reached through the clothing and brought out a guitar that was standing in its case against the wall. She watched him as he carried it, excited, back to the sofa and opened the case. His face showed wonder. Lifting the instrument gently, he plucked the strings one by one. "Out of tune," he said.

She had never seen the guitar before. Doug had not even mentioned it.

He sat down and tuned the guitar. To her ear, it was quickly and perfectly tuned. He began picking out the introductory notes to George Harrison's "Something."

Meredith tried to stifle a sudden sob, but it rose in her throat and came out as almost a whimper. He looked up at her, forehead creased for a moment, then broke into a wide smile. "I like this, too!" he said. With just a few mistakes, he played the melody through, and then began to sing. "Something in the way she moves …"

"Keep going!" she called to him as she rushed to the bathroom and closed the door. Sitting there, she could hear the song through her sobs. Unable to control her crying, she sat there until he tapped on the door. "Are you all right?"

Meredith stood up and wiped her face as she opened the door. Taking a deep breath, she said, "It's one of my favorite songs."

Doug took her hand. "Come, sit down," he said. "Why are you crying?"

She allowed him to lead her to the sofa. "I remember that song from a long time ago."

"Why is it sad for you?" He looked into her face, concerned.

It was all she could do to keep from throwing her arms around his neck and smothering him with kisses. "Sometimes, it's the memories that are sad," she said finally.

"Yes. I heard that George Harrison died. That was sad. He was a good musician. He had a spiritual side."

"Doug, he died in 2001," she said. "Do you remember?"

"I heard it somewhere." Then he thought for a moment. "I don't know what year this is!"

Meredith's heart was pounding. "That was ten years ago."

"Really?" He picked a few more notes, then strummed the chords she recognized immediately as the beginning of John Lennon's "Imagine."

"Imagine," she said. She wanted to flood him with questions, make him remember everything!

"Yes," he said, continuing to strum. "He's dead, too. I used to play a lot."

"I've never heard you play before. I didn't even know you had a guitar."

Doug stopped strumming and looked at her. "Did I know you before—before the accident?"

Her throat was tight, but she struggled to say the words, "Yes. We were in love."

He looked back at his guitar. "Then you're not really a nurse."

"No."

"Why can't I remember?" Absent-mindedly, he picked at the strings of the guitar. Then he looked up at her again and smiled. "I'd like to be in love with you again."

She had been holding her breath, and her lungs were still full of air as she tried to inhale more. Her words came out strained and high-pitched. "I'd like that, too." But then she regretted them, as he reached for her. She grasped his wrists and gently lowered them. "But not yet, Doug."

She moved away from him on the sofa. "Play some more, please?"

He smiled. "What do you want to hear?"

"What do you like, besides the Beatles?"

"Well, I like Rodriguez, but I never learned it very well." He began to play something that Meredith had heard many times but couldn't remember, a slow dance for guitar. "This is really hard on a folk guitar. It's supposed to be a classical guitar," he said, stumbling on occasional notes. "The strings are too close together."

She leaned back in the sofa, tears streaming unchecked down her face. He stopped, looking at her.

"No, no! Please go on!" she pleaded.

He played for a short time, then stopped. "I have to concentrate on the music when I play that," he said, "but I want to concentrate on you."

She sat up. "Doug, I said we were in love—but I never knew you played the guitar."

"Yeah, I took lessons in high school, and some of us guys played together sometimes at parties."

"Then you married Angie."

"Yeah, it just seemed the thing to do. All the guys were getting married."

"Were you in love with her?"

"I think so. She wouldn't …" His face turned red.

"She wouldn't go to bed with you until you were married." Meredith was more relaxed now, beginning to enjoy the game they were playing. Except that he wasn't playing a game.

"Yeah. How did you know?"

"That's something we used to do," she said, aware that it was not something she ever did.

"We used to argue a lot," he said, remembering things long past.

"And you went overseas, and she couldn't wait."

"Yeah. How did you know that?"

"You told me. You said you went to India." She waited. *One more step.*

"Did I? Yes, I guess I did. It's hard to remember."

They sat in silence for a long time. Doug had leaned back on the sofa, his eyes half-closed. Meredith wasn't sure if he were sleeping or trying to remember.

"Doug," she said, "it's very late at night. I need to sleep."

He smiled, his eyes closed. "Yes," he said, "me too."

She stood up and took the guitar from his lap and put it into the case. "Thank you for playing for me."

"I haven't played in a long time."

"I know."

He opened his eyes. "You know a lot about me."

"Not nearly enough." She reached her hand down toward him. "C'mon. You're sleeping in your own bed tonight."

"Where will you sleep?"

"Right here. This is your home. You get the bed."

He stood up, grinning. "I'd love it if you slept with me in my bed."

"Someday, Doug." She smiled up at him.

"Not until we're married?" He was playing the game!

"Well, maybe not that long," she said. "First, you have to remember me."

Scene 86

Dolly called when she got home from work the next day. Meredith was fixing dinner with the phone propped on her shoulder as she stirred something on the stove. "How are things going?" Dolly asked.

"We are having real conversations, at least. He gets a twinkle in his eye, and tells little jokes. You know he plays the guitar?"

"You never mentioned it."

"I didn't even know he had one! He just took it out of the closet and tuned it and began playing!"

"His memory sure isn't totally destroyed, is it? What's he doing now?"

"Reading, I think. He discovered his book shelves."

"Good! That's a good sign! Now, what can I do for you?"

"Dolly, you're sweet. Thank you. The only thing I've been wondering about is my poor bird. Could you go over and make sure he has food and a clean newspaper in his cage? Sally, next door, does that sometimes for me but I forgot to ask her before we went to Walter Reed."

"Sure. I might talk back to him if he gets too rambunctious, but I can feed him. Do you need any groceries over there?"

"Maybe tomorrow evening? Do you have plans?"

"You know me, Girl. If I have too much time on my hands, I get into trouble. I'll call you for a list tomorrow after work."

"Thank you, Dolly, you're a lifesaver."

"Seems to me that you're doing all the saving of lives. Speaking of which, have you slept with him yet?"

"Dolly, no!" Then Meredith chuckled. "Actually, he did ask me last night if I'd come to bed with him."

"And, Nurse Meredith refused—gently."

"I said not until he could remember who I am."

"Now, that's incentive for him."

"I hope so. I really wanted to cuddle with him. I also don't want him to burst his incision."

Dolly laughed. "I can think of a very crude retort to that. But I won't. It sounds like he's getting his groove back."

"He doesn't feel like Doug yet."

"Obviously, I don't know what Doug feels like."

"Dolly!" Meredith laughed. "You're incorrigible!"

"Hasn't done me much good so far."

"Hmmm. Dolly, have you been drinking?"

"Well, maybe a tiny shot—or two."

"Wish I could join you. I have 'responsibilities.'"

"It must be frustrating for you. How long are you taking off work?"

"Yes, it is." Meredith sighed. "I took two weeks vacation. I may need more."

"Hang in there, Girl. I'll come over tomorrow night and entertain your patient so you can relax with a martini."

"A friend in need."

"If you're going to hold out on him, maybe he needs …"

"Stop. Right. There. Goodbye."

Dolly laughed. "I'll call you tomorrow."

Scene 87

As Meredith and Doug were eating dinner, her phone rang. It was Janet. "How is he doing?" she asked.

"Not as good as you did," Meredith answered. "He's got serious amnesia."

"Oh. Sorry.

"He doesn't remember anything about the Company—or me."

"Oh."

"At first I was worried that he'd lost everything, but today he dug his guitar out of a closet and tuned it up and started playing. Pretty good, actually. How are **you** doing?"

"I feel like I'm pretty much back to normal," Janet said. "I'm not having as much fun, but I can do pretty much whatever I want."

"That's great. Have you been in touch with the group?"

"As a matter of fact, yes. I've gotten to know Gary Blanchard. Do you remember him?

"Of course." Meredith felt a twinge in her gut.

"He's the only one in the group who seems to understand what I'm going through."

"Yes, he's very insightful." The twinge was becoming a knot.

"Meredith, would it help if I came over and talked with Doug?"

Meredith was quiet for a moment.

"Would it help **you**?" Janet asked.

"Thank you, Janet. I really don't know. And I don't know why not. I have no idea how to handle this."

"Your call, Meredith. I'll come if you think it will help. If you don't, I'm okay with that."

"That's very kind, Janet. Let's try it."

"I'm free all day Saturday."

"Great. Call me before you come?"

"Are you at Doug's?"

"Yes."

"See you Saturday morning, late."

"Thank you, Janet."

Scene 88

Dolly was incredulous. "You're letting 'The Other Woman' come to visit him?"

"Maybe she can help him remember."

They were talking on the phone ostensibly to get a grocery list together.

"Remember what?!! He can't remember all the good times you two have had, and you invite her over to see if she can get him to remember playing in the Caribbean?"

Meredith sighed. "If it will trigger something, it's to the good. We need to get him back to today!"

"Even if you have to throw yourself on your own sword, right?"

"Yes. Even if." Meredith's eyes filled with tears.

Dolly was silent for a moment. "Okay, we've got a grocery list. I can be there with the stuff in about an hour."

"Thank you, Dolly."

"All right Saint Meredith, I'll see you in an hour."

When she closed her phone, Meredith looked up to see Doug watching her. She smiled.

"I'm feeling a little like a kid being talked about by his mom and his teacher." Doug had a pleasant look on his face, but Meredith felt ashamed to have been discussing him like that.

"I'm sorry, Doug," she said. "You have a number of friends who are concerned about you, and they all want to help you get your memory back."

"Who's Janet?"

Meredith was rattled. *When did he hear her name?* "She's somebody you used to work with," she said. She was trying hard to pick up what he might be thinking, but could get nothing but unintelligible fragments. *At least,* she thought, *that's more than I've gotten so far.*

"I try and try to remember things—I can't even remember yesterday! But I remember being a kid like it was yesterday. It's weird!"

"You had a surgical procedure the other day to remove an electronic device from your head." Meredith's breathing was shallow and her heart

313

was beating rapidly. *Slow down, Meredith. Keep it simple, and watch for a reaction.*

"What kind of electronic device?" Doug seemed simply curious.

"You worked for a government agency that wanted …" She stopped, and shrugged. "You were a spy."

Doug sat down in a chair. "I don't understand," he said, looking at the floor.

She knelt beside him and looked into his face. "Doug, look at me. You didn't want to be a spy, and so you told them to remove this device from your head. Do you understand that?"

He looked at her, then he looked away into the distance. "It sounds like science fiction!"

He laughed, and Meredith joined him, laughing until tears came to her eyes again.

"It does, doesn't it?"

"What did it do—the device?" Doug frowned.

"It let you hear what other people were thinking."

He looked at her for a long time. Then he said, "That's like cheating."

"Yes." Meredith thought about her own 'gift' and shuddered.

"So when they removed it, they removed my memory, too?"

"We hope that's just temporary. The brain kinda spasms sometimes when it's disturbed."

Their conversation was interrupted by the arrival of Dolly.

"Well, hello Dolly!" Doug said, laughing at his own joke.

"Well, hello Douglas!" She swept into the big room like her namesake had on Broadway.

Doug was obviously glad to see her. He met her halfway across the big room and took the two bags of groceries from her. "Let me help you!" he said.

She looked at Meredith with a surprised smile.

Meredith told Doug to put the bags on the table, and began taking out their contents. "Thank you, Dolly," she said, her face a mask.

Dolly looked at her quickly. "What's up?" she asked quietly.

Meredith shook her head. To Doug, she said, "You're in for a treat. You can have meat for dinner!"

Doug looked surprised, and then smiled. "I didn't notice."

"You're sweet," said Meredith.

"No, I didn't notice. I guess I forgot about meat. Don't you eat meat?"

Dolly helped Meredith sort through the groceries. "Doug, you're pretty perceptive," she said.

"I didn't notice," he replied.

"That's not what I meant. You did figure it out that Meredith doesn't eat meat."

He turned to Meredith. "Why don't you?" he asked.

"I don't want to harm animals," she said simply.

Doug looked at her for a moment, then said, quietly, "Wow."

Dolly picked up a package of port chops. "But you and I can have pork chops tonight."

Doug sat down at the table, a blank look on his face.

"Doug, what's wrong?" asked Meredith.

"Nothing—I don't know. I got this strange feeling all of a sudden, like I've been here before."

"That's called déjà vu," said Dolly. "What's it saying?"

"I don't know. It's like I half-remember something that I dreamed, only I can't remember exactly what it was, only the feeling." His face was pale.

"When did it start?"

"Just now. You said we can have pork chops tonight, and it was like this dream swept over me. Weird!"

Meredith pulled a chair up next to him and took his hand in hers. "Try to remember the dream."

"It's really fuzzy," he said slowly. "Like I'm in this restaurant, and somebody is there, and she picks up a fork full of food, and then puts it back down." He thought for a moment. "That's all I can remember. But the feeling is still here!"

"What feeling, Doug?"

"Like I'm ashamed, or something."

"Keep going. Stay in it. Tell us more."

"Who's she?" Dolly asked.

He looked at Meredith. "You have this earring that swings in that little space ..." He touched her hair where it covered her ear. "right there."

Meredith put her hand over her mouth to stifle a cry.

"Is it Meredith, Doug?" Dolly asked.

His eyes filled with tears. "I'm sorry!"

Dolly pulled a chair up next to Meredith. "What are you sorry about?"

"I don't know!"

Meredith took a deep breath and let it out. She continued to hold his hand.

Dolly stood up. "Okay, Doug. It's okay. When you want to talk more about it, we'll listen." She took a skillet from the bottom of the range. "We all need to eat something."

Doug looked at Meredith, then put his free hand on top of hers. "What are you eating?"

She fumbled with her words. "I have some Boca Burgers in the freezer."

"Boca Burgers?"

"They're like hamburgers, only made from vegetables."

"I'll eat those, too."

"Looks like I'm having pork chops all by myself," commented Dolly from the range.

Later, when Meredith asked Doug about his dream-like experience, he said it was gone, and he couldn't remember anything about it. Meredith asked him to play his guitar for Dolly. "Only not the Beatles, okay?"

He looked at her and smiled. "They make you cry," he said, and began playing and singing an old Bob Dylan song, "How many times ..."

The two women soon joined in, all the way to, "... before she sleeps in the sand."

That night Doug went alone to his bed again, but he lay awake for a long time. He thought about the dream experience he'd had—it was very uncomfortable, as though he couldn't think straight. The worst part was the feeling it had to it. For a moment he'd thought he might throw up.

Lying in bed, he tried unsuccessfully to capture the feeling again. *Maybe it's all the stuff I can't remember,* he thought.

Twenty feet away on the sofa, Meredith was also awake, thinking about what had happened that evening. It was as though Doug were about to recover, and then the window closed. Then she heard his thought, *Maybe it's all the stuff I can't remember.*

"Oh, Doug, I hope so!" she said aloud.

"What?"

Instead of replying, she got up from the sofa and went quietly to the bed. Slipping under the covers with him, she whispered, "You remember me!"

Scene 89

"Do we have a waffle iron?" Doug asked, poking through the kitchen cupboards.

Meredith had been in the bathroom prepping herself for the day, having slipped out of their shared bed without waking Doug—or at least, so she thought. Seeing him in the kitchen area, busily making breakfast, she had another moment of hopeful gratitude. "Yes," she said, "it's on the top shelf there—I can't reach it except on a chair."

"I remember how to make waffles," he said, and you seem to have all the ingredients."

"**You** seem to have the ingredients," she corrected him. "This is your place, remember?"

He turned and smiled at her. "I have to take your word for that." He extracted the waffle iron from the cupboard and plugged it in.

Meredith came up behind him and put her arms around him, laying her cheek against his back.

"Was I—was it okay, last night?" He continued to mix the batter.

She released him, and turned him around to face her. "I felt like I had you back again," she said softly, looking into his face.

He kissed her gently on the lips. "How could I have forgotten that?"

Meredith turned him back around. "I don't want you to forget you're making breakfast. I'm hungry."

"So am I. I was going to wait until you came out, and ask you if we could have waffles, but then I said, 'Well, dummy, do it yourself!'"

She leaned against the table facing him as he worked. "Doug, I hope you'll tell me if we—if I—am pushing you too hard. We have lots of time."

He smiled without saying anything.

"Today we have to take you to the hospital again for a follow-up with your surgeon. He'll probably take out your stitches and ask you a bunch of questions."

Doug set the table for breakfast. "You'll come with me, won't you?"

"Of course I will. I might have to tell them I'm your wife so they will let me in—is that okay?"

He turned and looked into her eyes. "It's more than okay."

"The waffles smell wonderful," she said. "I'll make us some coffee."

After they had eaten, Meredith brought up something she had been avoiding. "Tomorrow, we're going to have another visitor, someone you used to work with."

"Will I know them? I didn't know you or Dolly."

"I don't know. I'm hoping it will help you get your memory back. She asked if she could come and see you."

"Another nurse."

His lack of expression startled Meredith, but when she realized he was joking, she burst out laughing. "Have you had too many nurses?"

"Not if they all look like you."

"You are a smooth talker!"

He fingered his spoon. "You said we were in love, before."

"Yes."

"Last night, after …" He pursed his lips, thinking. Meredith caught fleeting impressions from his mind. "After we made love, I had another dream experience."

"You remembered something?"

"Just a feeling, like that déjà vu that Dolly said."

"Was it uncomfortable, like the last one?" She felt a growing apprehension.

"No, not really. But the feeling is weird."

"Be sure to tell the doctor about it. I think they will send you to a neurologist anyway."

He looked at the clock on the range. "What time do we leave?"

"Ten-thirty. It's not far." Meredith noticed that his thoughts were not as jumbled as they had been. She sensed that he was calculating time in his head.

"I should get cleaned up. I need to shave."

"All right, you go do that and I'll clean up the kitchen. Just don't get your bandage wet."

"I remember," he said.

Meredith looked at him quickly. "Doug, what do you remember?"

He laughed. "I remember that I have to keep my bandage dry!"

She reached across the table and took his hand in both of hers, and pressed it to her lips.

Scene 90

The appointment with the surgeon was quick and cursory. She removed the stitches in his scalp and replaced the dressing with a smaller one. "Give this another week, to make sure it's all sealed up. If you don't get any seeping into the dressing by next week, you can take it off and begin showering." She smiled at him. "It's healing nicely."

"He has amnesia," Meredith said.

"Yes, that's in the report. Something like that is to be expected for a while. I've made an appointment with a neurologist for Monday morning. Can you make that?"

"Yes," Meredith answered.

"Don't worry," the surgeon said. "He's going to be fine!"

Meredith tried to read the woman's thoughts, but she seemed not to have any. *If you can hear this, say hello.* Watching the woman's face, she decided that she didn't have an implant of her own. On the cab ride home, she told Doug what she had done.

"I don't understand," he said.

"One of the things about those implants like you used to have is that once the technology is developed, it will be seen as essential by more and more people, for different purposes."

"For different kinds of cheating."

Meredith looked at him. "You are so perceptive!"

Doug frowned. "How did it feel to you when I had the implant?"

"It didn't take me by surprise," she said, smiling. "I knew it the minute I first saw you. But for some reason it didn't bother me right away. Well, I guess it did a little bit. You were surprised that I wasn't intimidated by it."

"It's hard for me to imagine, right now, since I can't even read my own mind!"

Meredith became thoughtful. "Doug, I have to tell you something, and it scares me to tell you."

"Maybe you should wait, then." He looked over at her. "Maybe it will be easier."

"The trouble is, I don't want you to find out later and wonder why I kept it from you. Does that make sense?"

"Yes. And now you have told me that you have a secret, and when you can tell it to me, I will know that you waited for a good reason."

She had been leaning forward so that she could see his face clearly. Now she slumped back. "You are something else," she said.

"Now I'm worried," he said. "I thought I could wait for your secret, but then I started thinking about what it might be." He turned his head and looked at her. "Do you have a husband—or do I have a wife?"

Meredith laughed, and took his hand. "No, no, no. Nothing like that. Why?"

"Because you said we were in love with each other before, and that thought feels really good to me. It's like we are just getting to know each other, and already I don't want to lose you."

She smiled at him. "We haven't known each other very long, actually. Not even a year. There are things about you that I didn't know until just the other day, like your playing and singing. That was a delightful discovery for me!"

"Can you wait for me? What if I never get my memory back?"

"I will still love you." She almost stopped herself before saying it, but she had to tell him.

"Angie couldn't wait." He looked straight ahead.

"Do you miss her?"

"I don't remember."

"Will you tell me if you do?"

"Sure."

The cab pulled up before his building. "Here's your home, Doug," she said. Do you remember it?"

He looked out at the old building. "I think I do, but I'm not sure."

"We have lots of time."

As they made their way up to his loft, he kept looking at everything, trying to get clues to his past. When Meredith opened his door, he stopped, then walked deliberately to the center of the large room. "Pillows," he said.

Meredith threw her arms around his neck. "Pillows. Yes!" Kissing him quickly, she went to the closet and retrieved their meditation cushions. "That one is yours, and this one is mine. We sat together here to meditate."

Lines formed between his eyebrows. "I don't understand."

"You will, Doug. Now let's have some lunch."

That afternoon, the two of them explored his home. Meredith took things out of drawers, opened boxes that were stored in the big closet, and showed him his clothing. One box held photographs, tossed together in no order, hundreds of them. "Can we look at them together?" she asked.

"Sure. Maybe I can remember."

One by one, she took out a photograph, looked on the back to see if there was anything written there, and held it for Doug to muse over.

"Yes," he said. That's Charlie, uh, I can't remember his last name. He was in my class."

"In high school."

"Yes. We used to smoke pot together."

"Can I write that on the back?"

He laughed. "If you want."

"I'll separate them into ones you remember and ones you don't— yet."

To the next photograph, showing three young people, he said, "That's Marlene and that's Rich and that's—I don't remember his name. Marlene and I went together for a while. Her father didn't like me."

A small, formal portrait of a young woman gave him a reaction. Meredith looked at him as he studied it. "Angie," he said simply.

"She's pretty."

"Yeah."

"Doug, what are you feeling right now?"

It took him a minute to respond. "Sad."

"Why did you leave her?"

"She couldn't wait for me."

"I know that, Doug. But you left. Do you remember why you left?"

A tear fell from his face onto the photograph. He wiped it off and put the photo back in the box. "I just felt something—like I needed to find out something. I had to find out why I was alive, or something. I don't know."

Meredith lifted the photograph from the box and wrote "Angie" on the back, and put it with the first two. "A lot of us, when we're young, have that need to discover ourselves," she said gently.

They went through the pictures slowly. Some he could speak about and some he could not remember the faces on them. One showed a small group of young people standing before a building that looked foreign. "Ashram," he said. "I don't know who they were."

"Do you remember anything about that time?"

"We spent a lot of time there high on hashish. We were hippies, I guess. We didn't do anything useful or learn anything."

"Isn't that where you learned to meditate?"

He smiled. "Yeah, I guess I did learn that. There was this old guru, and he made me sit for hours and hours, and then go out and beg for food."

"Did you find out why you were alive?"

Doug laughed. "I don't think anyone ever does."

Another picture, of a soldier in full battle dress with his rifle at the ready, brought no recognition from Doug.

"Afghanistan?" she asked.

"I don't know," he said dismissively.

When they finally reached the bottom of the box, Meredith felt unsatisfied, as though something important was missing, a key that might unlock Doug's mind. "There's nothing here of recent years," she said. "You don't have any recent photos?"

"I don't know," was his only response.

"Oh, of course. You wouldn't have had any pictures of you in the CIA. Too dangerous."

He looked at her blankly.

"I wish we had a picture of us," she said, smiling. "When we see Dolly again, maybe she'll take one."

He returned her smile, but then said, "Pictures show only the outside."

"What does that mean to you?"

"I feel like I don't have any inside, like you do."

She leaned over and took his face between her hands. "Yes you do. We just need to let it show." Then she kissed him tenderly.

Scene 91

It was Saturday morning, and Meredith's heart was beating strangely. She felt as though she couldn't get her breath. After a moment of concern that there was something physically wrong—her heart was in good condition from her regular workouts—she remembered that Janet was coming to visit that day.

Casually, as she and Doug prepared eggs and toast for breakfast, she mentioned it to him. "Remember I told you one of your co-workers is coming this morning for a visit?

He thought for a moment. "I think so."

"Are you feeling up to it?"

He shrugged, and she let the subject drop. But later, when her phone rang, she was startled. *Relax, Meredith. It's a friend visiting!*

"Hi, Meredith, is this a good time for me to drop in?" Janet's voice sounded strong and friendly.

"Of course. I asked him again this morning if he remembered you, and he didn't. But he may when he sees you."

"How is he getting along?"

"He's improving every day."

"Good. I'll see you in about a half-hour."

Doug had noticed the phone call, and was watching her. "Is that the visitor?"

"Yes. Her name is Janet."

"Janet." His face showed no recognition.

Meredith tried to quiet her nervousness.

When Janet appeared, she was outgoing and bubbly. "Hi, Doug! How are you feeling?"

"I'm feeling good," he replied, and touched the bandage on his head. "They took out the stitches yesterday. I'm going to see a neurologist on Monday." Meredith detected no sign of recognition, and she began to relax.

"I had the same surgery," Janet said to him.

"You had an implant?"

"Yes."

"Did you lose your memory?" Doug was frowning.

"No," she said. "I did lose some feeling, though. It's getting better."

"I've got amnesia." He seemed once more a boy, describing things he'd been told about but didn't yet understand.

"I know. I'm sorry."

"So am I. I don't remember Meredith much, except once in a while, and it makes her sad."

Meredith and Janet exchanged wry smiles.

"Doug, do you remember Lucy?" She asked it in the same friendly, superficial tone that had been the conversation so far.

But Meredith reacted inside. *No! How could you! Don't ask about that!*

Doug's forehead furrowed. "Lucy. No." But he continued to think, to try to remember. Something was different. He put both of his hands to his head, as though trying to contain something. "I—I feel funny!"

Meredith and Janet looked at each other. Janet touched her lips with her fingertips. "I'm sorry!" she said softly.

Doug sat down, and then looked up at Meredith, smiling. "That dream feeling," he said. His hand shook on his knee.

"Just relax, Doug," Meredith said, and turned to Janet. "He's had a few of these spells. It will pass."

Janet looked concerned. "I thought it might help him remember."

Meredith squelched an impulse to cry out. *I don't want him to remember that!* "Sometimes strong feelings bring this on. It will pass."

"Meredith, you can read me! You know I didn't mean anything more!"

Meredith just looked at her.

Doug, still with one hand on his head and the other shaking on his knee, looked at both of them. "I don't understand."

Trying to control her breathing, Meredith said, "When you and Janet worked together on assignment, she had been given an alias of Lucy."

He turned to Janet. "I don't understand what you meant."

She turned red and looked at Meredith. "He doesn't know about you?"

"What about her?" Doug's voice was rising.

"Doug," began Meredith, "remember our conversation in the cab coming home yesterday, when I told you I had something I needed you to know?" She was shaking now.

"Yes. Your secret. You were scared to tell me."

Her eyes filled with tears as she tried to find the words.

"I said it would be okay when you could tell me."

"I wish it hadn't happened this way," she said haltingly. "Do you remember what your implant was for?"

"For spying. For cheating. I didn't want to do it anymore."

"Well, it happens that some people—a few people—have the same ability, and nobody knows how it came about."

"Without an implant?"

"Yes."

Janet was standing nearby, a look of anguish on her face.

Doug looked at Meredith. "You're one of them?"

In the midst of it all, Meredith marveled at his insight. He might not remember, but he could reason. "Yes," she said. "I don't know how or why, but I can—a little bit."

"You can read my thoughts?" He stared at her. In her mind, it was as though she were an alien being.

"Sometimes."

"Now?"

"No."

"Why not?"

Janet started to say something, but Meredith put her hand up. "Wait."

"I don't know, Doug. It's almost never easy to do, and some people are harder to read than others at different times."

"I can't think!" he said, almost in a whimper. "This feeling—this dream feeling!"

"Can we stop?" Janet's face was contorted. "I should go!"

"No," said Meredith. "We have to get through this!"

"I have a headache," Doug said, holding his head again with both hands.

Meredith pulled two chairs around the table for her and Janet. "We can slow down," she said. "Let's just breathe for a few minutes."

"Meditate," said Doug.

She smiled. "Yes."

Doug closed his eyes and put his hands on his knees. Meredith and Janet exchanged glances, then assumed the same pose. "Just breathe," Meredith said. She recognized that she spoke to herself even more than to the others.

She was surprised that it was more than ten or fifteen minutes before Doug began to stir on his chair. She opened her eyes.

He was looking at her. "It went away," he said simply. "That is so cool!"

Janet got up from her chair and moved toward the sink. "Would anyone else like some water?"

"Yes, thank you," replied Doug.

"Thank you," echoed Meredith. She took a deep breath and let it out. Looking at Doug, she asked, "How are you doing?"

Janet filled three glasses with ice and water and brought them to the others before sitting again.

"I'm confused," Doug said to Meredith. "Did I know this about you before?"

"Yes," she said. "You recognized it before I did."

"So we could read each other's minds?"

"Sometimes."

"Cool." He thought for a moment, then grinned at her. "Then for us it wasn't cheating."

"No."

"But now you can read me and I can't read you. Why did I have the implant removed?"

"Because with it you had to cheat others. That was your job."

He looked at Janet. "You had an implant, too?"

She nodded. "I had mine removed, just like you did."

Doug turned back to Meredith. "What am I thinking now?"

She smiled at him. "You're thinking, 'What am I thinking now?'"

"Aw." He thought for a moment, then laughed. "Okay." He laughed again.

Meredith stood up. "How about some lunch? I am hungry!"

"Me, too!" His response reminded Meredith of their meeting in the elevator, what seemed so long ago. His last words to her as she left was

328

to echo her own thought: "Me, too," when it began to sink in to her what a relationship with him might be like.

"Janet?" Meredith was greatly relieved that the crisis she had feared had ended with little heartbreak. "Will you have lunch with us?"

Janet managed a weak smile. "Please don't hate me!"

Meredith went to her and hugged her. "I don't hate you. Will you stay?"

"Okay. Thank you. Can I help fix it?

Scene 92

On the phone that afternoon, Dolly was impressed. "Nobody brought up the fact that she slept with him?"

Meredith laughed. "It was like, 'don't ask, don't tell.'"

"I'm glad it went well. I was worried."

"Me, too. It threw me for a loop when she mentioned Lucy. Doug went into one of his dream spells, whatever they are."

"You're seeing the neurologist next week, right?"

"Yes, and the following week I'll be back at work."

"God willing, as they say. So, Meredith—when can we get together to tie one on? Are you forever married to this guy?"

"Maybe. But eventually I will need to think about myself once in a while."

"Even saints need sex?"

"Well, …" Meredith began.

"You did it! Already! Good going, Girl!"

"It seemed the right time," she said.

"So, his **disability** doesn't extend to …"

"Not at all. Thanks for asking."

"Hey, that's what friends are for."

"I presume you're scheduled for tonight. Want to come over tomorrow? Or maybe we could meet at the bistro near my place. I should introduce Doug to my home."

"And your cockatiel. Don't forget your cockatiel."

"Thank you for looking in on him, Dolly."

"Don't mention it. I'm getting a little fond of the bird."

"What about tomorrow?"

"Okay. Lets coordinate things tomorrow."

"Love you.

"Hmm. Bye."

When she hung up, Meredith noticed that Doug was (on the far side of the big room) practicing on his guitar. He seemed not to have noticed that she was talking on the phone.

"Sounds nice," she said as she went near him. "I don't recognize it."

"Just noodling around," he said, looking up. Do you know Keith Jarrett?"

"Of course. He plays the piano, and he used to do improvisations in concerts all over Europe."

"I used to love to listen to him. I tried to improvise a little, but it never comes out like his."

Meredith sat down on the sofa next to him. "How do you feel about maybe going out tomorrow—like, dinner at a restaurant?"

"With Dolly?"

"You heard me talking with her?"

"Yes. I couldn't hear everything you said—you were far away."

"I wasn't being private. Well, maybe, a little."

He smiled. "That's okay. We've been together continuously since my surgery."

"And after next week, I have to go back to work, if you are able to get along by yourself."

"Don't I have to go back to work sometime?"

"You are on disability leave. It depends upon the doctors when you will be able to work."

"Can we talk about Janet?" It came out of the blue for Meredith. She had no idea he was still thinking about Janet.

"Of course."

"You said Lucy was an alias that Janet used in our assignment together."

"She was known as Lucy, and you were known as Daniel."

"We were both spies."

"Yes."

"Why did I go into that spell right then?"

"I don't know for sure, but I was very jealous of her after your assignment together, and maybe that affected you more than we thought."

"Why were you jealous?"

"Because you slept with her."

"Oh." Doug thought for a moment. "Oh."

"I might still be a little bit jealous of her." Meredith wiped her damp palms on her slacks.

"Did I sleep with her after the assignment?"

"I don't think so. No."

He grinned. "She is very attractive."

"How well I know!"

"Does it bother you that I said that?" He was watching her face.

"I want you to be honest with me, Doug. And I will be honest with you. But my feeling jealous shouldn't change that. Okay?"

"I like that. I remember a long time ago, somebody said that a liar has to have a good memory. That's not me, is it?"

They both laughed until suddenly, at the same time, their faces became serious. "I love you, Doug," she said.

He put his guitar down on the floor and wrapped his arms around her.

Scene 93

The neurologist agreed to set up some tests, beginning with a functional MRI, after which they could arrange for occupational therapy for Doug to help him recover his memory. "At least some of this," he told them, "might be related to migraine, brought on by the neurological stress of the surgery. We can't say for sure until after the tests. But it resembles the Transient Global Amnesia that some migraine sufferers experience. Those spells of dream-like feelings occur sometimes, too. It's like a temporary short circuit in an electrical device. Usually, it goes away without any long-term consequences."

Meredith took Doug out into the neighborhood around his loft, and showed him where the markets were. He had to get a new cell phone, since the one he had was confiscated by the Company, along with his firearm, badge and nametag.

They also took the subway into D.C., and she showed him how to get to her apartment. He was quickly losing his child-like responses, and took responsibility for his care and feeding. Meredith helped him with his finances for a while, checking his account balances online and arranging for automatic transfers and bill paying.

Scene 94

Meredith returned to her job after a two-week vacation. Doug had assured her that he could manage on his own, preparing meals and doing laundry and even venturing outside by himself to buy groceries and get exercise. They had resumed daily meditation together, and he found that he could access some memories on his cushion that had eluded him otherwise.

He tried meditating when his "dream spells" came on him, but usually they occurred when he was upset or confused about something, and he couldn't get himself to sit in meditation. Fortunately, the spells became less frequent. Music seemed to help. Listening to music or playing his guitar (even though it was more difficult to concentrate on his fingers) distracted the spells.

He read Meredith's book "Mindsight" and got a clearer picture of how his brain was processing (or not) his experiences. All of this activity, as the neurologist had suggested, helped him to feel and remember more clearly. Meredith ordered for him a copy of Daniel Siegel's other book on the subject, "The Developing Mind."

His memory of the recent past remained beyond his recall. He believed Meredith when she told him that he had served in Afghanistan, and had been an agent in the CIA, but he could not remember anything more than isolated fragments of his experiences.

One evening, as they sat with drinks before dinner, she told him how upset he had been after an assignment in which he had had to kill an enemy agent. "It really tore you up—you said you saw through his eyes for a moment as he died."

"It must have been hard. I cannot even imagine it now," he said. "How can a person kill another person? You say I had no choice, but how could I do that?"

"Like Daniel Siegel writes in his book, our brains evolved in sections, with the later sections being layered on top of the primitive sections, the brain stem and the limbic sections." She took the book "Mindsight" down from its shelf and pointed out to him the illustrations.

"When we are really threatened, we act out of those primitive sections even before our thinking sections get engaged."

He looked at her and smiled. "First, you were my nurse. I remember you taking care of me when I came home from the hospital. Now you are my teacher."

"You won't need the teacher very long, Doug. There were days during the weeks after you came home when I thought I would always have to take care of you."

"Really? You didn't tell me that." He pushed the little curl of hair back so he could see her earring.

"It's interesting," she said, "how our images of other people change with the situations we're in. I knew it was you—the man I fell in love with—inside your head, and I caught glimpses of you, but it was like there was a wall, or a closed door or something, that prevented us from seeing each other fully. You were like a shell or something of the Doug I loved."

He laughed, then caught himself. "I'm sorry—I'm not making fun of you, but I had this image of a stuffed animal ..."

"No!" She frowned, then her face eased into a smile. "I can't bring myself to imagine that. But I understand the image. If you had been somebody else, somebody I didn't love so much, I might be able to. Even the image of a shell of Doug makes me cringe!"

"It feels a little bit like I was born a couple of weeks ago," he said. "My memories from the past seem to dissolve slowly as time went by. And then, suddenly, I was here with you, and you acted as though it had always been like this. But it wasn't, was it?"

She touched his face with her hand. "In some ways, right now, it feels like it was always like this. But no, we've loved each other for less than a year. We've spent a lot of time together since then, but I didn't live with you before your surgery."

"I'd like that. Would you?"

"Would I like to, or would I live with you?" She smiled.

"Both."

"It sounds wonderful to me, but I'm not ready for that yet. A lot has happened in this past year, and I need to find out what it all means."

"I don't understand." Small creases formed between his eyebrows.

"When I began to read other people's thoughts, it was really upsetting for me. You were living with your implant for a specific purpose, but it just came on me, and I didn't like it at all. I found out that other people have developed the same ability, and I found a group in Silver Spring of people like that who were supporting each other and trying to make sense of it. I still need to keep in touch with them, because this thing is going to change the way people relate to each other."

"I understand the problem, I think," he said. "It doesn't bother me that you can read my thoughts, although I don't know how that works. But if you were a stranger to me, it might bother me."

"Yes, that's it, exactly. We're afraid it will create a division between people, and the world doesn't need one more division."

"Like the World Trade Center."

She looked at him quickly. "Do you remember that?"

"It's kinda fuzzy, but I remember about the planes and the way people reacted. It's how Afghanistan started, isn't it?"

"You do remember. We've always had conflicts between groups, but that was frightening—it still is frightening!"

"What can your group do?"

Meredith sighed. "I don't know. We have a little 'study group' that meets to share ideas. Would you like to come with me to one of their meetings?"

"But I can't read anybody's thoughts any more!"

"Neither can Janet. But she wants to help, and she can give us a different perspective."

"I'll come if you want me to. I can't think of any way I could help, but I want to be with you."

"I have an idea," she said. "Suppose I invite a few of them over to my place to talk some evening. You could get acquainted with them and see if you're comfortable."

"All right."

Scene 95

Meredith contacted members of the study group about an informal meeting. Gary agreed immediately, and suggested Janet. Meredith had some misgivings, but she felt that Doug might like to have Janet there, simply because he already knew her and because he and she had their implants in common—their **former** implants. George and Mary also agreed to come, but later backed out, saying they had "too many things going right now."

On the evening of the meeting, Doug insisted that he could make the subway trip by himself. He managed to get to the subway stop near her apartment, but then called for directions to her building. Meredith had been nervously waiting, trying not to give in to her imagination of all the things that could go wrong. When he rang her bell, she was relieved.

Gary and Janet arrived just after him, and the four of them settled in Meredith's little living room. They all accepted her offer of wine. She had moved her cockatiel's cage into the corner of the living room because she knew Chick would fuss if he heard voices in his usual place in the bedroom. Other than an occasional chirp, he remained quietly eyeing the guests.

"I guess we're the group," Meredith began. I invited George and Mary, but they couldn't make it."

"Good group," said Gary, smiling at the others.

"I wanted us to get together—just a few of us—so Doug could get a feeling of being in a group again, after his surgery." She looked at Gary. "You may have heard that Doug has amnesia, and we're trying to get him back." Meredith looked at Doug and laughed.

"I'm coming back," Doug said. "I still don't remember much at all from my recent history, but every once in a while, something reminds me, and I get another little piece. Meredith told me about why I made the decision to have my implant removed, but I don't remember anything about that. I'm taking it for granted that it's in here somewhere." He pointed to his head, where newly growing hair was beginning to cover the scar from the surgery.

"You said Meredith told you about why you had the implant removed," said Janet. "Do you have the same feelings that you had then?"

"I don't know if they are the same. Right now I can't imagine myself reading other people's thoughts, even though I know Meredith does it all the time."

"Not all the time," Meredith said.

"But from what Meredith has told me about your study group, I think it's a good thing, and I would like to help in whatever way I can."

"You know," Meredith said, "I'm coming to have a different point of view about reading people's thoughts than I did, like, six months ago. I still think it will change our culture when it becomes more widely recognized, and I still think that we need to prepare for the impact, if we can. But Gary and I were talking not long ago about it, and I agree with him that it's not so radically different from the way people have always related to each other."

"Say more about that?" asked Janet.

"Well, I may be out of my depth here, but it seems that people **read** each other all the time, in very subtle ways. We may not even be aware of how much we notice other people's gestures, tone of voice, even the way we look at each other. We're very good at knowing what's going on with each other."

Janet smiled. "I know that when I had my implant, I used what I felt was going on with other people to grasp what I read in their thoughts. When I first had the thing in my head, it was like I was overwhelmed by all the **noise** around me. I could no more make sense of all of it than I could understand Chinese. I learned a lot from meditating, because there I could see how chaotic my own mind was—how little I could actually control what went on in it."

"I'm just now getting to understand how wild my mind is," said Doug.

"Neurologists are still struggling with that," added Gary. "I'm reading a book, 'The Mystery of Consciousness' by John Searle. He talks about the mirror neurons in our cortex that fire in a kind of sympathetic reaction to those in other people we're with." He laughed. "I'm not putting that very well—I'm **way** out of my depth in this—but like when we watch somebody eat ice cream, the same neurons are firing in our heads that would be firing if we were eating the ice cream ourselves. They don't know how this happens, but it does."

"When I'm having a conversation with somebody, and it feels like we are exactly tuned in to each other—our mirror neurons are firing in synch?"

"Yeah, and like when we're making love with somebody ..." Gary stopped. His face became red.

Janet looked at him and smiled. "Like vibrating strings resonating with each other."

They all laughed.

Meredith said, "I find I'm not really paying as much attention to other people's thoughts as I used to when it first began to come on me. Like right now, I'm not picking up anything at all, because what's being said out loud is what I hear and what I'm aware of."

Janet nodded. "I'm just now getting used to not reading again. At first, it felt like my ears were stopped up or something. I was missing a lot of input from people around me. I'm curious about how Gary understands what's going on between us, because I'm not missing it like I used to."

Gary smiled. "I pay more attention to what you're saying—it's less work and it's usually clearer.

"There was a time," Meredith said, "when Doug and I had what we called a 'mind pool,' that contained both our thoughts, and sometimes we couldn't tell whose thought it was, but it was a really comfortable place to be, and it didn't matter who had come up with the thought first. And a lot of times we didn't have to say anything out loud to each other. Talk about vibrating strings!"

Doug looked at Meredith. "Do you miss it?"

She touched his hand. "Sometimes." Her eyes glistened.

Janet sighed. "I don't think I ever had that experience," she said.

Gary looked at her. "I hope this isn't too personal," he said, "but I feel that, the way she described it—mind pool—when we make love. I'm thinking, 'Yes, yes, yes!"

"Well, that's different," she said, blushing. "I'm thinking, 'Yes, yes, yes! then, too."

"We manage to communicate a lot, don't we?" Doug put his hands up to his head.

Meredith looked concerned. "Doug—are you okay?"

He grinned. "It's my dream thing again." Looking at the others, he said, "They say it's related to migraine. It'll pass."

Gary asked, "You have a headache?"

"No. Never had a migraine headache that I know of. That's just what the neurologist said."

Meredith felt an old tightness in her midsection.

Janet said, "When it happened before, Meredith had you meditate, and you said that helped. Do you want to stop and meditate?"

"Let's do," said Meredith.

The four of them sat silently, eyes closed, for a long time. After a while, the cockatiel chirped once, and someone stirred.

Janet laughed quietly. "Our time keeper."

Meredith touched Doug again. "How is it?"

"Still there. I can deal with it. Just let me sit for a minute." He looked at Janet and Gary. "Please go on. This will pass."

Meredith stood up. "More wine might help." She went into the kitchen and returned with another bottle. Pouring it, she said, "I have no idea whether alcohol affects those spells or not."

"My mom used to get migraine headaches frequently," said Janet. "She also drank, but not when she had a headache—that I know of."

"Well," said Doug, "we'll find out." He lifted his glass and drank it down.

"Wow," laughed Gary. "That's a really dedicated scientist!"

Doug smiled. "I have incentive. This isn't fun, although it's not painful. Just disconcerting."

The rest of the evening saw no more dramatic experiences. They found themselves comfortable with each other, and Janet and Gary left when the conversation began to lag. They all promised to meet again soon.

As Meredith and Doug picked up afterward, Meredith said, "You're not planning to go home tonight, are you?"

"We hadn't talked about that, had we?"

"Would you like to stay over?"

He looked at her. "What do you think?"

"Please stay."

"All right. If you insist."

She stopped with a glass in her hand. "I'd like to talk about something."

Doug took the glass from her hand and set it on the counter. Pulling her close, he said, "You want to ask about my dream thing happening just when Janet was talking about making love with Gary."

"I'm the one who's supposed to be reading minds." She kissed him gently.

"I thought of it myself. The last time we were with Janet, it happened then, too. While we were meditating, I was trying to get inside all that."

"Anything?"

"I'm not sure. It's strange—I see Janet, and I remember what you told me, that she and I slept together, but I don't feel anything. Now ..." He stopped and looked at her. "I won't deny that I think she's, uh, ..."

"Sexy is acceptable." Meredith smiled out of one side of her mouth.

"Okay, she's sexy. I could imagine, under different circumstances, ..."

"You would again." Meredith laughed. "We're finishing each other's sentences!"

"No, you are finishing my sentences. It's okay. You know what I'm thinking."

Meredith blushed.

"So," he said, "the question is, am I not remembering making love to Janet and the dream thing is some kind of symptom of my blocking that?"

"I'm having some kind of symptom right now." She took a deep breath. "I have a knot in my stomach, and my breathing is difficult."

"This subject seems to affect both of us."

"Yes." She tilted her head, and he suddenly remembered that he liked that.

"What can we do about it?" He took her hand and led her to the sofa. "Let's see."

They sat side by side, looking into each other's eyes without speaking for a long while.

Then she began in a near-whisper, "I'm going way out on a limb. I had another crisis, before you came home from your last assignment. I was meditating, and I was thinking about why I had kissed Dolly ..."

His eyebrows raised, but he said nothing.

"And I remembered a time when I was very young, a bunch of us were high on hash, and we decided to have an orgy." She dropped her eyes. "I found myself lying on top of a girl—my best friend—and kissing her passionately." She took a deep breath and let it out. "We didn't make love—although I don't know what else you'd call that. It didn't end well. She didn't speak to me for a long time afterward."

"You felt very guilty about that."

"Actually, I must have. But then I forgot it. Totally forgot it! It just came back to me on the cushion, and I could see that kissing Dolly was like that."

"Dolly was helping you through another crisis."

Her eyes widened. "I didn't tell you that, did I?"

"Not that you kissed her. You said you loved her."

"We'd been drinking. I gave her a peck, and then she invited me to 'do it right.' So I did. Then right away, I felt guilty, as though I had violated her the way I violated my friend."

"How did Dolly take it?"

Meredith laughed. "Like Dolly takes just about everything. She kissed me back, and then it was over."

"Does this have anything to do with Janet?" His fingertips pushed back a lock of her hair.

"Maybe. I don't know, Doug!"

"Are you attracted to her?"

She took another deep breath. "There's a piece of me. Yes! I have even had a dream of sleeping with her." She burst into tears.

Doug wrapped his arms around her.

After a while, she pulled away. "I'm sorry!"

"It's okay," he said softly.

"I feel terrible!"

"You're not terrible."

"When I was meditating, I finally got through the bad feelings, and I told myself it was okay. But there's a difference between just accepting my feelings and facing the fact that I love you and I wouldn't hurt you for anything."

He untangled them and got up. "Any more of that wine left?"

After going to the kitchen for wine, he came back and sat down again. "I don't know if this works, but I want to say it anyway, okay?"

"Okay." She wiped her eyes and smiled at him.

"We were talking earlier this evening about mirror neurons. It occurred to me that maybe that's what we are dealing with—you and I—right now. Maybe both of us are feeling sexual feelings toward Janet, that neither of us wants to admit. You know that I slept with her, and you have conflicting feelings about that." He took a sip of wine. "I remember. Meredith, I remember!"

"**What**?" Her red-rimmed eyes were wide.

"I remember how upset you were when you figured out that I had slept with Janet. You practically screamed at me that you didn't want to know."

"You remember that?"

"And I remember feeling so guilty! I kept telling myself to let it go, that it was just one of those things that happen, and it had nothing to do with you. That feeling ..."

Meredith blew her nose. "I know that feeling," she said quietly, taking another tissue from the box.

"A little while ago, when I had my spell—that was the feeling. I still didn't remember what it was for, and I didn't even recognize it. But now I do."

They sat quietly for a few minutes. Meredith took a drink from Doug's glass of wine.

"It's stupid, isn't it?" she said finally. "Here we are, totally in love—at least I am—and feeling guilty about our respective 'unacceptable sexual impulses.'" She laughed, and he joined her.

"Poor Janet," she said.

"Poor Janet?"

"None of this is her fault. She just happens to have a gorgeous body."

"I still don't remember sleeping with her."

"Too bad for you. I'm sure it was wonderful."

"Eat your heart out," he said, beginning to unbutton her blouse.

Scene 96

The next day after Doug left, Meredith picked up her phone and called George Randolph. "Do you have a phone number for Morgan Brown?"

"Yes," George answered. "I think so. Hold on for a moment."

Morgan Brown, the charismatic man she had met at one of the early meetings she had attended in Silver Spring, impressed her in some ways, particularly in his knowledge of the growing community of readers across the country. What she had not liked was his seeming elitism about reading.

The line was quiet for a few minutes, then George returned and gave her a phone number. "Meredith," he said then, as if he were going to say something else.

"Yes?" She was suddenly curious.

"You might also try online. There's a website."

Her pen was still poised over the pad. She waited, smiling at this peculiar man whom she had, inexplicably, grown fond of. Finally she said, "What's the address?"

"I can't remember," he replied. "You'll have to Google for it. Sorry."

"What do I look for?"

"George Harrison."

The hair stood up on her arms. "George Harrison," she repeated.

"Yes. Remember the song, 'Here Comes the Sun'?"

"Of course."

"At the bottom of the page there's a collection of links in small type. One of them is something like 'Here Comes the Sun.' It'll take you to a new page, where you have to register. It's a site where you can connect with other readers. I think they are planning some kind of gathering. I don't have time to go, but maybe you can."

"Okay," she said, by this time slightly annoyed. "I'll try to find it."

"I wouldn't use your real name," he said. "There are some crazies out there. I'd be discreet. But the site is moderated, so it's pretty safe."

"Thank you, George."

"Yes. Good luck."

Meredith opened her computer and Googled "George Harrison." The search listed the first few of more than ten million results. Scanning the page of results, she tried to ignore the little knot in her stomach. She was tempted to click on the YouTube sites that promised to play videos of George Harrison's performances, but she stayed on course to find what she was looking for. She clicked on the links one at a time and scrolled immediately to the bottom, looking for "Here Comes the Sun." The sites revealed a lot about George Harrison, but none displayed "Here Comes the Sun" at the bottom.

During her meditation that morning, she had become aware that her desire had been lagging lately, her wanting to try to help smooth the expected conflicts in society between readers and nonreaders. Lately, as she had felt more relaxed about her new ability, she felt less apprehensive about the cultural divisions. And with Doug now among the "others," she had actually been suppressing her gift in his presence. It occurred to her this morning, however, that the cultural problem was not going to go away. So, without mentioning it to Doug, who was meditating beside her, she decided to become more active. It was a cause she believed in, and she wanted to do something more with her life than take care of Doug—as precious to her as he was.

Well into the third page of search results, she scrolled down to the bottom of one more web page, not even noticing the other contents of the page. In a line of very small type that included "Contact the Webmaster" and "Sign up for free song downloads," was an inconspicuous link that read, "Here Comes the Sun."

Her hand shook as she moved the cursor to it and clicked the mouse.

The End

Afterword

"... *the skull can only swell so much and still pass through the birth canal. Even after the brain folded in, under, and around itself, it still needed to add important skills. The only solution was to drop some abilities to make room for more important ones. No doubt fascinating gifts were passed up or lost. ... But, of them all, the best survival trick was language, one worth sacrificing large areas of trunk space for, areas that might once have housed feats of empathy that would put extrasensory perception to shame.*"

—Diane Ackerman, *An Alchemy of Mind*

(From the blog YouHeardItHereFirst)

September 12:

> *For a couple of years, the online community has been buzzing with talk about CIA agents who can read minds; equipped with tiny chips implanted in their brains, they can pick up the thoughts of people in their vicinity, enabling them to outguess and outperform their rivals. Recently, we interviewed an ex-CIA operative, Doug _____ (whose full name we can't reveal for reasons of security), about the phenomenon:*

YHIHF – Doug, you were one of those mind-reading CIA agents, right?

DOUG – That's what they tell me.

YHIHF – That's what they tell you? Don't you know?

DOUG – I have global amnesia of the past six or eight years. I was told that it was due to the surgery to remove an implanted chip from my brain. My amnesia led to my discharge from the agency.

YHIHF – Did the Agency brain-wash you or something? Is that why you can't remember?

DOUG – No, nothing so sinister as that. It was simply the result of a kind of spasm of neurons from the surgery. I understand that it will eventually fade, and I'll be able to remember at least some of what I've lost.

YHIHF – In our research about your case, we came across the condition known as TGA, or transient global amnesia, a temporary condition sometimes related to migraine headaches.

DOUG – Yes, it's probably similar.

YHIHF – Well, what can you tell us about the mind-reading agents? Are their activities only overseas, or do they operate here in the United States?

DOUG – I can't say.

YHIHF – Did you operate here in this country?

DOUG – I don't remember.

YHIHF – You don't remember, or you can't say?

DOUG – Both are true, actually. If I could remember, I'm prohibited from discussing it.

YHIHF – Okay, can you tell us anything about the experience of reading other people's minds?

DOUG – Not from personal experience. Naturally, I'm as curious as you are, and I've looked into it through various means. To begin with, "reading minds" is a wild exaggeration. One can, with practice, sense in a crude way certain thoughts and images given off by just about everybody in the form of an electrical field.

YHIHF – You mean, we all broadcast radio signals from our heads, that with the right technology other people can detect?

DOUG – (Smiling) That's not far from how it works.

YHIHF – We've heard of companies marketing a kind of helmet that one can put on and control a computer.

DOUG – Yes, I've read about that, too. I've never seen one—that I know of, anyway.

YHIHF – Or that you could talk about if you could remember.

DOUG – Probably.

YHIHF – Anyway, let's talk about how it all works. Just what do you—does one—hear with this microchip?

DOUG – If you've ever paid really close attention to your own thoughts, like if you are a practiced meditator, you know that the mind is a very busy organ. Thoughts come up, but mostly they are fragments of thoughts, even single words, or sometimes a kind of image like you could remember—the face of your wife, for example.

YHIHF – So if you still had this chip, you could see my wife's face if I thought of it?

DOUG – Maybe. That's what I've been told, anyway.

YHIHF – Who told you—your former associates?

DOUG – (Smiling) You are persistent, aren't you? As a matter of fact—and this is something you can find online, as well—there are people who seem to have this ability naturally, without the need for electronic devices.

YHIHF – You mean, there are people walking around among us who can read our thoughts? That's a scary thought!

DOUG – To some, I guess. I've gotten used to the idea, and maybe because I used to have the ability, it's not such a scary idea. Think for a minute about how much you can pick up from even a stranger you meet on the street—not their thoughts, mind you, but their mood, perhaps, their state of mind. Are they smiling or frowning? Are they giving off what we used to call "vibes?" And if the person is someone you know, you can read all kinds of things about how they are feeling, what they're thinking, what they plan to do, even.

YHIHF – Body language.

DOUG – Exactly.

YHIHF – Something I'm not very good at, myself, reading my wife's face.

DOUG – Unfortunately, a lot of us are like that. But there are those who are very good at it. A salesman, if he's any good at all, is continually reading you as he makes his pitch.

YHIHF – But that's something we all know and can recognize and defend ourselves from.

DOUG – A good salesman can make good money, sometimes selling pure crap.

YHIHF – They tell us what we want to hear.

DOUG – And how do they know what we want? By watching us carefully.

YHIHF – I guess that's true. But let's get back to this mind-reading thing. It goes way beyond reading somebody's body language, doesn't it?

DOUG – Like I said a few minutes ago, our minds are full of fragmentary thoughts, feelings and images. When we want to say something, we often rehearse it in our heads first, so it will come out the way we want. First, it comes to us in pieces, and we have to put the pieces together. And there are always a lot of other things, alternative ways of saying something, irrelevant words and phrases, even conflicting stuff that gets rejected before you say what you want to say. It's all in there.

YHIHF – Like, how do you tell your wife you love her when you've been having a fight? You choose your words carefully.

DOUG – From a lot of other words.

YHIHF – What about feelings? You said your mind has these feelings. Can a CIA guy pick up the feeling? Does that mean that now he has the feeling?

DOUG – That's a really good question. I can't answer it—and I don't know if it would be classified if I could remember.

YHIHF – But you say that some people can do this naturally. Do you personally know any? Could you ask them about the feeling thing?

DOUG – (Smiling) I guess I don't have to. I can figure it out myself. Think about how you feel when you're watching a movie. Where do those feelings come from?

YHIHF – From watching the characters on the screen. You don't mean the movie screen gives off radio waves from somebody's head, do you?

DOUG – Of course not. But as you watch the characters on the screen, a part of your own brain—I think it's located behind your forehead somewhere—is mirroring the feelings portrayed on the screen. They are called mirror neurons. They're the basis for compassion and empathy that most of us experience.

YHIHF – So, besides reacting to scary situations, for example, we feel the fear that we see on the faces of the characters.

DOUG – Not so mysterious, is it?

YHIHF – What you're telling me, through all of this, is that it's not such a big thing to know that there are people out there who could tune into my chaotic mind, if they wanted to work at it. Other than, say, when I'm at the ATM machine, I don't want the guy behind me to hear me think my password.

DOUG – Or if you're a soldier and you and the enemy have your guns trained on each other, it might be important that you not give away your intentions.

At this point, Doug put his head in his hands, as though he suddenly had a terrible headache. We wanted to ask him if he remembered something, but out of respect called off the rest of the interview.

—*YouHeardItHereFirst*